Charleston Green

A NOVEL

STEPHANIE ALEXANDER

Cover and Interior Layout and Distribution by Bublish, Inc.
Cover Art by Caroline Staley

ISBN: 978-1-64704-050-5 (paperback)
ISBN: 978-1-64704-051-2 (eBook)

According to local lore, during the Reconstruction, the Union provided government issued paint to cover the damage to South Carolina homes. Charlestonians had no liking for the uninspired, flat black color. They added dollops of yellow and blue, subtly rebelling against its bland uniformity, creating Charleston Green— a shade of green so dark as to appear black to the untrained or uninformed eye. Today, the shade is found in subtle traces all over the Lowcountry: doors, shutters, porch trim, rocking chairs, and joggling boards. Joggling boards— long pliable boards supported on each end by wooden stands— are common on the porches and in the gardens of homes throughout South Carolina.

Charleston Green

*You said I killed you—haunt me, then! Be with me al-
ways—take any form—drive me mad! Only do not leave
me in this abyss, where I cannot find you!*

—Emily Bronte, Wuthering Heights

*We must be willing to let go of the life we planned, so as to
have the life that is waiting for us.*

—Joseph Campbell

Chapter 1

If Tipsy learned one thing from her divorce, it's that everyone in Charleston is at least a little crazy— even if they're already dead.

She had to move into Miss Callie's place to figure out that the dead carry on like the living do. She almost always ignored dead people, because early experience had proven that if she paid any bit of attention to them, they became a straight up nuisance. When she met Jane and Henry Mott, Tipsy had to stop avoiding and start listening. Some ghosts refuse to be ignored.

She wasn't worried about ghosts on moving day. She was thinking how damn lucky she was to be moving into Miss Callie's house, rent-free. By the time the movers cleared out at five o'clock, she was done in. Even the house seemed wiped out, and it hadn't done anything but sit there since the 1890s. Thank goodness it was Ayers's weekend with the kids; she couldn't have handled them running in and out and rustling through boxes. The whole crew, Ayers and all three children, had stayed with his parents for the weekend to avoid the chaos. Ayers had moved out six months ago, and now with Tipsy moving to Miss Callie's and him returning to their old house, she felt like she was in a game of musical domiciles. She had trouble remembering where anyone lived.

She carried the last box, the one containing Mary Pratt's American Girl dolls, through the white picket fence and up the porch stairs to the double front doors. Miss Callie's tea roses had run amuck since she passed on. The June sunshine woke the yellow blossoms, and they reached for Tipsy through the banister. Ayers's brother-in-law Jimmy had offered Tipsy this temporary solution to her housing problem. Jimmy's mother had recently died, and he was happy to let Tipsy move into Miss Callie's place and look after it for a time. She made a mental note to rein in those rebellious flowers once she got settled. Tipsy hadn't known Miss Callie too well, but she certainly owed her now. Her status as honorary caretaker would give Jimmy time to fix things up before selling the place, and buy Tipsy precious months to figure out her increasingly unpredictable life. She planned on earning her keep in the meantime.

Tipsy took the winding staircase to the second floor for the hundredth time that day. She couldn't help but compare this crumbling yet palatial house in the Old Village of Mount Pleasant—one of the most elegant neighborhoods in the Lowcountry, a place legendary for all things refined—with her grandmother's four-room 1950s rancher in the upstate town of Martinville. She grew up at the end of a dirt driveway. The nearest body of water: the aboveground swimming pool behind the neighbor's doublewide trailer. Now, her neighbors across the street sipped cocktails on their docks and watched the sunset over the harbor. On the other side of the Ravenel Bridge, the Charleston skyline wiggled through humid air. Bronze crosses grabbed at the sky, the Episcopalians trying to reach God before the Presbyterians. She could hear her Granna's voice: *My Tipsy, ain't you all fancy now.*

Shush, Granna, Tipsy thought. *Not too fancy in the bank account department at the moment. Besides, this place has seen better days.*

Tipsy dropped the box of dolls in the twins' bedroom. They grinned at her, reminders of the days when she and Ayers had casually doled out hundreds of dollars on smiling plastic little girls. She transferred her hands to the small of her back.

Glass of tea, sugar? Granna's voice rose in her mind again. Granna and she had shared that strange affinity for the dead, so although

Granna herself was many years gone, Tipsy still sometimes heard the voice that had steered her through her haphazard childhood. Truth be told, at times Granna resonated clearer than living people, with their yammering on about this or that. She didn't tell anyone this, of course, because that would qualify her own mental church as infested with a bad case of the batshit crazies.

Bats and belfries aside, Granna's voice had a good idea. As Tipsy backtracked down the narrow hallway she ran her hands over accent tables and the random chairs elderly people always place in spots where no one ever sits. Heavy wood and dark reddish upholstery in velvets and satins had an old-plantation-house kind of prettiness. While the mustiness made her nose itch, the well-worn furniture made the place homey. She hadn't wanted to take much of the furniture in her old house. Ayers had picked all of it, and he preferred stark modern styles. Made no sense for a hunting-and-fishing boy like him to have the aesthetic of an effete New York theater director, but that was Ayers. A study in contradictions.

Tipsy avoided her passing reflection in the glass covering Miss Callie's framed Duck Stamp prints. She let her long hair down from its too tight ponytail and rubbed her sore scalp.

That hair. Not blonde. Not brunette. Granna's sniffing laughter. *So sweaty dark it looks like you had a run in with the wrong shade of L'Oreal. Like thirty-four years of hard livin'!*

Thanks, Granna.

Oh, come now. You know I'm teasing. You've barely changed since seventeen. Who'd know you had three kids? But damnation, you need some of that Botox! You got my worrying brow.

You're biased, and then out loud, "Got to grow old gracefully."

"Is someone there?"

That shrill voice shot out of one of the guestrooms and knocked Tipsy sideways. Her ankle rolled. As she fell, she grabbed one of Miss Callie's antique porcelain lamps. She hit the Oriental rug with a thud. The three cavorting cherubs on the lamp reached out to her in sympathy. She thanked god those expensive little dudes were still in one piece.

Tipsy stood and rotated her foot until most of the pain dissipated up her leg. She peered into the cheery little room, with its yellow wallpaper and accent pillows in the shape of lemons and cherries. A woman sat on the four-poster bed. While she appeared to be about Tipsy's age, her tiny bare toes didn't reach as far as the lace bed skirt. Her pale, almond-shaped eyes stared into Tipsy's with startled curiosity, like a Siamese cat who unexpectedly found itself pinned down by the tail.

The woman jumped to her feet, buried her face in her hands and sobbed. She wore a sleeveless lavender dress with a dropped waist and a multi-layered lace hemline that ended below her knees. Her skin was translucently white, her hair black. Tipsy's initial assessment had classified the women's coiffure as a messy up-do, but her fidgeting revealed it to be a disheveled bob.

She whimpered with no break to gasp for air. It was too repetitive, too staccato. She wrapped her thin arms around herself. The edges of her dress smudged and faded and solidified again as she swayed. The fading spread from her clothes to her hair to her skin.

She's dead, Tipsy thought. *She doesn't need to draw breath.*

As a child, suffering from her own loneliness and tired of finding friendships in storybooks, Tipsy would speak to a ghost here or there, although most of them had lost their senses over time, like the teenage girl who haunted Martinville's single public park. She once caught Tipsy staring at her. She followed Tipsy, in her *Little House on the Prairie* garb, from the slide to the swings, begging Tipsy to help her find the family pig. By age ten, Tipsy had to swear off the park all together. It had been years since she made such a mistake, and not only because a ghost's desperate jabbering could annoy the hell out of a person in a skinny minute. Granna had warned her that while most were harmless, there were a few who were anything but. In educating Tipsy about their mutual peculiarity, she emphasized downplaying its existence, for everyone's benefit.

Something about this woman, though, made Tipsy pause. She reminded her of a little girl in the middle of some childish heartache. Grown women don't cry so hard without a good reason. This one was producing enough tears to fill the River Styx, and being damn loud about it—and in the bedroom right beside Tipsy's. Tipsy'd probably seen a hundred or more ghosts in her day. She'd run across them in places as predictable as the old Dock Street Theater— during a showing of *A Christmas Carol,* no less—and as random as the Mount Pleasant Whole Foods.

She'd never, however, lived under a roof with one, or tried to have a real, adult conversation with one. Tipsy wasn't really sure how any of it worked, from a ghost's perspective. Now suddenly, she and this lady were two chickens in the same coop. Tipsy would need to make her acquaintance sooner or later, if she didn't want to have the bejesus scared out of her on a daily basis.

Besides, from the antiquated look of the ghost's dress and hair, it appeared this had been her house a hell of a lot longer than it had been Tipsy's. Tipsy wasn't going anywhere, and this woman's ghostly existence meant she wasn't going anywhere either. Tipsy knew that much. The ghost couldn't leave the house if she tried, bless her heart. Trapped as a blind and clawless kitten on a high tree branch. Compassion, practicality, and a smidge of plain old curiosity overrode Granna's deeply entrenched wisdom.

"Can I help you with something?" Tipsy asked. She raised her voice to be heard over the woman's bawling.

The woman hugged herself tighter and rocked herself faster. "I can't say I know how to reply. Perhaps I did once, but I've forgotten."

Tipsy didn't know anyone other than Granna who shared her talent, so opportunities to speak probably hadn't come this woman's way too often. She tried a different route. "I should have introduced myself. My name is Tipsy Collins. Sorry if I startled you, but I didn't expect to find a ghost crying in the spare bedroom."

The woman's fingers twirled among themselves, as if she were knitting an invisible scarf. She sniffed and went solid. Aside from her pallor, she didn't look particularly dead. "Tipsy? Is that a French name?"

"No. My real name is Tiffany Lynn. Tiffany Lynn Denning, now Collins. The pastor's son couldn't say Tiffany when I was a baby. So I've always been Tipsy." She waited for the ghost to make the usual alcoholic comment, before remembering she probably wasn't familiar with booze-related slang.

"You can see me." Still her fingers spun, as if she were raveling together fractured pieces of thought.

"Yes."

That seemed enough of an explanation. "My name is Jane Mott. I was born a Robinette. The Robinettes of Water Street. My mother's people came from the Old Cannon, on the Wando." Jane ran both hands over her face, and giggled. She smoothed her hair a little too eagerly.

Uh, oh. Maybe I've popped the tab on a shook up can of Coke.

Too late, now, said the voice of Granna. *She might be crazier than a stoned possum, but now she knows you can see her. You're stuck with her.*

Tipsy backed toward the door. She would only need three of the house's six bedrooms. One for herself, one for her six-year-old twins, Mary Pratt and Olivia Grace, and one for her eight-year-old son, Ayers

Lee Collins V. Maybe she'd be able to steer clear of this diminutive spirit. "I live here now," Tipsy said. "So maybe we could, you know, mind each other's space."

The ghost's mouth hung open, as if she needed a straw to draw meaning from Tipsy's words.

"I guess I'll see you sometimes," Tipsy said, "but I'm usually really busy. So if I don't chat—"

"I'm accustomed to being ignored."

"Because no one sees you?" Again Tipsy felt the tug of sympathy.

"My husband ignores me. I ignore him. It's to our mutual benefit."

"Your husband is still alive?"

Jane looked at her with eyes as clear as Miss Callie's best Waterford vase. "He's just as dead as I am, Miss Tiffany-Tipsy."

"Oh, of course," said Tipsy, feeling slightly stupid. "Why do y'all ignore each other? It seems like a nice arrangement. Like a couples' haunting?"

For someone who wants to mind each other's space, you're asking a lot of questions, said Granna.

Tipsy ignored her. Sometimes Tipsy and Granna ignored each other, too. It could get crowded with both of them inside Tipsy's head.

"We don't get on," said Jane. "Haven't gotten on in quite a spell of time."

Tipsy found it odd to hear someone who appeared to be her own age speak in the soft drawl she associated with women of the grandmotherly sort, albeit rich Charleston grandmothers like the ones in Ayers's family. Jane seemed to blink when a particular word needed emphasis. The combination of bobbed hair, batting blue eyes and fey voice was reminiscent of Betty Boop. "If I can be frank, Henry and I don't get on *at all*." Blink-blink!

Tipsy did some rough math in her head. The woman's attire put her squarely in the 1920s category, like *Downton Abbey*, later seasons. "And you've been stuck in this house together for…ninety years?"

"Ninety-five."

Tipsy thought of being trapped in a house for decades with only Ayers for company. She couldn't bring herself to hate him now, despite the damage he'd dealt her over the past six months, but she damn sure would after a century. "That's understandable. Marriage is only supposed to last 'til death do you part. You're not meant to keep at it for all eternity."

"How can we *possibly* be *congenial*"—blink-pause-blink—"when he killed me?"

Boop-Boop-be-do! said Granna.

Tipsy sank into an antique chair. "Well, shit."

Jane scowled, and she remembered that proper southern ladies probably didn't drop the word *shit* very often in the 1920s. "Sorry. Wow, he did? How… or…" *Is it polite to ask a ghost the details of her murder?*

"Yes, he did. Although he still denies it." Jane balled her hands into fists. "But I *know* he did it! And then he killed himself." She hugged herself again and her black hair went smudgy. Tipsy saw right through her.

"Wait!" she said, and Jane returned to focus. "I'm moving my children into a house that's haunted by a murderer?"

The air around her cooled as Jane crossed the space between them. Jane's legs didn't move fast enough to explain her momentum, but she came on just the same, as if the wood floor had turned into a flat airport escalator. A lemony scent overrode the dusty smell of Miss Callie's antique quilt. Tipsy shuddered. She'd have had the same reaction if hands tipped a glass of lemonade down her shirt.

Granna! Tipsy thought as she stood. *Is she one of the bad ones?*

But Granna said nothing. Tipsy knew that if Granna had the answer, she'd give it. The thought brought her no comfort.

She took a step into the hall and Jane followed. "Henry will *never* admit to it," the ghost said, with blinking ocular italics. "He *won't*. But I *know* he did it."

"Of course. I'm sure it was horrible—but I have to—"

Jane's eyes filled with sparkly diamond tears. "Beg pardon. I'm frightening you." The sobbing again. "I *believe* he did it. In my heart..." She buried her hands in her hair. "But oh, my soul, I can't remember. I can never remember."

And with that, Jane Mott disappeared.

———•———

Tipsy wasn't keen to stay in the house that evening, but her girl-friends had been itching to check it out. So after a rushed tour, she sat on the late Miss Callie's front porch with Shelby and Lindsey. She gripped a cold Bud Light in a koozie emblazoned with the cheerful message, "Joe and Julie, October 18th, 2013—Love is Always a Party!" Tipsy had never met Joe and Julie, but she'd somehow acquired this token of their undying love. She wondered if they were still partying five years later, maybe with a couple kids and a mortgage and Julie's growing suspicions that Joe was shacking up with his assistant.

She took a long swig of beer and it stuck in her throat. *I live in a house with a murdering ghost and his discontented, possibly deranged wife. Hey Julie, want to trade?*

"And so there she is," Shelby said, "standing out on the driveway at three in the morning. Drunk as Cooter Brown. Screaming up at his window. *I know you're in there, Glen! I know you're in there!* And all the neighbors opening windows—"

"Wait—what?" Tipsy asked. "You lost me."

Shelby pursed her lips. "You're worse than a man with one eye on ESPN and the other on this month's Playboy." She crossed her eyes, as if Tipsy and Lindsey needed a visual.

Tipsy had first laid eyes on Shelby Patterson during a sorority rush skit at Carolina. Shelby's portrayal of Sandy from *Grease* was the stuff of legend in the Kappa Zeta house. Tipsy would never forget watching Shelby's skillfully teased blonde hair float across the makeshift stage. Her skintight black pleather pants had accentuated the purposeful shaking of her voluptuous butt.

"Glen's ex-wife," said Shelby, "y'all know she hates me—"

"You hate her, too," said Lindsey. Lindsey was always one for stating the obvious, but at least she gave Shelby her full attention. With her wide brown eyes and round face she resembled an early rising owl come to roost on the porch for Happy Hour.

Shelby sniffed loud enough to drown out the cicadas. "Hell, I don't hate her. But she is a tramp—"

Movement at the other end of the porch caught Tipsy's eye. Miss Callie's joggling board bounced ever so slightly.

Did you invite Miss Jane to your girls' evening? asked Granna.

Tipsy eyed the wooden contraption, just like the one Granna had kept on her own modest porch. No different from the boards she'd seen on umpteen South Carolina porches. Joggling boards were part lawn ornament and part outdoor furniture, a long single board with a dip in the middle, held up by two simple wooden pedestal ends. They had always reminded her of church pews without the back, or of saggy picnic table benches.

As a general gravitational rule, a joggling board didn't bounce unless the weight of someone's butt on the center plank made it bounce. Tipsy stared at the empty air above the board, but made out nothing beyond the haze of a summer evening punctuated by a few swirling no-seeums.

"Of course I was pissed. Who spends a whole Friday night with his ex-wife shooting at zombies?"

"Zombies?" Tipsy asked. *Aren't ghosts enough?*

Lindsey rescued Tipsy once again. Shelby looked like she might scream at the next interruption. "Glen and his ex," said Lindsey. "They took their son to paintball for his birthday. It's zombie paintball."

"Oh. He took his son. You can't get angry." Tipsy sipped her beer and glanced down the porch again.

A man sat in the middle of the joggling board, his elbows resting on his knees. He wore baggy tan pants and a white button down shirt. His bright red wavy hair suggested a failed attempt at flattering it with pomade. A man like that should have been pale all over. Instead, his dark eyes clashed with the rest of him. High cheekbones towered over a full, sensuous mouth. He was either one of the oddest looking men Tipsy had ever seen, or the handsomest.

"What are you looking at?" asked Shelby.

Tipsy cleared her throat. "The joggling board. It needs a fresh coat of paint."

"Charleston green," said Lindsey.

"Mmmm, hmmm." Shelby squinted at the board and tilted her head. "Nice shade."

Tipsy nodded. If she turned her head just right, so sunlight glanced off the board, the oily sheen of the paint revealed the true color. The green of a forest at midnight, under a full moon. "Probably hand mixed."

"Hand mixing always makes the best Charleston green," said Lindsey.

While most people wouldn't have noticed the subtle tone, Tipsy, an artist; Shelby, an art dealer; and Lindsey, a part time but unusually talented interior designer, could pick it out from a mile away. Or at least from across the porch. "I could work up a batch once the kids are settled in—"

"Good lord, Tips, I'm trying to tell a story!" said Shelby. "I know the three of us can make a whole conversation out of mixing paint, but come on now."

"I'm sorry," said Tipsy. The man on the joggling board picked at the peeling paint, but no flecks of blackish green drifted to the floor below him.

"Pay attention. You're about to send my train of thought off the rails and into a ditch."

"I've just got a lot on my mind." Tipsy got a peek at the yin and yang tattoo on Shelby's right wrist before Shelby took her hand. Years ago, Tipsy had taken to tapping that black and white symbol when Shelby needed to be talked off an emotional ledge. Shelby's ledges tended to be steep and high and loom over unyielding concrete and racing emotional traffic. The gesture had become part of their friendship's long code. *Come back to the light, sister.*

Sometimes, though, life turned the tables on them. Shelby was her rock during the dark days after the twins' birth, when sadness settled over her like a stalled low pressure system, soaking her in fear, worry, and inexplicable despair. While no challenge, before or since, equated with the emotional mêlée of postpartum depression, in the wake of her divorce, Tipsy was once again more of the sooth-ee than the soother.

"Honey, you must be so tired," Shelby said. "Let me shut up about Glen, Sexy Fishing Charter Captain Extraordinaire."

"That sounds like a better story than Glen, Possible Deadbeat Dad, and His Annoying Ex-Wife," said Lindsey. "Besides, y'all have only been dating two months. Story can't be that long."

"You know with me it can be." Shelby scooted closer to Tipsy on the wicker loveseat. "When is Ayers bringing the kids back?"

"Tomorrow afternoon," Tipsy said. "I've got to set up their rooms." She looked over her shoulder, but the redheaded man was gone.

"Y'all know I love to decorate!" Lindsey grinned and hopped to her feet. She wore obscenely tall platform wedges, despite Tipsy's and Shelby's flip-flops. Regardless, she barely reached Tipsy's chin, and even Shelby could still look down at the top of her head.

"It shows," said Shelby. "Your house is straight out of *Architectural Digest*."

"Thanks, honey," said Lindsey. "I had to get *something* out of my ex— that pathetic old goat!"

Tipsy laughed, and Lindsey joined her. She never minded being the butt of the joke, even after the intense public humiliation of her divorce from Barker Davies, one of the richest lawyers in town. Barker had left his first wife and kids for Lindsey. Ten years later, he had once again traded in for a newer model, leaving Lindsey a single mom with one daughter, a huge house, a fat bank account, and a great attitude. Tipsy thanked the good lord Shelby had introduced her to Lindsey after she left Ayers. Lindsey's positivity gave her hope.

"I might never have rustled up the nerve to leave him myself, so this new chick did me a favor." Lindsey's short blonde ponytail bounced. "Come on."

Tipsy's calves ached as she walked to the kitchen, the result of too many flights of stairs on Lowcountry legs unaccustomed to inclines of any sort. Lindsey called over her shoulder as she and Shelby headed upstairs: "Bring the beer to the nursery, Jeeves!"

Tipsy imagined the red headed man appearing in the doorway holding a levitating Yeti cooler and a butcher's knife. She assumed him to be Jane Mott's homicidal husband, Henry. Henry's flat, dark stare hadn't done anything to rouse the sympathetic curiosity that Jane had evoked.

By the time she reached the refrigerator, she'd squashed her burgeoning fear by donning the Armor of Mommy. Tipsy's children needed more than pretty rooms. They needed stability. She wasn't going to let a ghost risk their first opportunity at either in months.

Be careful, sugar, said Granna. *You already caught the attention of one loony spirit. Knowing you, you'll poke your head right into a Venus flytrap. You're not sure what he's capable of.*

That's what I need to figure out. And I will. Sooner over later.

Tipsy, that man killed his own wife.

What choice do I have? Tipsy grabbed hold of the perpetual panic that lurked in her stomach before it could poke her heart. *It's this or a friend's couch and blow-up mattresses for the kids.*

Ain't that the truth. What if Ayers wants the kids full time? Or his parents do? asked Granna.

No way. My children will stay with me, and I'll make a home for them. I will make this work.

Tipsy rose and fell on her toes to stretch her calves as she hunted through unfamiliar drawers for her Gamecock bottle opener. Tomorrow she'd go for a long run. She didn't have tolerance for wobbliness in her limbs or her living situation.

She watched for signs of Henry as she popped the tops on three beers: her own Bud Light, Shelby's Mich Ultra (always watching her carbs) and Lindsey's Corona Light (always with a lime). She carried them up to the second floor landing, where Shelby and Lindsey were examining a table covered with old vases.

"What's the latest with the ex-husband from hell?" asked Shelby.

"Okay, Shelby." Tipsy handed over her beer. "That's a bit extreme."

"Screwing your wife out of her alimony qualifies as extreme to me."

"Seriously," said Lindsey. "Even Barker didn't do me like that."

"Ugh, y'all, I don't want to talk about screwy South Carolina alimony laws." Tipsy walked faster. "What's done is done. He's paying me child support—"

"Not enough to come close to getting y'all by." Shelby gripped the skinny neck of a green vase as if she were choking it, or might knock someone upside the head.

"I know, but he's having a really hard time. I'm trying to give him a break."

"Whatever!" said Shelby. "He shouldn't even expect you to speak to him, after what he's done to you. Accusing you of adultery? When y'all weren't even living together anymore?"

"We all know the laws in this state." Tipsy had learned the ramifications of South Carolina's unusually conservative divorce laws the hard way. "You date someone before you have a settlement agreement in place and it's adultery. Ayers was depressed, and his lawyer talked him into it. And I left him. I don't know what that feels like."

"Jesus, Tipsy," said Shelby. "Why are you defending him? You left him for a hell of a lot of reasons. You were intimidated by his ornery ass when you were married to him." Shelby waved the vase in Tipsy's direction. Lindsey swiped it out of her hand and rearranged all the vases in neat rows. "Now add feeling guilty to feeling scared," said Shelby, "and it's a recipe for disaster."

Sometimes the truth can get under a person's skin. Shelby didn't sugarcoat anything, so her truth often came with a double dose of annoying. "I hear you, Shelby, but we have to get along for the kids."

"Right, but you're too nice. Ayers can go screw himself." Shelby grinned. "I've been engaged three times and never married so I'm the expert on ending relationships."

Lindsey stepped carefully over a stack of bubble-wrapped frames as Tipsy steered them into Little Ayers's room. "Time to move on," Lindsey said, "and we know who you need to move on with. Will Garrison."

Tipsy opened a moving box near the closet door. Soccer trophies, a Carolina piggy bank, a few framed photos from Little A's christening, and the antique toy cars her father-in-law had given him. The cars were heavy and cool in her hands. Solid craftsmanship, not like the flimsy Wal-mart specials that Ayers always bought. "Glen's fishing buddy?"

"Yes! He and P.D. were roommates at the College of Charleston, and they grew up together in Beaufort, too. He's handsome—"

"He didn't seem very friendly." She thought of the time she'd met Will Garrison in passing on the way out of a restaurant. He'd pretty much glared at her through a mumbled *nice to meet you* and *good-bye*.

"He's so sweet, once you get to know him," said Lindsey. "Wouldn't it be fun? We can all hang out."

"Hmmm," Tipsy said. Lindsey's boyfriend, P.D., was a gentle giant of a man who worshipped the ground she walked on, despite her post-marriage habit of philandering with the local college students. Tipsy trusted his good opinion. Glen's, however…

Shelby clapped. "He's a great dad, and he has a good job—"

"And good hair!" Lindsey tapped her head.

"Maybe. A little distraction can't hurt, right?" She held Little Ayers's old bunny in front of her chest like a tattered plush bridal bouquet.

Shelby reached over and hugged her, the embrace squashing the bunny between them. Little Ayers didn't need it every night anymore, so Tipsy hadn't sent it with his dad. For some reason the feel of that beloved toy against her best friend's hug brought tears to her eyes.

"You think about it, sister," said Shelby. "No hurry. Just think."

Tipsy gave her a watery smile. As she wiped her eyes, a shiny black shoe and one trouser leg disappeared past the doorframe.

When that ghost comes calling, you might as well ask him to set awhile and chat. Tipsy could have sworn she felt Granna's warm breath on the side of her neck. The smell of grits and apples and Prell shampoo. Memories like that returned to her, clear as day, at the most peculiar times. Sometimes they ran through her head like movies on a screen, or recordings of long past thoughts. The smells and sounds and tastes just as full and loud and flavorful as ever they were in the original.

When Tipsy was not long out of diapers, she'd seen a car hit a squirrel while she and Granna waited for a ride at the end of the state road. When she was eight, for no reason at all, the little creature's death had come back to her in all its gory detail. Granna found her crying in her bedroom. She'd tried to explain the blood shooting across hot asphalt, and the thump of a tiny body against an uncaring tire. Granna had barely remembered the squirrel at all. She'd said, *Sugar, maybe your talent serves you in other ways. Not just seeing ghosts. You find a way to use it.*

The next day, Tipsy drew a picture of the squirrel's demise instead of talking about it—much to the disturbance of her third grade art teacher. Drawing became her release, and then, as she discovered the comfort of a brush in her hand and a picture in her mind, she turned to painting. As the years rolled on, she stopped trying to explain the movie memories. That didn't mean they stopped coming.

———•———

Tipsy is seven and she's standing in the center of the joggling board. Up, down, up, down.

"Bouncy-bounce! Bounsa-bounsa-bounce!"

"Tipsy Denning! Get your hind end off that board this second!"

Granna never screams at Tipsy, not out loud and not when she talks to her in the way just the two of them do, without saying words at all. Her yell scares the patooties out of Tipsy and she falls right off the board onto her butt on the front porch.

Just when she's about to cry her eyeballs out, she feels Granna's arms around her. "Sugar! Are you okay?"

"Yes, ma'am, but I hurt my butt."

"Stand up and let me rub it."

Tipsy stands and Granna rubs and it feels better pretty quick.

"I'm sorry I yelled at you," Granna says, "but you can't jump on the joggling board."

Tipsy touches the board with her fingers. They're all stubby because she bites them when she gets nervous, and she gets nervous a lot. Granna told her the board belonged to her mama. She showed Tipsy, with a crow's feather, how the board wasn't really black, but green. Tipsy liked to look at the board at different times of day. Sometimes it was easy to see the green. Sometimes it was all black. She wasn't quite sure which color was hiding under the other. Granna says Tipsy's got a good eye, to see the light buried in the dark.

This spring past Tipsy sat outside and helped Granna paint the joggling board blackish greenish again. Sneaky fun color or not, it seemed silly to keep painting something the same color, over and over. Tipsy likes lots of different colors, like the paintings in the books Granna brings home from the Martinville library.

"Why can't I jump on it? You said the board is strong," Tipsy says.

"It is strong in the middle, even where it sags. But it's much stronger on the ends. We don't want to tempt fate and antique wood. Besides, look how you fell off and hurt yourself."

She kneels in front of Tipsy. It's getting dark, but her great big gray eyes, just like Tipsy's, catch the falling sunlight. Like the cloudy sky when it's just stopped raining and the sun is peeking through.

"There's often a soft spot in the center," Granna says, and Tipsy listens because Granna knows so much about everything, even the fuzzy people Tipsy sees around town sometimes, the ones no one else but Granna sees. "Pies and rainbows and joggling boards. We're all weak and wobbly there, so take care when you're in the middle."

Chapter 2

T ipsy never felt at home without art on the walls, but Miss Callie's art wasn't quite to her taste. Come Sunday morning, she stashed about twenty ornately framed landscapes, fruit bowls, and floral arrangements, mostly watercolors, in the attic. Many of them had hung so long that their outlines lingered in dark rectangles, squares, and ovals where the sun hadn't had a chance to dull the paint. Then she set about with her hammer and several packets of picture hangers in an effort to make the old house a little more her own.

She started in the kitchen (vintage posters of ice cream advertisements) and worked her way through the dining room and living room (oil studies of an abandoned barn and an abstract, respectively). She saved the more personal items for her bedroom.

Tipsy giggled as she hung a woman draped in a red blanket and apparently nothing else, oil on canvas, over the white dresser with the blue marble top. Would Miss Callie have been scandalized by the woman's breast peeking out from the blanket's edges, or moved by the patriotic color scheme? Two charcoal studies of horses, both Appaloosas with varying splashy dots and swirly spots, went over the wrought iron bed.

She picked up the last and smallest piece and held the frame against a bit of wall between two windows. The view through each narrow glass rectangle encased a section of the Ravenel Bridge. Charleston's largest architectural monument had replaced two older bridges whose rickety rustiness had given Tipsy heart palpitations when she drove downtown. She'd become accustomed to seeing the bridge from most vantage points around Mount Pleasant, like an architectural true north. The sight of it through her bedroom window reassured her.

"That's you."

"Jesus!" She spun around, the hammer slipping from her hands. She jumped in an instinctive defense of her naked feet. She held onto the frame, but the picture hangers sprayed across the dark wood floors with a *ping-ping-p-pa-ching!*

Henry Mott stood in the doorway. He looked as elegantly disheveled as he had in those quick moments on the porch. Stooping, he swept both hands over the scattered nails and hangers. They shot toward him, gathering in the air before his hands like a cloud of stingers with no bees. Floating bits of metal followed him to the bed. His black shoes made no sound on the wood floor or the fringed rug. When he closed his fists, the hangers and nails dropped in a neat pile on the quilt.

"*Please* stop *sneaking up* on me!" Tipsy said—or rather, hollered, if she were to call a spade a spade.

Henry's eyebrows went north and the corners of his mouth went south. "Pardon. I don't believe I've snuck up on you before now."

"I'd call it sneaking up when you appear out of thin air with no warning. And your wife scared me yesterday. I've been in this house twenty-four hours and about been driven to cardiac arrest three times, near broke an ankle and came close to losing a toe."

"Let me again beg pardon. I've never been an adept conversationalist." He stepped closer. "May I look closely upon that portrait?"

His dark eyes weren't brown. They were a deep blue, the color of the ocean. They narrowed in concentration as she held the painting out before her chest like a shy child at show and tell.

"And a goodish likeness. A self-portrait." He pointed one long finger at her name in the corner. "But I think you exaggerated your features. Your nose isn't that big."

"I thought it was. Or maybe I've grown into it. I painted this when I was fourteen. Freshman year in high school. My mama framed it for me. It won a little award."

The painting left her hands and floated toward Henry's. It spun in mid-air. He read the faded purple ribbon Tipsy's mother had glued to the back of the frame. "Grand Prize, High School Division, South Carolina Arts Council." He directed the frame to the wall with a nonchalant wave of his hand. A nail and a hanger shot from the bed and into the drywall. "I shall hang it."

"It's not very good," Tipsy said. The lack of depth around the throat and shoulders had always annoyed her, as did the amateurish overuse of bright color on her lips and eyes and sweater. "But Mama loved it, so I've carried it around."

"I think it's rather beautiful. *And there she weaves by night and day, a magic web in colors gay.*"

"Tennyson."

"Do you like poetry?"

"I love art. So I've studied history. History begot literature. Literature led me to poetry."

Henry moved closer to the painting and she stepped aside. "Most women of this day are nothing but improvements and falsification."

While Jane had smelled of lemon, Henry smelled of mint. *A spectral mojito*, Tipsy thought. *Anointing of the dead. Lemon, frankincense and mint.*

"Charleston has always claimed pretty women. In my day they were of all colors. All shapes. Now, I can't help but notice that many of them look the same." His hand traced the outline of her fourteen-year-old face in the painting. "Your beauty is timeless. I may have seen such likenesses in the castles of France and Spain. Or perhaps in an old Papist church. A Madonna."

Tipsy's mouth had fallen open of its own accord. She snapped it shut like a fish that senses the worm is attached to a hook. *If I'm feeling low enough to take a dead man's flattery I need to hang around some construction sites.*

"Are those recent works?" Henry asked. He gestured toward them, but didn't look at the lady with the blanket or the horses. He seemed to have eyes only for the portrait.

Tipsy detested such questions, predominantly because she didn't have much in the way of recent work. She cleared her throat and pushed her painter's block back into its hated corner of her mind. Granna had suggested she get answers from this ghost, and she had always listened to her Granna. "I've just moved into this house. My children are returning tonight."

"Welcome," said Henry.

"I didn't prepare for roommates, but it looks like I got 'em. So I'm telling you straight up, stay away from my kids."

Tipsy, you take care now, said Granna. *Flies and honey and what not.*

"Mother Bear," said Henry. "Your children won't see me. You're different from most people. We both know that. I'll have no way to speak to them."

"That's of no account. I saw how you..." She waved at the nails and the picture hangers in their little pile on the quilt. "You can move stuff around."

"You noticed!" He smiled, as if she'd complimented a new haircut.

"And yesterday, on the porch. I couldn't even see you, and you were bouncing the joggling board."

The smile widened. "Wasn't it funny? I could see you."

"So you can see me when I can't see you?" Since she'd never had the opportunity to ask a ghost about the mechanics of such things, she might as well get some answers. The idea gave her the heebie-jeebies.

STEPHANIE ALEXANDER

Henry or Jane, watching her from behind a wall of invisibility in her very bedroom.

"Yes. But I'll try not to. It seems impolite."

"Don't touch any of my children's things. Not their toys or clothes or toothbrushes or anything."

"Their clothes are of no interest to me," Henry said. "But I do find your little machines fascinating. Everything in this day is a machine." Tipsy's electric toothbrush rose a few feet from its spot on her bed beside a pile of miscellaneous toiletries. "Even the brush for your teeth."

"My kids have plain old plastic toothbrushes," she said. "Nothing interesting about them at all." Her panic built as the conversation drifted further into the realm of absurd. If Henry went all *Poltergeist* on her, she had no way to defend herself. "So leave them alone. Not just the toothbrushes, everything."

"Certainly."

"Don't even go in their rooms."

"Yes, ma'am."

His agreeableness unnerved her more than his expected ghostly wrath. Her bluster trembled. "Fine. Okay." She crossed her arms over her chest, as if Henry might find something more dangerous than a picture hanger to fling in her direction. Her eyes darted around the room for potential projectiles. Her hammer. Her coffee table book of 19th Century Impressionists. Her god-forsaken hairdryer. *I'm about to join Jane and Henry in haunting this house via a well-aimed Conair. Oh, please, will you just disappear now?*

Ask him while you can, said Granna's voice. *Nicely!*

Tipsy took a deep breath. "Did you kill your wife? She said you did."

"No."

"So your wife wasn't murdered? And you didn't commit suicide?"

"Supposedly she was murdered. Perhaps I did commit suicide." He narrowed his eyes and looked at the ceiling, as if the answer lay somewhere among the rafters, then he shook his head. "But I didn't kill her."

"She says she can't remember what happened."

"Nor can I. I remember my life until a week before, and then it's all gone. I woke in my home on a cold February morning, dead as a rock."

"Then how can you be sure you didn't kill her?"

"I know because I know myself. I have faults. Too many to name. But I'm not a murderer." He walked past her, trailing mint in his wake. The closer he got to the door, the blurrier the edges of his silhouette. Smeared, like the charcoal roundness of the haunches of her horse drawings.

She followed him. "You can't blame me for asking—"

"I do not," he said, in a voice sonorous enough to make Rhett Butler jealous. He took a right as he departed the bedroom.

Tipsy followed him into the hall. "I meant no offense—"

She shut up. There was no use talking to musty air.

———•———

Tipsy returned to the bedroom and plopped into the wrought iron chair at Miss Callie's dressing table. Her befuddled face looked back at her, a grown-up Alice on the other side of the looking glass. She tilted her head and ran her finger over her nose, which she'd always hated. In Tipsy's twelfth year, a high school boy in her church youth group had announced that she "looked like the Noxzema girl, but with a big nose." What had started out as a compliment ended in mortification. She glanced up at the self-portrait on the wall.

A Madonna. Warmth filled her stomach.

Don't get all moony, now, said Granna.

Maybe he didn't do it. He seemed so reasonable.

They said that about Ted Bundy. Not every man deserves the benefit of the doubt.

Tipsy thought of the boats that crisscrossed Shem Creek every Sunday afternoon. Right about now, revelers en route to the restaurants after a long day on the beaches of Morris Island and Capers Island were waving and calling out boozy greetings and updates between vessels. News of a double murder in the Old Village would have gotten out, via land or sea, even a hundred years ago. The idea shimmied around Tipsy's head like drunk, bikini-clad college girls cavorting on the boats in the creek.

The screen door slammed downstairs. Little Ayers yelled, "Mama!" and Mary Pratt and Olivia Grace's dueling flip-flops slip-slapped across the kitchen tile.

"Buddies!" Tipsy called. She yanked her brownish hair, which couldn't accurately be described as curly or straight, into a ponytail. Today's sweat had glued it to her neck like a splat of overcooked egg noodles. She'd never bothered coloring it. Henry Mott was on to something in his observation of the local women— a monochromatic, symmetrical tribe marked by blonde highlighted blowouts and breast implants. On more than one occasion, she'd fumbled through awkward exchanges with comely blonde women at the gym, or in the grocery store. *Hey Tipsy! So good to see you! Can the twins come play with Maddy? Who is Little Ayers's soccer coach this season?* As the years went by, even their features seemed similar. Tipsy smiled while struggling mightily to place the ubiquitously pretty face in front of her. Charleston had developed a uniform for female attractiveness that extended beyond attire, at least for white women. Even her close friends stuck to the code. Shelby's hair hadn't really been blonde since eighth grade, and in addition to a beautiful house, Lindsey got a tasteful boob job out of her marriage.

A sudden thought wiped the first trace of an appreciative smile from Tipsy's face. How could Henry know about the Charleston Dress Code Blondes, if he'd been haunting this house for a century? Miss Callie hadn't had many visitors for the past twenty years or so, other than her children and grandkids.

Mary Pratt met Tipsy on the landing where the stairs made their tight curve and jumped into her mother's arms. Olivia Grace scampered up behind her with a look of grim determination on her face. "M.P., move!" She tugged at her sister's skinny waist. Mary Pratt squealed and kicked one long dangling leg.

"Leggo!" Mary Pratt said, and she wasn't talking about little plastic blocks. "Leggo, O-Liv!"

"Girls, come on now!" Tipsy returned Mary Pratt to the ground and knelt in front of them. She faced four identical light brown eyes, four curly brown pigtails and two sets of pouty lips. "Y'all just got home and you're about to knock all three of us down the steps." She poked each one in the belly and got twitchy smiles in return. "Go see your room. Remember where it is? Look under the pillows. There might be something special there."

She kissed each one's cheek in passing as they raced to their room. Whooping yells let her know they'd found the bags of pastel M&M's, Swedish fish, and gummy worms she'd left under their pillows.

Little Ayers trailed behind them up the steps. "Hey, Mama," he said.

"Hey, sweet boy." Tipsy kissed his freckle-covered cheeks. Those childish dots belied his serious expression. She tried to tell herself he'd always been this way, but these days he reminded her of an idealistic young lawyer who'd just realized he was going to spend his life defending thieves and liars.

"Did y'all have fun with Daddy this weekend?"

"Yes, ma'am. We took the boat to Capers with Aunt Mimi and Uncle Jim and all them."

"Nice!" She squeezed him and he smiled. "I got you a treat, too. Just promise me you'll brush your teeth super clean before bed."

They high fived and Tipsy smoothed his dark blonde hair as he headed to his bedroom. She clipped down the rest of the stairs with a growing hollowness in her stomach.

Big Ayers stood in the kitchen, leaning against the magenta countertop. His inherent manliness against the color scheme, along with the fruits-and-veggies-themed wallpaper, gave the impression that someone had dropped a lumberjack into a Chiquita banana advertisement. Tipsy inhaled his presence, as she had for years, trying to read the vibrations in the air around him.

"Hey," she said. "You doin' okay?"

He nodded. He hadn't shaved, but that wasn't too unusual. He wore a baseball cap, and had for the past few years since his hair had started thinning. The visors of his twenties didn't cut it anymore on boat days, what with the sun beating on his scalp. He'd lowered the brim almost to his eyebrows, but his height necessitated that she look up at him. She had a decent angle on his big brown eyes, so like his daughters'.

He crossed his arms over his increasingly round belly and scuffed his feet against the old tile. "Place looks good, but this kitchen needs a damn update." He spoke around a wad of gum. Another habit that made no sense. Big-city taxi drivers chewed endless splats of gum, not the sons of genteel southern families.

At least I don't have to try to explain his idiosyncrasies anymore. Or live with them. Aloud, she said, "I guess old ladies don't care too much about granite countertops and Viking ranges."

Ayers grunted his agreement. "I kinda always pictured us in a house like this."

"You don't like old houses. Too much maintenance."

"Something *like* this. Not *this house.*" He rolled his eyes.

"Right." Tipsy hadn't argued with Ayers in years. There was never any point in it. Not about cleaning the bathrooms or universal health care, about the children's aversion to vegetables or Russian collusion. Over the years she told herself, *choose your battles*, but truthfully, her internal army had dug deeper into the trenches and refused to engage, resulting in an emotional No Man's Land between them. Even post-divorce, she preferred to stay safely on her side of the battlefield.

"We could have built. In a couple more years, on the water." He grabbed a paper towel, spit his gum into it, and threw the wad into the sink. He took a pack of gum from his pocket and started the whole chewing process over again.

"Have you had any offers on the property?" As soon as she said it, she wished she hadn't, but the mention of building on the water inevitably reminded her that Ayers had lost all their savings in a bad land deal. One fraudulent environmental survey, plus a few determined twenty-something conservationists and fifteen endangered nesting birds had equaled financial disaster for Ayers Lee Collins IV, and hence disaster for Tipsy. All well and good to have a financial settlement that said he owed her one hundred and fifty thousand dollars, but if he didn't have it, she wasn't getting diddly squat. He'd gotten out of paying her monthly alimony with his trumped up adultery charge, but she was still entitled to the value of half their assets. Unfortunately, their liquid assets had disappeared.

"I've told you. That land isn't worth the grass growing on it. Can't build a damn thing. No one's going to buy it."

"I'm sorry. I didn't mean to bring it up. I guess I'm still hopeful."

"Thanks for reminding me I'm a goddamn failure living off my daddy at thirty-nine years old."

"Ayers—you're not a failure."

He covered his eyes with his hands, and Tipsy gripped the door handle of the ancient beige Frigidaire. He might yell, or he might cry. In the days of their marriage she would have guessed the former, but since she'd asked him to move out six months ago, she'd gotten more of the latter. When the land deal went south in March, she'd lost any ability to predict how he would react to anything.

"Tomorrow's an early morning," she said in the kind of voice she might have used had Ayers been the one she'd be sending off to soccer camp in the morning, instead of his namesake. "I should get the kids moving toward bed. You should do the same."

"I would have changed, Tipsy," he said, and while she thanked god he wasn't bringing the hysterics, she breathed in his heavy sadness until her lungs felt like sandbags in her chest. "We would have gotten through this, if you'd given me some kind of chance."

A girlish, gleeful screech came from the second floor, followed by the roar of Little Ayers doing his best zombie impression. The kind of game that starts fun and ends up with someone bruised or crying or both. "I should check on them," she said.

"Yeah." Ayers wiped at his eyes. "I'm going home. Empty house on a Sunday afternoon. Shit, why talk about it."

Tipsy backed away. "Have you been taking your medication?"

"Screw that. That doctor didn't know what the hell he was talking about."

"If you need anything, call me."

"Yeah." He paused in the doorway. "By the way, Jimmy decided to put this place on the market by next spring. Plenty of time for him to make improvements and then offload it."

"I see," said Tipsy. She'd been hoping for at least a year, but she wouldn't look a gift brother-in-law in the mouth. Every month saved her a few thousand bucks she didn't have.

Ayers mirrored her thoughts. "Almost a year for you to figure something out. You should be happy with that."

"I am. Tell him I'm grateful."

"I don't want my kids living in some shitty apartment eighty percent of the time. No yard to run around in. No place to have friends come play."

Tipsy's voice dropped to a whisper. "Neither do I."

"Minding the desk at Shelby's art gallery isn't going to cut it forever, you know."

She wanted to strangle him. "I haven't really worked since Little Ayers came along. That's a pretty big gap in the resume. Right now I'm grateful I have a job."

"You should try painting. You know, *your thing*." She pictured sarcastic quotation marks around the last two words. "You made a little money off it back in the day."

In truth, Tipsy had supported them the first two years of their marriage, while Ayers job-hopped from one unsuccessful venture to the next. They hadn't been rich, but for a Charleston-based artist, she'd done pretty damn well. She wanted to remind him of that, and add, *at least I have a "thing" that's mine,* but instead she said, "Hopefully I'll sell something soon."

"Yeah, well, unless things change, maybe every other weekend will be all you can handle. It's a good thing I have a proper home for them, should the need come to that."

Tipsy drew in a sharp breath. Ayers had never flat out suggested the kids live with him.

"It won't come to that," she said. "It will not."

"Right," said Ayers, and he left with Eric Church blasting out the open windows of his truck.

The hollow feeling in her stomach didn't dissipate during the kids' baths or story time or tucking in. She sat cross-legged in the landing between Little Ayers's bedroom and the girls' bedroom and sang *Sweet Baby James* until all three children stopped rolling around and their breathing came in soft, unsynchronized puffs. Only then did she let the tears come.

She climbed into bed without washing her face or brushing her teeth. *What am I doing?* she asked herself, or maybe she asked Granna, but Granna didn't answer. Besides, she'd asked herself that question a million times over the last year. She had good days. She got up every morning, and hugged her kids and did what she had to do and laughed when things were funny. But the sadness over her failed family— her failed life— never left her. Ayers had known her a long time. He'd stood in the wings, a somewhat interested observer, while she wrestled her postpartum depression into submission. He probably sensed melancholy churning under the ice sheet of her can-do attitude.

She lay there in the dark, on her children's first night in Miss Callie's house. *Pros. Cons. What if this. Maybe that.* She'd never been able to consider staying in her old house herself. She couldn't pay the mortgage. She could have forced Ayers to sell it, but she'd chosen the divorce. It had seemed heartless to take his home, and the only home her kids had ever known, in the neighborhood where all their friends lived. At this point, even if she pushed for him to sell, she knew he'd fight her. She didn't have spare cash for lawyers and court battles.

He would never really take the kids. He's just blowing smoke, like he usually does. She tried to convince herself, but foreboding swelled inside her. Ayers would say ten things—good or bad— and nine of them would fall by the wayside, never to be heard of again. He'd choose one, however, and vehemently see it through until the end. She could only hope this wasn't unlucky number ten.

She had about twelve thousand dollars left from Granna's life insurance policy, enough to keep her going for a few months, as long as she didn't pay rent. By the time Jimmy put Miss Callie's house on the market she'd be past this worry, one way or another. The only scenarios she didn't actively consider were prostitution and returning to her marriage. As devastating as the ramifications were, Ayers's vengeful behavior since their separation had only justified her decision. She pictured him, earlier that evening, smug in his ability to pay the bills, which in his mind, made him the superior parent. She'd never buy that man another pack of Wrigley's Spearmint, much less sleep in the same bed with him.

The tears kept coming, but she didn't cry out loud. Olivia Grace slept lightly. God forbid she wake to her mama having a meltdown on her first night in her new home.

Is there any point in calling it home if Jimmy is going to sell it within a year?

She must have fallen asleep, but it seemed that only a moment passed between crying and waking up to Jane Mott's pale face. In the dark Jane looked less solid. She emitted a kind of bluish glow, like a dying flashlight.

"I would find a way to ease your mind, for you seem to have many preoccupations," Jane said. "But I cannot bring you a glass of tea. That's what my mama would have recommended."

Tipsy propped her head on her elbow and sniffed. "She sounds like my Granna. Sweet tea solves all problems."

"That gloomy large round man. Is he your husband?"

For some reason the description struck Tipsy as both hilarious and accurate. She giggled. Soon the ghost smiled back at her in a way that wasn't spooky at all. "Ex-husband," Tipsy said. "We're divorced."

The grin left Jane's face—as if Tipsy had declared Ayers to be a leper and herself a carrier of the bubonic plague. Jane blinked in exclamation points of dismay. "How *truly awful.*"

"It's not. Or, maybe it is. Hell, I don't know."

"Mama and Daddy would have sent me to a lunatic asylum or a convent before allowing *that*. Were you unhappy for a spell before your…" Jane lowered her voice. "…*divorce?*"

Tipsy thought of her years of tiptoeing around Ayers's temper, the conversations like pruning roses. She needed to find just the right grip to avoid the thorns. She nodded. "He was, too, but for different reasons. Were you unhappy?"

"Most obviously, since one doesn't kill one's wife and oneself in a fit of *joy.*"

"Many people are unhappily married. They don't commit murder."

"Henry killed me for my inheritance." Jane's fingers spun in her lap, just as they had during Tipsy's first conversation with her. As if she were knitting together her explanation.

Tipsy frowned. "You couldn't have been struggling too badly. Y'all lived in this huge house."

Jane oozed rationality and blinkiness. "Many people live in large houses but have modest bank accounts. I knew families who lived on South Battery and barely put *food* on the *table*, bless their hearts."

"You're right," said Tipsy. "Look at all the people who took out interest-only mortgages and are upside down."

"Pardon?"

"Never mind. Were you due a large inheritance?"

"When my parents passed on, yes. Not Vanderbilt standard, but a decent sum."

"Were they ill?"

"*Heavens,* no. I come from hardy stock."

"It wouldn't do Henry much good to kill you and wait twenty years for your parents to go, too. Besides, you think he killed himself, too!"

Jane's face darkened from translucent blue to a shade reminiscent of anti-freeze. "Have you been speaking with him?"

"I did. Yesterday, for a few minutes."

"Ha! I *knew* it!"

Tipsy sat up. Her bedroom glowed with Jane's blue anger. "I can look into what happened. Maybe check the old newspapers?"

Jane shook her head. Her black bob whipped back and forth like the ears of a wet spaniel.

"Maybe Henry didn't do it," Tipsy said. "You'd have no reason to hate him—"

"You're convinced of his innocence!"

"No! Listen to me." Tipsy threw back the blanket and climbed out of bed. "If we can find proof that he did kill you, he'll have to admit it and apologize. If you have to haunt this place for all eternity, at least you'd do it in peace."

Jane paced the bedroom. Her effervescence pulsed as she faded and solidified. As she slowed, the room lightened. Her blue anger faded away in a cold dawn. She stopped in the far corner of the room, near the tiny closet. "Thank you for your thoughtful sentiments. And I'm sure Henry beguiled you, in his Henry way of beguiling." A wry smile twitched the corners of her purplish lips. "But I have no desire to turn over stones that have long since anchored into the ground."

Tipsy plopped down on the edge of the bed. "Jane, that's ridiculous. How can it hurt to know—"

"Goodnight, Miss Tiffany-Tipsy." Jane strode toward Tipsy with her hands clasped before her chest, like a high priestess approaching a sacrificial altar. A dismissive, irritable noise from the back of her throat—"*Hmmph!*"—and electric blue light shone from her pallid face.

Tipsy held one hand before her own face. Her eyes scrunched shut of their own volition.

Before she could open her eyes, she fell backward. Tipped right on over, like a spilt glass of tea. And in those seconds— *or minutes? or maybe hours?* — between her eyes closing and her head hitting the mattress, something happened. Something supernatural, the likes of which had never happened to her before.

———•———

A waterfall flows through Tipsy's head. She can't see, it's all yellow and silver and she's opening her eyes but, Jesus, why can't she see? What happened to the sun?

She blinks and—what the hell?—she's standing in a bedroom. Planked wooden floors and wallpaper that's green and brown and gray and tan stripes. A four-poster bed, just big enough for two people, is adorned with dark green curtains. Someone's tossed the curtains over the posters, perhaps to make a path for the breeze. The sheets are a jumbled mess at the foot of the bed. The gray quilt is in a pile on the floor. The room smells of oranges, the source of which Tipsy locates in a crystal bowl on the desk by the open window. The door to her left is open. There's a delicate hand holding the doorknob. Female voices chatter away in the adjacent hallway.

A man hunches over the desk with his back to Tipsy, but his hair gives him away. Bright red on top has sweat-darkened to auburn at the base of his neck. He glances toward the door, his mouth set in a firm line of irritation, then returns his attention to the pile of paper in front of him.

"Henry!" Tipsy crosses the floor. Her bare feet make no sound against the wood planks. Her voice doesn't either, because Henry doesn't flinch, much less turn around.

The door opens wide. Jane steps into the bedroom, but not the pale fragile Jane Tipsy knows. This woman has bright pink cheeks and reddish lips, and she looks like she's been drinking the sunshine like Tipsy's girls slurp down glasses of cold lemonade. She's wearing a white dress and stockings and shoes. Her hair is twisted into a bun at the base of her neck. She's tucked a white magnolia blossom into the swirls of dark hair.

The colors and sounds and smells are so vivid, Tipsy feels like she's stepped into one of her own paintings. She stares at Jane in wonder. She can almost feel Jane's pulse— see the very blood rushing through tiny veins under her skin. Happiness and love seep from her pores. Vibrant emotions and a thumping heart create the perfect blush on that lovely, amazingly alive face. The perfect work of art—the painting to end all paintings. What Tipsy has always hoped to produce.

Jane calls cheerfully over her shoulder to someone in the hallway. "We'll be right there—just give me a moment!" She closes the door behind her. "Dearest, are you coming down?" she asks, as she walks toward Henry.

"No."

"Aren't you finished? I don't think you even slept last night. When I woke"—Tipsy automatically steps out of Jane's way. Jane puts her hands on Henry's shoulders—"there you were, lamp burning and all. And now here you still sit!"

He shrugs her massaging hands from his shoulders. "I'm not finished."

"What are you writing? A story, or a poem?"

Henry turns around, and Jane backs away from him. "You'd never understand," he says, "and I won't finish it if you don't leave me to it."

"Oh, please, Henry. Come down for a bit. Tomorrow is Thanksgiving Day."

"It is." Henry mops the back of his neck with a green handkerchief. "Although how it can be so damnably hot I don't know. We should have stayed home. Maybe we could have caught some wind off the harbor."

"Silly!" Jane's dimples must be an inch deep. World-record-setting dimple depth. "We always spend the holiday at the Old Cannon."

The Old Cannon, *Tipsy thinks.* Jane said her mother's family came from the Old Cannon, on the Wando River. It must be some kind of country home.

"Come, it's past lunchtime," Jane says. "Mr. and Mrs. Barnwell are on their way from Columbia. You know Mrs. Barnwell plays a nice piano. And the Hugers are coming, and they're bringing Johnny along with them. He's such a fine singer—"

"John Huger is a fop. He cares for nothing but playing tennis and smoking cigars."

"That's unkind. You shouldn't about him speak so. We've been friends since we were children, running about in bows and short pants. I thought we could all have a bit of a sing before supper! Remember that Christmas when we sang—"

Henry snorts. "You can't sing worth a damn, Jane."

She flinches as if he'd spit at her, but she keeps smiling. "You're right, but who cares among friends? Oh, and my sister and little Luisa will be here, and I believe the Reverend is going to ride with them from town! They'll all stay a few nights—"

"Wonderful."

"—and we won't have to miss church. The Reverend can give the service right here at the Old Cannon."

Henry returns to his notebooks. "I'm not coming down until I'm finished."

"But Henry, you're never finished—"

"For the love of god, what are you? A fretful child?" He spins around again. "There are more important things in life than picnics and tone-deaf sing-alongs and suppers with people who only come together to talk about everyone in the state of South Carolina who isn't currently participating in those trivial activities!" Henry's face goes redder and redder as he speaks, for he doesn't stop to draw breath. His dark blue eyes bulge. While Jane looks *markedly different from the ghost Tipsy has spoken with a few times, Henry isn't far off the mark of familiarity. Perhaps it's lack of sleep or too many hours ensconced inside, but he's almost as pale and cavern-eyed as ever. He whacks his pencil against the paper. "You think you know beauty, Jane, in your flowers and frilly dresses. But you know nothing of it."*

Jane's grin has become fixed on her face, as if she'd offered to smile for a photographer, and he took too long adjusting the lighting. "It's clear you'd rather stay here."

"It is, isn't it."

"I shall tell everyone you've a headache. And send Beatrice up with a plate of lunch."

"I'm not hungry, thank you."

"Certainly." Jane walks to the bedroom door, a stiff mannequin version of the buoyant woman who'd entered not ten minutes before. The exquisite emotions Tipsy saw so clearly are gone, and Tipsy wants to cry out in mourning for the loss of their beauty.

Henry is already scribbling by the time Jane shuts the door behind her. Tipsy wants to stay, to see what will happen next, but the black and yellow lights return and she can't hold on. Her own life is calling her, and she has to answer.

———————•———————

When Tipsy woke up, she was lying on her back. She strained for something to focus on in the dark room, and finally picked out the outline of the cracked glass light fixture over Miss Callie's bed. She sat up. A quick glance around the room told her that Jane had disappeared. She climbed toward the pillows, and slid under the sheets.

So strange, she thought. Perhaps the blue light flashing in her face had brought on some kind of supernatural seizure— induced a dream of some sort. But whatever she'd just seen, it hadn't felt like a normal dream. Or a dream at all, really. It felt more like one of her movie memories— but from someone else's life. The smell of ripe oranges; the sweat-soaked, russet and flame colored chunks of Henry's hair; and most of all, Jane's transition from ebullience to rigidity—she'd never had such a vivid dream, and the longer she lay there thinking about it, she remembered more detail, not less.

If only I could capture that version of Jane on canvas. My worries would be over.

She checked her phone. It was nearly three o'clock in the morning. She rolled over and closed her eyes, and tried in vain to sleep. Life and death, with all their facets and conundrums, climbed into the bed and pressed against her like frightened children. She lay crammed between the two, but no amount of repositioning brought her comfort. She couldn't dismiss the feeling that Jane and Henry weren't the only ones trapped in a no man's land between one life and another.

Chapter 3

The next day, Tipsy woke Little Ayers and the twins for soccer camp and art camp, respectively. She hustled them through their usual routine. Get dressed, brush teeth, fix the girls' pigtails and flatten Little Ayers's hair with water, tramp to the kitchen for breakfast. All three sat around the table with bowls of cereal and sliced bananas. The smell of the peanut butter and jelly sandwiches she'd tucked into their lunchboxes permeated the room. The magenta kitchen clashed with the girls' red polo dresses and Ayers's red tee shirt.

"Did y'all all plan on red today?" she asked.

Mary Pratt's grin revealed a few pastel marshmallows between the spaces left by her lost teeth. "It's a rosy day!"

"An apple day!" said Olivia Grace.

Ayers growled at them and held up his hands in claws. "It's a zombie day!"

"Good lord," said Tipsy. "Ayers Lee, that's unpleasant. And what is it with zombies lately? Everyone loves zombies."

"Zombies are gross," said Mary Pratt.

"That's why I love them," said Ayers.

"Goddamn you!"

Tipsy dropped O-liv's empty cereal bowl. By some miracle it didn't shatter, but both girls jumped.

"You okay, Mama?" Ayers asked.

"Yes—I'm fine. I just slipped—"

"If I could throttle you now, I would, I swear to all that is holy!"

41

Tipsy grabbed for the cereal bowl. Jane's shrill voice joined Henry's as Tipsy clunked the bowl into the sink.

"So you're admitting it?" Jane asked. "Finally? You did it! You did it! You did it!"

Tipsy spun around and gripped the edge of the counter behind her. She stared past her children's wide-eyed faces.

Jane and Henry stood at opposite ends of the kitchen. Henry's face had contorted in rage, while Jane looked as if she were watching some hilarious stand-up comedy routine.

"No. I'm not admitting it!" yelled Henry. "I'll never admit it because I didn't do it!"

"Mama—you sure you're all right?" asked Ayers.

Tipsy grinned at him, and hoped her expression conveyed more sanity than Jane's did. "Yes, of course baby. I'm—"

"You did!" Jane spoke around hysterical laughter. "You did! Mama said you did—"

"Your mother was an idiot!" Henry screamed, and the faucet behind Tipsy blasted water into the sink.

"The water!" Olivia Grace shouted. "Water, Mama!"

Tipsy spun around as Henry and Jane continued to berate each other. She spoke in a voice that seemed to come from outside her own head. "Oh, it's okay. Just old pipes!" She yanked the faucet's handle into place, and the water shut off. "Time to get going!"

"I'm not finished with my cereal," said Ayers.

"Let's take a granola bar—we have to—"

"Damnit!" Henry shouted, and the bookshelf Tipsy had set up in the corner of the kitchen crashed to the ground. The kids screamed as cookbooks, family pictures and knick-knacks scattered across the tile.

"It's okay! It's okay!" Tipsy herded the sobbing girls into the hallway. "Don't be scared, buddies. Mama must not have put that thing together correctly—"

Mary Pratt gripped Tipsy's hand. "But it was so loud—"

"And my plate broke!" Olivia Grace looked up at her with tearstained cheeks. "My Christmas plate with my handprints on it from when I was little!"

"I'll glue it together, baby, I promise," Tipsy said.

She grabbed their little summer camp backpacks. Ayers patted his sisters' shoulders. "Don't worry, y'all. I knew that bookshelf was cheap anyway."

If she had any ability to calm her thoughts as well as she'd calmed her voice, Tipsy would have laughed at his typical Little Ayers man-of-the-house response. She hurried them outside. The whack of the front door slamming behind them cut off the sound of Jane and Henry's battle.

The kids heard nothing, said Granna. *They never hear or see a thing. No harm done.*

Tipsy's children had never shown the slightest sign of clairvoyance, so she wasn't worried about that. Regardless, she didn't share Granna's nonchalance. *They did see their mother on the verge of a panic attack. I'm not even going to pretend I played that one off.*

Will you get used to it?

How can you get used to people no one else can see screaming at each other in your presence? And that bookshelf... what if one of the kids had been standing beside it? Tipsy's mind raced as she buckled the girls into their booster seats.

"I can do it, Mama," said Mary Pratt.

Tipsy kissed her daughter. "I want to help you, baby."

She got into the driver's seat with new and grim determination. Solving Jane and Henry's conundrum wasn't just about curiosity, or about bringing them the peace of a resolution. She needed to protect her children, and if she was lucky, her sanity.

———•———

After dropping the kids at their camps, Tipsy spent a queasy two hours scrolling through dizzyingly small type and inhaling the vinegary smell of decaying film before admitting she'd ridiculously overestimated the amount of information she'd get from the College of Charleston's microfiche files. She planned to peruse issues of the February 1923 *News and Courier* and *The Evening Post*, read about the murder, and grab coffee before heading to her job at Shelby's art gallery on Queen Street, the Good Queen Bess. Drop kids at camp, check! Solve murder mystery, check!

Maybe she'd expected a glaring headline, "Double Murder on Bennett Street," followed by the subhead, "Lovely couple killed by Mr. John P. Murderer, who shall now rot in jail before he rots in hell." Or, "Double Food Poisoning Mistaken for Murder! Lovely couple victims of spoiled chicken." She would have settled for, "HE DID IT! Henry Mott murdered his lovely wife."

She found Jane and Henry's obituaries, nestled amid advertisements for hair tonics and social announcements, but not one mention of how they died. At half past nine, she gave up and headed to work. She prepped the gallery for opening: dusting, sweeping, laying out some pamphlets and brochures, wiping down the bathroom. After restocking the toilet paper, she leaned on the reception desk and reread the photocopied death announcements to herself for the twentieth time, as if some new information might be gleaned from them.

Henry Whitestone Mott (January 31, 1894 - February 19, 1923) and Jane Alice Robinette Mott (May 3, 1895 - February 19, 1923) of Mount Pleasant entered into eternal rest this past Sunday. Henry was the son of Frederick and Patience Mott (née Lewiston) of Bull Street, Charleston. Jane was the daughter of Pierre and Theresa Robinette (née Beckett) of Water Street, Charleston. The unfortunate deceased are survived by their parents. Surviving siblings include Edward Mott and Constance Bishop (née Robinette), and a niece, Luisa Bishop. Henry Mott was in the employ of Mott & Phipps Wholesale Company, with responsibility for the firm's warehouses East of the Cooper. He studied English Literature at the University of South Carolina before traveling extensively throughout Europe and Canada. Jane kept their home on Bennett Street, in Mount Pleasant, and was known as a gracious hostess both in her own home and at the Beckett family plantation, the Old Cannon, in Berkeley County. The congregation of St. Philips' Episcopal Church will miss her high spirits and gay laughter. Church picnics will suffer without her well-regarded pecan pie recipe. The family will receive friends at the home of Pierre and Theresa Robinette on February 23, from 12 to 4 o'clock in the afternoon, with burial services at St. Phillips' on February 24 at 9 o'clock in the morning. Services will be officiated by the Reverend Proctor James. Requiescat in pace.

"Peace," Tipsy said, as Shelby whizzed through the door with blonde hair flying and cleavage bouncing.

"Mama might be coming in to check on things this week!" she shouted over the clanging bell. The bell settled into miffed silence. Shelby and that bronze sentry always tried to out-yowl each other, and the bell always lost.

Shelby dropped a pile of files and art magazines on the desk. "Calm down." Tipsy tapped Shelby's yin and yang tattoo. Her off button. "We're having a pretty good month."

"It's been okay, but it's tourist season. We need to be slingin' some art."

"You're a Picasso pimp. You're a Hans Holbein hustla." Tipsy did a suitable white girl bootie grind against Shelby's rear end, but Shelby had no sense of humor when it came to appeasing Elizabeth Patterson. Besides, although Shelby could easily live off her family's money, she took pride in her work. She'd been running the Good Queen Bess Art Gallery for her mother for years.

Tipsy had first visited the GQB in college. It occupied two floors of an old tenement building in the French Quarter. The neighbors included two other art galleries, an antiques dealer and a shop that sold high-end, handmade home accessories and lighting fixtures. Elizabeth Patterson had been the first person to sell Tipsy's work in those post-college days of overflowing ideas. Tipsy adored everything about the GQB, from its foggy old windows to the smell of ceramic dust to the tiny bathroom where she had to pull her knees toward her chest to take a pee.

"We show some good stuff in GQB, but no geniuses," said Shelby. "Only genius around here is the one working behind the counter."

Here it comes, said Granna. *If she weren't so right I'd say that nag was walloped dead five times over.*

"You painted anything yet?" Shelby continued as she alternately tossed some papers in the trash and added the rest to the pile under the desk.

Tipsy saw no need to pussyfoot around. "No."

"Honey, you promised!"

"I'm trying. People keep saying to me, you're going through a hard time, so pour it into your work. That doesn't happen for me. When I'm stressed, or sad—" She shrugged. "I'm not good at the tortured artist routine."

"I hear you. I'm not going to patronize you by going on about your creative outlets and all that bullshit. That last painting—"

"It felt like a fluke."

"It sold for four grand in five days."

Tipsy rubbed both hands across her face. That painting, Tipsy's first real work in over eight years, had woken something in her. It had followed months of increasingly frenetic sketching. First a few times a week, then every day, until she'd come across Mary Pratt sitting on Ayers's parents' dock, holding the string of a bright blue birthday balloon. The image had burned a hole into Tipsy's mind, like sunlight after she'd closed her eyes. It dogged her until she transferred it to canvas, just like in the old days. It hurt to think about it. In the act of rousing Tipsy, it forced her to face reality, and therefore abandon the passion it had revived. She'd asked Ayers to move out soon after, and hadn't painted a thing since.

Shelby put her hands on her hips. "Look, Tipsy. I love you, so I'm telling you true. You should be exhibiting in this place. Not minding the desk and directing lost tourists to the carriage rides. How are you and the kids going to survive once you have to leave Miss Callie's? Do you think Ayers will pay up?"

"I'm not getting anything else from him but the fourteen hundred bucks a month he pays me in child support."

"So he lives high on the hog with his parents bankrolling him on the side, while you're scraping by without any GD freakin' alimony." Much to Tipsy's discomfort, Shelby delved into the reason for the lack of said GD freakin' alimony. "You're finally done with Saint Dave, right?"

"Haha," Tipsy said. "He goes to New Day Church—"

"New Dazed," said Shelby. "That place is a cult for the self-righteous. The holier thou art, the greater chance thou art a lying, philandering drunk. And that holds for the women as much as the men. I just want to know you got rid of him."

"Need I remind you, *he* got rid of me when Ayers went psycho on him. Not that I really blame him."

"Why not? Blame him, Tips! Dave knew you were just getting out of your marriage. He came on like high tide at the full moon."

"Ayers threatened to talk trash about him all over town. Guess it was too much for him." She'd put the fiasco of Saint Dave behind her, but their relatively brief but intense relationship wasn't without emotional residue. "Yes, it's over. We say hi when I see him at the gym. That's about it."

"Thank god. I hope he prays to his savior every night over the hearts he's broken until his shiny white teeth hurt. Sure wasn't worth losing alimony over a set of nice pecs."

Tipsy walked through the gallery while Shelby's rant shifted from Dave's pecs to Ayers's scheming. "…so that asshole *tells* you he doesn't care if you're dating after y'all separate. Who would hire a PI, he says. That's crazy psycho shit and a waste of money, he says, let's both just move on! And then once you fall into the arms of Saint Dave, Ayers slams you with adultery and you get no alimony. Not even a couple years to get you back on your feet. After living with him all those years and taking care of his babies and tolerating his crazy moods—"

"We've been over this a thousand times. It's just South Carolina law." Tipsy understood Shelby's frustration. The State of South Carolina wanted people to get married and *stay* married. Until recently, the state recognized the antiquated legal concept of common law marriage. South Carolina didn't legalize divorce until 1949 and still did not recognize legal separation. In the eyes of the law, until the ink dried on a Final Marital Settlement Agreement, approved by the Family Court, the spouse that strayed outside the bonds of Holy Matrimony was a cheater, case closed. It didn't much matter if the parties lived apart for years, nor did the Court care that Ayers told Tipsy to go ahead and get on with her life. The state's alimony statute clearly defined marital infidelity as a valid basis for denying spousal support to the cheater, and this punishment affected women far more often than men. While the supporting spouse, usually the husband, might get a stern look from the judge for being unfaithful, the unsupported spouse, usually the wife, got the full Scarlet Letter treatment.

"Adultery means no alimony," Tipsy said. "Seems like every divorced person we know has either hired a private investigator or been followed by one. Why would Ayers be any different?"

Shelby leaned against the wall. The blue heron in the painting beside her loomed over her with beady yellow eyes, as if it would spear her if she didn't agree. "You're right, but—"

"I shouldn't have risked it. I know I have to take everything Ayers says with a grain of salt, good or bad. I shouldn't have believed him when he said he didn't care if I dated. But I was lonely and scared and I wanted to believe him because it made things easier for me."

"He still manipulated you for his own good," said Shelby. "You're too hard on yourself and too easy on him. And Dave. Like always. You have a studio art degree and you're working for me. At least make it worth your while. Paint something."

Tipsy opened her mouth, but Shelby held up her hands. "Enough—damned if you shouldn't have gone to New York with your god-given talent and skipped college altogether."

"I promised my Granna I'd go."

"Tips, watching you is the art dealer's equivalent of a birdwatcher eyeballing an albatross that thinks its wing is broken and won't even try to fly."

Tipsy had no reply. That analogy felt too close to the truth.

———•———

Shelby exited the GQB in another huff, on her way to a meeting. Tipsy circled the five exhibit rooms as a few tourists wandered into the gallery. Her admiration of the varied paintings slowly turned to gnawing jealousy. Why did other artists produce and she did not? In the old days, she'd felt like she would never have time to bring to life all the paintings in her head. Now, her mental gallery contained a row of empty frames. The lights shone on bare walls.

She returned to the desk with grim determination. A mere doodle on a piece of copy paper would suffice, but she would draw something. The bell announced a visitor as she started sketching her grandmother's face.

"Hey, Tipsy," said a man in khakis and dark blue polo shirt. Tipsy took in his hair, thick and black and curly, and remembered Lindsey tapping her own blonde head. *He has good hair.*

"Hey, Will," Tipsy said. "You here to see Shelby? She went to meet a client."

"She asked me to come by and measure some flooring that's got water damage. In the hallway by the second exhibit room."

"Oh, right! I know what you mean."

She led him down the narrow hallway and pointed out a patch of discolored wood in the midst of the wide antique planks. "You work on floors?"

"My company specializes in historic restorations. Plank wood floors. Moldings and built-in libraries. Rebuilding porches and staircases." He crossed his arms over his chest. He had pretty greenish eyes, and a Marlboro Man jaw line, but he watched Tipsy as if his comment had been a test question and there were no multiple-choice options. No different from her first passing meeting with him. His glare had the kind of weight that made a person feel the need to stoop under it.

"Oh, that's neat," she said. Will continued to stare at her, as if he expected her to keep talking. "Good town for it. There's so much hard wood around here." She grimaced. "Oh, lord. That didn't sound right."

Will laughed, a high, almost boyish sound. The glare disappeared. When he smiled, it seemed like his whole face grinned at her, not just his mouth. For a moment Tipsy thought he was teasing her. "I'm sorry," he said. "Thanks for making this less awkward."

She smiled tentatively, and exhaled her own giggle. "No problem, but why is it awkward?"

He rubbed his jaw before kneeling and pulling a measuring tape from his pocket. "Man, I'm not doing this very smoothly. I asked Shelby if you were working today. I kind of thought… after meeting you for a minute a few weeks ago…I wanted a chance to ask you out."

"That's…" *A complete and utter shock.* "…so sweet. Most guys would just text."

"I'm a terrible texter," he said, and Tipsy had the urge to touch his hair. "Besides, a girl like you, sure you get plenty of texts. I wanted to rise above the pack."

Tipsy waved a dismissive hand at the top of his head. "Silly. There's no pack." She'd never seen someone who could manage to appear on the verge of laughter while simultaneously scrunching his eyebrows together. Will had a slightly crooked smile, and could be evidenced in the deep dimples on the right side of his face. The result was endearing in a decidedly goofy way.

"Listen to you," she said. "So much for awkward and being unsmooth."

"I take a bit to warm up."

"Slow boil," Tipsy said. Maybe that first quick introduction hadn't given him a chance to turn on any kind of heat.

"Gotta dig deep for the charm. Am I charming?"

"In an odd way." She blushed, but to her delight she got another dose of his boyish laughter. "That sounded awful," she said. "Maybe I'm a slow boil, too."

"Been out of the game a while?"

"Yeah. For about sixteen years."

"I've been back at it for a couple years now, but I'm not sure what I've learned. My daughter thinks I'm hopeless."

"How old is she?"

"She's almost fourteen."

"You don't look old enough to have a fourteen-year-old." Tipsy gave in and reached for his hair. "No gray."

"I'm thirty-six. Got started early."

"Wow, just out of college?"

He nodded. "Didn't have much choice, if you know what I mean. Isabel was coming whether we planned it or not. Shotgun wedding."

"Oh, I see." Not all twenty-two-year-old guys would have risen to the occasion of fatherhood. "Is Isabel your only child?"

"No, two others. My ex-wife waited a good while before agreeing to more kids. Then we had Ella and Rosie. Boom-boom. They're five and four. I have them half the time, since before Rosie was two."

"Really? Seems like most guys do the every-other-weekend thing."

Will pulled the tape measure from its plastic casing and let go. It retreated back inside the casing with a *zip-snap*. "No way. Not me. I made sure it was fifty-fifty. I'd hate to be away from them that much."

"Daddy's girls," said Tipsy, before filling him in on the basics of her own situation.

He pried up a few boards as she talked. He hmmm-ed and asked quiet clarifying questions at the right times. Despite his perpetually wrinkled brow as he stared at the wood below him, that half smile played on his lips when he looked up at her. "I'm listening," he said several times as she yammered on. He stood again. They were about the same height. "So here is where I officially ask you out. Get ready."

"I'm waiting," she said, and she leaned over to scoop up a few splinters of wood by her shoes. Sharp edges dug into her tender palms as she swept away the remnants of his work. She walked back down the hallway and flicked the shards into the trashcan beside her desk. She kind of hoped he was watching her. Her pulse quickened pleasantly, and she bit the inside of her cheek to keep from grinning.

You sure this is a good time? Asked Granna. *You just moved. How about getting settled in?*

It's only a date.

You just ended it with Dave. Plus you were married for twelve years, and been dating Ayers since you were eighteen.

All the more reason to have some fun.

You can have fun without a man.

Granna's commentary felt sort of Shelby-like in its annoying truthfulness, but Tipsy forgot her grandmother's wisdom, and her million other problems, when she looked at Will Garrison's lopsided smile.

"Do you have your kids this weekend?" he asked. The standard divorced people question. "If not, maybe we could—"

Tipsy cut him off with a gasp. Henry Mott peered over Will's shoulder, as if Will had sprouted a second, fiery red head, like a ginger hydra. Henry's dark blue eyes, cold and flat, met Tipsy's. A three-foot-tall ceramic statue of two entwined lovers floated above Will's head.

An unfamiliar vibrating heat welled up inside Tipsy. It came on like a sneeze through her eyes. She felt as if her mind had somehow taken hold of the statue. She cut a glance to her right. It struck the wall and exploded. Shards and chunks of ceramic sprayed across the hallway like shrapnel.

"Shit!" Will grabbed Tipsy around the shoulders and pulled her head to his chest. He covered her exposed cheek with his hand. "What the hell?"

She pulled away from his embrace. Her pulse beat a wild staccato that she felt from her head to her stomach to her toes. No sign of Henry in the hallway.

What just happened? Vibrations lingered in Tipsy's cheeks. Whatever had shot from her field of vision had made her eyes water. Her eyes drew a frantic triangle from the vacant display pedestal to the empty air above Will's head to the mess on the floor. She'd somehow diverted the statue's seemingly intended concussive path. Her hands shook. *Was that really Henry—and how the hell did he get here?*

It sure looked like Henry, said Granna, *but in all my years I've never seen the same ghost in more than one place. And I certainly never saw anyone – dead or alive – who could chuck a big 'ol inanimate object against a wall under the power of eyesight.*

You never did something like that?

Uh, no. But listen, sugar, that don't mean nothing. We might share headspace these days, but you ain't me and I ain't you.

"Are you alright?" Will asked. He gripped Tipsy's shoulders.

"Yes. Thank you—but you're not!" A thin line of blood ran down his arm. "Oh, Will, I'm sorry—"

"No big deal, just a scratch," he said. She grabbed a few tissues from the reception desk and dabbed at his arm. To her relief, once she wiped the blood clean, she saw he was right.

"I'm so sorry. I don't know what happened."

Again with the crooked smile and gentle eyes beneath his knitted brow. "Why are you apologizing? Not your fault. That thing looked precarious on that stand anyway. Like those pottery people were hugging while walking on a tightrope." He eyed the bits of ceramic covering the floor. "But damn, no putting it back together."

"Nope. Humpty Dumpty all over again."

"My little Rosie says *Humper-Dumper*." He nodded and pointed at the mess on the floor. "That's some Humper-Dumper, right there. You won't have to pay for it, will you?" he asked, with genuine concern. "If you have a broom, I'll help you clean up."

She shook her head. "Honestly, Miss Elizabeth will be happy it's gone. A friend of hers made it in a pottery class. Miss E's kept it there because the woman can't sculpt worth a damn, but she'll buy up some art." Tipsy blessed Will for coming up with a reason the statue had fallen so she didn't have to.

She ushered him to the front door, and they exchanged numbers. He said he'd be in touch, and she promised to show up at one of his job sites and accost him with hideous artwork. After he left she sat at her desk. "Henry?" she called out, unsure if she wanted a response or not. "Henry? Are you here?"

Henry said nothing, so Tipsy swept up the ruins of Miss E's charitable exhibition and tried to convince herself that it hadn't been Henry at all, but some other spirit. She'd never seen a ghost in the GQB, but anything was possible.

The rest of the day passed without incident. She locked the gallery's doors at half past five and walked the few blocks to the parking garage to retrieve her truck. As if Henry's appearance weren't strange enough, Tipsy had no idea where she'd gotten the supernatural wherewithal to chuck the statue at the wall. She'd experienced many odd supernatural occurrences in her life, but nothing like that. It shook her. What else could be lingering dormant inside her?

She focused on a positive. *It's nice to know one thing, Granna,* she thought as she drove over the Ravenel Bridge.

What's that?

Maybe I don't have to be quite so afraid of Mr. Mott. Looks like I have my own ways of defending myself, even if I never knew it before today. Nothing like a ride over one of Charleston's myriad bridges to remind her that you never can stop looking for new ways to rise above.

———— • ————

Tipsy is eight and she's watching her mama walk from one end of the kitchen to the other holding a strainer full of spaghetti that's dripping all over the floor. Daddy follows her and slips on the wet linoleum. His big brown work boots leave skiddy mud footprints everywhere and Tipsy grits her teeth, because guess who's going to be cleaning that up?

Daddy and Tipsy just got home from her first Clemson baseball game. It was real fun cheering for the Tigers until Daddy got in a fight with two men who had been sitting behind them on the stands.

"You got in a fight in front of Tipsy? Jesus, Randy."

"Don't swear in front of the girl!" He puts a hand on Mama's shoulder. He's taken off his orange hat, and his brown hair that's short on top and long in the back is smooshed onto his head. "Denise—" He stops when she wiggles out of his reach. The strainer lands—clunk—in the metal sink. A few bits of spaghetti fly out of the strainer and stick to the walls, like one of those sticky octopus guys that come in Tipsy's Happy Meals sometimes.

Daddy reaches for Mama again and she holds both hands up, like he might hit her. Her eyes are round gray circles of fear framed in black eyeliner. But that's crazy, because Tipsy's daddy is the most gentle guy ever. He didn't even hit those men at the game, he just yelled at 'em good, but Mama always squirms away when he touches her.

But now Daddy does seem kind of mad, and he picks up one of the old chairs he refinished for Granna and slams it down again. Then he goes to the fridge and grabs a Pabst. When he opens it beer sprays out and joins the spaghetti water on the floor and Tipsy wants to say, "Hey, lay off that floor!" but she keeps her mouth shut.

"More? More?" Mama laughs. "That's just what you need, after drivin' forty miles to Clemson and back with your daughter in the car. Your daughter *in the* car." *She tries to whisper those words, Tipsy thinks, but it's hard to whisper when you're mad.*

"I'm fine. I was fine to drive." He has to talk down at her like she's a kid, because she's so short and he's so tall. Mama is like Granna, a midget. Tipsy is like Daddy, a giant. It seems like Mama gets smaller all the time. She's so skinny that Granna brings home whole milk from the Piggly Wiggly now. Not that mama drinks milk. She only drinks Diet Pepsi. Her jeans look like her whole body would fit in one leg.

"Right," says Mama. "So fine you start yelling at some stupid rednecks over a damn baseball score."

"It wasn't that!" Daddy glances at Tipsy, and she wants to hide under the table. "Tipsy was having fun. Just wavin' that little pom-pom I bought her—" Daddy clenches the back of the chair. "Wavin' it—"

"What does that have to do with anything?" Mama grabs the other chair, and Tipsy wonders if they'll both fall over if they let go.

"Those damn boys behind us kept tellin' her to stop. Said they couldn't see. That she was bein' too loud." Daddy drops the chair. "My baby girl was just having a good time. I'll be damned if those fools were going to tell her what to do or keep her from enjoying her first Tigers game."

Tipsy feels like she's swallowed an ice cube and it got stuck on the way down. Like when you have to wait for your body to warm it up and melt it so it will keep moving. Daddy tilts the beer back and it drips down his chin and then onto his hand and arm and off the end of his elbow. More wet on the floor. Please, Baby Jesus, no more dripping. No more muddy beer spaghetti mess.

But more wet is coming, because Daddy starts crying. "I just want to show my baby a good time. Let her have a bit of fun. And those white trash assholes ruined it all. No respect for a man and his only child, and the great American pastime." Tears and beer and oh no, oh no. Snot and tears and more beer. Tipsy presses against the wall. Bits of peeling plaid wallpaper tickle her bare arms.

Mama turns away, but Tipsy can't. Someone has to comfort Daddy.

She can't do it. The beer and tears have glued her Keds to the floor. She can't help him when he's like this, no matter how hard she tries. Sometimes she brings him something: the sports page from the paper, a pack of cigarettes, or one of those scary Stephen King books he likes. The covers of those books terrify her, especially the one with the flaming dog's skull, Cujo. *She carries them face down when she delivers them. Sometimes she brings him another beer. But when Daddy gets sad, Tipsy can't ever make it right.*

So she watches her Daddy cry until he falls asleep with his head on Granna's dinged up kitchen table. She shuffles and drags her heavy shoes to the table and eats her spaghetti while he sleeps. She watches him snore till Mama lifts her up, right out of those Keds, and takes her to bed.

Chapter 4

Tipsy's weekend with her kids came and went in a hustle of birth-day parties at swimming pools and play dates on the beach. Each excursion required age- and gender-appropriate gifts, snacks and sunscreen, wiped noses and properly applied band-aids, brushed hair and matching clothes. She tried to forget about her ghostly roommates, but it wasn't easy. Jane didn't seem to realize Tipsy had somehow dreamed up one of her memories, however it had happened. But when Tipsy walked into the kitchen, or her bedroom, she often found Jane sitting at the table, or in a chair, with her hands spinning in her lap. She'd smile and bat her eyelashes, and go back to her invisible knitting. She didn't say anything, so Tipsy grinned back and carried on with whatever she was doing. After every weird but inoffensive interaction, an annoying nineties pop song ran through her head. *If you want to destroy my sweater… pull this thread as I walk away…*

Jane herself was benign, but the combination of Jane and Henry was not. She didn't see Henry, but she heard them, screaming at each other, at least once a day. Sometimes in the middle of the night. She jumped every time she heard his booming voice. *How dare you!* or *You insufferable witch!* or just your basic *Goddamnit!* Jane fought back, but Henry always yelled louder. She eventually deteriorated into sobbing and laughing hysterically, which only frustrated him more. Their ar-guments ended suddenly, as if someone had lifted the needle on a vinyl record. One of them probably reached the end of his or her rope, and disappeared. Still, they lived—or died, or however one could rationally describe it— to fight another day. Tipsy found chairs tipped over, broken photo frames, and once, a pillow with all the stuffing ripped and strewn across the living room.

Thankfully, the kids didn't notice the messes Jane and Henry left amidst their own happy chaos. Tipsy had a gnawing fear, however, of something more major happening. What if the ghosts got really pissed, and like, dropped a chandelier on someone's head? And it was exhausting, listening to them rage at each other. The stress she'd been under for the past year or so had taught her how to function in a state of constant fatigue, but she sensed their anger draining her further. Or maybe it was merely their close proximity. Tipsy felt frustratingly uninformed. She asked Granna, but for once, Granna wasn't much help.

Never lived even close to a ghost, sugar, Granna said. *I don't know what to tell you.*

I have to make the best of this. The kids can't hear them. Seems like they're at least trying to stay out of our way, and a ripped up pillow can't hurt anyone. And let's face it, even with these undead lunatics, I got it pretty good in this big old beautiful house.

That's my girl, stay positive.

You know it, Granna.

The next week, Tipsy dropped all three kids at Pelican Surf Shop on Coleman Boulevard, where they caught the early morning bus to surf camp on Folly Beach. Tipsy enjoyed a steady flow of texts from Will Garrison. She teased him that his texting impressed her, but he needed to learn proper use of emojis. He replied, *That's not my thing... ok fine* ☺. So far, he had yet to plan dinner, or ask her to see a movie, but she played it cool. Shelby and Lindsey stressed that she must not come off as needy via text. Texting-and-dating made Tipsy highly anxious. When she met Ayers, she couldn't even afford a cell phone. If he wanted to talk to her, he had to call the sorority house. Now, an entire relationship could sink or float based on whether she texted Will the right message, within the right time frame.

She forewent running or lifting weights over several balmy mornings in favor of getting to know her new neighborhood. She'd traversed most of the picturesque downtown streets and had run at least a thousand miles on the beaches, but she'd never done much exploring in Mount Pleasant. Tipsy and Ayers's house, in an agreeable if cookie-cutter subdivision off Long Point Road, bumped up against several similar neighborhoods, none of which offered any interesting architecture or breathtaking vistas. She'd driven through the Old Village, Mount Pleasant's quaint historic district, before moving into Miss Callie's. She had met friends for coffee, and taken her kids to the park at Alhambra Hall, but she hadn't had much reason or opportunity to take in the minutia of its charms. If anything, the Old Village smacked of a secretive private club. While she and Ayers hadn't had any financial worries until recently, they'd been light years from contemplating membership. Unlike downtown, where homeowners were accustomed to tourists gawking at their pastel paintjobs and brushing up against their window boxes, residents of the Old Village noticed strange cars and out-of-place people. Let the visitors overrun the Battery and King Street; the Old Village had no inclination to draw attention to itself.

Tipsy had an address these days, so after introducing herself to the neighbors and making sure that everyone on her street knew her face, she set about exploring. Haddrell Street, which ran along Shem Creek, had to be one of the few thoroughfares in the world where one might admire multi-million dollar mansions and buy fresh seafood straight off a shrimp boat. Hibben Street claimed the oldest house in Mount Pleasant, the Hibben House. It dated to 1755, but its extensive additions and renovations made Tipsy think of the Golden Age of Film, as if Greta Garbo might poke her head out a window and declare that she wanted to be alone. In the business district on Pitt Street, residents ate candlelight dinners, bought gourmet cupcakes, picked up medications at the old Pitt Street Pharmacy and shopped for home accessories.

And really, what more do you need in life? asked Granna.

Tipsy didn't have to worry about talking around a mouthful of cupcake when she replied, *Not much.*

With every block she fell more in love. The oak and magnolia trees provided the perfect combination of shade-sun-shade as she walked. There were few sounds beyond birds, lawnmowers and the smack of boat hulls against waves on the streets closest to the water. The streets smelled of freshly cut grass and pluff mud, the viscous marsh muck exposed by the retreating tides. The condition of the houses ran the gamut from *Town & Country* spread to in need of an Extreme Makeover. Will had worked on many of them, and Tipsy pledged to ask him which ones. If she could find the right time to introduce that into the text conversation.

Even Big Ayers seemed reasonably content. At least for the moment, he'd stopped threatening to highjack her children. She still hadn't figured out how Henry showed up at the GQB, but disgruntled ghostly stalkers were the problem of crazy people, not Tipsy Collins. She was managing her undead roommates, a job, three kids, an ex-husband, and a possible new paramour with ease. She might be broke, but fiddle-dee-dee, said Scarlett, I'll think about that tomorrow. The only thing missing, besides a decent paycheck, was real painting inspiration. She stared into faces and at buildings and across rivers, but like a camera with a broken shutter, her mind refused to click on anything and capture it.

Thursday night, however, found Tipsy uncomfortably alone. The solitude rattled her fledgling peace of mind. The kids went straight to Ayers's house after camp. Tipsy closed up the gallery and ran a few miles through the tree-lined streets South of Broad. She couldn't think much, because she had to watch her feet. Roots had pushed the sidewalks into concrete mountain chains. The walkways around the Battery pitched at an angle, like the floors of a funhouse. She started her cool down at the corner of Meeting and Broad Streets, near several sweetgrass basket stands. The basket weavers sat in folding chairs, surrounded by their craft. The complicated baskets, wreathes, trays, and woven floral arrangements were a testament to the timeless techniques brought from Africa by their ancestors.

Tipsy waved and said hello as she passed. They returned her friendly greeting, and went back to talking amongst themselves. The enslaved people of the Lowcountry had developed a unique creole language, known as Gullah or GeeChee, with its own mix of African and English words and syntax. Tipsy had heard Gullah storytellers and historians at libraries and museums—the people who worked tirelessly to preserve their culture and its language after decades of stigmatization and an intentional effort in schools to force GeeChee children to standardize their speech. Remnants of the language lingered in the basket weavers' distinctive accents. A carriage tour guide's enthusiastic history lesson and his horse's clomping hooves provided accompaniment to their lively conversation.

Once the basket weavers' chatting faded behind her, Tipsy's own mind went quiet. She couldn't stand any more ruminations on her meager bank account, so she mulled over the conundrum of Jane and Henry's murder, which brought her back to Henry's unexplainable appearance at work. She couldn't fathom how he'd shown up. Ghosts were supposed to stay in one place. When Tipsy wasn't much older than five, she'd asked Granna if the shy little boy who haunted their church could come home to play. Granna had told her with a great sadness that the little boy couldn't leave the church, not ever. Tipsy had been horrified.

Although Granna didn't approve, she continued to wave and smile at the quiet, melancholy child in the first pew that no one else could see.

Tipsy still wanted to convince herself that it hadn't been Henry at all, but some other spirit, but that answer didn't set well with her. The shadows lengthened as she walked and pondered, and pondered and walked. When she looked up she found herself in front of St. Philip's Episcopal Church on Church Street.

This is where they held the memorial service, she said to Granna, and Granna sniffed her agreement.

The idea that Jane and Henry might be buried in St. Philips' cemetery lit a fire under Tipsy's curiosity. She strode into the larger of St. Philips' two graveyards, the one across the street from the church. She paced the rows of tombstones. Wind and rain had worn many of the oldest stones to the point of illegibility. A shame, because some of them gave not only names and dates of birth and death, but fascinating annotated life stories. The slate stones had weathered the years better than the granite ones. Some of them had stayed crisp since the 1700s. For some reason those early slate-loving colonists had included strange carvings of swooning angels and sorrowful faces. Their memorials stood out in macabre Gothic relief against the larger but more sedate granite headstones.

A few other curious visitors wandered the cemetery, but their numbers dwindled as the sunlight did the same. Tipsy ignored the impending darkness, except to be annoyed by its hindrance of her ability to read the stones. After all, graveyards strike fear into people's hearts because their cold fences encircle the unknowns of death. If she went around fearing death, in all its manifestations and possibilities, she'd spend her life in bed with the covers over her head.

Eventually she had to give up, for fear she'd do permanent damage to her eyesight. As she left the cemetery, she noticed that one last figure remained with her in the dark. She'd been too preoccupied with her search to notice the slim man with the white beard, but his pearly bluish glow made it hard to miss him in the fading light.

Tipsy turned away from the ghost with the intent of ignoring him as Granna had always encouraged her to do. She stopped before she crossed under the stone-and-wrought-iron gate and looked over her shoulder. The ghost met her eyes. One white eyebrow lifted in surprised acknowledgement.

Oh, lord, said Granna, *keep going, sugar! Haven't you learned enough, what with almost getting sliced to bits by flying ceramics?*

In for a penny, in for fifty pounds. Tipsy walked back into the cemetery.

The man didn't speak as she approached. His white hair and beard gave him the look of a skinny Santa Claus. Tipsy tried to judge his era by his clothes, but didn't come up with anything better than mid-twentieth century. He wore some kind of undershirt and black slacks. A pair of suspenders held up his pants.

"Hello," she said.

He nodded.

"I wondered if you knew the stones very well? Seeing that you're here all the time."

Another nod.

"I'm looking for the graves of Jane and Henry Mott."

The ghost took a moment to appraise her, as if she were the apparition that might disappear, before motioning her to follow him. He stopped before a largish but otherwise nondescript granite tombstone. Deep hash marks spelled out the name MOTT near the top of the stone, below a cross. Henry's name and dates of birth and death followed, then Jane's. No revealing biblical quote or anguished, skyward-gazing stone angel. Not even a pretty tree branch to hang Spanish moss overhead like the bell sleeves of a bereavement gown.

Tipsy giggled at her own silly disappointment, and then cleared her throat. "Sorry," she said to the ghost. "It's just anticlimactic."

"I've found that most things in life and death are so." The ghost sounded as if he'd either died of emphysema, or hadn't spoken in a few decades. "Might I ask why a young woman would come seeking the graves of those ninety years dead?" He raised his hand and the glow made Tipsy's own nose look bluish before her eyes. "I will say," he went on, "you being what you are, I have a hankering why."

"What I am?"

"A seer of sorts. I didn't believe in such things in life, being a man of the cloth." A smile sent a fissure of deep wrinkles across his cheeks and forehead. "I suppose I must believe now, owing to the circumstances of this conversation. I'm pleased to make your acquaintance, Miss Seer. I'd shake your hand, but..." With a graceful lift of his shoulders, a shrug became dance step. "My name is Proctor James."

She introduced herself, and as she said her own name the ghost's unusual moniker tickled her memory. "Proctor—Proctor James! You officiated Henry and Jane's funeral!"

He chuckled. "It seems you have done a bit of digging, should you pardon the pun."

"How well did you know them?" Tipsy fairly stood on tiptoe in her excitement.

"How well do *you* know them?"

She'd never had a conversation with one ghost about another, but she supposed it didn't make an odd situation any odder. "I live in the house where they died. Only for a couple weeks, but I've spoken to them both a few times."

"Indeed. And how do they fare?"

"Not great, honestly. They hate each other with a red passion."

"Red passion. That's a good way to describe Jane and Henry."

"What do you mean?" She wanted to grab Proctor by his shoulders. "And how did you know they were…um… still hanging around?"

"I didn't know, but given the circumstances of their demise, it doesn't surprise me."

Tipsy didn't know which questions to ask first. "Why? Because they were murdered? Because Henry killed Jane? Can you leave this place? We'll visit them!"

The old man stroked his beard, and now he reminded her more of Father Abraham than Father Christmas. "No. I cannot leave here. This city of stones has been my home since 1949. As for Henry and Jane's continued presences on this Earth, I believe that those who linger have unresolved matters that weigh on their souls. That keep them from God, or the Other, depending."

"They don't remember how they died. She says he killed her, but he says he didn't. Do you know anything about what happened? I figured people must have talked. People in this town love to talk. That can't have changed."

"I heard rumors of such as you said, sad story that it was. But both families avoided the topic. Jane's heartbroken family couldn't stand to hear talk of it. Her father never forgave himself for letting her marry Henry. I believe Henry's family was more humiliated."

"Why? Why didn't they want her to marry Henry—and why were the Motts—"

Proctor raised both hands in five-fingered bluish stop signs. "Perhaps I can tell you what I know of them and save you from your questioning. Although—I've always admired a questioning mind. One doesn't answer the call of God unless one seeks answers to great questions." He pointed to a stone bench under a magnolia tree. "Let us sit."

Tipsy trotted over to the bench. By the time she reached it, Proctor already sat there, as if he'd been waiting on her for hours.

"I was born seven or eight years before Jane and Henry. My grandfather was rector here at St. Philip's, so I grew up in this place. My own father was a man of the law. He didn't have much use for church other than as a venue to impress his neighbors and hear tell of their potential legal problems, but I knew from a young age that I wanted to follow Grandfather on the Lord's path. I imagined no vocation would bring me greater joy than that of ministering to the hearts and bodies of my neighbors. The Robinettes were one of our oldest families, although Pierre's ancestors originally came to Carolina from France, with the Huguenots. Somewhere along the way, some Robinette must have loved a girl so fiercely that he agreed to cross the English Channel of religion. That's neither here nor there, really, but you know how we love our family lineages."

Tipsy nodded. Ayers's family had balked at the idea of their son marrying a girl from upstate who had an offensive redneck accent, and an offensive redneck name, to boot. While many found Tipsy's lifelong nickname to be odd indeed, Mary Penelope and Ayers III, otherwise known as May Penny and Tripp, had been relieved by it. "Tiffany Lynn? Bless her heart," May Penny had said one Thanksgiving when she didn't realize Tipsy was standing behind her. "That's as bad as Tammy, or lord help us, Crystal."

"I knew both Jane and Henry as children. Jane, bless her, she was the most precocious, precious child. Her parents doted on her. She never sat still in church, but they rarely reprimanded her." He smiled at the memory. "The older ladies of the congregation found it all to be in very poor taste. That lovely little girl bouncing from pew to pew, smiling and giggling and singing hymns at the top of her lungs. But even the most critical eyes eventually fell to her charms. No matter how they might have twittered about her parents' lack of discipline at the parish picnic.

"Henry was a different sort of child altogether. His mother and father also felt the barbed end of the gossipmongers' tongues, but not because Henry sassed and ran wild. He was an odd, and dare I say it, odd-looking little boy. So pale and freckly, skinny as a starved egret, with that mop of bright orange hair. He wasn't friendly at all. In fact, he'd hardly say *hello, ma'am* or *thank you, sir*, and he'd shove his hands in his pockets if you so much as tried to shake his hand. He was always peering around." Proctor's hazel eyes bugged from his head in imitation. "Little Henry Mott, staring at lights and candles. It drove his parents quite mad, but never so much as when he'd talk to himself. Carry on a proper conversation with no one, as if the empty air were one of those newfangled telephone machines."

Tipsy's stomach cramped up as Proctor talked. How many times had Granna told her as a child, *Don't talk to 'em when folks are around, Tipsy, they'll think all your marbles ran out your ears and rolled away into the storm drains.* Perhaps Henry Mott hadn't had anyone to warn him.

"He was like me. A seer."

Proctor nodded. "I assume so. His conversations with unseen persons make sense to me now, in light of my current predicament." He crossed his legs in the way that once had been perfectly acceptable for a man, and now would seem distinctly effeminate. The lower half of Proctor's body progressed from solid enough at the hips to misty at his feet. Tipsy thought of Jane's habit of fading in and out when she was agitated. Henry sometimes did the same before he disappeared, but generally speaking, he was either there or he wasn't. Maybe such things became afterlife mannerisms, like a tendency to grind your teeth or talk with your hands. "Henry's parents weren't as firmly placed in society as

Jane's," said Proctor. "The Robinettes were a rare combination in those days. A family with an old name and a small fortune."

"They didn't lose it all in the Civil—the War Between the States?" asked Tipsy. "I thought everyone in Charleston went broke."

"Most did," Proctor said. "Jane's great-grandfather lost the Robinette rice plantation on the Edisto River, but he'd attended Harvard College. He had the foresight to keep some money in northern banks, in the care of an old school mate from Boston. I heard tell he invested in railroad interests in Colorado Territory. He founded the Edisto Bank and Trust. Jane's father, Pierre Robinette, took the bank's helm before Jane's birth. Pierre helped anyone who needed it and showed gumption. He financed Mott and Phipps Wholesale Dry Goods."

"Henry's family's business?"

Proctor nodded. "The Motts were comfortable enough by the time Henry came along, and I tell you, Miss Seer, comfort was quite an achievement in those hard years. Frederick Mott bled sweat and tears building Mott and Phipps."

"So the Robinettes and the Motts were old friends."

"Not exactly." Proctor tugged his beard again, as if each time he yanked on it, a new memory resurfaced. "The two families knew each other, but if the Motts populated Charleston for a hundred years and were as wealthy as the Rockefellers, they still would not be the Robinettes. So the critical eye fell more heavily on them. Patience Mott wasn't having that."

"Did they keep Henry home from church?"

"He didn't go to church, but he didn't stay at home, either. They sent him off to boarding school in Virginia by his tenth birthday. About that time I left for divinity school at Sewanee. By the time I returned and my grandfather took me on as junior rector, Henry had been gone for years. But Jane remained."

"Did she ever learn to behave?"

Proctor laughed. "Not really, but no one cared. As a young woman, she acted in plays, mostly at the Dock Street Theater. She charmed everyone, in town and out at the Old Cannon. The Robinettes would spend a few months each winter there, with Theresa's parents. Usually for Thanksgiving and Christmas. I joined them on several happy occasions."

Tipsy pictured a crackling fire and a family gathered around an upright piano for Christmas carols. What Proctor said meshed with what she'd seen in that weird dream.

"Once I saw Jane don a pair of her father's trousers under her dress, belt them tight, and jump right into the Wando on a dare," said Proctor. "A warm day in November, mind you, but Theresa Robinette nearly swooned from shock. When Jane climbed out of that river, she walked the yard serving bourbon and sweet tea to her grandmother's guests. Sopping wet, because she didn't want to take the time to change and have anyone go thirsty. Theresa wrapped her in a wool shawl, but Jane shrugged it off and kept on playing the gracious hostess. Cold be damned, she refused to be a wet blanket." Proctor's eyes twinkled. "Pardon the pun. Theresa made her lie down for fear she'd succumb to some form of ague. Maybe she would have been a film star, if she'd been born twenty years later. Or a senator, if she'd have been born a man."

Tipsy rested her chin on her hand and her elbow on her knee, so that anyone who passed might have mistaken her for a female replica of *The Thinker*. Flashes of that energy and warmth still shone through the cracks in Jane's fragile paranoia. "What about Henry? He returned at some point."

"He went from boarding school to the university in Columbia, but he didn't last long. I heard tell that he refused to participate in some classes, failing outright, and passed others with the highest marks while making no apparent effort. The university's literary magazine published many of his stories. One found its way into *The North American Review* and another into *The Atlantic*. Eventually, the university asked him to leave. No one knows exactly why, but I heard he accosted his roommate during an argument over the merits of *Heart of Darkness*. When he left Columbia, his parents sent him to stay with a cousin in Montreal. Then he spent several years in Europe. He returned to Charleston in, oh, 1915?"

"From how you're describing them, I can't see how Jane and Henry ended up married."

Proctor laughed again. Tipsy's unwitting ability to entice chuckles out of that long silent voice gratified her. She imagined it felt pretty nice to laugh after decades of lonely wandering amidst the gravestones of your friends and neighbors. "When Henry returned to Charleston," said Proctor, "he'd changed quite a bit. He'd grown into himself in the most surprising way. That ugly child became a most handsome man."

Tipsy nodded. She pictured his wild red hair and too-dark eyes. "Strangely so."

"Agreed. Not the kind of face you'd see in a Coca-Cola advertisement. But he mesmerized women nonetheless. His worldliness shone in a provincial town. And he had an air of... how best to put it? Mystery."

"He still does. I thought maybe it was because being dead automatically makes you somewhat mysterious."

"He intrigued us all in life as well. Always scribbling away on scraps of paper during church and spouting off about obscure New York poets at luncheons and picnics. It became known that Henry Mott was writing the next great American novel. Our homegrown, quirky genius. It helped that he'd finally stopped talking to shadows in public."

"So Jane fell for him?"

Proctor nodded. "Her parents weren't convinced, but Jane begged and pleaded. Henry presented himself as normal enough when he asked her father to marry her. Pierre Robinette did insist that Henry take gainful employment. Pierre didn't want to support a starving poet, and hence his own starving daughter and potential grandchildren. So Henry began working for his father, first on the peninsula. When the navy built the Rifle Range during the Great War, he and Jane moved East of the Cooper. It was hard on them, what with having to find transport on a boat or take the ferry into town." Proctor's old Charleston brogue turned *Cooper* into *Cupper* and *boat* into *bow-ut*. "Mount Pleasant wasn't much more than a village with a post office and a few churches. The neighbors' goat destroyed Jane's rose bushes."

"I can't imagine the Henry you described jumping for joy at having to take a normal job."

"No, but he loved Jane. I spent many hours talking with them throughout their courtship. I married them."

Tipsy pictured Jane and Henry, both impossibly beautiful and desperately in love, standing under the thick white pillars of St. Philip's. Young lovers in the counsel of a priest they'd known all their lives. "But what went wrong?"

"That I can't tell you. But it did, and tragically so in the end."

"So Henry did kill her?" Tipsy's heart sank.

"So it's said. Their ending is shrouded in years of whispered gossip." Proctor stood. His white hair looked to be running into his beard, as if someone had poured a glass of milk over his head. "So much speaking is wearing on me. I'm sorry, Miss Seer, I must leave you now."

"All right. Thank you for talking with me." She rushed on before Proctor got any fuzzier. "Last question. Have you seen Henry since you died?"

"No. How would I have seen him?"

"He can leave the house." Tipsy told Proctor of Henry's appearance at the GQB.

"Jane and Henry died in the same place. So there they haunt, together. I've not seen another like me in all the years I've been in this cemetery. It's not as if I can go calling on nearby deceased inhabitants. Then again," he said as he faded away, "Henry always was an unusual fellow."

Tipsy checked the time on her phone as she left the graveyard. She'd promised to catch a beer with Lindsey and Shelby, but it was past ten. She sent apologetic texts that claimed exhaustion and an imminent bedtime.

An unusual fellow is right, said Granna.

Tipsy slowed as she crossed Church Street. She leaned against the wall that surrounded St. Philip's and stretched her hamstrings. The sign on the pedestal beside the locked gate of the smaller cemetery bore a friendly message: *Welcome to St. Philip's! The only ghost in our graveyard is the Holy Ghost.*

If y'all only knew, Tipsy thought. She pushed her weight into her heels until it hurt. *You're right, Granna. But Henry is more than your usual oddball.*

She'd bet her last dollar, and she'd just about reached it, that Henry's lifetime ability to see ghosts was directly correlated with his current ability to travel as one.

* * *

Tipsy didn't expect to return home from her Friday morning gym session and find Ayers's truck in the driveway of Miss Callie's house. She checked the time on her phone. Quarter till nine. He must have dropped the kids at camp and come straight over. Foreboding swelled in her stomach. Maybe someone was sick, or hurt.

Or maybe he needs a few more pairs of Disney Princess underwear for the weekend, said Granna. *No use panicking yet.*

Tipsy got out of her truck and walked to his. Ayers was fiddling with something in his lap. She tapped on the window. Johnny Cash's diatribe against rich folks and their fancy dining cars got louder as the window slid down.

At least the man in black is good country, said Granna.

Tipsy agreed in her head before speaking with her mouth. "What's up?" she asked Ayers.

He took a few good smacking chews on his gum before answering. "O-Liv had a nightmare last night."

Tipsy frowned. "Did she? Could she tell you what it was about?"

He shrugged. "Not really. Loud noises and broken china."

"Oh." Tipsy's heart sank. "Did she say anything else?"

"She said the new house is scary."

"She's told me it's big. The house. But she's never lived in such a big place. She'll get used to it."

Ayers returned to his phone. He checked a text or maybe an email, and responded while Tipsy stared at him. He lowered the volume on the radio. "She also said you seem sad."

"I'm just tired."

"Little Ayers mentioned how you freaked out in the kitchen a couple weeks ago. Dropping shit and spraying water all over the place. Some bookshelf almost landed on the kitchen table."

"I'm doing the best I can, Ayers," Tipsy said. "Like I'm sure you are."

Chew, chew, chew. Pink bubblegum flashed between his teeth. Johnny Cash had moved on to Jackson, Mississippi, and a lot of messing around. All the women were going to stoop and bow. "Those first months were rough," Ayers said. "I admit it. But I think we've been doing a pretty good job of keeping it civil for the kids lately."

"I agree."

"I'm telling you, though, if you can't figure out a way to support them, I'm not afraid to go back to the lawyers and change our arrangement. Or if you, you know, fall apart."

The specter of those months after the girls' birth hovered over Tipsy and her kids' father. A different, somehow scarier kind of ghost. Endless nights when she lay in bed, crying and unable to sleep, even if her babies gave her the chance. She pictured herself, sitting on the carpet in their happily messy playroom, with little Ayers toddling around and both baby girls in bouncy seats. That playroom had felt like a cage, that she was nonetheless afraid to leave, lest something terrible happen to the children. The sound of rain on the rooftop and jingling mobiles. The smell of the lavender lotion that was supposed to soothe the girls into sleeping through the night.

"Kids need peace after all this," said Ayers, jerking her back to the here and now.

"I know that." Tipsy's eyes stung. "I know it."

Ayers shrugged. "All right. Just make sure you give it to them. If you can't, I will."

Tipsy opened her mouth, but nothing came out.

"I'm going to work. I'll text you if anything comes up this weekend." He closed the window and stepped on the gas. He left before June Carter's fiery re-entry into the song skewered Johnny for his carousing down in Jackson. There was no retaliating female voice, in the song or the conversation.

Inside the house, Tipsy kicked off her shoes and straightened the children's jackets on their hooks by the front door. She walked into the kitchen, washed a few plates and put them into the dishwasher. She wiped down the counters, swept, and changed the trashcan liner. Once she'd run out of things to tidy, she stood in the center of the magenta kitchen. She stared at the four walls around her and the still unfamiliar pattern in the wallpaper. The house closed in on her like a superficial embrace. Cold and quiet and foreign.

She covered her face and cried into her hands. She cursed herself for not rising to Ayers's challenge. For not looking him in the face and demanding that he stop his two-pronged threats. The truth was, he was right. It wasn't the noxious haze of postpartum depression, but she was sad and tired around the children at times. Sometimes her smiles and hugs felt false. They must sense that. And she'd chosen this for everyone in her family. For the children and for herself. Whether he deserved it or not, she'd also chosen it for Ayers. Everyone's current state of discontent had a direct line back to Tipsy's decision to end her marriage.

As always, things she should have said ran through her head after the fact. *Screw you, Ayers! No judge will give those kids to you. You couldn't handle them anyway! Three days without your mama's help and you'd be begging me to take them back, you self-righteous, delusional asshole.*

Then the imaginary Ayers struck back. *At least they'll have the security of a stable home. And remember, Tipsy, you made this goddamn bed. It's not made of feathers. You're going to have to sleep on it if you can. So get yourself some Ambien, baby.*

Tipsy gripped the edge of the sink. Maybe he *would* try to take the kids.

Forget one day at a time, said Granna. *One hour at a time. What do you need to do right now?*

Tipsy sniffed and swiped at her eyes. She cleared her throat, although she had no cause to speak. She needed to shower before heading to the GQB. The kids were safe. Ayers was gone, for now. She had to go to work. She picked up the phone to determine how much time she'd wasted sobbing in the silent kitchen. She swiped across a text from Will Garrison.

No kids tonight, right? Want to have dinner?

She sniffed again, and swallowed, and typed out a quick reply.

Okay, sure. Where?

***

"Good evening, Miss Tiffany-Tipsy."

"Hey, Jane." Tipsy wiggled her fingers in a wave at the ghost's reflection in the bathroom mirror. She gave herself a pat on the back. Jane's voice drifting over her shoulder didn't cause her to spin around in terror or drop her deodorant in the toilet.

Jane stood on tiptoes in an attempt to see over Tipsy's shoulder. It didn't work, so she peeked under Tipsy's upraised arm and into her makeup bag. "Are you going to a party?"

"I have a date." Tipsy messed with the edges of her hair. Sometimes she wondered why anyone bothered using a hair dryer during Charleston summers. Despite the whirring air conditioner, the act of blasting heat onto her head only resulted in sweaty-wet hair instead of shampoo-wet hair. At least Jane's presence cooled the bathroom somewhat. The last remnants of her shower fog dissipated from the mirror. "Like, a gentleman caller," Tipsy said as she picked up her round brush.

"How nice," Jane said.

"You haven't been very chatty lately."

"I've been keeping to myself. Our *last* conversation made me think on things I *don't like* to think on." *Blinkety-blink-blink!*

"Think about it tomorrow," said Tipsy, altogether aware that she'd recently developed an annoying propensity for *Gone with the Wind* colloquialisms. She giggled. "After all, it is another day."

"Pardon?"

"I'm being silly. I'm just jittery about my date." She gave up on her hair and returned to the bedroom. Shelby and Lindsey had descended upon her as soon as word got out that she was going to have dinner with Will. They'd spent the after-work hours sorting through possible first-date outfits, while Shelby railed against Glen's ex-wife and Lindsey pretended to be shocked by a series of increasingly provocative photos sent to her by a twenty-five-year-old medical student.

Jane followed her like an independent shadow. "Is he a good man?"

"I don't know him well, but…" Tipsy thought of Will's crooked smile. "I think so."

"I'm sure your mother told you this, but, if you *truly* want him, *hold fast*," said Jane in an almost conspiratorial voice. "You *know*, don't be too…" Jane colored the faintest bit, like a thawing rose.

"My mother didn't teach me much," said Tipsy. "She and my daddy disappeared before that kind of talk was necessary." She straightened her strapless maxi dress. Pink flowed toward purple at the hem, a melted Popsicle gown on a hot summer night. It showed off her shoulders and months of stress-busting weight training. Tipsy had always been thin, a genetic gift that somewhat compensated for her nose, but for the first time in her life she felt strong. She grabbed a pair of strappy wedge sandals from her closet, made a quick determination that she wouldn't be taller than Will, and she slid them onto her feet. A spritz of perfume and a dab of lip gloss and she'd finished her prep. "Don't worry, Jane. I might kiss him up a bit, but that's it."

Jane crossed her arms, and her black bob became a nun's habit. Mother Superior had come to chastise a potential sinner before the act could be committed. "I can't approve of *that*, now. You said you *hardly know* him!"

Tipsy wished she could hug Jane. That strategy always worked when Shelby got caught up in bitching about something and forgot that the grass still grew and the sun still shone. "That's tame, Jane. If you'd heard some of the stories—"

"I haven't!" Jane's eyes widened. "But *perhaps...*"

Tipsy laughed. "Come with me. I'm going to wait on the porch."

So Tipsy sat on the joggling board beside Jane. She sipped a pre-date anxiety-reduction beer while she gave the ghost a taste of modern life in Charleston. "...so Lindsey married a much older man, but he left her for a woman who's even younger than she is. After they got divorced she... umm..." Tipsy struggled for the right words, because she couldn't exactly call Lindsey's conquests *dates*. "...kept company with much younger men."

"That's very odd," said Jane.

"Not so much. Most of these young guys have some weird MILF fantasy."

"Milk?"

"Never mind," said Tipsy, for fear that the shock of that definition might send Jane toppling off the board. Not that she'd hurt herself, but surely swooning wasn't pleasant for anyone, alive or dead. "Anyway, the last guy was maybe twenty-four, and gorgeous. In the Air Force. Lindsey met him at the BP—where you get fuel, for your car. They started texting. She met him for dinner... and well...let's just say he revved her engine. Right in the back seat of that Mercedes."

Even if the specifics of the description were lost on Jane, she seemed to get the message. "Dear lord. She didn't?" Jane's blinking eyelashes were like hummingbird wings. She clutched at her chest. "Did she *really?*"

Tipsy nodded. "Why not? Her husband wasn't exactly..." Tipsy propped her elbow on her knee. Her fingers pointed at the ceiling fan above their heads. She let her wrist go weak. Her hand flopped like an empty banana peel.

"My word." Jane's mouth worked, and for a moment Tipsy thought she might cry. Instead she burst out laughing. "Oh, my word. *My word.*"

"I don't want you to think badly about Lindsey. Now she has a boyfriend she loves, and he loves her. But you'd be amazed. Seems like everyone around here has a story that would make for a torrid romance novel."

"In my day, a girl would be ruined. She'd be locked in the house with a cup of strong coffee. And a bible."

"Speaking of bibles, I met someone you know!"

"I don't follow you."

"A ghost, of course!"

Jane's giggly, girlfriend-ly demeanor disappeared. "You're still looking for information about Henry and me?"

"Don't you want to know who it is?"

Jane stood with a huff. Tipsy glanced down the driveway. She didn't want Will to pull up and see her talking to the humid air. Jane faded, then went solid, then faded again, in a display of ghostly indecision. Her curiosity evidently got the better of her, and she settled on substance. "Who was it?"

"Proctor James."

Jane's nostrils flared, like a horse about to spook. "Proctor James? Where?"

"In the churchyard at St. Phillips. He haunts it."

Jane covered her mouth with one hand. Chirping birds and the laughter of the neighbor's children punctuated the long, silent minute before Jane's eyes resumed their normal rate of blinking. "Pardon. I haven't heard that name in years. He was an old family friend. *Very* close to my parents. I never knew what became of him. I don't know what became of *anyone* other than Henry and me."

"He looked about seventy years old."

"Did he seem… in good spirits?"

Tipsy chuckled. "In good spirits. Yes, very spirited!"

If the neighbors had been able to hear Jane's laughter, they surely would have peered over the fence to see what was so funny. She threw back her head, and quaking humor blurred her silhouette. She solidified and wiped her eyes. "So he lived long beyond us. He was a dear man."

A blue pick-up truck pulled into the drive. "Here he is." Tipsy's pulse fluttered from her chest down though her legs, as if her body was a birdcage and someone had riled up the canaries. She sought reassurance from the only someone around. "Do I look all right?"

Jane flashed the brilliant smile that had charmed all of Charleston with its good-natured vivacity. "You're *beautiful!* Pretty as can be!"

"Thank you," said Tipsy. "Goodnight, Jane."

Will got out of the truck and waved. He walked around to the passenger side and opened the door. He wore a crisp white dress shirt and a pair of dark jeans. Tipsy clipped down the stairs. His smile and his hands on the doorframe so absorbed her attention that she forgot to look over her shoulder to see if Jane still stood there.

It wasn't until she got into the truck that she saw it, through the open passenger side window as Will pulled away. Jane remained on the front porch. She leaned against the pillar at the top of the stairs. She'd draped one arm over her head, and the other across her waist, so her own limbs formed a picture frame around her face. She looked into the late afternoon sun, as if she might soak it in and warm a perpetual coldness. Her purple dress and black hair swayed despite the still air, and the animated, cheerful woman from that long ago Thanksgiving shimmered beneath her quiet pallor. The tea roses turned their yellow faces toward her, as if she were a fragile sun-below-the-sun. Jane was an animated Renoir, a woman trapped in a painting that Tipsy must paint.

Tipsy's first date jitters disappeared by the time the waiter asked if she'd like dessert. Excitement about a potential new painting made her even chattier than usual, and the conversation flowed as boats slipped past the wide windows of Water's Edge on Shem Creek. Tipsy and Will checked the usual first date conversation boxes: where they'd both grown up and gone to school, their families (Will's seemed more normal than Tipsy's, so she glossed over that part), music and food preferences (both gave the Allman Brothers the thumbs up and avocadoes the thumbs down). She pointed past competing restaurants and a few waterfront mansions, toward the rooftops of the Old Village on the other side of the creek. She wondered aloud if one of them could be Miss Callie's place. Will asked how she'd come to live on Bennett Street, which led them to a topic divorced people inevitably discuss. *What happened to your marriage?*

"Ours was pretty textbook," said Will. "We fought all the time. About everything. She spent tons of money. I spent too much time fishing. She wanted to talk all the time, I guess I didn't. I wanted—" He cleared his throat. "I wanted more intimacy, and she wasn't buying it. It's a bad cliché. We get on pretty well now. She's a good mom. She's a nurse."

Tipsy nodded. "I guess we get along, as long as I'm agreeable and he's in a good mood. It's sort of day-by-day. Ours is harder to explain. Our life never satisfied Ayers. Me, the kids. I felt like we were tying him down. But I don't know what from. He was angry all the time. So I started ignoring him to keep the peace. Guess I woke up one day and realized I didn't care anymore. Not if he came or went. I wasn't even mad. Just, ambivalent. We tried to work it out, but..." She shrugged.

"Your heart wasn't in it."

She nodded. "I think you have a better chance if you fight. At least you still care."

"Maybe," said Will. "Hmmm."

"I got the wrong impression of you. I thought you were kind of... unfriendly?" She blushed, but he laughed.

"I get that sometimes. Don't mean to be." He pointed at his brow. "I think it's my permanent facial expression. Sort of pissed off."

She giggled. "You need Botox."

"Dudes don't get Botox. We play the cards we're dealt."

"Now I think you were just trying to figure me out."

"I'd like to figure you out." He took her hand across the table. His was warm, although they'd been sharing a chocolate sundae. He had a trace of fudge on his lower lip.

Maybe three beers made her bold, but she reached for it. "You have chocolate...right there."

"Help me out," he said. She brushed it away with her thumb and cupped his cheek in her hand for a moment. He kissed her palm and she felt small spasms in places that Jane would wholly disapprove of.

"Place is emptying out," he said, once her hand rested on the table.

She glanced at the empty tables around them and started to agree, until she saw that someone occupied the booth across from them. A pale, red-haired someone. A busboy approached the booth, but he didn't put a hand on the remaining plates and glasses and soiled napkins. He grimaced and changed course, as if traffic control had warned of invisible turbulence ahead.

"Henry," Tipsy whispered.

"Excuse me?" Will looked over his shoulder. "Someone you know?"

"I thought—I—" She pulled her phone from her purse. "Do you mind if I call my kids to say goodnight?"

"Of course not—"

"I'll step outside—"

"Meet me at the Cabana Bar for a drink? Unless you want to head home now."

"No—please. I mean, yes. Cabana Bar."

He said he'd get the check. She thanked him and headed toward the door. As she passed Henry, she put her phone to her ear. "I'm walking out to the dock!" she said in a pleasant, mommy-like voice. "Wish you could come with me!"

Henry beat Tipsy to the end of the dock. He stood beside a charter speedboat and a dilapidated shrimp boat. Some fool captain had turned the speedboat into a grinning, psychotic gingerbread man with a custom paintjob that included emblazoning *Can't Catch Me! Harbor Tours* on both sides of the hull. The boat's painted googly eyes watched Tipsy approach as if it might flop onto the dock like a beaching shark and swallow her whole. Seagulls screeched over her head. She prayed she wouldn't feel the warm splat of gull poop on her bare shoulders. That smell would certainly drown out her perfume. She kept her phone pinned to her ear, lest she appear to be conversing with the gingerbread man or the birds. Her breath came in anxious bursts, and she inhaled and exhaled the smells of oyster shells and wafting cigarette smoke.

"What are you doing here?" she asked Henry.

He pushed his pale hands into his pockets. "I'm not certain. I felt you here, so I came to see you. But you have company. Again."

"Okay Henry—" she didn't know how to begin. "This is all flattering... but you're a ghost... and I'm not... so..."

A blush lit Henry's pale cheeks. "I have no such intentions. I'm a married man."

"Uh, okay... sorry. I guess that was presumptuous of me." She thought about reminding him that in addition to being dead, he and his wife hated each other, but she didn't want to make things any more awkward. "Still, I'm having the best night I've had in months and you show up here like—like a lost cat or—an undead chaperone—"

"I only wanted to confirm the intentions of your new friend." He pointed at the phone in Tipsy's hand. "I sometimes watch over people's shoulders when they tap on those telephones. They're photographic devices as well, correct? And you can write letters on them?"

Tipsy was in no mood to give Henry a technology lesson. "Something like that. Whatever. I'm not so sure about *your* intentions— not after you almost dropped that sculpture on our heads."

"You didn't see him, that day. When you walked back to your desk, he looked at you in a manner that was— well, it was salacious." Henry crossed his arms over his chest and looked down his nose at her. It was all rather fatherly.

"He was checking me out?" she asked, while she thought, *oh, good,* and *my outfit was cute.*

"I don't know what that means. But you and he were alone in the shop. Who knows what he could have done."

"I appreciate the gallantry, but I'm a grown woman. And nowadays, politely checking a woman out is tame. He didn't do anything inappropriate. Will is no Weinstein."

"I don't know what that means, either."

A gull swooped low and she ducked. "Right, but *I know* something. I know what you *are*, Henry. It lets you travel from place to place. Because you were like me when you were alive."

"Yes—I—" His closed his eyes, and they became dark hollows in his face.

Tipsy laughed into her phone. "No wonder you've checked out the makes and models of the local ladies. You zip around town, looking and listening!"

"It's not quite that simple. Or enjoyable. And I've never known anyone like me. You're the first."

"No one in your family? My Granna taught me about our talent. As much as she knew, anyway."

"No, no one. Perhaps that's why I find you so fascinating, and want to keep you safe. Finally, a kindred soul. Perhaps you can teach me about this talent? Although I've always thought of it as more of a curse."

Tipsy's annoyance drained away, as it always did in the face of someone else's sadness. "It must have been hard for you, facing it alone. Of course I'll tell you what I know, but honestly, since you're a spirit, you're more in the know than me at this point. So please stop following me around. If you're so worried about me, I would think you'd be a bit nicer. Especially since you want me to believe you're not a murderer."

"I know my behavior at your art shop did nothing to convince you otherwise. I've always felt things very deeply. More so in my current state of existence. During my lifetime I wrote. Writing provided a release."

"Right. You're like a male Virginia Woolf. But instead of writing your spouse a letter and stepping into the river with rocks in your pockets, you killed your wife and then shot yourself."

"The talk I've heard in the house over the years says so. That I shot her and then myself. But I swear I couldn't have done that."

"The man I saw in the gallery could have done it." Tipsy put a hand on her hip. "It doesn't matter. Because I'm going to find out what happened."

His face split into a blindingly beautiful grin. "Would you?"

His reaction so differed from Jane's that Tipsy had to choke back an insisting reply. She'd expected to have to convince Henry, too. "Yes. I'm trying to, anyway."

"Please—Tipsy, do find out. I've lived so long with this question. Please answer it for me. You can prove that I didn't kill us." He tilted his head. "I'm certain you can unravel the truth. It takes a powerful mind to produce the paintings I saw in your bedroom. Layers of history. Layers of paint. I believe you can create whole pictures."

Henry Mott sure did know how to deliver a compliment. Tipsy lowered the phone. She doubted the surfacing dolphins cared for much beyond the dead fish that the shrimpers threw overboard, and most of the human occupants of the dock would soon be too drunk to notice her talking to herself. "Jane doesn't want to know."

"I do." His red hair melted into the colors of the sunset behind him. When he sidestepped he reminded Tipsy of a toddler who needed to use the potty *right now.* "I have to go. I can only leave the house in short increments before it starts calling to me. Hollering inside my head. As if instead of the lunatic screaming to get out of the asylum, the asylum is screaming at the lunatic to return to his cell." He hunched over, as if he'd been punched in the gut, and vanished.

Tipsy wandered back to the Cabana Bar. Will pulled a stool from under the bar. "Everything okay?"

It might have been preemptive, but Tipsy rested her head on his shoulder. "Yes. It's just hard sometimes."

He kissed her hair with a sweet, reassuring pressure. "I know. I have to escape sometimes, too. So I fish. And hunt deer in the fall."

"Where do you hunt?" Ayers had always participated in a hunt club to the north of Mount Pleasant, near Eutawville. In the early days of their marriage she'd sometimes gone with him. As their family evolved, she resented him for leaving her alone all weekend to manage the kids by herself. The last few years of the marriage, however, she looked forward to deer hunting season. It gave her respite from him.

"Way out Route 41, near Huger. Friend's parents have some land that butts up against a plantation. Old Cannon."

Tipsy sat upright at the mention of Jane's family home. "Old Cannon Plantation?"

"Yeah. It's pretty as hell out there. I actually did some work on the house, for the owners. It's one of the few antebellum plantation houses still standing out that way. Rebuilt their library. Solid oak shelves from floor to ceiling, with new crown moldings. It's one of my signature jobs. You heard of that place?"

"Someone mentioned it to me once. Feel like a drive to the country?"

Chapter 5

The next day, Will's truck turned off one quiet state road and onto another before wheeling onto a half-mile avenue of oaks. The road to the Old Cannon wasn't unusual by the standards of Lowcountry plantations. The well maintained dirt road needed no signage. Stooped limbs, silent witnesses to years that had seen carriages turn horseless and slaves go free, welcomed visitors onto the estate's grounds. The truck's tires kicked up dry dust, but Tipsy craned her head out the window anyway. Her face met surprisingly cool air. Spanish moss hung overhead in a shading, waving canopy.

"Are you sure Mrs. Childress doesn't mind visitors?" She raised her voice to drown out the rattle of pebbles against the undercarriage.

"No, she's a sweet old bird. She's used to curiosity about the place. Lots of history out here. Sometimes the College of Charleston archeology students come out and dig. They find all sorts of things. Bullets. Slave tags. Bits of old tools. Mrs. Childress has a big basket of stuff people have found in the dirt, all bagged and labeled. It's damn interesting."

"What did you tell her when you called?" Tipsy doubted Mrs. Childress had run into her kind of curiosity.

"Just that you were interested in her family, since you were living in her Aunt Jane's house." Will spit tobacco juice into an empty Coke can. He spoke around a puffy lip. "Sorry. I know it's a disgusting habit. Trying to quit."

"Cancer," said Tipsy, with a shrug. "Did Mrs. Childress say anything about her aunt? Or her uncle?"

"She didn't know them." Will stopped the truck, opened the door, and spit the wad of dip onto the dirt road. He popped a few Altoids and stepped on the gas again. "They passed on before she was born."

Tipsy put a hand on Will's knee. "So it's not a shock… the aunt and uncle. They were murdered. Supposedly. In the house."

Will grimaced around his mints. "Really? Damn."

"You think I'm morbid?"

"No. It's kind of interesting actually. In a very morbid way," he said. As usual, his eyebrows stayed glued together, so he simultaneously scowled and smiled. She swatted his arm.

"So that's why we're out here," he said. "Amateur sleuth?"

The house's appearance saved Tipsy from having to answer. "There it is," she said.

When viewed head on, the Old Cannon appeared to be unimpressively large, like the house that's not the biggest in the suburban subdivision but not the smallest, either. A two level white porch fronted an even brick façade of seven skinny windows up and six down, with a door in the middle. As the driveway curved, however, a rambling whiteboard addition off the back of the house blew the symmetry all to hell. A disorganized hodgepodge of flowering trees filled the yard. Tipsy picked out evergreen and deciduous magnolias, dogwoods, crepe myrtles and some variety of flowering cherry. *In bloom most of the year*, said Granna, in the approving and slightly envious voice of one avid gardener admiring another. On this early July morning, fuchsia crepe myrtles ruled the day.

The drive ended in a circle, and within that circle stood a black cannon atop a tiered granite pedestal. "It's from the Revolutionary War," said Will as they climbed down from the truck. "No one even remembers how it got out here."

White rose bushes surrounded the cannon. A bed of red pansies lined the roses, like puddles of paint left by the Queen of Hearts' errant playing cards. Flowers in colors and varieties too numerous to count spilled over the porch railings.

Will whispered to Tipsy as they approached the porch. "Her name is Billingsford."

"Her maiden name?"

"No, her first name."

Tipsy whistled. "That's a doozy, even by Charleston standards."

"She goes by Billy."

"Every southerner loves a good nickname."

Will put an arm around her shoulder. "Yes we do, Miss Tipsy."

Mrs. Billingsford "Billy" Childress welcomed them both with hugs as Will introduced Tipsy. Mrs. Childress had already laid out tea and homemade chocolate chip cookies on the porch. She insisted on showing Will's library to Tipsy. Tipsy didn't know much about building, but she couldn't help but be impressed. He'd not only rebuilt the shelves, the floors and ceilings had been refinished with some kind of antique-looking, wide-planked wood. She would have never guessed an entirely wooden room could work so well, but it did. Rows of old books and framed black and white photographs lined the shelves. The white marble mantels on each side of the room stood out in elegant relief against the rest of the earthy tones. She smiled at Will. "It's beautiful," she said.

He shrugged, but she sensed his pride as he ran a finger down the closest bookshelf.

They returned to the porch. Mrs. Childress sat in a rocking chair, in front of a tall window, framed in long shutters painted a glossy Charleston green. Tipsy sat across from her and examined the woman's face for a hint of Jane, her blood kin. She was close to eighty or just past it, with the healthy glow of a long, happy life and country air. She beamed at Will and Tipsy. "It's so *nice* to have visitors!" she said, and Tipsy found the sought after resemblance in her wide blinking eyes and a smile that managed to be simultaneously coy and genuine.

"Thank you," said Tipsy. "What a lovely place. Do you live here alone?"

Mrs. Childress waved her hand. "Psst, no. My husband Martin is out on the grounds somewhere. We have armadillos digging up the tomato plants, the rose bushes, everything."

"That's a country problem, ma'am," said Will.

Mrs. Childress threw back her head and laughed, again reminding Tipsy of Jane. "It is indeed," she said. "Martin's out on the four-wheeler, laying live traps. He thinks I'm silly, but as much as those critters are an ugly nuisance, I can't see them tortured." She fingered the gold cross around her neck, as if her mercy on the armadillos were in penance for a mild sin. "Anyway, my children and grandchildren are usually out here on the weekends, too. You caught us on a quiet day!" She handed Tipsy a cookie on a delicate blue china plate. "Now what can I tell you, dear?"

Tipsy took a bite of her cookie. The smells of chocolate and a million flowers swirled in her nose like the world's yummiest, sweetest perfume. She told Mrs. Childress the annotated story of how she'd come to live at the house on Bennett Street. "And I heard, ma'am, about Jane and Henry Mott, and how they were killed in the house. It made me curious—"

"A curious cat doesn't die. She finds the mouse," said Mrs. Childress with a knowing nod.

"I can't find any details about what happened," Tipsy said. "I know Jane spent a lot of time here. I wanted to see a place she loved. And honestly, I thought you might know something."

"All I can tell you is what my mother told me. What was said in the family. I'm no... whatcha-callit." The old lady waved her hands in the air, as if she were swatting at unseen extraneous words. "Forensic person. And honestly, no one said much. My mother never got over losing her sister, and under such circumstances. No one wants to talk of such painful things."

Tipsy deflated a bit. "So Henry did kill Jane?"

Mrs. Childress nodded. "Yes." She took a sip of tea. "That's what everyone said, officially."

"Officially?"

"It's what was commonly *known* to have *happened.*" Mrs. Childress' eyelids weren't quite as active as Jane's, but she appeared to know the exclamatory value of a good blink.

"I don't understand."

"Our family had connections, and not only in Charleston. Throughout the state. Those deaths weren't a mere tragedy. They were scandalous. The Robinettes didn't do scandal. The last thing my grandparents wanted was a lengthy investigation that would drag poor Jane's name through the papers. They were found dead in their home. Jane shot through the heart and Henry through the head. The murder weapon in his hand. What more needed to be said?"

"Pardon, ma'am," said Will. "It wasn't just her name being dragged through the mud. What about his?"

"His family didn't fight the obvious. Mother said the Motts almost seemed unsurprised." Mrs. Childress crossed one tan leg over the other. "Although, there's always something that did strike me as odd, when I thought on it. And I did think on it in my younger years. Henry and Jane were my family's Heathcliff and Catherine."

Tipsy perked up again. "What struck you as odd?"

"You see, while my Mother went to her grave cursing Henry for stealing her only sister away from her, she always wondered if Jane knew what was coming."

"You mean she was afraid of him?"

"Mother said she acted very odd in the weeks leading up to the murder. Mother found her crying in her bedroom out here"—she pointed into the house—"at the Old Cannon. Several times. She said Jane never cried. She went through life in a happy whirlwind. But before she died, she was sad and quiet and distracted. And Mother caught her in a few lies. Nothing too terrible. Jane said she would be in one place and turned up in another, but Mother said it wasn't like Jane to be dishonest. They told each other everything."

"Hmmm," said Tipsy. "What about Henry? Did he act strange?"

"That's the thing, dear. It's hard to say, because according to Mother, Uncle Henry was *always* strange. I've heard he was handsome and told wonderful stories about his travels. When he and Jane were young they laughed and had a gay old time like any couple in the midst of first love. But as the years went by, Jane stayed full of laughter and gaiety and Henry lost his. She always tried to bring him around, but he wouldn't have it. He only left the house to go to work and attend necessary family functions." She smiled. "And with the Robinettes in those days, there were many family functions and they were all necessary. I suppose my mother saw a good bit of him. The family knew Jane and Henry weren't the happiest couple. But as far as acting out of the ordinary, no. Same solemn Henry. It was Jane who seemed distraught."

"Maybe he was threatening her," said Will.

"Or maybe…" said Tipsy.

Maybe everyone's got it wrong, said Granna.

Mrs. Childress's eyes widened in a positively Jane-like manner. "No. Oh, no. I didn't mean to suggest…"

"Jane did it?" said Will. "But the gun was in Henry's hand."

"It doesn't sound like there was a very secure crime scene," Tipsy said. "No police investigation."

Mrs. Childress shook her head. "No, dear girl. My aunt Jane would never have—"

The squeal of tires on dirt and gravel cut her off. A four-wheeler careened into the driveway. "Martin!" Mrs. Childress called as the gray-haired man yanked the brake.

Martin Childress, dressed from head to toe in camouflage hunting clothes, strode up to the house with the bowlegged gait of an old cowboy. "Hey, now!" he called. He settled into the ornate white wicker couch across from Tipsy like a camo cake topper. "Who we got here?"

Will and Tipsy said hello, and as Mr. Childress started talking, Tipsy got the distinct feeling that their discussion about Jane and Henry had ended. Their host, like any good Southern storyteller, reveled in an audience, and Tipsy and Will were prisoners of manners. Mr. Childress launched into what could only be accurately described as the Epic Armadillo War of the Old Cannon Plantation. For the better part of an hour, he regaled them with tales of the largest, cleverest, most devious creatures known to man, who were personally intent on destroying both his tomatoes and his sanity. He was the Swamp Fox to the armadillos' Red Coats, or maybe vice versa, but either way, Mr. Childress wasn't having any conversation that didn't revolve around invasive marsupials.

"...but goddamn those little buggers. I swear this new trap will be the end of them. And guess what I'm using as bait? Ever lovin' tomatoes! The very fruits they're stealing from me will be what brings 'em down." He sat back on the couch, full of smug irony. His camo clashed majestically with the blue and yellow striped cushions.

"Heavens, Martin." Mrs. Childress gave his knee a squeeze. "Let me get you a bourbon."

"Thank you, Billy, darlin'. But I wouldn't be so hard pressed if you'd just let me poison the things."

Mrs. Childress scowled.

"I'm kidding you now," her husband said.

She kissed the remains of his springy hair and disappeared into the house. "I tease her," he said to Will and Tipsy, "but truth is, I'd never kill those stupid critters. My angel is too tenderhearted for that." He swelled with pride. "I'll get rid of them, and they'll all come on back. I'll trap 'em all again, if that's what Billy wants me to do."

Mrs. Childress returned with a tumbler of iced bourbon, wrapped in a cocktail napkin. "Here, love," she said to her husband. She handed Tipsy two black and white photographs. The first was of Jane and Henry Mott on their wedding day. June 5, 1916. Jane would have been twenty-one, Henry, twenty-two. Jane's hair must have been long then, in the days before those first women on the cusp of modernity took scissors to their locks. She'd piled it on her head in loose, dark layers. Henry's face was fuller, almost babyish, as if the years between his marriage and his death had worn some of him away. While neither subject smiled, the photo portrayed tenderness. Jane leaned into her new husband. His chin brushed the side of her face, as if he were about to whisper in her ear.

In the second photo, Jane wore a long, medieval looking gown with bell sleeves. That long black hair cascaded over her shoulders. A Romanesque column, draped in ivy, stood behind her. She held one hand aloft, her expression beseeching, as if asking a favor of the sun. Tipsy read the back. *Romeo & Juliet. April 7 till 13, 1912. Dock Street. Chas.*

"You can keep them," said Mrs. Childress. "I've been digitizing all my family photos." She grinned at her husband. "We're old, but we're not above learning new things. Like computers and pest management."

"Where was this photo taken?" Tipsy held up the wedding photo.

"At my grandparents' house, on Water Street. Jane and Henry lived there before they moved to Mount Pleasant. Mother lived there for a time, too, with my sister. In the days after her first husband died in the First World War."

"How sad for your mother," said Tipsy. "She lost her husband and her sister within a few years?"

Mrs. Childress nodded. "Tragedy followed tragedy in my mother's early years. Her first child, my sister Luisa, passed on from influenza not two years after Jane and Henry died. I never knew her, bless her heart."

Will whistled. "That's too much for anyone to bear. If I lost one of my girls... man, I'd go completely insane..." He trailed off, and blushed. Tipsy didn't see how his comment necessitated it, but she had a hunch Will wasn't one for emotional proclamations.

"Mother wasn't insane, but she was a hard woman," Billy Childress said. "She married my father many years later. I came along late in life; she was over forty. She didn't have much left for me by then, but she showed me what love she could. Well...enough of this sad talk, don't you think?"

They chatted about armadillos and summer vegetable gardens for a few more minutes before Tipsy thanked them for their time. She asked if Mrs. Childress would mind a phone call if she had more questions. The old woman said, "Psst, of course! But we miss a lot of calls, running this big place." She wondered if Mrs. Childress had appreciated her husband's trapping tirade. It had saved her from having to defend her mother's beloved sister from suspicion.

"That was interesting. I do like coming out here," said Will, as they drove down the dirt drive. "Get anything useful?"

"Yes. No." Tipsy stared out the open window. "Now I have more questions." She juxtaposed the Childresses' obvious dedication to and enjoyment of each other with the slow decay of her own marriage, and Will's, and Jane and Henry's. They had all gone from newlywed tenderness to varied manifestations of unhappiness—mundane and macabre. The Childresses had done something right that other couples did wrong.

Will pulled the truck to the side of the road and put it in park. He took her chin in his hand and kissed her. He'd done so the night before, when he dropped her at her house after the Cabana Bar. This kiss left their polite first date peck in the dust. Under the oak trees, the clean country air and the afternoon ahead of them. No kids, and nothing much to do but kiss. There would be time for pondering such questions, but this most certainly was not it.

Sunday morning found Tipsy in Miss Callie's yard with a blank three-foot tall by five-foot wide canvas and an easel. She'd pulled her workbench out of Miss Callie's shed. This pre-painting phase didn't require many materials. She placed a few watercolor pencils in grays and browns beside the gray lump of a kneaded eraser. She'd felt this mixture of terror and excitement hundreds of times. The flat, blank canvas existed in stark contrast to the multi-layered, colorful picture in her mind. Unfeeling whiteness competed with the myriad emotions that had called the picture into being in the first place. She always began with the fear that she wouldn't be able to do justice to any of it with her hands. Jane's upturned face, hipshot stance and the set of her shoulders had a story to tell—a narrative that needed a million chattering pages but got only Tipsy's single silent one.

Kids will be home in six hours, said Granna. She'd already spent an hour mixing a perfect shade of Charleston green, to match the house's door and shutters. She poured it into a small jar and tightly sealed the lid. An important touch, but it was time to get down to the real business.

She closed her eyes, and Jane returned to her mind, as she had been on the porch on Friday evening. The minutiae of detail included the smell of Tipsy's own first date perfume and the sound of some unseen neighborhood child's motorized scooter. Tipsy rarely worked from a model. She could have sketched in her bedroom. She'd chosen to work in the garden because it relaxed her, not because she needed to look at the house in order to paint it accurately. Like the memory-movies that had sparked her first drawings and still rose, unbidden, to torment her with past emotions, Tipsy attributed her photographic artistic memory to her supernatural talent. Unlike those memories, however, she always welcomed the ethereal painting experience.

I've done this before. It's been a while, but I can do this.

And then the living, effervescent Jane from the Old Cannon overlapped with the image of the subdued woman on the porch. The picture roared to life, a lion that demanded to be fed.

Tipsy fought her way to creativity's shore four hours later. She stood back, heaving and gasping, on a beach that had seen the wreckage of many artistic endeavors these past few years. She found that this painting had survived those early, roughest tides. She'd filled the canvas with sketchy drawings. The house. The grounds: bushes, trees, and flowers. And the figure of Jane, small yet dominant, in the center of the porch.

"Thank you," Tipsy said aloud. She wiped her face on her tee shirt and removed a layer of sweat and the final vestiges of last night's mascara from her face. She smiled down at the smudges of gray and brown watercolor pencil that covered the shirt like badges of productivity. A clickety-clackety noise brought her attention back to her work. She panicked at the thought of raindrops splattering off her painting, before she remembered the cloudless July sky. Her watercolor pencils jittered and jiggled in their cup. The kneaded eraser bounced along the workbench, as if someone were dribbling a tiny gray basketball.

"Henry?"

Henry materialized on the other side of the workbench. A playful smile tickled the edges of his mouth.

"That was a nice gradual entrance," she said.

"I've learned it's best if I don't surprise you," he said.

"Thanks for that consideration. I don't have the money to dye my hair if it starts going gray."

Henry tipped his head, like an earnest child asking for a well-earned treat. "Promise me you won't ever change your hair? I've never seen anything like it. The color and the texture remind me of ripples on a lively creek. Just after a spring rain. When the soil is stirred up and the flow might burst the banks."

Tipsy chuckled. Only Henry could work such a hopelessly romantic statement into a casual conversation. He spoke as if men said such things to women all the time, like *how-do-you-do*. Nothing smarmy about it. No hidden motives. Just the observations of a man whose thoughts manifested themselves in poetry.

Henry focused on the painting, just as he had gotten into a staring contest with Tipsy's self-portrait upon the occasion of their first conversation. "Might I look on your work? I saw you out here, but I didn't want to disturb you. I understand what it's like to be bothered when you're deep into a story."

Tipsy picked up her kneaded eraser and squished it in her palms. An old habit that always relaxed her. "I don't write. That's your art."

"But it's the same, isn't it? One form of art to another. They're all stories."

"You're right. And it is difficult to get back in the right frame of mind once you're distracted. Hence me working now before the kids get home."

"I didn't have any children to distract me. Just Jane," he said, and Tipsy wasn't sure if he sounded wistful or vengeful. He pointed at the figure in the painting. "That will be her, won't it? My wife."

Tipsy nodded. "Yes. I saw her standing there on the porch. She caught my eye."

"She catches everyone's eye. She caught mine, when I thought nothing could distract me from words on paper. Have you had any luck, with your inquiries into the circumstances of our lamentable demise?"

Tipsy thought about telling Henry what Mrs. Childress had said about Jane's state of mind in the weeks before the murder, but decided it would be best to confer with Jane before speculating. "Nothing much, really."

"Jane still doesn't want to know, does she?"

"I haven't spoken with her about it much more—"

"It's so like her. She'll carry on believing Mama and Daddy's assumptions and accusations for all eternity." With each word Henry's pleasant afternoon picnic manner became more barroom brawl in tone. "Not a brain in her head to craft her own thoughts. Stupid girl."

"Henry. Calm down. Maybe we can convince her."

"I don't care. She'll be proven a fool when you've proven my innocence."

Tipsy still gripped the kneaded eraser in her hand. She held it out toward Henry like a peace offering. "Listen—don't get your hopes up. I haven't proven anything yet, except that I can still paint."

Henry spun around and made to storm off in the direction of the shed at the back of the yard, before pirouetting and lunging in Tipsy's direction.

"Whoa!" Tipsy sidestepped left, and he went the same way. She sidestepped right. So did he, but while she stayed stationary, Henry moved

forward. She looked deep into his eyes, cold dark blue pits of stagnan
well water, and he stepped through her.

———•———

Yellow and black and silver lights flash before her eyes. The waterfall roars between her ears again—just like it did when she thought she dreamed of Jane and Henry arguing at the Old Cannon. Now she understands, however, that wasn't dream, and this isn't a dream either.

Henry walked through her, and now she's seeing smack dab into his memory. Jane must have walked through her the last time, with the same result. She was a psychological, supernatural voyeur.

If this is a memory, Henry is around here somewhere. She tries to pick him out of a sea of white dinner jackets and high, stiff collars. Every man in this ballroom has slick pomaded hair— the look Henry must have been going for right before he died, but he somehow mussed up, leaving him stuck with a disheveled red mop for all eternity. Women swirl past in versions of the loose fitting, mid-calf dress that Jane always wears, but layers of beading and gauzy muslin embellish these exquisite numbers. Jaunty feathers sprout from beaded headbands, as if they've accessorized with captive fireworks.

For a frightening second, as pleasantly benign jazz music wafts over her, Tipsy feels like she's stepping into the ballroom scene in The Shining. *Thankfully, no creepy butler appears beside her, to wish her good evening,* Miss Collins, *and hand her a glass of champagne.*

Ridiculous. If anyone is creepy in this ballroom, it's me. If I'm here, I'm damn sure gonna get some info.

On the short sides of the rectangular room, tall mirrors almost entirely cover the walls. They're crisscrossed with faded patches, lines, and speckles. People pass, their reflections muted, as if they're already ghosts. A few or-nate marble fireplaces, and old family portraits in elaborate frames, line the long walls, reminding Tipsy that she's in old Charleston, not New York _ty, or a haunted hotel in Colorado. Gas lamps provide muted, flattering light— each face Tipsy looks into, fresh and smiling, until she sees Henry._

He's reading the small plaque beside the portrait of a man with mutton chop sideburns who wears a Confederate uniform. His hair is satisfyingly slicked down, and he's sipping from a coffee mug. Someone calls out his name. He turns away from General Muttonchops, toward the other party-goers. A tall man beckons Henry. Henry's nostrils flare, but he goes to the man. Tipsy follows close behind him.

Jane stands beside the man who waved, but she's so short, Tipsy couldn't see her from across the room. Now, Jane fills her eyes, slender in a silver brocade dress that about knocks Tipsy's eyes out with its sparkling, and long white gloves. Her lipstick is bright red, her bobbed hair styled in neat finger waves. She wears simple pearl earrings, but no headdress or other accoutrements. She doesn't need them.

The three other men standing around Jane snicker as Henry approaches before disappearing into the crowd.

"Henry, you old stump," says the remaining man, "aren't you going to wish me a happy birthday?"

"Happy birthday, John Huger," says Henry, with a noticeable lack of enthusiasm.

Tipsy remembers the name from Jane's memory. John Huger is a fop, _Henry had said._ He cares for nothing but playing tennis and smoking cigars…. And then Jane— _we've been friends since we were children…._

John reminds Tipsy of a young Peter O'Toole, like from the Lawrence of Arabia _days. Tipsy watched that movie with Granna, and honestly, she only stuck it out for four hours because of O'Toole's jawline and bright blue eyes._

Jane stands between the two men, smiling. "Henry, dearest," she says. "Johnny wants me to give a monologue."

"What will your mother think of that?"

"You know what she'll think. I'm not going to ask her. She's in the tearoom with her lady friends."

"That's our girl," says John. "A little rebel, like my granddaddies and great uncles on the wall."

"Should I?" Jane asks Henry. "Awful lot of people here. I haven't been onstage in a few years. Maybe I won't remember the words."

"If you make a fool of yourself, most of these people will be too drunk to remember." Henry waves away a black waiter who offers him some brown liquor in a crystal tumbler. "How'd y'all get so much booze in here, anyway?"

"Daddy asked President Harding to repeal Prohibition in honor of my birthday," says John.

Henry gives him a sarcastic ha ha, but Jane's face has frozen in the same hurt grin Tipsy saw out at the Old Cannon. "Maybe I shouldn't," she says. "I'm a little tired."

"Hell, no, Janie," says John. "I want some birthday Shakespeare."

"I'd rather she not."

The two men are like the opposite sides of the coin of masculine energy. John—robust, confident, and hearty— he's heads. Henry—glowering, mysterious, a bit dangerous— tails.

"Son, it's my party," says John. "And I'd rather she do."

He takes Jane's arm. She looks over her shoulder as he leads her to a baby grand piano. He tells the elderly black man to stop playing.

"Hello, there, hello!" John calls out over the crowd. Tipsy doesn't pay much attention to what he's saying, something about thanking everyone for being there. She's too busy watching Henry watch his wife. He seems to be chewing on the inside of his cheek.

Once she focuses in on him, she feels the same minutiae of emotional detail that she experienced in Jane's vision, at the Old Cannon. This time, however, his sensibilities are not warm, or joyful. There's a coppery taste f blood in his mouth—and Tipsy's—from his cheek chewing. He lays off that tender flesh, and grinds his teeth together. Tipsy can hear the sound between her own ears. He's crushing his resentment and his annoyance into a fine powder. He wishes he could spit it out. She's knows that deep inside, he hates himself for feeling this way.

But he can't let it go. Those sour emotions have mixed with saliva and blood in his mouth, and he's swallowing them. He's poisoning himself.

John is still talking. "…so everyone knows our Janie could have been a great star of the stage. Y'all remember how she played Mary in the Christmas play? Those nights she brought down the house at the Dock Street Theater?"

Jane blushes, and looks at her folded hands. She blinks at the floor.

"Now she's all grown up, so those days are long gone, of course. Not much need for Shakespeare in the kitchen. Or the nursery, once that fine day arrives, when we're blessed with little Henry Junior!"

The crowd laughs, and whistles. Henry's face is mottled red, as if his freckles have spread across his face like an allergic reaction. Some man claps Henry on the back. Tipsy is surprised Henry doesn't punch him in the face.

"…so now Janie is going to give us a little Romeo and Juliet." John steps away from the piano. A slim blonde woman sidles up to him, and he puts his arm around her waist.

As the crowd quiets, Jane wriggles her shoulders. Her jaw moves as she clears her throat. Henry stares off into space, as if purposely avoiding her eyes. Now Tipsy wants to punch him, for not smiling any encouragement across the room as Jane begins. For allowing his own insecurity to override the conscience that she knows is in there, somewhere.

"O Romeo, Romeo, wherefore art thou Romeo? Deny thy father and refuse thy name. Or if thou wilt not, be but sworn my love, and I'll no longer be a Capulet."

The familiar soliloquy rolls out of Jane's tiny frame, surprisingly powerful. She's not looking for Henry's eyes, or the eyes of anyone else in the room. She's Juliet calling to Romeo, trying to rectify her love for him with her family's hatred. "…a rose by any other name would smell as sweet…"

The subdued partygoers chit chat and laugh quietly among themselves, sipping their drinks. Tipsy doubts anyone in the room cares much for Shakespeare. Even John, so intent on this recital, is more interested in whispering in the blonde woman's ear.

"…doff thy name, and for that name, which is no part of thee, take all myself."

Jane's far off gaze returns to her friends and neighbors before her. As suddenly as the lovely, serious thespian appeared, she's gone. She's replaced by the Jane they know and admire: flirtatious and gracious, complete with fluttering lashes and flashing dimples. To the crowd's credit, they cheer enthusiastically for her. John whistles, his teeth folded over his lower lip. He pecks Jane's cheek. She gives out and receives more kisses as she makes her way toward Henry. He sees her coming, and turns away.

Damnit, Henry. Tipsy follows him. Don't you dare end this memory on me now.

Jane catches up to him. She tries to grab his hand, but he won't take hers. He's heading back to the corner, and the company of the esteemed General and his whiskers. Jane refuses to give up. When Henry stops under the General's gaze, she's standing beside him.

"I'm sorry," she says. "For the Shakespeare."

"Your mother will be not be pleased. Nor your father."

"I don't understand why they're so adamantly against my acting. When I was a child, they loved it."

"That's because you were a child. Now you're a woman. A wife." He glares down at her. "And apparently, John thinks it's time that you're a mother."

"Oh dear." Jane covers her mouth with one gloved hand. "That was very embarrassing, wasn't it?"

"You seemed happy with all the attention. Although you couldn't have picked a more worn out monologue."

"I wanted something most everyone knows, a little bit."

"Perhaps this would have been more appropriate— I am ashamed that women are so simple, to offer war where they should kneel for peace."

For once, Tipsy senses the beginnings of anger behind Jane's hurt. "So now I'm a shrew to be tamed?"

"Men have always played all *the roles in Shakespeare's plays. Seems a shame to change three hundred years of tradition."*

"Henry, what is the matter with you? When we were young, you cheered me on at the Dock Street. Don't you remember A Midsummer Night's Dream?"

"That was a long time ago, Jane. You dragged me to this party, and now you've embarrassed me. That idiot Huger made a spectacle of you, and impugned my manhood for good measure!" His mouth is close to her ear. A passer by might think he's sensually kissing her neck.

"You're right. I said I'm sorry. I should have told him no." She grips his arm, smiles, and tries a different route. "By next year, it will be you *in front of everyone. Reading a passage from your* novel!"

Henry looks toward the heavens with flaring nostrils, as if asking God to deliver him from his wife's presence, this house, and all its company. "Remove your hand from my arm," he hisses.

Tipsy wishes Jane would tell Henry to stick it where the sun don't shine, but Jane says, "Please don't be angry. We can go back to Water Street. You can go to bed."

He rubs his forehead. "Please. I can't stand it here."

Jane's anxious face softens. "Does your head hurt?"

Oh my god, Jane, *thinks Tipsy.* What he needs is a good knock upside his head!

"Yes. I've had a headache all night."

"Why didn't you tell me? Let's get you some water—or better— they have sweet tea. And finger sandwiches. Are you hungry?" Jane finally succeeds in getting Henry's attention by making the conversation about him. The memory fades as Jane takes her husband, with his poor aching head, to find sustenance.

Chapter 6

When Tipsy woke up from another brief look into Jane and Henry's life-before-death, she lay on the grass beside her easel with her arms wrapped around her knees. She'd been deep into her painting when he showed up, and wasn't sure how much time had passed. The kids were due to arrive any time, however, so she'd been out for at least a few minutes.

She saw him that evening, sitting on the joggling board talking to himself, but like Jane the first time, he didn't seem to realize anything unusual had happened. Part of her felt like she should tell them, but she didn't want to give away a potential method of seeing what had really happened to Jane and Henry that February afternoon in 1923. Or maybe it was all a fluke. She'd have to be careful, though. She couldn't let herself zone out like that around the kids.

Still, she couldn't stop thinking about Henry's coldness. Or Jane's hurt feelings, and her attempts to appease him. She'd been there herself, back when she still cared enough to make an effort to rouse Ayers from one of his blue moods. The words and gestures and body language of both Jane and Henry caused her investigative compass to spin wildly through long runs and cooking sessions. Between Mrs. Childress' frustratingly vague speculations and Tipsy's first hand glimpses into Jane and Henry's unhappiness, her quandary had skewed toward a quagmire.

She hashed it over on Wednesday evening as she drove to Sullivan's Island to pick up her kids from her in-laws' house after camp. The victim of bad drawbridge timing, she spent fifteen minutes parked at the foot of the Ben Sawyer Bridge. Normally Tipsy didn't mind watching whatever grand vessel had necessitated the opening of the drawbridge. The skinny stick of manufactured land that supported Ben Sawyer Boulevard wasn't much wider than the asphalt, so she had a view of the marsh from every window: acres of brownish grass and fingerling creeks at varying depths depending on the tide. She usually opened the windows, put the truck in park, and inhaled the smell of salt air until the attendant lowered the bridge. As the minutes ticked past her promised kid pick-up time, however, she forgot about Jane and Henry. Trepidation about what awaited her won out over trepidation about events long past.

May Penny and Tripp's house wasn't the biggest on the island, but that didn't mean anything. Sullivan's prided itself on being somewhat tattered and messy yet still highbrow, sort of like Henry. Tiny ramshackle cottages and not-so-tiny perfectly kept Cape Cods hobnobbed with 1970s ranchers on stilts and palatial new houses that could have been transplanted from the Hamptons. They all sat on large lots surrounded by brambles and scrubby beach trees. No one seemed to mind the conflicting styles. A multi-cultural architectural utopia, occupied by wealthy white people.

The Collinses' house was somewhere between Cape Cod and the Hamptons, on the Intercoastal Waterway side of the island rather than the beach side. They'd moved into it in the late-1990s when Ayers's sister Mimi had joined her brother at Carolina. Ayers and Mimi had grown up in Mount Pleasant and attended the Pinegrounds School, a place famous for sending many of Charleston's brightest off to the Ivy Leagues each year. The Collinses were a Gamecock family through and through, however, as evidenced in the garnet and black flag that flew from the house's front porch and the stone rooster in the middle of May Penny's bed of day lilies. Tipsy had originally expected her own kids to follow Ayers and Mimi to Pinegrounds, but she had pushed him to try the public schools when he started exploring investment opportunities outside of his job as a jack-of-all-trades at the Collinses' construction company, ColSouth. Pinegrounds wasn't cheap. Tipsy blessed her rare success at influencing him, in light of their current financial circumstances. She couldn't imagine the humiliation Ayers would have felt had he been forced to withdraw his kids from his alma mater, or worse yet, ask his parents to pay the tuition.

She found May Penny and Mimi on the screened back porch. The children splashed around in the pool below them. Little Ayers begged for more time with his cousins, so she gave him the twenty-minute warning, then sat on the edge of a cushioned lounge chair across from May Penny. Her mother-in-law wore dark Gucci sunglasses and a white straw hat. Even in the synthetic shade of the screened porch, she could feel May Penny's blue eyes crawling over her, even if she couldn't see them. May Penny had at least twenty pairs of oversized sunglasses, and had a great appreciation for a dash of bling. Her current selection had rhinestone flowers on the frames. Tipsy picked at a streak of gray paint on her knee that she'd somehow missed in the shower, and tugged her sundress down to cover it.

Mimi broke the silence by asking about the gallery and her new painting. "The girls said you've been staying up late…painting away." She tucked her keratin-straightened blonde hair behind her ears and crossed her slim legs at the ankle. The picture perfect Charleston wife and mother, from her tastefully whitened teeth to her Lily Pulitzer dress to her gold Jack Rodgers sandals. "Can you tell me… about the painting?" A lifetime of fighting asthma had worked its way into Mimi's speech over the years. At this point, Tipsy didn't think Mimi's breathy voice had anything to do with an inability to get enough oxygen. It had simply become part of her, like the inhaler she always kept in her perfectly matched handbag. Tipsy imagined plenty a man had found himself hanging on Mimi's next airy word.

Tipsy smiled her appreciation. Mimi had always quietly defended her from May Penny, as if Tipsy were an adopted mutt in a litter of bullmastiffs. She'd learned to navigate her relationship with Ayers by watching Mimi steer around May Penny's flattering-yet-somehow-insulting banter. No matter the tension in the air, mother and daughter never fought. Tipsy's opinion of the effectiveness of this strategy had changed since her divorce—perhaps if she'd told Ayers exactly how she felt about his behavior years ago, they'd have never come to their current unpleasant circumstances. She didn't begrudge Mimi, however; after all, she couldn't divorce her mother.

Tipsy rambled on about the painting for a while before May Penny found a spot to jump in. "It's good you're doing something." Her leg bounced. The sole of her own Jack Rodgers tapped lightly against the bottom of her foot. "With all this mess…" She sighed. "My word, my word. It's good you're finding a way to fill your time that might earn you some money eventually."

"I hope so," said Tipsy. "I've been trying to focus on the children—"

"Of course you have, dear. As you should. But you can't expect Ayers to support you. Now, it's none of my business, but you made this decision. You have to face the music." May Penny removed her hat, revealing bobbed blonde hair that magically remained fluffy. "Or, in this case, stare down the orchestra."

"Yes. I know. It's a lot for all of us—"

"The children seem to be handling it tolerably well." May Penny removed her glasses as well. She peered through the porch rails at Mary Pratt and Olivia Grace as they joined hands and leaped into the pool. "Poor little loves. And you. Finding yourself and all. Creative fulfillment,

la-la-la. But what about my son? What about Ayers? Heavens, heavens."
Apparently it was May Penny's business, after all.

"Mama," said Mimi, "Ayers… seems to be doing better—"

"Don't sass me, Mimi. I'm his mama. It's my job to look after him. If I don't, who will? Obviously not his wife."

The blood drained out of Tipsy's face and pooled in her bladder. She suddenly had to pee. In six months she'd had only passing conversations with Ayers's parents about the logistics of the divorce. She had expected this at some point, but she still wasn't ready. "I'm sorry—"

"You should be. My son loved you. He took care of you and kept a roof over your head, a mighty nice one if I recall. And how do you repay him? How, how? You ruin his life and humiliate him by running around town with that holy-roller."

Tipsy had no idea May Penny had known about her brief rela-tionship, if it could accurately be so labeled, with Saint Dave. "May Penny—I understand how you feel—"

"No. You don't. God forbid you ever sit in my place and have to tell some ungrateful woman who broke your son's heart into a million pieces exactly what she needs to hear." May Penny's lip quivered. "After you appeared in our lives out of nowhere, from lord knows where. What heehaw town was it? Mauldin? Manning?"

"Martinville."

"Wherever. We took you in. And now this. My poor, poor son." She grabbed a SpongeBob beach towel and buried her face in it. Squidward and Gary the pet snail glared at Tipsy with accusing cartoon eyes from between her mother-in-law's clenched hands.

"Mama." Mimi tried again. "You don't know what happened… between Tipsy and Ayers. No one knows. Let's be honest. Ayers isn't the easiest person to get along with, no matter how much we love him."

Squidward and Gary disappeared into May Penny's lap, to be replaced by Mr. Krabs' equally hostile face. *Who knew SpongeBob characters are so opinionated about family matters?* asked Tipsy's frazzled mind.

Hold on, now, baby. Don't lose it, said Granna.

"That's not the point! Tipsy promised to love and cherish him, in good times and in bad—"

Oh, for the love of god, said Granna.

"—not abandon him in his time of horribly stressful financial need."

"He wasn't *in* a time of financial need when we separated," Tipsy murmured. *But he was angry and depressed and mean and miserable. He screamed at the children and I was too scared to tell him to shut his fat mouth, God forgive me. I steered them around him as best I could, but it wasn't enough. Now at least he sees. He sees what he's become and maybe he can change. Maybe someone else can reap the benefits of that, but it can't be me. Please, can't you understand that?* It all sat on the tip of her tongue, but all she said was, "I'm sorry."

"He needs you now! He needs his family, so he can recover from this!" May Penny flopped into her lounge chair in a backwards, land-locked swan dive.

"I'm sorry—" said Tipsy.

"Sweet mother of mercy, is that all you can say?" asked May Penny. "I'm sorry, I'm sorry, I'm sorry?"

"I'm—I'm sorry," said Tipsy, as if there were no other response and that one would give her permission to run away. She called to the children, bade them hug and kiss their grandmother, and ushered them out the door. She put her truck in reverse as Mimi ran out the door.

"Wait—Tipsy, wait! Can I talk to you—" She eyed the wet kids, who were all puffy eyed from the chlorine. "—in private?"

"Do you need your inhaler?" Tipsy asked.

Mimi shook her head. "I just need to talk. And calm down."

Tipsy nodded, although every cell in her body wanted to drive away from this house as fast as the Tahoe would take her. She switched on the DVD player, and fought back a peal of hysterics when the SpongeBob theme song blasted through the truck. *Who lives in a pineapple under the sea?*

"Hang on a sec, buddies. Watch SpongeBob while I talk to Aunt Mimi."

"Whoo-hoo!" said Little Ayers, and both girls said, "Yes, ma'am."

Tipsy got out of the truck and shut the door. Mimi apologized for her mother's behavior, before launching into the real reason she needed to talk.

"I need to tell someone— please, Tips, swear you won't say anything? Not to Ayers?"

"Lord, Mimi, I don't talk to Ayers about anything personal anymore." Tipsy wiped at a tear that had slipped down Mimi's face. "Are you okay?"

"I'm thinking about… leaving Jimmy."

For a moment this didn't register with Tipsy. She considered herself close to Mimi. They'd talked intimately about their kids, their friends, Tipsy's art and Mimi's volunteer work… but come to think of it, Mimi never said much about her marriage. "I always thought y'all were happy."

"I always thought y'all were happy, too." Mimi swiped at her eyes. Her perfect makeup smeared toward her hairline in uneven brown stripes. Her breathy pauses became stutters. "I'm—I'm having an affair."

If May Penny had labeled Tipsy a tramp for seeing another man after she and Ayers were living in separate homes, she'd hardly approve of her own daughter seeing someone while she and Jimmy were still as married as June and Ward Cleaver. "With who?" Tipsy asked.

"Brad Humphries."

"Holy hell, Mimi!"

"Please—promise me—"

"I won't say anything—but—Brad Humphries? He works for your father! With Ayers! And he's—he's married and has what, two kids?"

She nodded. "We've been seeing each other eight months."

"And Jimmy has no clue?" Mimi shook her head. "And y'all are going to—you're going to leave him, for Brad?"

"I want to… but Brad, I don't know. He's not ready. He wants to keep doing what we're doing."

Tipsy shook her head. "No. If he's saying that, he's not going to leave. He's got his cake and he's eating it. What about his wife?"

"He says they don't have any relationship—they live separately in the house. She's horrible—"

"You don't know that. He's lying to her, why won't he lie to you? And hell, you're lying to Jimmy—"

"I don't love Jimmy anymore like that. We've been in and out of counseling for years. I never told anyone about it. How did you tell Ayers? Did you just sit him down and say it?" Mimi finally pulled a blue and white inhaler from the pocket of her dress. She fired it into her mouth and took a deep breath.

"Stop now. If you're going to leave, you need to do it for you. On your own. Not for freakin' Brad Humphries who doesn't even want to leave his wife, anyway!"

"I thought, if I left first…"

"Mama, the DVD is skipping!" Mary Pratt had rolled down the window.

"Okay, baby, I'm coming." She took Mimi's hands. "Listen—don't do anything yet."

Mimi's lip quivered. "I didn't mean to dump on you… but I'm not like you. You're so strong and independent. And you have your art. It's so beautiful. I don't have anything, and I'm getting so paranoid. What if Jimmy suspects something and hires a PI? I'll lose alimony, and I haven't worked in twelve years. I don't know what I'd do. At least if I leave with Brad I'd have someone to lean on." She clutched the inhaler to her chest as if she could find support in the bit of plastic that she'd depended on her entire life.

"But Brad's not talking about leaving—"

"If I have alimony, I'll be fine. And child support. I can stay in the house—be home with the kids. Jimmy will *have* to do that—right?"

"Mimi, I'm not a lawyer—"

Olivia Grace squealed inside the car, and Tipsy heard a muffled, "M.P., give it *back!*"

"I'll call you tomorrow. Promise me you'll sit tight."

Mimi nodded, and wiped her eyes again. With her smudged eye shadow, she looked like she belonged on the record cover of Granna's soundtrack to that Broadway musical, *Cats*. Tipsy kissed Mimi's cheek and hopped into the car.

"Okay, buddies, simmer down now. We're going home!" As Tipsy wheeled out of May Penny's driveway, she wondered how Mimi had sat through May Penny's interrogation and come out thinking Tipsy was strong and independent and brave.

On Thursday, a quick check of property records online during a lull at the gallery led Tipsy to the address of the old Robinette house, near the corner of Water and Church Streets. As it sat a few blocks south of the GQB, she decided to stroll past on her lunch break. The house, built in 1845, was one of the largest on the street of meticulously maintained homes. Charleston singles, most of them, a uniquely peninsular design consisting of a long, relatively narrow house with multi-level porches on one side. The porches, or piazzas in Charleston-speak, all faced in the same direction. Each house looked out over its own pleasant side yard abutting the non-piazza wall of the neighbor's place.

In most cases, a solid wood door fronted the street level piazzas. Ayers had taken Tipsy on a walking tour on the momentous occasion of her visit to Charleston. The simultaneously quirky and harmonious homes, like soldiers in the same army that wore different uniforms, had appealed to Tipsy's artistic sensibilities. The practical country girl in Tipsy, however, had been struck by the dysfunction of the piazza doors. It seemed pointless to lock out trespassers who could simply jump the railings and help themselves to your potted plants and rocking chairs. She'd recently mentioned her observation to Will, and expected him to launch into a discussion of angles or symmetry, or some other build-er-ism. To her surprise, his answer bespoke aesthetic over rationality.

"The doors are beautiful. Unique," he said. "Beautiful things don't always have to make sense."

Annuals in full riotous bloom exploded from window boxes and through fence rails and over garden walls. Squadrons of butterflies landed on the blossoms, as if their fluttering wings might push them back where they belonged. Tipsy exchanged friendly hellos with several puttering ladies in wide hats, each armed with clippers and gardening gloves and bags of fertilizer.

The Robinette house had passed out of the family in the 1930s, and the last sale in 2001 appeared to have been to an out-of-state buyer. Tipsy ran her hands along the brick and stucco wall that surrounded the garden. She squinted up at the gray stucco house. It sat about fifteen feet behind the wall. She doubted the new owners would be keen on a request to wander the house in search of a little girl who died in 1925.

She thought that Luisa Bishop, Mrs. Childress's long lost half sister, might be able to give her a first hand account of the days leading up to or following the murder, but Tipsy had never sought out a ghost. They'd always turned up uninvited. Now she wanted to find one, and she had no clue where to begin.

Granna? She asked.

Not sure what to tell you, sugar. Never tried myself. Maybe close your eyes and do what comes natural.

Tipsy leaned against the wall, resting her bottom on stucco and her back against wrought iron. The former felt sun-warmed and the latter felt cold from the shade of a climbing wisteria. She tapped her fingers on her lap, one-two-three-four-five-four-three-two-one, again and again. The numbers in her head drowned out the cars on busier Church Street.

Her fingers slowed to match her heartbeat, and she spoke with her mind. *Luisa? Luisa Bishop? I'm a friend of your Aunt Jane. I'd like to talk to you. Are you here?*

She repeated herself until the pattern of her thoughts and the sun's warmth on her head and her shins made her sleepy. She wiggled her toes, and the rhinestones in the center of her strappy sandals winked at her like plastic doll's eyes. She'd had a low grade headache all day, probably from the heat. She pressed her fingers into her temples.

This isn't going to work, she thought, but when she peered through the web of wrought iron and wisteria branches, she saw a small, still figure in the middle of the four stairs leading up to the porch's pseudo-security door.

Tipsy scooted to a spot where she had a clear view. The little girl's head moved with her, like a rabbit who has seen the hawk, but isn't yet sure if it's mutual. She wore what appeared to be a long pink night-gown with a sailor collar, slouchy woolen socks and some kind of soft shoes that reminded Tipsy of her girls' ballet slippers. A giant bow perched atop her chin-length blonde hair, further adding to her rabbit impersonation.

Tipsy smiled, her headache forgotten. She beckoned through the fence. *Here, bunny foo-foo.*

The little girl glided toward Tipsy and stopped on the other side of the wall with a poochy lip and round blue eyes. She looked to be about ten years old.

"Hello, Luisa," Tipsy said.

"Hullo," said Luisa. She scratched at her head, as if to loosen her bow. "You can't know my Aunt Jane. She's dead. I know because I remember when she died. Like me. I'm dead, too."

"How do you know you're dead?"

"How do *you* know you're alive?" Luisa vanished, but before Tipsy could panic, she reappeared about a foot closer to the wall.

"I guess I just know. And I'm breathing."

"I just know, too. And I'm not." Her lip stuck out further. "So you can't know my Aunt Jane. Because she can't be an old lady, because she's dead."

Tipsy treaded lightly. "She couldn't be an old lady now, anyway. Too much time has passed—"

"It's hard for me to follow time. I was just learning all about it from my nanny."

"—but Aunt Jane is still here. Well, she's at her house. She's like you—she's a ghost."

The girl smiled, revealing a mouth full of too big adult teeth she'd never grow into. She blinked in and out as she giggled. Trying to focus on her flickering form made Tipsy dizzier.

"Goodness!" Luisa said. "I always wondered if I was the only one. Except for Virginia, but she's long ago gone. I wish I could see Aunt Jane."

"That would be nice, wouldn't it?" Tipsy said. "But she can't leave her house. Can you?"

Luisa shook her head. "No. I wish I could." Her eyes brimmed with sparkly tears. "I get so lonesome."

Tipsy leaned her forehead against the wrought iron. Luisa wasn't so much older than her own girls. As twins, they'd never spent more than a few hours apart. This poor child had been without family or playmates for decades. "I'm sure you do—"

"How can you see me?" Once again she vanished and reappeared a few steps to the right.

"It's a special thing I can do."

"It must be very special. I've been here a long time, and no one has ever seen me."

Tipsy felt as if she were talking to a child and an adult, one actor playing different roles in the same scene. "I wondered if you'd mind talking to me about Aunt Jane. And Uncle Henry."

"Uncle Henry killed my Aunt Jane. When I was eight."

"I wondered if you'd know that. Maybe a child wouldn't have heard."

"At first Mother didn't tell me. She was so sad. She'd always been sad, because my father died in a big war across the ocean. In a ditch in a place called Argonne." Luisa looked past Tipsy, as if she saw that far off forest through the neighbors' houses, over the Charleston Harbor and across the Atlantic. "Mother got sadder when Aunt Jane died. She first told me that Aunt Jane and Uncle Henry had an accident. But one day, she drank a lot of wine, and she cried and said, *Henry! Henry Mott, you killed my sister!* And she said other words that I'm not allowed to say, like taking the Lord's name in vain."

"Do you remember much about your Aunt and Uncle?"

She smiled and clasped her hands together. "Oh, yes! My Aunt Jane was the prettiest, sweetest of ladies. She baked pies with me and taught me to sew, and to dance. She was always laughing. Uncle Henry was grouchy sometimes, but he did tell me stories. My favorite was when the toy soldier fell in love with the china doll, but she sat on the highest shelf. So he stole ribbon from the little girls to climb to his sweetheart…" She scowled. "But he never told me the end. Or maybe I don't remember. There are some things I can't remember."

Tipsy thought of Jane and Henry's inability to remember their deaths. "Like how you ended up this way?"

"Yes, ma'am."

Tipsy didn't want to disturb the child with ruminations on her own passing, so she steered the conversation back on to the pre-planned route. "Did your mother say anything else that night? When she drank too much wine."

"She spoke about letters… how Aunt Jane wrote so many letters during that Christmastime, at the Old Cannon. She said she wished she had those letters. And then she cried harder, because she thought Aunt Jane told her troubles to another lady. Mother and Aunt Jane were the most dearest of friends. She looked through Aunt Jane's things and didn't find any letters anywhere."

"Did she speak of it anymore, after that?"

Luisa's round white cheeks bounced when she shook her head. "She stopped drinking wine. My grandmother made her stop. Said it wasn't right for good Christian ladies to drink so much wine. She feared the police would come take Mother away. And Grandfather for giving it to her."

"Police—oh, right. Prohibition," Tipsy said as Luisa flickered. She remembered her headache. "Sugar, could you stay still? It makes my eyes hurt when you move so much."

"Yes, ma'am," said Luisa. She folded her hands before her waist, the way Mary Pratt might after being chastised for squirming too much at the dinner table. "After I died, Mother moved out of this house. She only came around sometimes. At first I yelled and screamed at her, but she never heard me. In the stories I heard about ghosts, they throw things and blow out candles and slam doors, but I can't do any of that."

Tipsy thought of Henry's manipulation of inanimate objects. She'd never seen Jane do the same. "I think only some ghosts can do that."

"Oh. Virginia couldn't touch anything either. We both tried, but our hands—" She made a chopping motion at the wisteria branches above her head. The knobby wood never moved, and no blossoms were knocked loose. Her arm passed through it all.

"So I stopped screaming at Mother. I followed her through the house instead. Then my grandmother and grandfather moved out to the Old Cannon for good, and I didn't see any of them anymore. Mother had a new husband by then. A man from up north."

Tipsy's heart caught in her throat at the thought of mother and daughter, so close but unable to ease each other's pain. "I'm sure your family missed you very much."

"I missed them, too, but my sadness got worse when Virginia went away."

"Who is Virginia? You've mentioned her several times."

"The ghost who was here when I woke up dead."

"There was another ghost?"

"Yes. She was my friend. We talked and rested together, and she sang songs. And we played chase in the garden. When I was sad she cheered me. And I tried to cheer her, too."

"I don't understand. What do you mean, she went away?"

"One day she was here, and then she was gone. She apologized for leaving me, but she had to go home."

"That's odd. How did she—"

"Can I help you?" A man stood about fifteen feet to Tipsy's right, at the house's front gate. His accent was New York or New Jersey, or maybe Boston. "If you wanna look, fine, but don't pick any flowers. This is a private home."

Tipsy peered though the wrought iron again. Luisa was gone. She touched a wisteria blossom and grinned at the man as if the flower had left gold dust on her finger. "Oh, of course not! I'm just looking. Your flowers are gorgeous."

He swelled like an overstuffed calzone. "Thank you. Our gardener is a genius."

"Yes, sir," she said. She bid him a nice day and set off down Water Street with a line of sweat dripping down the back of her sundress. She cursed the owner's unfortunate timing; he'd surely recognize her if she returned. On a street with so many floral choices, only a person who was up to something suspicious would continually choose the same place to stop and smell the roses.

<hr>

Tipsy still had twenty minutes of lunchtime left. The abrupt end to her conversation with Luisa flustered her, so she decided to walk past St. Philip's.

I want to see if Proctor is… like, haunting around.

Don't see the harm in it now, said Granna.

Tipsy entered the graveyard and was pleasantly surprised to find it relatively empty, perhaps due to the heat. The thick, moist air could probably support a school of small fish. She sat on the bench where she'd last sat with Proctor. He must have felt her, or saw her. He materialized on the bench beside her as she was replying to a hope-you're-having-a-good-day text from Will. His messages and late night phone calls were becoming a source of joy and comfort to her. He'd taken to stopping by her house after her kids were asleep. They sat on the joggling board on the front porch and hashed out problems as significant as global warming and as mundane as why Will's neighbors insisted on leaving their Christmas lights up all year long. Tipsy always talked more than Will did, but the observations he made and the opinions he offered continued to surprise her with their insight and thoughtfulness. As she got to know him, she had trouble believing she'd ever thought him gruff and unsociable.

"Always people are staring at those machines," Proctor said, and he crossed his legs. He held his hand before his pallid face. He stared into the air with buggy brownish eyes and wiggled his thumbs.

"You're right." Tipsy stuck the phone in her purse. "We spend too much time on them."

"None of you understand that your time is limited."

"What a pleasant thought," said Tipsy. "I spoke with Luisa Bishop, Jane's niece, just now. She's a ghost. And this past weekend I spoke with her other niece. She's alive, by the way. The other niece, I mean. She lives out at the Old Cannon."

"You're a wonder, Miss Seer."

"Or maybe I'm a clairvoyant with OCD." She laughed at his puzzled expression, and then filled him in on the basics of her visits with Mrs. Childress and Luisa. She told him about Jane's supposed strange behavior before her death, the letters, and the mysterious Virginia. She left out the visions of Henry and Jane arguing at the Old Cannon, and John Huger's party. It felt too much like revealing a secret, or malevolent gossip.

"I remember Luisa Bishop," said Proctor. "A sweet child. She didn't look much like her Aunt Jane, but she had the same impish manner. A dead ringer, pardon the pun."

"Mrs. Childress said that Jane's sister…" Tipsy pushed her thumb into her temple. "What was her name?"

"Constance."

"Yes. I got the impression Constance became bitter after Luisa died."

Proctor folded his arms over his mid-section. His white beard touched his chest, and he gave it a good memory-inducing tug. "A terrible thing, that child's passing. I was there. Pierre Robinette asked me to come. To pray for healing. I stayed on when it became apparent that Luisa wouldn't recover. I hoped to offer comfort, but as we all know, such efforts are menial in those circumstances."

"Hopefully she went peacefully."

"I'm sorry to say it, but she did not. Constance held her through that last night, while she burned up. Luisa cried out all manner of nonsense in her delirium. Constance begged her for hours, to stay, please stay. Screams echoed throughout the house, all night. Luisa wailing and Constance beseeching her. The child died in her mother's arms as the sun rose."

Tipsy shivered. "And to think, nowadays she might have spent a few days in bed and then been back at school."

"Jane's death opened a dam of sadness for the Robinettes. Luisa's death, and then a few years later, Black Tuesday."

Tipsy had read enough about the Wall Street crash of 1929 to guess the answer to her next question. "Were the Robinettes hit hard?"

"Edisto Bank and Trust folded. Pierre lost everything. He had to sell the house on Water Street. He and Theresa moved out to the Old Cannon. He died not long after. It was too much for him. If not for Constance's new husband, they would have lost the plantation, too."

"Luisa said she married a man from up north."

Proctor nodded. "No one liked him much at first, but he was a godsend in disguise. He was a rich New Yorker. He and Constance took up full time residence at the Old Cannon, and old Miss Theresa lived out there with them."

"No wonder Constance never recovered. Her first husband. Luisa. Her father. Jane."

"Constance and Jane were always close. They had a whole group of chums from childhood. The heirs apparent of Charleston society."

"Like who?" Tipsy asked. Perhaps Jane's friends had descendants, like Mrs. Childress.

"Let's see. There was Annie Rose Middleton—she married Charles Chalmers. He and Andrew Bishop, Constance's first husband, were cousins. And Tradd Smith and Reed Hamilton. They both married girls from Walterboro. I conducted all those ceremonies. And John Huger."

Tipsy sat up straighter at the mention of John. "Who was John Huger?" Tipsy asked, sensing an opportunity to get some useful information. She used the local pronunciation, *You-gee*.

"Son of another old family. The Hugers had a plantation near the Old Cannon—"

"In Huger, no less."

"Yes, in that community—one can't really call it a town— named after their family. And a grand home at the south end of Meeting Street. A cottage out on Sullivan's Island, on the Moultrieville side. They weren't as wealthy as the Robinettes, but they managed. In fact, John's father—" Proctor lowered his voice, as if someone might hear him gossiping about someone who had been dead for at least seventy years. "— he rebuilt the family fortune by bootlegging spirits."

Well that *explains his illegal booze party*, said Granna, rather disapprovingly.

Proctor continued. "The Hugers and the Robinettes spent time together out in the country. John, Jane, and Constance were like the Three Stooges when they were children. Always making mischief. You do know the Three Stooges?"

She nodded. "Moe and his boys were before my time, but I gotcha. Who did John marry?" Perhaps he had living grandchildren!

"No one. John never married."

"Oh." Or maybe not.

"He died about ten years after Jane and Henry. He used to take swims out on Sullivan's at least once a week during the warm months. Drowned. Mighty sad. He was quite a character. Anyway, I don't remember Jane acting particularly mysterious in the weeks before her death, but Constance would have known better than I."

"I'm not sure what to do with that information. Jane refuses to talk to me about the past. I suppose I could ask Henry. But if he threatened her, and he wants me to believe that he's innocent, would he admit it to me?" She stood. "I'm sorry. I'm talking to myself. I should go back to work."

"No pardon needed. I often talk to myself."

"You have good reason. I'll think about it some more. Maybe I'll call Mrs. Childress and ask her about the letters. But on another note, I don't understand what Luisa said about the ghost she called Virginia. How did she haunt the house and then just—not? And it sounds like Virginia knew she was going away forever. She said she was going home. Like going home to a house she'd live in? Or *going home*. Sometimes people say that for—you know—" She pointed at the sky.

"Heaven. Being with God."

Tipsy nodded. "It sounds like she'd figured out how to escape her haunting." She spoke under her breath as she walked toward the cemetery gate.

Proctor slid along beside her on his misty legs, as if the cobblestone path had turned to ice. He stopped several feet from the gate. "If only everyone could be so lucky."

———————•———————

Two days later, while the kids watched a pre-bedtime movie downstairs and Tipsy folded laundry in her room, Jane materialized at the foot of Tipsy's bed, apparently intent on one of their pleasant evening chats. Tipsy promptly ruined Jane's mood by giving her the details of her visits to Mrs. Childress and Luisa. The ghost glided from one end of the room to the other, in zigs and zags and aimless circles, like she stood on a Roomba. "I've told you. I don't want to *know* these things!"

"But Jane, isn't it a relief to know what happened to your family and friends? How things turned out for them after you passed?"

"Yes—no. My sweet little niece. I can't stand the thought of her wandering my parents' house, as lonely as I am. To think of my father, heartbroken and destitute. Dear old Johnny, dead before his time. And my poor sister. A life of such great *sadness*." She sat on the bed.

"Your family had its share of sadness, for sure, but there must be some closure—"

"Closure?"

Tipsy backtracked. "That's probably a later twentieth century concept. What I mean is, at least you don't have to wonder anymore. And it's not all sadness. Your mother and Constance lived out their lives at the Old Cannon. Constance had another child. Now that child is an old woman and she lives there still, content as a clam in mud. Billy Childress has children and grandchildren, and a husband who thinks she hung the moon. The Old Cannon is still a happy place."

"I'm pleased the family has hung onto the Old Cannon, if we lost the house on Water Street. But Tipsy, I *truly* don't want to talk about it anymore."

Tipsy decided to press on until Jane cursed at her or disappeared. "What about what Mrs. Childress' said about you being distraught in those last months, or the letters Luisa mentioned? Do you remember any of that?"

Jane looked down at her hands. "I always kept up with my correspondence. Constance always sought all my time and attention—"

"She was possessive?"

"Yes—that sounds about right. Possessive, bless her heart." She shrugged. "Henry and I hadn't gotten on in a goodish amount of time. I hated to let anyone know our troubles. It was humiliating and it made me so *very sad*, but perhaps the sadness finally wore through my attempts to hide it."

A male voice entered the conversation like a sudden baritone aria amidst a soprano chorus. "Of course. You were distraught, so the fault lies with me."

"Oh—Henry," Tipsy said. She slid off the bed as Henry approached Jane.

Jane stood and clenched her fists. Her chin jutted. She backed away from Henry, a runty hen flapping her wings at an incoming fox. "You let me be."

"I will not." Henry jabbed a finger in Tipsy's direction. "Tipsy here is trying to help us. And yet you stonewall her at every turn, and always turn the blame on me."

"That's the truth! We were unhappy. Or have you forgotten, just as you forgot shooting me through the heart?"

"Always the melodrama with you!" Henry sneered down at his wife. "Why don't you want to know what *really happened?* Perhaps you're *hiding something?* What's sweet little Janie *hiding?*"

"Stop it!" said Jane. "I'm hiding nothing—I'm—" She covered her ears with her hands.

Henry roared laughter in her face and slapped both hands on his thighs. "You don't want to hear it! You don't want to know the truth. It might not be the same story that has given you an excuse to make me even *more miserable* in death than you did in life!"

"Okay—Henry—okay," said Tipsy. "This isn't productive."

"Your own *parents* didn't defend you!" Jane spit back at Henry. "Even your own blood kin knew you were *crazy!* They only associated with you because you managed to marry me. They wanted to elevate *themselves* through *my family!* If not for me, they would have sent you off to some other relation and spared themselves the embarrassment of you!"

Henry's nostrils flared, like a greyhound at the starting line. "How dare you."

Jane smiled. "Now they're all dead, and no one living but Tipsy even remembers us." She laughed, and then sobbed, then giggled again. "Why bother reminding anyone?"

"Because you're hiding something, you neurotic bitch—you goddamn—"

"Henry!" Tipsy stepped between them. "That's enough!"

She felt those vibrations behind her eyes, like she had at the GQB. The same inexplicable sneeze-like force that had heaved the ceramic sculpture against the wall before it crushed Will's skull. This time, however, she didn't need to fling anything to get her point across. The force of her intercession smeared the snarl on Henry's face into a scowl and blew his hair toward the ceiling in red shock waves.

He stepped away from Tipsy and Jane, in the direction of the door. His hands hung at his sides. "My apologies. For using language hardly befitting a gentleman. Y'all enjoy your evening." He pointed toward his wife. She hugged herself while humming a tune that sounded vaguely like *Shoo-fly, Don't Bother Me.* Her hands met before her middle. She set about knitting with her invisible needles.

"I know something isn't as it seems here." He went fuzzy and drifted through the floorboards, a wax man melted by his own temper.

Whoa, Tipsy thought. *What was that?*

Seems like you're asking me that question a lot these days, Granna replied. *Same thing that happened at your gallery, I suppose.*

Tipsy's neck hurt, but it was probably stress-related, like that mild headache that sometimes simmered behind her eyeballs lately. Intervening between two battling phantoms surely counted as stressful.

Jane smiled at Tipsy in her deranged way. "I don't like fighting," she said.

"You did the right thing." Tipsy flexed her neck from side to side. "He shouldn't talk to you like that."

Sounds like something I would have said to you, about Ayers.

Yes, Granna, I know. Her reply felt very teenager-y, but she wasn't in the mood for a lecture. She turned toward the bathroom, intent on splashing some cold water on her face and maybe popping some Tylenol.

Henry stood behind her, his face a mask of hatred. Before Tipsy could move, or try to summon her supernatural powers, he rushed at his wife. Tipsy instinctually stumbled backward. She reached for Jane— in another instinctual attempt to pull her out of the path of a raging bull. Jane's eyes widened in fear as Tipsy's grasping fingers passed through her arm. Tipsy had just enough time to witness Jane blink out of existence in her own defense. Then, like before, she saw nothing but black and yellow and silver, until light rose on crackling flames in an ornate fireplace.

———•———•———

It takes only a moment to recognize the front parlor of Miss Callie's house. The furniture is different, but it's one of those rooms that really only has one sensible configuration: a couch before the fireplace and an armchair on either end of the couch. Unlike the present day, there is no mahogany coffee table. Instead, several small end tables dot the empty space between the furniture like channel markers. The wallpaper is fleur-de-lis rather than the floral pattern Tipsy sees every day. Firelight and a single lit gas lamp bathe the room in varying tones of brown and orange. The fire hisses and snaps and its sparks spit a faint smoky smell over the room.

Jane and Henry sit in the armchairs. She holds some kind of knitting in her lap. Real knitting this time, and Tipsy finds she's relieved that Jane's nervous habit of weaving unseen tapestries had some basis in real life. "I enjoy these cool early summer nights," *Jane says.* "The firelight is pleasant."

"Yes, it's peaceful," *says Henry.* "Until your parents and sister descend upon us."

Jane laughs. "Silly. They'll only stay a few weeks. Walk along the beach. You can't blame them for wanting to escape town in this heat."

Henry squints into the book in his hand. He leans toward the gas lamp on the table beside him. Tipsy can see the book's title, This Side of Paradise, *by F. Scott Fitzgerald.*

"I've taken on a new gardener," *Jane says.* "He lives on Pitt Street. A strong, solid fellow. He promises he can save my rose bushes, but it will take effort. Can we afford for him to come three times a week?"

Apparently Jane knows how to interpret Henry's grunting response. "Wonderful," *she says.* "I'm pleased you've taken an evening free of working."

"Reading is part of my work. I can't write if I don't read." He closes the book. "This man, this Fitzgerald...I think he has something. He's asking questions about happiness and privilege. Do they go hand in hand? What is the meaning in any of it, for Amory, or any man?"

Jane leans toward Henry as if he's quoting scripture and she might miss the key to salvation. "I'm sure if he saw our blessed life, our beautiful home and our family and friends, he'd find answers."

Henry exhales and rubs his eyes. "That would be your conclusion." He stands. "I'm going to bed. I'm to be at the warehouse early tomorrow. I'm taking the car."

"Are you sure you're tired?" Jane blushes. She sets her knitting on the sofa. She creeps toward him, and gingerly eases her arms around his waist. Her head rests on his chest. His hands are stuffed in his pockets. It must be like hugging a pine tree. Stiff and prickly.

Her fingers wander over his back and across his chest, but when they meander toward his belt, he steps away from her. "If you want to lie together, if this is about producing a child, you can say so."

"Goodness, Henry...I could never say—" She picks up her knitting, and the ball of yarn, as if she needs something to do with her suddenly empty arms. "I suppose it is about that... but not only that. I miss you. I'm..." Her lip trembles. "I'm lonely."

"Why the tears? Didn't you just say we have the most blessed life?"

"I believe we do," she whispers.

"I'm sorry I make you sad. It's never been my intention. But until I finish this novel, the story must be my highest priority."

"You haven't really started it yet, and you're gone all day...at the warehouse—"

"Where I labor at your father's request. Just as we live on this side of the river, surrounded by bumpkins and Negros and chickens and goats. All owing to your father's insistence that I work for mine."

"You're right. Thank you. I know you'd rather be in town, and maybe you could spend more time on your real work...but I do wish—"

"If you're so lonely, Jane, you can find other distractions."

"What do you mean? I'm not going to find companionship in—" She holds up the ball of yarn. "—knitting. I'm trying to befriend the neighbors, and I adore my sister and my mother—but I long for my husband."

Henry walks to the parlor door. "There are other men who can provide you companionship."

She shakes her head, her brows knitted together much tighter than the lumpy stitches of her knitting. "Pardon?"

"Such indiscretions happen all the time in modern life."

"You're telling me to...take the favors of another man?"

He shrugs. "I could accept that, if it will make you happy. Just be discreet. And be careful. But you're a big girl. You know how that all works." He opened the door. "I'll see you tomorrow, at breakfast."

"Yes."

"Will you have Beatrice make grits and gravy?"

She nods. He says goodnight, and closes the door behind him. The fire pops and fizzles, almost as if it's laughing at Jane, the stone woman in the silk dressing gown. Her surprise, embarrassment, and confusion wash over Tipsy like dirty water from an overflowing storm drain. Jane's shoulders start shaking. Tipsy feels so polluted, she may cry herself. Maybe tears will sterilize these intolerable emotions.

Jane covers her mouth with one hand, and the half knitted sweater-scarf-something-or-other falls onto the rug. The ball of yarn rolls down her leg and over her bare foot. It unravels, getting smaller and smaller, as it heads toward the fire. Jane watches it end in a knot on the hearth, a thin reminder of what was recently full of potential warmth.

Tipsy couldn't hold on to the vision, but she couldn't wake up, either. She vacillated between knowing she was asleep and dreaming that she was already awake. Small hands grabbed her, fingers ran over her face. She couldn't make out what the high-pitched, frantic voices were saying. Tipsy's mind turned away, like a bear that had emerged from hibernation and realized it's still winter. She wanted to let all her thoughts, and the sickening residue of Jane's emotional trauma, spiral away down some deep, dark drain. *Damnit, why won't they leave me alone?*

The voices sharpened. "Mama. Mama, wake up! Ayers, why won't she wake up?"

"She's all sweaty."

"I— I don't know. Maybe she's sick. I'll text Daddy."

Little Ayers. The girls. Tipsy's mind cleared, but she still couldn't open her eyes. The inside of her head was a room with one light switch, but the single bulb had burned out. She strained to wake the rest of her body.

"Mmmm." Some weird sound came out of her mouth. "Ahhhh." Another one.

Wake up, Tipsy! Granna yelled inside her head.

I'm trying. What's wrong with me?

I don't know, but you got to open your eyes.

Suddenly, Tipsy saw the kids and her own bedroom, as if she were spying on them like she just spied on Jane and Henry. She lay on the oriental rug, outside the bathroom, on her right side. Mary Pratt, in her hot pink jammies, was taking off her socks. Olivia Grace knelt beside her, holding one of her limp hands. Little Ayers stood beside the bed in his little boy boxer shorts and a tee-shirt, typing on her phone. *Am I dead? No. I am not. I'm not!*

She gasped, and sat up. The girls screamed. Little Ayers dropped the phone.

"Mama!" Both girls threw their arms around her.

Tipsy's heart banged in her chest. Her hands shook as she tugged the girls toward her. Her tongue felt like a lump of cracked clay in her mouth. Thank the good Lord, she was very much alive.

"I'm so sorry, buddies."

"What was wrong with you? You made weird noises." Mary Pratt illustrated with groans and rolling eyes.

"We heard a crash. We thought—I thought—" Olivia Grace's messy nighttime ponytail drooped beside her face. She couldn't seem to spit out *we thought you were dying*, and why should any six-year-old have to say that about her mother?

"I'm okay, y'all. I'm just really tired. I... uh... I sat down to stretch. And I guess I fell asleep right here on the floor."

Ayers handed her the phone. "Sorry. I texted Daddy. I didn't know what to do."

"It's okay, honey. Really. You did the right thing."

She looked at her texts. Big Ayers hadn't replied yet, but it had been over ten minutes since Little A sent the first message.

Its ayers mama is asleep she wont wake up what should we do

Dad should i call 911 maybe shes choking

Daddy anser please

So the kids had been trying to wake her up for at least ten minutes, probably more. "I'm so sorry I scared you."

"Why are you so tired?" asked Ayers, his brow furrowed.

"My painting." She smiled. "Y'all don't remember what it was like when I used to paint all the time. It totally wipes me out!"

"Oh." Ayers looked up at the paintings on the walls around them. The horses and the lady with the red blanket, and Tipsy's self portrait. "Yeah. I guess it must take a long time."

"And make you really tired," said Olivia Grace.

"I bet your eyes are crossed when you're done," added M.P.

The kids seemed to want an explanation as much as she did. She crossed her eyes and stuck out her tongue. "Exactly!"

She stood on shaky legs. The room spun. She grabbed one of the bed posters, and waited for it to settle back into place. A painful goose egg had bloomed on the side of her head, from where she hit the floor. Thank goodness for the Oriental rug, or she might have split her noggin wide open. "Y'all head to bed. I'll come tuck you in."

The girls ran into the hall, but Ayers lingered. "You're coming?"

She nodded. "Potty break and I'll be right there."

He walked out, and she went to the bathroom. Her head throbbed, and not just where she'd bashed it on the floor. The mother of all headaches settled in behind her eyes. Even her eyeballs themselves were throbbing. The back of her neck ached, too, like it did when she felt a fever coming on.

Worst of all, the bathroom walls would not stay put. Tipsy's stomach lurched. Jane's hurt and sadness, and the creepy crawly horror of her humiliation, refused to abate. Tipsy was sick in body, and sick in soul. Hot tears further scorched her inflamed eyes. She spit into the sink.

Her mind raced. She'd just experienced two powerful supernatural encounters in the span of an hour—the intervention between Jane and Henry, and the vision of the two of them in the parlor. And Jane's feelings in the vision—holy hell. They were as agonizing as anything she'd ever felt in her own life.

Maybe it's too much for you, said Granna.

Tipsy couldn't reply. Saliva filled her mouth. She made momentary eye contact with her own grayish face in the mirror, before she spun around with her hands over her mouth.

She retched into the toilet.

Oh god, Oh god. She reached up and shut the bathroom door, while praying the kids would wait patiently for their goodnight kisses.

Right on cue, Olivia Grace yelled out, "You comin', Mama?"

Tipsy yelled back, "Yup! Give me a minute." She gagged again, silently, then coughed. "I'm in the bathroom!"

Once her body ridded itself of everything she'd consumed in the past few hours, including Jane's unhappiness, she felt a little better. She took a few deep breaths, wiped off the toilet seat with some toilet paper, and then flushed. She washed her hands and splashed water on her face. Then she sat down to pee with her forehead in her hand. Despite herself, she wondered if she could somehow work the sentiments she'd seen in the memory into her painting of Jane on the porch.

Good lord, she thought, cringing internally. *That's so selfish of me.*

And crazy, given that Exorcist *impersonation and what just happened with the kids,* said Granna.

She was about to acknowledge Granna's point, when her phone rang in her lap. She jumped on the toilet. "Jesus."

Big Ayers. She waited until the call went to voicemail, and then typed out a text.

Everything is fine. I fell asleep hard after painting.

He replied right away. *U sure? Little A sounded scared.*

It's okay. Really ☺ gotta go tuck them in.

He didn't reply, and that was fine with Tipsy. She'd had enough for one day.

ipsy threw herself into painting in ways reminiscent of her prolific college years, even though she felt like dog shit after the vision. The headache nestled behind her forehead like a nest of rats. She felt mildly nauseous most the time, like she did when she read in the car. Everything she tried to eat tasted like sawdust. After a week, she felt a little better, but her appetite didn't come back, and she couldn't stand bright light, so she religiously kept her sunglasses perched atop her head. She took precautionary Tylenol each morning, and stopped drinking her usual green tea. Her stomach suddenly couldn't tolerate it.

Still, she finished the painting in nine days, from first sketch to final brush strokes. When she finally stood back and looked at the finished product, she had trouble holding back tears. Her hungry eyes raced over the canvas and devoured the earthy palette that she'd interspersed with the colorful pop of flowers. She relished the contrast between the house's solidity and Jane's muted fragility. The dusky figure looked as if she might blow off the porch in a strong wind. And finally, and most important, a sense of some hidden sentiment on Jane's upturned face. Even Tipsy wasn't sure how to define the conveyed emotions. She only knew they came from Jane's own memories, and that she'd never painted anything more beautiful.

"Thank you, Lord," said Tipsy. "Thank you, thank you."

Acrylic paints dry frightfully fast, but Tipsy took an extra day before she risked transporting the painting and scratching it. She transferred it from room to room in a somewhat obsessive search for the perfect combination of temperature and humidity. Once she had no more excuse to keep it hidden, she asked Will to help her take it to the GQB. She removed the Tahoe's third row seats and stored them in Miss Callie's gardening shed. She laid a soft chenille blanket across the back of the truck and slid the painting onto it.

Will drove the Tahoe on their delicate art delivery mission. She sat in the passenger seat and turned sideways so she saw the painting out of the corner of her eye.

He tipped his head toward the painting. "I'm really impressed. I knew you were talented, and I'm no expert, but I've never seen anything like *that* before."

"Thanks," said Tipsy. She rubbed at a dark spot on his bare arm. Probably some kind of wood floor stain that would require a scrub brush to remove it, but it gave her a reason to touch him. "I'm happy with it."

"You should be. It's pretty amazing. I don't know how you do it."

She shrugged. "When the idea is flowing like it did with this painting, it's not hard."

In a rare unfurling of his permanently scrunched brow, he raised one eyebrow.

"It's really not," Tipsy said. "I mean, it's exhausting in a way, but it doesn't feel like work." She bit her lip. "Now I need a new idea. Shelby wants me to fill up a whole wall at the GQB." She looked out the window as they crossed the Ravenel Bridge, as if she might see stories on faces in passing cars, or in the clouds.

"Give yourself a day or two to rest. And don't strain your hands," said Will. "I need you to rub my back."

She swatted him. "Artists have strong fingers."

"Yeah, you're stronger than you look." He reached over and massaged her shoulders. Her neck still felt stiff, and she leaned into his hands. She wasn't used to a man having much concern for her welfare. She'd always been the one to do the caretaking. Last night, after the kids fell asleep, Will showed up at her house with a homemade yogurt smoothie and a box of high efficiency light bulbs. She'd followed him around the house, sipping the smoothie, while he switched out most of the light bulbs and promised her a reduced electric bill.

"Something else on your mind?" he asked.

She took a moment to collect her thoughts before replying. "Yeah, but it's hard to explain."

"Try me."

"I have these…friends. Or people I know, anyway. They have this problem, and I'm trying to figure it out for them." Over a month of living with Jane and Henry had proved she couldn't avoid them, or their mutual enmity. She'd come up with only one solution: force Henry to acknowledge his crime, or force Jane to acknowledge he didn't do it. At the same time, she was at a bit of a loss for how to do so after the disaster of her last significant interaction with them.

Will scowled. "I don't get it—who has a problem?"

"I can't tell you. It's personal."

"Okay…you're not…like talking about yourself and don't want to tell me? Are you in trouble or…you have some weird secret?"

She almost laughed, because of course she did have a very weird secret. "This problem has nothing to do with me. Let me try again." She thought about Henry's targeted viciousness, but also considered Jane's hands, covering her ears. *What is sweet little Janie hiding?* She faced Will. "The one person, he sort of seems…he can be a real asshole. So part of me thinks it has to be his fault. But I think the other person might be lying to me, for her own benefit. Like to screw him over."

"Sounds too damn complicated for me. Like they both have is-sues." He switched lanes abruptly and Tipsy reached back to steady the painting.

"Yeah, they do," she said, "but I can see both sides in a way, so I don't know who to believe."

"I'd get out of it if I were you. If it's not your problem."

"It's not that easy."

"Make it easy." He shrugged. "That might not be what you want to hear, but they both sound like assholes to me."

"That's not fair. They have good points—"

He laughed. "Most people have something good about them some-where, buried beneath a lot of B.S."

"I feel like you're being so skeptical."

"Well, you're just flat out naïve."

She turned to the window again. He put a hand on her knee. "I'm sorry," he said. "I'm trying to help, but that didn't come out right."

"You probably have a point. Or two or three. Forgiven."

He took her hand, but his comment hovered between them as they drove down East Bay Street. They double-parked in front of the GQB. Shelby burst through the door onto the sidewalk in a reversal of her usual dramatic entrance. She grabbed Tipsy's keys and mashed a button. The rear hatch opened like the doorway to Ali Baba's treasure cave. Shelby stuck her head under it as it rose. She squealed and hugged Tipsy. Shelby had shown unusual restraint when Tipsy dropped hints that she was working again. She hadn't asked for a progress report, perhaps in fear that the added pressure would only prolong a positive outcome.

"Oh, praise the Lord!" Shelby said. "I knew you could do it!"

Tipsy grinned. "Thanks."

Shelby pointed at the figure. "I love her. There's something different about the look on her face. What *is* it?"

Tipsy replied honestly. "I'm not sure myself."

"What's it called?"

"I call it *Stepping off the Porch*."

"Perfect! What's she waiting for, anyway? Oh, I adore it!"

Will and Shelby carried the painting into the GQB. Tipsy followed behind them, the high priestess following a golden calf, while Shelby barked instructions at Will. They lay *Stepping off the Porch* on a folding table that Shelby had set up in the front exhibit room. "Set it here for now," Shelby said. "I want to move some things around. It needs a prominent display."

The door's bell clanged and Lindsey walked into the gallery, resplendent in a pair of mile high wedges and a strapless lime sundress. A tall man in a dark blue sport coat, tan pants, and a polka dot bow tie followed her. He had a shock of gray hair, the kind that many wealthy older Charleston men seemed to retain, as if they'd all won some kind of collective genetic hair lottery. "Ooooh, is that it?" Lindsey ran/shuffled to Tipsy's side. "Oh, honey." She looked between Tipsy and the painting. For once Lindsey didn't have words. She just put an arm around Tipsy and gave her a squeeze.

"Hi, Barker," Tipsy said to Lindsey's ex-husband.

"We were having lunch and talking about Barker's new fiancée!" said Lindsey with a wide but potentially poisonous grin, the smile of a snake about to strike. "She'll be meeting Emma for the first time this weekend. Isn't that *nice?*"

Tipsy nodded, all the while imagining the new girlfriend attempting to befriend Lindsey's ten-year-old, noticeably spoiled daughter. "Very nice. Good luck with that."

"Thank you," said Barker. He eyed the painting. "Your work?"

Tipsy nodded.

"I like it—"

"Barker does love his art." Lindsey tapped his arm. "That's why I dragged him in here. I want to help him out. He likes to impress all his New York friends out on Kiawah."

Barker cut his eyes at his ex-wife and said, "I have a friend in town. From New York, coincidentally. Vivian Greenblatt. She's interested in local artists, but she doesn't want the same old paintings of Rainbow Row. Maybe I'll bring her by this evening. We're having supper at Hall's."

Shelby smiled, suddenly all business. "I'd be happy to keep the gallery open until y'all finish your steak."

Barker nodded, said a cold goodbye to Lindsey, and left.

"Don't let the door hit you on the ass on the way out," Lindsey said, as soon as he rounded the corner. Her happy façade cracked. "Hope this chick gets the kind of reception I got from Barker's older kids when I first met them. Karma is a bitch, I tell y'all."

"Will he come see the painting?" asked Will. "I hope so."

He took Tipsy's hand. This time, when he squeezed, she genuinely squeezed back.

Lindsey nodded. "If he can tell his New York friend he made a discovery, he'll be all over it."

One of Will's foremen turned up to give him a lift to a jobsite, and Tipsy puttered around the gallery for the rest of the day before leaving to pick up her kids from camp. Shelby promised to let her know if Barker and his New York friend showed up. Tipsy kept checking her phone all evening, until Mary Pratt said, "Mama, do you have a fun new game on there?"

So she silenced the phone and forced herself to put it away until the kids were in bed. Once everyone slept soundly she walked toward the charger as if pulled by a tractor beam. She tapped on a text from

Shelby. Tipsy heard her friend's boisterous voice in her capitals and exclamation points.

HOLY HELL!!! That woman bought it right on the spot for 3K!!!!! You're a genius! ☺

———•———

In Charleston and the surrounding environs, it was common knowledge that any occasion worth commemorating is best celebrated on the water. Birthdays, graduations, engagements (including the popular romantic evening boat ride proposal), anniversaries, first communions, bar mitzvahs, new jobs, new houses, new dogs, new spouses, Memorial Day, Fourth of July, Father's Day, Mother's Day, Easter if it comes late in the spring, Labor Day, various regattas, and post-funeral boat cruises. If a party was required and a boat was available, it behooved the planners to hold the celebratory event on said waterborne vessel.

So, as they were both kid-free for the weekend, Will suggested Tipsy invite a few friends on a Tipsy-Sold-Her-Painting Saturday Boat Day Funfest. Tipsy hummed her way through the aisles of Harris Teeter in her beach cover up and flip-flops, and arrived at Will's house with several grocery bags and an eighteen pack of Bud Light. She'd cooked dinner with him at his place a couple times, so she was starting to get the lay of the land. She flitted around his kitchen, packing a cooler with fried chicken, fresh salsa, Palmetto Cheese, and a pasta salad she'd made the night before. She added a few peaches, because her conscience told her she must include something with obvious health benefits. As a precaution, she took an Aleve and a Dramamine. Extra protection should her headache come back, or she suddenly developed susceptibility to seasickness.

Will sprayed down and mopped out the boat, an older model Grady-White he kept on a trailer in his driveway, and then filled Yeti coolers with beer. She handed him the food cooler, a few bags of chips, and her beach bag of towels and sunscreen. He opened a beer.

"I have koozies in my bag," she said.

"I keep some onboard. I have extra sunscreen, too," he said.

"You got it all covered." She climbed the ladder by the engine and kicked off her flip-flops.

"Amen."

Lindsey and P.D. arrived first, followed by Glen and Shelby. Glen and Shelby had guests in tow, two guys and a girl that Tipsy didn't know. Tipsy gave them all vague smiles, but found she didn't want to engage in much small talk. All three had a distinctly barfly look about them. A certain air of hard living— the eternal adolescents with no kids, or kids out of wedlock, who had either never been married or had been married too many times. Glen himself fit that bill. His most recent ex, the mother of his son, had been his third wife. She watched him puff away on a cigarette and toss the butt onto Will's driveway before pouring a bunch of vodka into a plastic cup of orange juice. Tipsy wondered once again what Shelby saw in him, or what Will saw in him for that matter.

Will probably don't care as long as the fish get caught, said Granna.

Tipsy frowned, but before she could reply to Granna in her head, a Volvo station wagon pulled up in front of the house. "She's here!" Tipsy called.

Mimi climbed into the boat and sat beside Tipsy on the bench seat in the back. "You made it," Tipsy said, as Will climbed into the truck.

"Thanks for inviting me," said Mimi.

"What's Jimmy going to do with the kids?"

She shrugged. "Not sure. We've been fighting. Think he was happy… to have me out of the house for a few hours."

"You still haven't said anything about leaving, right?"

Mimi shook her head.

"Good," said Tipsy. The boat jerked a few times as Will pulled out of the driveway.

They put the boat into the Wando at the neighborhood ramp and set off in the direction of the Ravenel Bridge. The Allman Brothers blasted over the speakers, but once they got moving, Tipsy heard nothing but the engine. She smiled up at the cloudless blue sky through her sunglasses. The combination of hot sun on her shoulders, cold beer on her tongue, and glancing droplets of salty water on her shoulders made her shiver. For the first time in over a week, she felt pretty darn good, as if her supernatural hangover had finally worn off. They passed under the Ravenel Bridge and she wondered if the drivers above watched Will's boat and thought, *oh how lucky!* It was her turn to feel fine, and thank the good lord, she did.

They pulled onto the beach at Morris Island after cruising back and forth to find a space to squeeze in and drop the anchor.

"Whoa," she said to Will as she eyeballed the boats crammed in on the shore and anchored just off it. "I haven't been out here in years."

"You mean you and Ayers didn't bring the kids out here?"

"Right, because it's so family friendly." Something about his choice of the biggest public party scene in town worried her. "I don't know, Will. Maybe we should just cruise up the intercoastal?"

He laughed. "It's only one day, baby. The best part is the people watching."

"Oh, I'm watching."

Beer flowed and the sun shone, and despite her initial trepidation, she relaxed. Unlike Tipsy, no one out here seemed to have a care in the world, and it was contagious. The partiers skewed toward their mid-to-late twenties, but Tipsy's thirty-plus generation made a loud and proud showing by blasting the classics, like the Notorious B.I.G. Some revelers wandered the beach, while others stood in the water with red plastic cups and bottles in koozies. A few diehards sipped from flasks. The boats anchored off the beach tied up to other like-minded vessels, sometimes half a dozen in a row. Music blared from at least fifty conflicting speaker systems.

On the boats, men sang at the top of their lungs while women climbed onto the fiberglass tops and perched precariously on railings, shaking and swerving in ways that were sexy on some but downright embarrassing and scary on more. Tipsy found herself standing on the bench seat of Will's boat, bopping up and down to some pop country song she'd heard a dozen times but couldn't place, and waving her beer over her head. She leaned over and kissed Will's hair as he reached into the cooler, and then said to Mimi on the bench beside her, "Lord, sister, if only Ayers and Jimmy could see us now."

"I know." Mimi giggled. Tipsy hadn't glimpsed her inhaler all day. "This is the most fun I've had in forever."

"Moms gone wild!" shouted Shelby, who was not a mom, but didn't seem to make that connection after slurping down a few Jell-o shots.

"I'm done drinking," said Tipsy. "Let's eat something. I don't want to feel this tomorrow." No nausea so far, but she didn't want to push it.

She passed fried chicken to Mimi, Shelby, and Lindsey. Even Lindsey's boat-day flip-flops had a wedge heel. Tipsy had to admire Lindsey's sea legs. It took talent to maneuver up and down the rocking vessel in those kicks. The four women congregated at the front of the boat.

"Who *are* those people?" Lindsey asked. She pointed at the two guys and girl who had shown up with Shelby and Glen.

"I don't know," said Shelby. "Guess Glen knows them from… somewhere. Think one of those guys works on his boat. Helps when he takes big groups out fishing."

"That girl's too flirty." Lindsey glowered at the bouncy, unfamiliar woman who stood between Glen and P.D. and flashed alternating smiles at both. Another Charleston Dress Code Blonde, like the women who had asked Tipsy for playdates in the grocery store, but judging from her thong bikini, Tipsy doubted she was a mom.

"P.D. isn't paying her any mind," said Tipsy. She watched the two men's markedly different reactions. P.D., who stood at least six-foot-three and could have played football for Carolina if he'd had an aggressive bone in his body, towered over the girl's head. He responded when she asked him a direct question. Otherwise he kept up his usual jolly banter with the rest of their party, and shouted through a week's worth of scruffy beard at people he knew on the surrounding boats. Glen, on the other hand, rested one elbow on the driver's seat and leaned toward Blondie. He never wore a hat, so his slightly-too-long, wavy blonde hair floated fetchingly in the breeze. "Oh, *hell no*," said Shelby. Blondie ran a finger over one of the tattoos on Glen's arm, some kind of tribal symbol that circled his admittedly buff bicep in an inky souvenir of his college glory days.

Tipsy tapped Shelby's yin and yang tattoo. "Don't make a scene. The quarters are too close."

"Whatever. I've got bigger fish to filet."

"What do you mean?" asked a round-eyed Mimi. She'd not had this much beer, or drama, in years.

"It's coming to a head with Glen's ex."

"Oh, lord, Shelby," said Tipsy. "You're going to let her drag you into some redneck mess?"

"She's always in his mix. Blowing up his phone. Asking him to meet for lunch and dinner and drinks. She's like a disease that I'm trying to treat with antibiotics, but the germ is resistant."

"Maybe he needs to do something about it. Not you."

"That woman needs to back off. Okay—now I've had enough of this chick, too."

Tipsy grabbed her arm. "You're already fighting one other woman for him."

Shelby shrugged her off. She made her wobbly way toward Glen and the blonde girl. She smiled sweetly as she slid her hands around his waist.

"Hey, baby!" Glen said. Shelby and Glen kissed, a gratuitous, in your face smooch if Tipsy had ever seen one. Shelby was probably skewering the competition with one open eye. Blondie sipped her beer and transferred her attentions to one of the men Tipsy didn't know.

"I can't believe Shelby comes from an old money, downtown family," said Tipsy. "Sometimes she's like country come to town."

"At least she's herself," said Lindsey.

Tipsy held up her Solo cup of rehydrating water. Even if Tipsy didn't agree with her methods, Shelby was always Shelby. "Cheers to that. Maybe I'm feeling sappy because I'm tipsy—"

"You're always Tipsy!" Lindsey laughed. "That never gets old."

"I'm thinking how lucky we are. Living here in Charleston." She swept an arm over the wide expanse of the harbor. "People pay money to come here and vacation, and it's home. So beautiful."

"It's not only how beautiful it is," said Mimi. "It's how we live in it."

Lindsey bit into her chicken. "Y'all are getting too deep for me." She swallowed and gave greasy cheek kisses before leaving Mimi and Tipsy to it.

"When I lived in D.C.— " said Mimi.

"How long did y'all live there again?"

"Four years. That's how long Jimmy's firm... kept us up there. People there don't know how to live. They have all these possessions and all these—acolytes—"

"Accolades," said Tipsy.

"Right. But they never take time to enjoy any of it. I had to move away from home… to appreciate how we do things." She leaned closer. "I didn't know one divorced couple up there. Not one."

"Maybe they're happier."

Mimi shook her head. "No one really knows anyone. People stay for a few years and leave, like we did. So nobody knows who is really an alcoholic, or living off credit cards. Or having an affair. We have to work harder to keep up appearances. And secrets." She laughed. To Tipsy, it sounded just a little bitter.

"Right. This town forces us to own up to our dirty laundry sooner or later," said Tipsy. "That stinky sock? It's mine. And that depressed husband that drives me to drink too much wine after the kids are in bed? He's mine, too!"

Will joined them. "What are y'all laughing about?"

"We're saluting Shelby for being a genuine nutcase," said Tipsy. "And pondering happiness and marriage and a bunch of other crap."

"I wonder if I know anyone who's really happily married," said Mimi.

Tipsy hugged her with one arm. "I've seen truly happy couples." She told Mimi about Mr. and Mrs. Childress. "I'm still trying to figure out how they do it, but they're out there."

"My sister and her husband are happy," said Will. "And I believe it's genuine."

"How do you know?" asked Tipsy.

"They have four young kids, and they both work. So they have plenty of stress. But they still—they get a kick out of each other. They laugh, and they're always touching. And, man, when they talk about each other it's like talking about someone you just met, before the person starts getting on your nerves. You can tell she has total faith in him, and him in her. It's like they're a team. Team Lisa and Darren, against the world, or something." He rubbed his Saturday scruff and chuckled. "Maybe that doesn't make sense."

"Oh, no," said Mimi, "is that—it's my neighbor's stepson. There, on that boat!" She ducked and burst out laughing. "I don't want him telling his mama… he saw me drunk and shaking my butt out at Morris Island." She crept toward the console and slapped a wide straw hat on her head.

Tipsy slipped an arm through Will's. "You make perfect sense. Maybe you're not such a skeptic."

He kissed her. "Maybe you're right."

* * *

Days on Morris Island started early, so they ended early, too. By five o'clock, the boats cleared out as the tide came in. Will let Glen drive the boat back. Tipsy sat tucked under his arm as they pounded across the water toward Shem Creek. She wasn't in the mood to drink anymore, but Glen insisted on a margarita at the Water's Edge Cabana Bar. Tipsy yawned and closed her eyes. Her cheek felt warm against Will's tee shirt.

She decided to stay on the boat. She'd had enough partying for one day.

Or one summer, she told Granna. *That was fun, but ugh. I cannot imagine doing that every weekend.* She watched a woman who appeared to be at least forty-five trip over the railing as she climbed into the boat beside Will's. Her bathing suit top slid precariously askew, and both her frozen margarita and her flip-flop fell into the creek. She hiked up her bikini and let out a curse that would have made Proctor James call for his bible.

Tipsy told Will to go ahead and join everyone else at the bar. "I like the quiet," she said, when he asked if she really didn't mind. "I'll watch the boats go by. And I do have some company." She pointed at one of Glen's friends, a compatriot of flirty Blondie; he'd passed out on the back seat.

Tipsy sat on the front of the boat, munching chips and salsa and waving to boating passersby. She recognized a few people from the kids' school or the gym or her old neighborhood, but she lifted a hand to everyone, because that's what you do on these waterways. She laughed at an older couple whose boat couldn't have been more than sixteen feet long, but managed to stay afloat with five matching white labs perched on the bow. The man and his wife waved at her through a wall of waving tails and doggie drool. Children in neon life jackets crammed the family boats. They squealed at the dolphins that popped up throughout the creek like swimming Whack-A-Moles. Tipsy's hand stopped mid-wave when a navy blue Cobia slid into view. She recognized it by the tiny red and white palmetto flag that flew from the bow. The Citadel's unofficial banner. Mimi's husband took pride in his alma mater.

Jimmy stood at the steering wheel, with Ayers beside him. All six of their kids had piled on the front of the boat. "Mama!" yelled Little Ayers.

All six kids began yelling in a cacophonous mix of "Mama-Mommy-Aunt Tipsy!"

She stood and waved maniacally. "Hey, y'all! Hey! You having fun?"

"We're coming to get *chicken nuggets!*" yelled Olivia Grace.

"And Daddy said we can have a *Coke!*" added Mary Pratt.

"Great! That's so great!" Tipsy shouted back.

"Is Mimi with you?" Jimmy called.

"She's in the bathroom."

Jimmy spun the wheel. The boat had been on a trajectory for Water's Edge, but it turned hard right toward Red's Ice House on the other side of the creek.

Tipsy waved to Ayers, but she couldn't tell where his gaze fell, since he wore sunglasses. He didn't wave back; he just chewed away on his gum.

"Bye, Mama," said Little A.

"Bye, sweetheart. Use your good manners!"

"Yes, ma'am!"

"I'll see you tomorrow—" He'd already turned back to his cousins. She removed her own sunglasses and pressed her thumb and forefinger to her eyes. When she opened them, a tall figure stood on the back of the boat.

"Henry!" she screamed.

The nameless drunken man on the back of Will's boat sat up. "What? I'm here—Daddy—fix that tire—" He shook his head and passed out again.

Tipsy clenched the railing, and this time she screamed with her mind.

Henry! Get off that boat! Leave my kids alone!

He turned around.

Please, Henry. Please don't do anything crazy. The girls aren't strong swimmers—

I'm not going to hurt anyone, Tipsy.

What are you doing then?

Their father came to the house this morning. To get a bucket one of the little girls had left on the porch. His steps weren't strong. He smelled like whiskey. Henry pointed at the boat's dashboard. *I can see moving dots on this small film screen. It says Fish Finder?*

It's for when Jimmy goes offshore— Tipsy shook her head and cleared her mind of Henry's latest techno-puzzle. She wanted to know exactly what the ghost was getting at. *Ayers was drinking whiskey this morning?*

With the kids? Ayers enjoyed his beer, but she'd never known him to drink hard liquor during the day. Not since college, anyway.

Yes. I found them here, on the water. All seems well. He's not drunk anything else but water since I've been here. And the other man is drinking beer, not spirits.

Thank god. Maybe it's worn off. She wanted to kiss Henry's cheek, but of course that wouldn't have been possible even if they hadn't been separated by thirty yards of water. *Thank you! Thank you for checking on them.*

He doubled over as he had that evening on the dock. *I have to go home now. I've stayed too long. But I believe they're safe.*

Thank you—

He vanished. The kids piled off the boat. Mary Pratt remembered her mother and waved. Tipsy waved back. She returned to her seat, but she didn't pay attention to the boats anymore. Finally, after what seemed like hours, Will returned with P.D., Lindsey, and Mimi. "Glen and them are gonna stay here. Take an Uber back," he said.

Tipsy nodded.

"You tired?" Will asked.

She nodded again. She suddenly wanted out of here, pronto. "I'm too old for this."

He squeezed her. "It's been fun, but let's go home," he said, and pushed her hair out of her eyes.

That night, when Tipsy climbed into Will's bed, she'd already made up her mind. She'd slept at his house once, when Ayers took the kids on an unusual mid-week overnight, but she hadn't been ready to make love to him.

"You okay?" he asked her, as he pressed against her.

"Yes."

"You sure?"

"I'm a little nervous, but I guess that's to be expected."

"We don't have to. I'll keep trying and you can keep shooting me down."

His blunt honestly always made her laugh. "You win," she said.

He smiled as he kissed her. "Yeah!" he said.

Afterwards, as she lay tired and happy in Will's arms, she thought again of Jane and Henry. She'd seen enough of their lives to know that Henry hadn't been a particularly nice guy, to his wife or anyone else. Tipsy couldn't rectify that person with the ghost who risked great pain to make sure her children were safe.

Chapter 8

A yers brought the kids home an hour later than Tipsy expected on Sunday evening. She was waiting on the porch when his truck pulled into the driveway. She'd had a pot of spaghetti on low heat since the estimated six o'clock arrival. The smell wafted out through the screen door.

"Are y'all hungry?" she asked as they raced past her on their way to the backyard.

"We had McDonalds," said Little Ayers, by way of answer.

"Chik-fil-A was closed!" added Olivia Grace.

"It's Sunday!" Mary Pratt slammed the screen door behind them.

Big Ayers trailed up the stairs after them. He wore an ancient Sigma Alpha Mountain Weekend tee shirt and a pair of gym shorts.

"Can you text if you're going to be late, please?" Tipsy asked.

"I figured you'd be at your new man's house today." Ayers spit his wad of gum over the porch rail into Miss Callie's tea roses. Tipsy swallowed the sour taste of undiluted disgust. "I wanted to give you some extra personal time," he said.

"Okay, Ayers."

"I know who that guy is. Jimmy's brother knows him, through his contracting work."

"I'm sure he said he's a nice guy."

"I didn't ask. I don't care what you do."

She changed the subject by stepping onto the delicate tightrope between her lingering fear of Ayers's temper and her need to defend her children. "Why were you drinking whiskey when you had the kids?"

He went red. "It was a family outing. I wasn't drinking whiskey on the boat."

"No, you got sauced up beforehand."

"Who told you that—" He stopped, a general gathering his troops for a quick change in battle plan. "Don't you talk to me about drinking. Some neighbor kid of Jimmy's saw you and Mimi all lit up like Roman candles out at Morris, bumpin' and grindin' on the back that Will dude's boat!"

"I didn't have the kids."

"That's not exactly the kind of shit you expect from a woman with three children. Not a classy woman, anyway. That's some white trash bullshit, right there."

"That's the first time I've had more than a few beers in months. And it was a one-time thing. We're entitled to blow off some—"

"How about you passing out the other night, with the kids in the house!"

"I told you, I fell asleep after painting—"

"Don't attack me, damnit."

"I'm defending myself! You started in about Will. I just asked you to give me a courtesy text—"

He stepped onto the porch. Close enough that she could have counted the red hangover-induced lines in his eyes. "Put a *goddamn sock* in it, Tipsy! *Jesus*, I come over here and you start givin' me shit the second I get out of the truck. I can't even say goodbye to my *children* in peace!"

"Mama?" Little Ayers peeked though the screen door. "Can I have some Oreos?"

She smiled at him, a wooden mommy puppet. "Eat a banana. If you're still hungry you can have two cookies."

"I'm going, A," said Big Ayers. He jerked the door open, kissed his son's cheeks, and ruffled his hair. "Give your sisters a goodbye kiss for me."

"Do I have—" His father stopped midway down the stairs, but before he turned around, Little Ayers said, "Yes, sir."

"You changed your name yet?" Big Ayers asked.

She shook her head. When they separated, she decided to resume her maiden name. She justified it by reminding Ayers that she'd sold a lot of paintings under the name Tiffany Denning. In reality, it was more about reclaiming the girl who created those paintings than about selling future work. When she first raised the idea, he'd been offended, but lately he mentioned it whenever he saw an opening. As if it pleased him to be rid of her.

"Haven't had time to go to the Social Security office."

She sat in one of the wicker rocking chairs as he backed down the driveway. No Eric Church or Johnny Cash coming from his open windows. Brad Paisley this time. Little Ayers joined her in the next chair with a banana. "Can you open this?"

She nodded and obliged. The sweet banana smell stayed on her fingers as she chewed her pinky nail.

"Daddy was mad, huh?"

"I'm sorry, baby. You shouldn't have to hear that. Grownups fight sometimes."

"It's okay. Daddy gets mad a lot."

"Does he yell when y'all are at his house?"

Little A licked his lips. "Not as much as he did when we all lived there. He's a lot more fun now."

Tipsy nodded her agreement. She had a hunch that Ayers's parenting had improved without the pressure of daily interaction with his kids. "He doesn't see us as much," his son said. "So maybe we're not there to make him mad all the time."

Tipsy bit down on her nail. "It's not your fault Daddy gets mad, honey."

"Yeah, but I've been trying real hard to be extra good. To make him happy." He jumped up. "Can I have my Oreos now?"

"You may, Ayers, but... look at me." She held his small serious face in her hands. "You aren't responsible for making Daddy upset, and you're not responsible for making Daddy happy, either. Daddy is a grownup. He has to take care of those things for himself. Do you understand?"

"Yes, ma'am." He raised his eyebrows. "Oreos?"

She nodded and let go. Her finger returned to her mouth. She thought of her father, long ago. Wet, cheap linoleum, and sadness that she hadn't had the nerve to comfort. She'd spent her life offering comfort, and not getting much in return. How could she expect Little Ayers to understand, when she still didn't really understand herself?

———•———

Tipsy is sixteen and she's in a foul mood, but that's not unusual. Granna says it's the hormones, but Tipsy thinks there's more to it. Some of it is Martinville, which for the past two years has started to feel like one of those mousetraps with the glue inside. Like she's stuck in this place until she either starves or chews off her foot to escape or someone puts her out of her misery. And now Granna is giving her hell because she caught Tipsy talking to the ghost that haunts their church.

"No one saw me, Granna!" Tipsy's voice echoes through the kitchen. She's perched on the edge of the Formica countertop, beside the microwave.

She used to sit up here and help Granna cut apples for the Thanksgiving pies. Her skinny butt still fits. "He's harmless, anyway."

"I don't care. I've been telling you about talking to that boy since you were as old as he looks." *Granna takes a drag off one of the cigarettes she's always smoking, the ones Tipsy thinks are slowly killing her, but as Tipsy will find out in a year or so, are actually killing her pretty quickly. She's cut her hair short. Tipsy doesn't like it, because Granna has always had long hair, and when Tipsy was little she liked to brush it. Granna's hair has been gray and sort of prickly Tipsy's whole life, but Tipsy doesn't have a sister and her Mama always wore her hair in a feathered bob. She only had Granna's hair to brush. Maybe she's too old for that now, but it still felt like Granna ripped up an album of family photos when she chopped off her hair.*

Granna pretty much always wears the same thing, which is a pair of jeans and a tee shirt in the winter, and a pair of jean shorts and a tee shirt in the summer. Except when she goes to her job at the Piggly Wiggly. Granna worked her way up from cashier to second assistant manager at the bakery. She wears khakis and a polo shirt with the smiley pig on it to work.

Tipsy jumps down from the counter and plops her rear end into one of the kitchen chairs. She picks at a scratch on the edge of the chair that's in the shape of a T. *She carved it into the wood with a charcoal drawing pencil when she was eleven.* "Who am I allowed to talk to?" *Tipsy asks.* "You won't let me go on dates, or go to friends' houses. Not that anyone asks me anymore." *Tipsy slumps in a miserable heap against the table.* "They give up when you keep saying no over and over."

"I've told you. You can have friends come over here."

Tipsy looks around the tiny kitchen. The wallpaper she leaned against on the night her daddy cried over the Clemson baseball game is still there, just with a lot more peeling. The doorway leads to an equally small living room. An old black and white TV rests on the floor, like maybe Granna and Tipsy should sit in front of it in poodle skirts and watch Howdy Doody or Mister Ed. *No cable. Sure as hell no computer or Internet, like some of the kids from school are talking about. The carpet is bare in patches. She thinks of her tiny room with its twin bed and cheap Wal-mart comforter she's had since she was eight. Hello Kitty, for goodness sake.*

"No, thank you," Tipsy says.

"You got friends that are too uppity to come to your house, they aren't friends."

Tipsy rests her elbows on the table, and takes in Granna's work-roughened hands. She feels like the world's biggest brat. "I'm sorry, Granna. It's not that. Besides, I really don't have any friends. Guess that's why it doesn't seem to matter if people see me talking to ghosts. They've been thinking I'm odd for years."

"They think I'm odd, too, sugar. It's this town. Too small."

"Why didn't you ever leave?" *Tipsy has always wondered what kept Granna here, in this Podunk town. Estelle Ann Myers McNair, stuck in a crevice where the Piedmont Hills arch their rocky backs in an effort to become the Blue Ridge Mountains. Stella McNair, who works at the Piggly Wiggly but feels most at home in the library. Miss Stella, who encouraged Tipsy to read* To Kill a Mockingbird *but still refers to the black family who lives in the trailer down the state road as* those people. *Her Granna, who scrapes together change to buy quality paints and brushes for Tipsy and lives off bologna and Wonder Bread.*

"Your grandfather never wanted to leave. His own daddy worked his whole life to buy this land. Pop-Pop loved the fields around this house, small as the house itself is."

Tipsy thinks of the ten rolling acres that surround Granna's house, and the stream. Tall stands of pine trees block the view of the road out front, but open up to let in a distant mountain-scape out back. The air around Granna's house never smells of anything but pine needles and grass and soil. Dirty-but-clean smells. Tipsy knew her grandfather until he died from bladder cancer when she was five. Granna thinks he got cancer because he drank too much Diet-Rite mixed with bourbon. She swears that can't be good for your excretory system.

"Pop-Pop never thought I was weird," Granna added.

"Did he know about the ghosts?"

She nodded. "Only person I ever told."

"How will I know who I can tell?"

"I think you just know." Granna took her hand. "I'm only trying to protect you. Have you really tried to make some friends? The boys surely call a good bit."

"Well, the girls don't. Seems like they all hate my guts. And you won't let me go on any dates."

"I don't want you ending up like your mama. We got you, and that's all that matters, but if you ended up with a man like—" Her lips set in a thin line.

"Like my daddy."

"Almost two years they've been gone. Two letters and a collect call from her. Not a word from him, or a bit of money to support his daughter." Granna leans toward Tipsy. "Now, you don't complain, but I know it's hurtful. No parents in a right frame of mind up and disappear on a four-teen-year-old girl."

Tipsy shifts in the chair. "It's fine. Whatever." She's wearing a pair of Converse Chuck Taylor All-Stars that Granna found at the Salvation Army store. She pulls her knees toward her chest and picks at the shoelaces. Her hair falls into her eyes in a wavy brown shower curtain. Granna invades Tipsy's privacy when she pushes it back.

"I say this, hurtful or not, because I want you to have a clear mind when you meet a boy that turns your head. You got a measure of damn amazing talent in your artwork. You're going to go to college, and you're going to visit places I ain't never been. But someday you're going to pick a *man. Every woman does one day or another. So you pick one that will help you, not hinder you."*

Tipsy says yes, ma'am, *but she just wants to go to the movies and hold someone's hand and get kissed. She wants to be a normal sixteen-year-old girl who doesn't see weird fuzzy people out of the corners of her eyes all the time. But she's always promised Granna that she'll go to college, and she damn well plans on it. No way in hell she's sticking around Martinville and following Granna up the ladder at the Pig.*

Granna stands and kisses the top of Tipsy's head. "Thanks, sugar. It gives me some peace of mind knowing you'll make a good decision someday."

"I will, Granna," Tipsy says, because she does want to give Granna peace of mind. The worry on Granna's face when she opens the bills at this table each month breaks Tipsy's heart more than seeing Darryl Peters kiss Tracy Scruggs by her locker each morning before math class. And the good lord knows, that's saying something.

Granna might be strict, but she loves Tipsy. Sometimes Tipsy doesn't understand her, and sometimes life in general makes no sense, but Granna understands everything.

After Ayers laid into her in person on the porch, he started laying into her via text. At first she tried to reason with him.

Ayers: *I can't believe the mother of my children is still whoring around town. And a drunk to boot.*

Tipsy: *Please stop. We went to Morris for a little fun. Will and I are dating. We're in a relationship.*

I told u. I don't care what u do.

Then why are you texting me this?

Because I care about MY CHILDREN of course.

If you care about them, please don't yell at me in front of them.

Then came a tirade. She turned off the text tone on her phone so she wouldn't hear it dinging.

Ayers: *They'll see u for WHAT U ARE.*

Ayers: *U better not be losing your shit. I know u passed out the other night when the kids could not wake u. How much r u drinking?*

Ayers: *U know I'll never forget when u lost it after the girls were born and I had to take over. I'll take over for u again.*

Ayers: *U better not doubt it. If u r not able to take care of them I will.*

Tipsy couldn't stand when grown adults used letters in the place of words. She almost replied with a one-word message (*YOU*), but she decided correcting Ayers's grammar would only provoke more ire, and more texts. She also wanted to point out that Ayers had hardly taken over all the parenting during her depression— he'd hired babysitters to watch the kids on the weekends when Tipsy begged him to give her a break. Shelby had helped out more than he had.

Again, she decided silence was a better reply.

She tried to go to bed on the early side that night, but she tossed and turned with Ayers's threatening messages swirling in grammatically uncouth circles around her head. Finally, around midnight, her numb mind gave up and shut down. She woke in a cold sweat as dawn leaked through the plantation shutters and drew stripes of light on her bed. She'd dreamed of fluffy orange and white Clemson pom-poms that had turned to baseballs, which an unknown someone started chucking at her head. She didn't open her eyes.

Granna? Granna!

Only a dream, sugar. Go back to sleep.

I wish Will was here. Tipsy heard a girlish whine in her mental voice, like a child asking for a well-loved teddy bear.

I like that man, but you're a ways off him sleeping under the roof with you and your children.

Oh, I know, Granna. But I miss him.

Fallin' in love comes with a lot of missin'.

Tipsy rolled over and opened her eyes. For a moment she thought she was still dreaming, and Will lay in the bed with her. Will didn't glow blue, though, not even in her dreams.

The male shape shifted on the bed beside her, and Henry's sleeping face turned toward her. He tucked one hand under his cheek. His long eyelashes lay against his cheeks like the wings of a butterfly at rest. His chest didn't rise and fall, and no pulse beat in his neck. She hadn't known that ghosts slept.

As she watched him, she remembered what she'd sensed during John Huger's birthday party. How down deep, Henry had wanted to do the right thing. But in the end, his ego wouldn't let him. The dichotomy that she felt within him made her eyes sting.

How terrible, to live like that, she thought. *I wonder if Ayers ever feels the same way.*

She didn't want to disturb him, so she decided she'd paint him instead. Just as he was, not as an oddball creative genius, a neglectful husband, a psychotic murderer, or even the guardian who'd looked after her kids. A sleeping man, like any other under the Charleston sky.

Tipsy wanted to start the new painting as soon as possible. Shelby allowed her to set up in the GQB's storeroom on Tuesday morning. She left the door open, and listened for the clanging bell to announce arriving customers. Not as pleasant as the garden at Ms. Callie's, but at least during the sketch phase, she didn't need to drag paint into the storeroom. Just Tipsy, a canvas, her pencils and kneaded eraser, and a spotlight to cut through the dust eddies floating around her head.

Despite the distraction of a few window shoppers and the UPS guy, Henry's unusual face inspired her. She delighted in the minutiae of his arched nose and flaring nostrils. She wanted to make sure she captured the depth of his eyes, even though they'd be closed in the painting. The only real damper on her vibe: Ayers's continued texting. He sent four messages in an hour. She had to keep her phone turned on, in case one of the kids got sick or hurt at camp.

U going to work today?

Yes.

Regular time?

Yes. Why?

How r u feeling?

I'm fine. Why?

Are u working on any new paintings?

Yes. As a matter of fact I'm trying to work on one right now. At work.

Thirty minutes after his last text, the bell clanged. Tipsy wiped her hands on a rough cloth she kept beside her easel and walked into the front showroom. A man stood beside the front desk. He wore jeans and a collared shirt and held a large manila envelope.

"Hey, welcome," said Tipsy. "Can I help you with something?"

"Tiffany Collins?" the man said.

"Uh, yes."

"I have legal papers to serve on you."

Tipsy's heart dropped from her ribcage into her pelvis. "What? What are you talking about?"

"I'm just here to serve you, ma'am, in accordance with South Carolina law."

Tipsy signed the man's paper, but she couldn't open the envelope. She left work with it tucked under her arm, the seal unbroken. She dropped it on the floor in front of the passenger seat and picked up the kids. She left it on the table in the foyer as they walked into the house, as if it were a piece of junk mail. Little Ayers helped her mash ground beef into hamburger patties and the kids had dinner. She watched an episode of a new tweeny-bopper show on the Disney Channel with the girls. Once everyone was asleep, she could no longer ignore the manila envelope. She sat at the kitchen table, reading the Summons and Complaint for Modification in the Charleston County case of *Ayers Lee Collins, IV v. Tiffany Lynn Collins, a/k/a Tiffany Lynn Denning*.

The parties were divorced by an Order of this Court… Three children, to wit: A.L.C., M.P.C., and O.G.C… The Father is informed and believes that the Mother has a history of mental illness, including severe postpartum depression… A.L.C. texted the Father that the Mother was asleep on the floor and they could not wake her…the Children tried to revive her for approximately thirty minutes, during which time she made incoherent mumbling sounds, frightening the Children… the Children have observed the Mother acting erratically, for example, knocking over a book shelf in the kitchen… the Mother has shown no signs of being able to support the Children financially…the Father is informed and believes that the Mother's deteriorating mental health and financial instability are substantial changes in circumstances warranting a modification in the parties' custody and visitation agreement, both temporarily and permanently…

There was more at the end, a list of petty demands, like the suggestion that Tipsy somehow pay Ayers's attorney fees, since her cray-cray had brought the burden of this litigation upon him. Only one line, however, really mattered.

WHEREFORE, the Father requests an Order of this Honorable Court granting him sole legal and physical custody of the Children, temporarily and permanently.

Tipsy had thirty days to provide the court with an answer to Ayers's complaint, lest she be held in default. A Notice of Motion informed her that she was to attend a hearing in the matter in six weeks. She slid the papers across the table. She rested her forehead on her arms. Her shoulders shook, but as usual, she cried silently, so as not to wake the kids. She sucked in short, gasping breaths of increasingly lemony air.

Jane spoke softly from behind her. "There, there. All will be well, Miss Tiffany-Tipsy."

"No," said Tipsy. "I don't think so."

Jane hummed, *shoo-fly, don't bother me.* The lemon scent grew stronger. Tipsy raised her head. Jane's blue-white arms encircled her, in a nebulous hug.

It's not the usual transition from her modern life to a ghostly memory. Light sears through her eyelids. The shape of her own corneas is almost psychedelic, bright yellow flashing against black. She tentatively opens one eye, and then another, and realizes it's sunlight—the kind of Charleston morning she'd once heard Tripp Collins refer to as "severe clear." Sky so blue you'd almost think it's fake—a swath of periwinkle crayon drawn in the heavy hand of a child learning to grip a pencil. She recognizes the steeple of St. Phillip's Church, and the brick wall surrounding the graveyard Proctor will haunt in about thirty years.

It must be Sunday, because people stream out of the church. They wear coats, so it's fall or winter, although Tipsy can't feel any temperature one way or another. She looks into the female faces that peek from under cute bell shaped wool and felt hats, searching for Jane.

And then there she is; in a dark purple coat. Her black hair peeks from below a brown hat with two short purple feathers in the brim. Those bobbed tresses hug her cheeks, lending definition to a face that's still cherubic. She turns south as she leaves the church. Tipsy guesses she's walking to her parents' house.

Tipsy runs to catch up. A male voice calls out, "Janie!"

Tipsy and Jane both turn around. It's John Huger, the dashing man from Henry's party memory.

He falls into step beside Jane. She slips a hand through his arm. "Johnny, where is your hat? You'll catch your death. And your Mama's wrath."

John sticks out his chin and gives Jane the side eye, one eyebrow raised. "Why are you all by your lonesome? Where are your parents and Connie? And…" —he pauses, perhaps for dramatic effect— "where is our esteemed literary virtuoso?"

"Daddy and Luisa have colds, so Mama and Connie stayed home to keep watch over them. Henry—he's in Mount Pleasant. I came Friday evening to help Mama and Connie with the nursing."

"Mister Pierre and Luisa must be in a bad way if your mother is willing to miss church. Connie, now, her being so protective over that child, she'll keep her wrapped up in blankets and gargling chicken soup, after one sneeze."

"You can't really blame her. Since she lost Andrew, she feels like Luisa is all she's got."

John bumps Jane gently with his hip. "You know I'm teasing. I loved Andrew like a brother. You and Connie are like my little sisters. That tragedy about near broke my heart."

"We are lucky to have such true friends," Jane says. "But Henry doesn't like how it's always the same people we visit with, over and over."

John scowls. "I'm sorry we bore him so. Maybe if he spoke with me, or Charlie, or Tradd, or Cousin Reed, he'd see we're a pretty swell group of fellows."

"Don't take it too personally. Henry isn't partial to anyone, really."

"Even when we were all children, at bible study, he never talked to us. How can an eight-year-old boy be such a snob?" He chuckles. "We're the ones who are supposed to be looking down our noses at him. Better breeding

and all that. Somehow he got luckier than all of us, though, and won your heart."

This finally elicits a smile from Jane. "Must you always flirt? Even with your supposed little sister?"

"No sensible man could avoid flirting with you."

"You're a silly man; not a sensible one."

They walk on in companionable silence for a while, until John says, "Now, what's bothering you? Usually we're both talkin' over each other, like two happy blue jays that just found a bird bath."

"We both do tend to go on."

He stops. Tipsy looks for a street sign, and the rickety one to her right confirms they've reached the quirky diagonal corner of Church and Water Streets. "I'm worried about you. You haven't seemed yourself lately."

"I was festive enough *at your birthday party, wasn't I?"*

"By the end of the night, you lost all the pep in your step."

She looks back around his shoulder, toward the church. Then she blink-blink-blinks up at him. "Reverend James gave a lovely sermon today, didn't he?"

"You know I don't pay much attention to the preaching. You're changing the subject."

"I'm not... But the Reverend talked about rules. How sometimes, the Lord might want us to break them."

"I remember something about that. Reverend James always manages to come up with a new way to deliver the same old message."

"What message is that?" Jane stares into his face, as if she hopes he can provide a simple answer to a complex question, and thus save her the frustration of ruminating on it herself.

"Love thy neighbor as thyself. And don't forget your tithing envelopes."

"Johnny, I'm serious."

He shoves his hands into his pockets. "I don't know. Jesus broke lots of rules, right? Preaching things that the Pharisees didn't want anyone to hear. Keeping company with the wrong sorts of people, like Mary Magdalene. Maybe he meant something like that."

Surprisingly thoughtful, *Tipsy thinks.* Maybe John Huger has more going on in his head than Henry gives him credit for.

"Perhaps. It struck me in a—"

Tipsy senses her desperation to make someone else understand, or agree with her, or at least listen to her. Like her other emotions in past visions, Jane's overwhelming sense of urgency is equally Tipsy's, but this time it's confusing, because she doesn't really understand the source of Jane's agitation. It's frustratingly hidden from her.

Jane hops in place in her purple coat. "A way that has nothing to do with church," she finishes, lamely, and Tipsy is equally deflated. Maybe even Jane doesn't truly know what it is that's bothering her.

"Everything is about church to the Reverend."

"Why do I always do what I'm supposed to do, Johnny?"

"That seems like the kind of question Henry might write about in one of his books."

"I don't know what Henry's writing about. I don't know my own story anymore, let alone his."

John takes both of Jane's gloved hands and squeezes them. "Our stories aren't near finished yet. So if you want to change yours—maybe add some new characters or even get rid of a few chapters, I think you should go right on ahead and do it."

"You're sweet. As always."

"Don't go gettin' yourself crucified, now."

"I won't."

John pulls a pocket watch from his overcoat. "Mama probably already has Sunday dinner on the table, and she'll raise all colors of holy hell if I'm late." He walks backwards, across Church Street, toward Atlantic Street.

Jane lifts her hand in a little wave, and he spins around and starts jogging. A car comes bouncing down Church Street. Whoever the passengers are, they shout hello *and wave to Jane, perhaps reminding her that her own Mama won't be happy if she's late for dinner. She waves back at the Sunday drivers, and hustles down Water Street. For Tipsy, severe clear fades to black, and Jane disappears.*

Tipsy woke with her head on the kitchen table. Her mouth hung open, and she'd drooled on the scratchy woven placemat below her cheek. Her arms were asleep. Jane sat in the chair across from her. As Tipsy closed her gaping pie-hole, Jane started chattering.

"My word, you gave me a fright. Moaning and groaning and what not."

"Sorry, I…" Tipsy lunged toward the Formica counter. Saliva filled her back of her throat. She braced herself, and vomited into the kitchen sink.

"Good gracious!" Jane fluttered around Tipsy, helplessly wringing her hands. "Help! Help!"

"Shush, Jane, please." Tipsy spit into the sink. Her stomach rolled again, and she gagged. She had nothing left to puke up, so her midsection clenched in the painful, ineffective cramps of the dry heaves. "Oh, god," she moaned. This was worse than the other night in her bedroom. She hadn't puked like this since college, after a night of too many shots of Evan Williams Green Label bourbon.

"Evil Evan," she gasped. That long gone night, Shelby had done her the consummate girlfriend favor of holding her hair. She choked on a few giggles, imagining Jane trying to do the same, and accidentally killing her.

"What? Who? Tipsy!" Jane said. "We need help!"

Tipsy rested her forehead on the edge of the counter. "Only Henry can hear you. I don't need to listen to y'all rippin' into each other while I'm trying to barf."

"Bark? Bart? Does that mean vomit? What about your son? He can call a doctor—"

"No." Tipsy collapsed into the nearest chair. "He can't see me like this."

"What happened—"

"Jane." Tipsy gave Jane a wan smile. She ran water into the sink to wash away the nasty remains of her puking session. She dumped some Lysol in for good measure and turned on the garbage disposal. "Thank you, really, but I'm okay. Probably ate some bad lettuce. There's a lot of bad lettuce going around."

Jane's brow furrowed, but Tipsy didn't have the energy to explain e-coli contamination to someone who had lived before the discovery of antibiotics. "Thank you for being sweet to me. I'm going to get some water and go to bed."

She bid Jane goodnight before the ghost could ask anymore questions, or touch her again. In the moment, she'd found some perverse humor in the idea that Jane could unintentionally do her serious harm. But she really wasn't sure she could tolerate another psychic interaction between them so soon on the heels of hurling her guts into the kitchen sink.

She walked up the stairs on marshmallow legs, checked on the sleeping children, and retreated to her room. She fell asleep straightaway, without having much time to think about Jane's memory. Her alarm blasted her out of a deep, dreamless sleep the next morning. She got up, drank a huge glass of water, ate two bananas, and took some more Tylenol before she woke the kids.

Her efforts to stave off another supernatural hangover failed epically. If anything, this one was worse than the last time. She threw up again at work, and the Tylenol didn't put so much as a dent in her headache. Still, as she made her foggy way through the rest of the day, she thought of Jane and John. How good it must have felt, after Henry's callousness, to have someone comfort her, and be kind.

━━━━━━━━━●━━━━━━━━━

Whether she felt crappy or not, when Tipsy had work to do, she did it. The lawsuit certainly upped the ante. So much for hoping that Ayers was just blowing smoke. Part of her wanted to rationalize it all away. *Now that he's got me really scared, he'll back off. He's just being dramatic. He just wants to punish me more. He doesn't really want to be a single parent to three kids eighty percent of the time.* She never thought he'd take it this far, however, so she reached a grim conclusion. She was still on Ayers's roller coaster. There was no stopping the ride once it got going, no matter how much she screamed to be let off. So she had to buckle her seatbelt, hang on, and prepare for the first big hill.

Her most reliable safety mechanisms: money and a good attorney. She wasn't getting the latter without the former. So even if she had to keep a bucket beside her easel, she was going to paint.

As if inspired by his paradoxical complexity, the study of Henry's face and torso came to quiet life before her eyes. She worked on the porch, in the evenings, after the kids went to bed. Once the sun disappeared, she angled her spotlight so as to avoid bugging the neighbors. She covered her workbench with a palette, tubes of paint, flat and liner brushes in varying sizes, masking tape to give precision to the painting's few hard lines, and texturizers. She kept two full misting bottles at her feet to use as watery weapons against the acrylic paint's propensity for drying out on the palette.

She blended the paints into an autumnal spectrum, tinting burnt orange to pumpkin and shading white to cream to caramel. Most of the lightest tones went to his shirt and skin. A gradual fade of auburn to russet brown in his freckles and brows and lashes eased the bright red shock of his hair.

The fact that sleep lent no emotion to Henry's face gave the work an appropriate enigmatic air, as if he might open his eyes and betray some secret to the viewer in those first vulnerable moments of consciousness. She somehow infused his quirky features and atypical coloring with what she knew of the deeper workings of his mercurial heart and mind. The result surprised even her. The man in the portrait exuded cryptic sensuality. She'd never considered her paintings to be sexual, but she had to admit that there was something mildly erotic about this one.

She wondered if Jane watched her work, unseen. As Tipsy sensed the painting finishing itself, she became more convinced that Jane *needed* to see it. It didn't seem right to gently portray the man who had treated Jane so cruelly. Tipsy had seen that first hand, murder speculations notwithstanding. What's more, Jane still laid claim to Henry. For another woman to see him so intimately, no matter the circumstances, didn't set well with Tipsy. She wanted Jane's approval.

Three days after she started sketching, with the paint drying on the final product, Tipsy found Jane sitting mutely at the kitchen table. The girls were at a friends' for a sleepover, and Little A had zonked out well before dark, exhausted from a long hot day at Outdoor Adventure camp on Shem Creek. With the house quiet, Tipsy beckoned Jane to the front porch. There, she stood beside Tipsy, a shadow made of light, casting a glow over her sleeping husband's larger than life visage.

"I remember him that way," Jane said. "When he slept. Serene, yet still confounding. You certainly captured the essence of him."

"Is it okay? Can I sell it?"

"What would you say if I said no?"

Tipsy thought about legal fees. "I'm not sure. I need the money. I want your approval, but I want to provide for my kids more."

Jane nodded. "I never had children, but I *always* wanted them. You have my blessing."

"Thank you." Tipsy sat on the wicker sofa beside the easel.

Jane turned to Tipsy with those sparkly tears in her eyes. "It's beautiful. *Truly*. It's hard for me to look at it."

"Because of what he did to you?"

She shook her head. "Because of what he was. Or what I thought he was. I've had nothing but hours to think about my life, in which I thought I'd gone mad from loneliness and anger and even boredom. But I'm not as addled as Henry thinks I am. Those hours taught me what I might not have learned in a longer lifetime. I know that I never should have married Henry."

"Why? Didn't you love him?"

"I did. With a passion I can't explain. But it was the love of a girl who didn't know herself, not a woman. It should have been allowed to burn bright and fizzle out." She tugged at her dress, as if even those willowy layers of fabric encased her too tightly. "I believe my father *knew* that."

Tipsy looked at the sleeping man in the painting. "I understand why you fell in love with him."

"My wandering minstrel, whose favorite song was a sad tune. I thought my heart would explode if I couldn't touch that place inside him where all those sentiments lived, like..." Jane clenched both fists, as if she might catch the right words in her palms. "…would-be martyrs, hiding in the catacombs. And even now, something in him stirs me."

She stepped away from the painting. "But that's not the stuff of a lifetime together. It's what I should have looked back on, as an old woman, with a pang in my chest but the satisfaction of peaceful and fruitful years behind me."

"I wish you'd had those years."

"Do you mind, since you've asked for my blessing, if I observe your children at play? Or when they sleep? I did that for years, when Miss Callie's were young. It brought me some joy, and some of that *peace* I've been sorely missing."

"Of course I don't mind." Tipsy pictured Henry on the back of the boat, keeping watch over Little A and the girls. "No harm done in a kind pair of eyes, even if the kids can't see them."

Jane reached toward the painting, and on a whim, Tipsy lifted her own hand. She could easily reach the petite ghost, even while seated on the sofa. Perhaps she could see something else from the past. Something that could help Jane finally find some peace.

And— selfishly— with this painting finished and her legal defense fund at basically zero, she needed fresh inspiration more than ever. Since she met Jane and Henry, she was two for two on completed and— dare she say it— pretty freaking amazing paintings. Jane could be hiding a beautiful piece of art somewhere in her befuddled psyche.

She pictured their fingers intertwining. *Pinky swear,* she thought.

Sugar! Don't!

Granna's voice startled her, and she dropped her hand. She leaned back against the springy cushions.

Something ain't right between your health and these ghosts. Little Ayers— if he wakes up— or what if you end up in the hospital—

Tipsy sighed. *You're right, Granna. It's not worth it.*

Maybe you can help Miss Jane, and find new painting ideas, in some other way.

Tipsy watched Jane's lissome fingers brushing against her husband's painted, freckled cheeks. A lone tear escaped one bright blue eye. It wiggled down her face in a glittery line. Her delicate sadness squeezed Tipsy's heart.

In a few overwhelming seconds, Tipsy realized the totality of her moral and practical vicious circle. She wanted desperately to help this poor trapped spirit. She even wanted to help her irascible, changeable husband. Bring them peace, and in turn live peacefully herself, without their battles beating her down. But she could fathom only one way to bring them the closure they needed, and that entailed accepting more unpredictable and serious physical risks associated with seeing into the past. Which could in turn contribute to the worst scenario imaginable: Ayers getting custody of the children, and succeeding in his ultimate vendetta against her. In order to stop him, however, she needed money to hire a lawyer. Which meant she needed more paintings. Which of late, only seemed to come from her real and past time interactions with Jane and Henry… whom she wanted desperately to help… and so on, and so on, et cetera, et cetera.

She sensed Granna's befuddled sadness. *When you put it that way, sugar…*

It seems like there is no solution.

Granna didn't reply. Tipsy brushed away her own tears, and watched a moth banging against the ornate sconce beside the front door. Attracted by the glow, and repelled by the dusty glass covering it. Eventually, it would exhaust itself. It would die trying to reach the light.

Tipsy stood and turned off the sconce. The moth finally landed. Whatever compelled it to keep futilely beating its wings was gone, so it rested, quivering, on the darkened glass.

———————•———————

The next morning, Tipsy still felt terrible. She needed help getting the sleeping Henry painting out of her truck and into the GQB, even though it wasn't as large as *Stepping off the Porch*. She didn't trust her shaking hands and wobbly knees.

"You look like hell," said Shelby, confirming Tipsy's self diagnosis.

"Thanks," said Tipsy. "Think I had some bad lettuce."

"Yeah, it's going around. You're even skinnier than usual. And too pale."

"Okay, Shelby." Tipsy glared at her friend over Henry's oversized bushy red eyebrows. "Lookin' rough. I got it."

"I'd like to build up some inventory," Shelby said, once they hung the painting. It did look lonely, on its own wall in the GQB across from the work of several more prolific artists.

"Okay. I haven't started anything yet," said Tipsy.

Shelby nodded. Apparently Tipsy's production of two paintings in a relatively short period of time had restored Shelby's faith in her. "I've had a couple more inquiries, and that New York friend of Barker's is supposed to get back to me. Vivian Greenblatt. She's madly in love with *Stepping Off the Porch*."

Tipsy followed her. "I really need to sell this one. Especially now that I'm facing this lawsuit. Are you sure you like it?"

"It will sell fast. I love it. It's stunning. Unlike anything you've put out." Shelby took hold of the mouse and pulled up her Facebook account on the front desk computer. "Why?"

"You're usually more enthused."

"Sorry. I'm just—"

"Hey-yeee!" Lindsey peeked around the edge of the front door. She'd cracked it gently, so the bell barely had reason to ding. Lindsey slipped inside and did her I'm-Having-Trouble-Walking-In-These-Ridiculous-Shoes Shuffle to the desk. She reached out to shake Tipsy's hand.

"Ummm…" said Tipsy.

"Come on now!" Lindsey's hand whipped up and down.

Tipsy thrust out her right arm to humor her, then switched arms in confusion. "What are you—that's your left hand—" A sparkle on Lindsey's finger. "No!"

Lindsey held her hand before her face, bling side out. "Eeeee! P.D. and I are getting *maaa-rried!*"

"Oh, jeez! Shake your hand? Please!" Tipsy hugged Lindsey. Lindsey hopped in her embrace. The top of her head bumped Tipsy's chin, exacerbating her headache, but she didn't mind.

She gibbered on about the proposal, how it all went down (on P.D.'s boat, naturally), and what her parents and his had said. She whipped out her phone. "Which picture should I put on Instagram?"

"You ready for this?" Shelby asked. "You and Barker have only been officially divorced for a year."

"We've been talking about it for a while, and P.D. wants kids. I only have Emma. I've always wanted a big family. We're both thirty-six. I don't have forever." She did another little hop and Tipsy grabbed her elbow for good measure, so she didn't roll an ankle upon landing. "I'm so happy, y'all. That man is the sweetest, the kindest—oh. I adore him."

"So much that you still text with all your little boy toys?" Shelby said.

Lindsey shrugged. "That's silliness. I sent a few texts this morning, letting them know I'm going chat free. Besides, it's not like I've actually *seen* any of them in months. Not since P.D. started hinting that he wanted to get serious."

"He's always been serious."

"Umm, no. He told me when we first started dating that marriage terrified him." Lindsey put a one hand on her hip. "I wasn't going to put my whole heart in that basket—not after what I've been through—and have him turn out to be some typical Charleston man-boy. Doesn't feel so good when the man you love tells you he might never make a commitment to you."

"Let her be, Shelby," said Tipsy.

Shelby stood and hitched up her khakis. Tipsy glanced at the baggy rear of those pants. Shelby's sexiness had always been the curvy goddess kind, but Tipsy wasn't the only one who'd lost weight. Shelby's famous derriere didn't have quite its usual *umph*. "Well now you got him," Shelby said.

"*Got him?* You're acting like I stopped taking birth control pills or something. What is your problem?" Her free hand went to her other hip. Two sharp elbows poked at the tension between Lindsey and Shelby.

"Nothing—nothing." Shelby closed the Internet browser and sat back in her chair.

Tipsy knew better. "Sister, what's up?"

"You want to know…fine. I'll tell you. Glen's going back to his ex."

Lindsey leaned over the desk, her anger apparently forgotten. "You're kidding."

"And according to the messages she's been sending me on Facebook and Instagram, they've been sleeping together the entire time we've been dating." Shelby pressed her fingers into her eyes.

"Shelby—that asshole," said Lindsey.

"Now I've got the ex all on my social media, and Glen blowing up my phone saying he's sorry, but asking me to *lie to his ex*. He says it all has to do with his son—that he doesn't love her."

"Send her those messages!" said Tipsy.

"He doesn't write them—he's been calling. Telling me he still loves me, and maybe we can keep seeing each other." Shelby held up her phone. Three missed calls from Glen. "All this time, I've been so suspicious of him. And the drama with her about turned my hair gray. But the thought of starting over, *again?* Y'all know how it is in this town. How we're outnumbered."

Tipsy scowled. "Not that again."

Tipsy had arrived in town right after college. She immediately heard about Charleston's supposedly skewed male-to-female ratio. Of course she expected congratulations when they got engaged, but everyone acted like she'd won the Y-chromosome sweepstakes by landing Ayers Collins. The urban legend started at the College of Charleston. Historically, more women than men attended the College. In calculating the entire young adult population, however, she figured the numbers were pretty equal, given that the overwhelmingly male Citadel stood around the corner.

Somehow, that rumor lived on, following the women of Charleston through all stages of life. As a result of this mythical lack of men, women felt the need to compete ferociously among themselves for male attention, resulting in myriad never-ending, catty quarrels like Shelby's feud with Glen's ex-wife. Many of the men, in turn, had perceived carte blanche to do whatever they wanted to do, and act however they wanted to act. Which included being entitled to eternally play the field with little to no consequences.

Since her divorce, numerous people sympathetically expressed doubt that she'd even date again, let alone get remarried. At first, Tipsy resigned herself to a life of loneliness. Once she got out and about around town, however, she started to think it was all a bunch of bullshit, propagated by men to keep women perpetually desperate.

"When we go out to dinner," Tipsy said, "or to get a beer, or the beach, there are dudes everywhere. Every place we go is a sausage fest."

"But most of them are terrible! I don't get it, y'all. How do I get myself involved with these men? Three fiancées? Guys like Glen?"

Tipsy also suspected that many women preached the Gospel of No Men to justify their dysfunctional relationships. "Yes, there are plenty of men like Glen. But they're not all like that."

"Honey," Lindsey said, "maybe you keep chasing possums up the wrong tree. And then putting up with them pooping on your head."

"For a minute, I almost agreed to keep seeing him. I must be completely crazy." She covered her face with her hands. "And I *am* happy for you, Linds. It's just so hard to watch someone else succeed while I keep failing."

Tipsy knelt beside her. She collected her thoughts. "Shelby. Stop beating yourself up. You loved him—of course you were tempted to keep seeing him. It's like…when you have insomnia, sometimes even a nightmare sounds appealing."

Lindsey chimed in. "You didn't agree to it. That's the point."

Tipsy nodded. "Now, you told me true when I needed to hear it. So I'm telling you. Stop talking to him. Block his number. Unfriend him. Whatever. You cannot communicate with him at all."

Tears finally leaked over Shelby's eyelids. "I'll try."

"Give me the phone," said Tipsy. "Hand it over."

Tipsy hit Glen's number. The phone rang once, before his frantic voice came on the other end. "Baby—Jesus, what took you so long—"

"It's Tipsy, Glen."

"Oh—where's Shelby?"

"She's not talking to you."

"Put her on the damn phone, Tipsy."

"No, you asshole."

"What the hell—"

"Listen to me. Don't call her. Don't text her or Facebook message or tweet at her or Insta-snap her or whatever the hell y'all do. You made your choice."

"You don't know my business. Don't tell me what I can and can't do."

"Go back to your wife. Be miserable. Drink your life away. I'm sure you'll find someone else to screw around with you. Like that blonde chick from the boat. She looked ready to go."

"Put Shelby on the phone!"

"I swear to god, Glen, you keep calling Shelby I will go all trailer park on your ass and you will regret it. Move on. With your wife or someone else. It's not going to be Shelby." And she hit the end button.

"Lord, it used to be so much more satisfying when you slammed the phone down in someone's ear." Tipsy looked up at Shelby and Lindsey. Both stared at her with eyes on stalks, like two startled praying mantises.

Lindsey started laughing. "What exactly does going trailer park on someone entail?"

Shelby joined her. "You going to empty a septic tank in his front yard?"

"Set a bunch of coon dogs on him?" Lindsey doubled over. "Shoot his tires out with a twelve gauge?"

Tipsy snorted. "Maybe I'll force feed him SPAM covered in hot sauce and steal all the toilet paper in his house."

They laughed until Shelby's sad tears had turned to happy ones, at least for the time being. "Thanks, Tips," she said. "And I'm sorry, Linds. P.D. is a good guy. And he's not too old, or too young, for once." Shelby walked toward Tipsy's painting, as if seeing it for the first time. "Damn. This one is going to go big."

She turned around. "You know the thing about you, Tipsy, that makes me wonder? Artistic genius aside."

"Haha," Tipsy said. "What's that?"

"You protect everyone, even when your own life is going to shit. Your friends. Your kids. Annoying old boyfriends. Sometimes you even protect your ex-husband— the cause of all your problems. You should try sticking up for yourself the way you stick up for other people."

———— • ————

Tipsy sat on the front porch the next day, a pretty Saturday morning. She held a spiral notebook and pencil in hand, but she wasn't drawing. She was compiling a packing list for Ayers. May Penny and Tripp had offered to take Ayers and the kids to Disney World for a week. Packing for an eight-year-old and two six-year-olds was easy-peasy when compared to the old days. Bouncy seats, pack-n-plays, bottles, baby food, diapers, bedtime lovies, and baby toys that played annoying jingles on permanent repeat. All doubled with twins. Still, she knew if she didn't spell it out precisely, Ayers would never remember things like socks and Little A's retainer and story books for the girls.

She took a moment to contemplate the irony of her helping Ayers keep it together, while he tried to take the kids from her based on his claim that she was losing her mind and couldn't handle being a parent. She remembered a conversation she'd had with Lindsey, not long after they first met. Lindsey had reminded her that divorced or not, she'd always have to deal with Ayers, and suggested she learn to ration out her good will.

"But you can't let him know you're doing it. It's all for the kids, anyway." Lindsey had shrugged and taken a sip of her bright green kale juice. "There will be times when y'all are in the middle of World War

Collins, and you'll still be having a totally mundane, even pleasant conversation. Welcome to the Divorce Twilight Zone."

So Tipsy had put aside her increasingly heavy heart and offered to text him a checklist. He'd sent her a terse gratitude text (*thank u*), but then followed up an hour later by stating that he'd already registered Little A for fall soccer, and he didn't ask her to pay half the seventy-five-dollar rec league registration fee.

Small victories.

The kids were playing some kind of werewolf-zombie chase game in the yard below the porch. "Don't get too tired out, buddies!" she called. "We're going to the beach in a bit."

"Who we going with again, Mama?" shouted Ayers.

"A friend of mine. And his kids."

"What kind of kids does he have?"

"The nice kind, I'm sure."

"No, boys or girls or what?" Little A stopped and looked up at her. The girls latched onto his legs. He paid them no mind, as if they were large, shrieking soccer shin-guards.

"Girls. Three of them."

"Blah." He brandished a light saber in his mother's direction. The toy flashed and flickered in seizure-inducing red.

"Come on now, A," Tipsy said. "You're having fun with girls right now. And there will probably be kids from school out there anyway."

He returned to zombifying his sisters and she returned to her list, but she couldn't concentrate. Unfortunately, headaches and queasiness were status quo lately, but she had another reason to be distracted this morning. They had a fun day planned, but meeting Will's children for the first time, and him meeting hers, and them meeting each other... it kinda felt like another pancake on her anxiety stack. She'd always promised herself she'd be very choosy about who she brought around her kids, and the nagging little voice in the back of her head wondered if it was too soon.

"Your son makes me laugh," said Jane.

The ghost sat on the edge of the joggling board. "Hey Jane," Tipsy said. She smiled her welcome, relieved to have some distraction from her newest worry. "Yes, he's a hoot."

"Is your new friend a good father?"

"I haven't seen him in action yet, but I'll find out today. I'm sure he is." Tipsy reassured herself with her own honest opinion. "If he's half as sweet to those girls as he is to me, they're lucky kids."

"There's something about a man and his daughters." Jane smiled. "My sister and I certainly loved our father. What a *man* he was."

"From what Proctor James said, you ran all over your daddy at Sunday church."

Her smile widened. "I suppose I did run wild. But still, Daddy took a hand to my bottom a time or two. I surely deserved it more often."

"Your father was a fine gentleman, for sure." Henry had joined them on the porch. He stood near the far end of the joggling board. "Everyone in town held his opinion in the highest esteem."

Jane fidgeted in Tipsy's direction. "Thank you. It's kind of you to say so."

Henry pointed into the yard. "I came to watch the children. That is, if their mother is in agreement."

"Of course," Tipsy said.

"I'm doing the same," said Jane. "It does *amuse* me."

"Yes. It's a pleasant distraction." He pointed at Little Ayers. "I would have loved such a toy as a child. I would have played with it after dark. It's like holding a shooting star in your hands."

Tipsy watched them watch her children. She expected one to fade or disappear from the discomfort of the other's close proximity, but they stayed pale and solid.

"Might I sit?" asked Henry. He pointed at the board.

"Certainly," said Jane. Their decorum struck Tipsy as ridiculous. After all, they had known each other longer than any couple Tipsy had ever come across. Longer than any couple had a right to know each other.

Jane scooted over as far as she could scoot without falling off the edge. Henry took the other end. They sat in stiff silence with their eyes on the yard.

"Mama!" yelled Olivia Grace. "Can you fix my ponytail, please?" Her hair had escaped its ribbon and hung in her face in sweaty brown strings.

Tipsy walked down the steps. Warm wood gave way to prickly grass beneath her bare feet. She pulled a hair band from the pocket of her shorts. It seemed that with three females in the house, Tipsy always had a spare hair band on her person. She fixed O-Liv's ponytail, and Mary Pratt's while she was at it.

"I'm going in to get our beach stuff ready, buddies. Y'all need more sunscreen."

Someone might have said okay, but Tipsy had already turned back to the house. Her mental list shifted from what Ayers needed for Disney to what she needed for an afternoon at Sullivan's. If Ayers forgot socks, well, they had to have Wal-marts in Orlando.

She looked up as she climbed the stairs. Her eyes sought her notebook, but she stopped on the middle of the steps when she saw something more interesting.

Henry and Jane, on each end of the joggling board, like bookends that held up invisible volumes. The blackish-green joggling board against the white house. The two figures in symmetrical poses, stiff formality in legs crossed at the ankle and hands folded in laps. The center of the board didn't dip, and it wouldn't have even if they'd sat there, for they had no weight. Still, Tipsy imagined pushing each one toward the middle. Jane and Henry sliding down the gentle incline toward the place where you were supposed to sit. A bit of gravity would force them to bump hips.

They were so close together, yet so very far apart. And Tipsy had first hand, intimate knowledge of the dark history that divided them. Her heart banged happily in her chest.

Shelby said she wanted inventory. She had found her next painting.

As Tipsy opened the front door with a smile on her face and the new painting in her mind, she heard Jane's nervous chattering behind her. "It's been so nice to see you. Truly. But I have to— I must really—"

Henry: "You don't need to go— I can leave—"

"No, no, no. Thank you. Yes. Very much. Good afternoon."

Apparently, Jane didn't have the wherewithal to sit beside Henry for long. If she were alive, she would have elbowed past Tipsy in her effort to get into the house and away from him. Instead, Jane walked right on through her.

Tipsy's stomach dropped sickeningly. Her elevated pulse, pleasant just a few moments ago, beat too hard against the inside of her skull. Her field of vision narrowed. Yellow splotchy lights cut through the descending darkness. *No, not now. Not with the kids right outside.* She fought, trying to hold onto her own reality. She pushed back against Jane's mind as it tried to cover her own in a tear-soaked blanket of painful recollections.

The memory was too strong. Tipsy willed herself to keep some control, lest her children find her, unconscious in the foyer, her nose busted open from face-planting on the hardwood floor. She braced herself, and held on.

———————————

The dock that she's on leads to a sluggish river. Tipsy peers over the edge, where the wood planking ends like an unfinished sidewalk. A canoe is tied to the pilings. The tide is so low that the rope is taut, and the edge of the canoe lifts out of the water. If the river recedes anymore, the canoe may capsize.

She turns around and sees the brick and clapboard plantation house of the Old Cannon behind her. Jane sits further down the dock, close to the grass. She's hunched over a book. The earthy smells of pluff mud and maybe a beached fish are harsh in Tipsy's nose as she walks toward Jane. Tipsy looks down at exposed oyster beds. There's something creepy about the dozens of small gray crabs that click over the shells like scuttling castanets.

Jane is scribbling in the book. She sniffs and swipes at her nose, and at one point throws back her head and aims her face at the washed out blue sky. Tipsy has seen her do this before, in laughter, but her teeth clenched on her bottom lip tell Tipsy nothing is funny. Her heartbreak shimmers before Tipsy's eyes, almost palpable in its combination of longing and grief.

Tipsy walks around Jane and looks over her shoulder. She starts reading.

Dearest,

I fear that I've placed you in a position of danger, for if we are discovered, it would go harder on you than me. It breaks my heart, for how can you show so much kindness to one who isn't wholly yours, and also threatens you with ruin?

I feel that I don't deserve your devotion. Oh, I know you say I do, that I should be someone's sun and moon, and bless you for those words. But I'm in a state of utter and depraved dishonesty. So it was condoned, does that make it acceptable? Does one who caves to such selfish needs over sacred duties deserve your affections?

Know that I do love you tenderly, and I wish I could change our circumstances, but I do not see how that can ever be! As Ms. Wharton says, we can't behave like people in novels. So here, I add my tears to the brackish water of the Wando.

Christmas will be over soon, and I'll return to Mount Pleasant. It's a shame that you couldn't be here this season, but perhaps a blessing in disguise. It would be difficult to hide my tender feelings. I'll come into town and stay with my mother and father for a spell, just as soon as I am able.

With love, always!

Jane

Jane rereads the letter. Her fingers trace her own pretty penmanship. She rips the page from the journal and stuffs it in an envelope. She looks over her shoulder and then tucks the envelope into the pages of another book. Tipsy reads the title, The Age of Innocence. *Jane scoops up both novel and journal in one hand and pulls a handkerchief from her pocket with the other. She presses the silk to her eyes and nose, and clears her throat.*

Tipsy wants to follow Jane. She would take her by the shoulders. Who is this Dearest? *She wants to ask.* Is he worth dying for?

It must be John. Henry found out, and went crazy. And Jane's parents didn't want to sully her reputation, so they kept it under wraps.

Jane calls out as she walks toward the house, "Beatrice? Has Jackson left for the post office yet? I have a package."

———————— • ————————

It worked, at least somewhat. She woke up in the living room, on one of Miss Callie's antique upholstered lounge chairs. She lay there for a few minutes with her eyes closed, willing her stomach to stay out of her throat. Her head kept on hurting, but her belly slowly calmed down.

She didn't know how she'd safely made it to the chair, but it didn't matter. She heard the kids, still outside, blissfully clueless that their mother just went on a paranormal time-traveling jaunt. She dozed on the chair for about thirty minutes, letting her mind and her body recover their twenty-first century sensibilities, until she heard the girls yelling in the front yard. Ayers had pulled a very amateurish parenting move, and bought one sparkly unicorn bathing suit, because *you girls can share it*. Instead of following his fatherly advice, the girls were about to go all Henry and Jane on each other over who would wear the suit to the beach. Tipsy grabbed her purse, opened a bottle of Tylenol, and downed three.

"Girls!" she yelled, and winced. Despite her pounding head, she had to lay down the hammer on their bickering. "*No one* is wearing the unicorn bathing suit! It's staying in the drawer, tags on, until y'all can figure out a way to *get along. Got it?*"

Wish you had a sparkly unicorn bathing suit to use as a bargaining chip with the Motts, said Granna.

You and me both.

———————●———————

Tipsy always made the kids carry stuff on the walk down to the beach. Little Ayers had a boogie board slung over his shoulder. Mary Pratt hauled the bag of beach toys. Olivia Grace peered into the snack basket as she walked and kept tripping over her own feet. Neither wore the infamous unicorn bathing suit. Tipsy figured she might as well frame it and hang it on the wall, as each girl would each rather go naked than let her sister win that battle.

That left Tipsy with the big beach bag (monogrammed with COLLINS in purple lettering), a small cooler and a beach chair. They traipsed over the dunes toward the beach at Station 19 on Sullivan's Island. The trail, just wide enough for one person and surrounded by flowering thickets on both sides, always reminded Tipsy of a storybook path. The tiny butterflies might be joined by flittering fairies, and the rabbits she heard scurrying though the brambles might pop their heads up and wish Tipsy and her kids a good day. The clear air made for precise delineations from one shade to the next, a salad bowl of colors: dark green bushes, cloudless blue sky, creamy sand, white butterflies, and yellow and purple flowers.

When Will saw the Collins crew crossing the dune he jogged over and took everything from Tipsy's hands.

"Thanks—wait, now I'm not carrying anything," she said. She kicked off her flip-flops. The sand was warm, but not yet too hot to handle.

"I got it." He set all their accoutrements under his umbrella and called to his daughters. Tipsy watched them approach. His dark haired oldest, tall and thin and leggy like a yearling filly, and two stocky little blonde girls with pigtails and matching Dora the Explorer bathing suits.

They introduced all six children. Rosie, Will's four-year-old, grinned up at Tipsy. She pointed at her little potbelly. "Dora Spa-lora!" she said.

Tipsy poked at the goggle-eyed monkey beside Dora on Rosie's suit. "And Boots!"

Tipsy's twins promptly joined Will's girls in digging a hole and filling it with water. "I'll fill up my bucket!" Mary Pratt said. She pointed at Will's five-year-old daughter, Ella. "You come with me!"

"Mary Pratt, try again," said Tipsy.

"Will you please come fill up buckets with me?" She handed a pink one to Ella.

Ella looked up at her big sister, Isabel. "I'll go with you, El," said Isabel. "How about we all go?"

"'Kay!" shouted Rosie. She raced toward the water on chubby legs with a bucket waving in each hand.

"You going to help them, Ayers?" asked Will.

Ayers watched the girls filling their buckets in the surf. "No, sir. I'm going swimming."

"Stay right in front on me. Pay attention to the current. It will push you that way." Tipsy pointed toward the lighthouse, the black and white monument that watched over Sullivan's Island's slow erosion like an ineffective, bored security guard.

"That wasn't so hard," said Tipsy. She wore her darkest sunglasses, but her head still hurt. She sat on a towel, and sipped a cold Coke. Fizz mitigated her lingering queasiness. "Funny how kids can be friends in a minute."

"Did you think it would be hard?" said Will.

"Maybe. I haven't introduced anyone to my kids yet. Have you?"

"I dated a girl for about nine months. She came around."

"Oh." Tipsy hadn't known Will had any other steady girlfriends, although since he'd been single for a few years it made sense. "What happened?"

He shrugged. "She wanted to have kids, her own kids. I don't want to have more children. Plus, I like to have a good time, but she drank too much for me."

Tipsy nodded. She had given Shelby good advice about the plethora of men in Charleston, but now she had a specific one she wanted to keep, and she hated the thought of him with someone else. Suddenly, the beach teemed with umpteen pretty Charleston Dress Code women in skimpy bathing suits, all with better figures and perky fake boobs. The kind of curvy, bouncy girls she'd envied in high school. Cheerleaders with button noses, cuteness incarnate. Tipsy was many things, but cute was not one of them. Tall and gangly with a patrician nose did not equate with adorable. She imagined every damnably cute one of them watching Will from behind her sunglasses and knowing how wonderful he was, and hence wanting to steal him.

She chided herself for playing into the un-sisterly, competitive mentality she hated. "Sounds like you made a good decision."

"Who's that guy? In the new painting."

The abrupt change of topic took Tipsy aback. "Uh, no one. Just someone I made up in my head."

"I thought artists look at models." Will looked at her, his face impassive. He'd made a rational observation, and he clearly expected a rational answer.

"A lot of artists do. When it comes to painting figures, probably most. I don't."

"How do you remember all that detail?"

"I don't know. I just remember it."

"So you do see it in person first."

Damnit, she thought. *Why do you have to make so much sense?*

She backtracked. "Not this painting. I saw a guy with red hair like that. A great color…so I…made it up." Tipsy didn't even believe herself.

Tipsy…maybe he's the one who needs to know, said Granna. *Maybe you should tell him.*

I can't. Will doesn't even like Star Wars. *I doubt he believes in ghosts.*

Suit yourself, said Granna.

"Hmm. Okay," said Will. He returned his gaze to the water. On anyone else, the furrowed brow would have been a sign of confusion. Since Will always looked like that, Tipsy had no idea what was going on in his head.

Tipsy's eyes swept the beach for her own change of topic, and settled on the five girls by the water's edge. Isabel led the little girls in a game of red light green light. "Isabel looks like you."

"That's what everyone says. The little ones look like Michelle."

He didn't talk much about his ex, but even after her visceral reaction to the passing mention of a former girlfriend, Tipsy pried at the top of that can of worms.

"She still lives in the house y'all had together, right?"

"Yeah. I rented for a bit, then bought mine."

"You didn't want the house?"

"No. Too much history. And she wanted it. So it was easy."

"When you left her—"

"I didn't really leave her." He continued to watch the ocean.

"Oh. For some reason I thought you did."

"She first asked for a divorce." He leaned back on his elbows. "I wanted to work it out. For the kids. At least try. She wasn't interested." He lifted his shoulders toward his ears in an awkward shrug.

Tipsy's heart cramped a bit. Will's nonchalance about his divorce, which she'd attributed to indifference toward his ex, suddenly had implications of heartache on his part.

"Eventually, I realized it was the right thing. Then she backtracked." He sat up again and brushed sand off his legs. Tipsy sensed he wasn't enjoying the conversation. "Once I wanted out, she wasn't sure. So in the end, I made the final decision."

Isabel ran toward them. "Daddy, can I go swimming? Ayers wants me to boogie board with him."

"Sure, baby. I'll come in with you. Your sisters will follow you."

"I'll come, too. My girls won't want to be left behind."

Will stood and tugged Tipsy to her feet. As she stood, her nausea returned. She paused for a moment and stared at the horizon, willing it to stay in a straight line. Once she was confident that her Coke would stay down, she followed Will and Isabel to the surf.

"Mama!" yelled Olivia Grace. "You comin' in the water?" She jumped into Tipsy's arms, cold wet child against warm dry skin.

"Lord, you're freezing me!" Tipsy squeezed O-Liv and then plopped her into the water.

"It's not cold if you jump right in!" said Little Ayers.

"Daddy—Miss Tipsy!" Little Rosie took one of Tipsy's hands and one of Will's. "Swing me in the waves."

Will grinned at Tipsy. To her relief, the retreating ocean sucked away any remaining tension between them. "How are we going to do this?" he asked.

"As long as no one drowns, we're succeeding," she said.

Rosie let go of their hands and jumped up and down. "I can't see my feet!"

Tipsy splashed her girls, who returned the favor until she gave up and dove under the waves. She still wore her sunglasses, so she held on to their frames. The water felt wonderful—cool and clean.

There's something healing in the ocean, said Granna.

Tipsy smiled at Granna under the water. She popped up to Will's voice, calling after Rosie.

"Come back this way—Rosie! This way!"

In the span of a minute the current had pushed Rosie out of his reach while he tossed Ella into the air. Rosie fought the current hard to walk back to them. "I'll get her," said Tipsy.

She hop-walked over the waves in Rosie's direction. Little Ayers called out from behind her, "Here comes a big one!"

The wave in question wouldn't be big to Tipsy, but Rosie's crumpling face as it bore down on her showed it to be tsunami-like to a short four-year-old.

"Damn—she's going to get pounded!" yelled Will. He shoved Ella in Isabel's direction. Rosie braced for impact with both arms held straight before her in a futile attempt to hold back the ocean.

The vibrations started in Tipsy's eyes, as they had before, but this time shot through her arm, as if she'd tried to insert a light bulb into a live socket. She pointed at Rosie and swung her buzzing arm toward the beach. She grabbed at her shoulder and grimaced.

She opened her eyes to Will reaching for a crying Rosie, who appeared to be at least ten feet closer to the shore. The remains of the wave swirled around them, the gurgling layers of water weaving through their legs like a pack of guilty puppies.

"Whew," said Will. "That was close. Must have been another wave that pushed her back. Lucky girl." He kissed Rosie's cheek.

Tipsy continued rubbing her shoulder. She felt like she'd attempted an overzealous tennis serve, or struck her funny bone. Moments ago, the sloshing waves had rejuvenated her. Now she couldn't tolerate such jostling of her delicate stomach. Her headache was back with a vengeance, and she had a few hours before she could take any more.

"You okay, sweetie?" she asked Rosie.

Rosie nodded. She stuck her fingers in her mouth and buried her face in her daddy's chest.

"Daddy's right," she said. "You're a lucky girl."

Especially since I have no freakin' idea what just happened. She'd have to pack it in earlier than planned. She could no longer tolerate the glare off the sun-kissed waves, even through her sunglasses.

Same thing happened at the gallery when you smashed that sculpture on the wall. And in your bedroom when those ghosts were having at each other.

But what is it, Granna?

Can't help you there.

———————•———————

That evening, Tipsy wanted an early bedtime. Once again, she'd experienced two intense supernatural occurrences in one day: the vision of Jane on the dock, and her intervention between Rosie and the indifferent Atlantic Ocean. The aftereffects were in full bloom. The requisite headache and nausea, plus exhaustion and muscle aches. She was even hungry, but she couldn't eat. It felt like early pregnancy symptoms crossed with the flu.

The kids were happily wiped out. She folded laundry after dinner and bath time, and as she put a few tee-shirts and sundresses away in the girls' dresser drawer, their conversation made her smile to herself.

"M.P., I think Ella is nice. Do you?" Olivia Grace sat on her bed with two My Little Ponies in her lap. She held one before her face. "Did you like her, Rainbow Dash?"

"Ella is nice." Mary Pratt lay under her covers, staring at the ceiling. "And Rosie is too. Even if she is only four. She's sassy." She dropped her voice to a whisper. "I like sassy people."

Tipsy bit her lip to keep from laughing. She gave goodnight kisses to both girls, then said goodnight to Ayers, who grudgingly offered his own assessment of Will's kids ("Isabel is pretty cool for a teenager"). She went downstairs to the foyer to tackle the beach bag. She pulled out a clump of wet, sandy towels, a few empty Capri-sun bags, and a damp bag of Goldfish that would have to be tossed out. She removed goggles and sunscreen bottles and a random plastic shovel and set them all in a pile by the closet. She'd throw the towels in the dryer and pitch the trash, and wipe down everything else tomorrow, when she had more energy.

Will had already texted goodnight, but she checked her phone one last time anyway. She frowned at the alert on the lock screen.

Ayers Collins Text Messages (4)

She swiped the screen. Her pulse quickened unpleasantly as she read.

U already got that guy around my kids?

Do u even know him?

Your judgment is terrible. It's getting worse all the time.

Hope your PLAYDATE was worth it.

Tipsy took a few minutes to think before she replied. She had to admit, it irked her that Ayers had called her out, when she'd already questioned the wisdom of today's beach outing. She typed a few versions of the message before she hit send, and to her relief, she found that her genuine explanation once again soothed her.

Ayers, Will is a very nice person. He's got two girls who are almost the twins' age and an older daughter who is sweet and fun. Even Little A liked her. I told them he is my friend. Nothing else. They won't know he's anything but my friend unless you decide to tell them that. I think that would be inappropriate. But I understand that I cannot control what you do.

His typing bubble lit up immediately. She waited anxiously for his reply.

No. U will never control me ever again.

She rolled her eyes and tried another track. *I didn't see anyone I knew at the beach for once. So who saw us?*

Ayers: *Don't u worry about that.*

Tipsy typed faster. *Did you hire a PI? Again?*

She waited, but Ayers didn't reply. In his silence, Tipsy figured she had her answer.

● —— ◆ —— ●

Two days later, on Monday morning, Tipsy and her lingering supernatural hangover arrived at May Penny's house to drop off the kids for their Disney trip. May Penny planned for the children to ride with her and Tripp, and Ayers to follow behind in his truck with all the luggage. Tipsy's former father-in-law pulled up behind her Tahoe as she unloaded the children's bags onto the driveway.

Tripp Collins got out of his white Suburban, a tall man with a round belly and a permanently ruddy face. Tripp must not have sipped enough water from the magical Charleston fountain of good hair, because his had receded to the point where his noggin was mostly forehead. He wore khaki pants and a white polo shirt. Tipsy assumed he'd come from the golf course.

"Hey there, Tipsy," he said, and gave her a hug.

She hugged him back. He smelled like Old Spice aftershave. "Hey, Tripp." Tipsy had always had a genuine fondness for Tripp, the male version of Mimi in the Collins family. They formed a gentle buffer against May Penny and Ayers and their excitability.

"You leave that stuff. Ayers and I will load it in his truck when he gets here. I'm going up to get a sweet tea. You want one?"

"No thanks," she said, and pulled a couple bags from the back of the Tahoe. She wanted to get out of here before Ayers showed up.

"You've brought everything else they'll need?" said May Penny over her shoulder.

Tipsy turned around to face her mother-in-law in her blue visor and matching polo shirt atop a white tennis skirt. "Yes. If you could remind Ayers to make sure Little A wears his retainer I'd appreciate it."

"All right." May Penny's latest sunglasses, leopard print frames with gold swirls on the arms, sat atop her head like designer Mickey Mouse ears.

"And the girls still don't brush their teeth well," Tipsy said. "Sometimes they need help."

"Anything else?"

Tipsy leaned against the truck. "No. I don't think—"

"If you were coming along you could take care of those things your-self. Men have trouble managing these things." May Penny unzipped one of the bags, as if a brief glance would determine what Tipsy might have forgotten. "That's why children need both parents around."

"I guess Ayers will have to learn, right?"

"Then again, a mother who doesn't put her children first… maybe it's best the father step into both sets of shoes."

Tipsy felt as if someone had placed cold hands on the sides of her tender head and commenced squeezing. "What are you saying?"

May Penny sniffed. "I don't want to have another argument. That's not how I like to start my family vacations."

"That wasn't an argument we got into on my last visit," said Tipsy. "Two people have to be fighting for it to be an argument."

"I'm not going to apologize for telling the truth. It's not my problem you couldn't defend yourself."

For the first time in sixteen years, Tipsy allowed herself to see red when she looked at the woman who had spawned Ayers. "What is this? Am I on trial?"

"Don't raise your voice. The neighbors might hear you."

"I will raise my damn voice," said Tipsy, and she did. "You think I'm not putting my kids first. When I left Ayers, that was me putting them first. We all lived in a house walking around on eggshells—and let me tell you—those things had sharp edges. I didn't want my children thinking that's normal. That it's what a marriage should look like."

"That's ridic—"

"You weren't there, May Penny!"

"Ayers loves those kids—"

"I didn't say he doesn't love them! But I don't want Little Ayers growing up to bully his own family. I don't want my girls thinking it's right and normal for a woman to be a doormat! I'll be damned if they're going to repeat my dysfunction."

"For heaven's sake. You don't have to be so angry."

"I am angry! You know why? Because I finally can be! I had no room in my life to be angry, or sad, or frustrated, because Ayers's anger and sadness and frustration took up all the space! So now I'm pretty damn pissed you're insinuating that my children aren't my first priority!"

May Penny crossed her arms over her chest. "Well. I never, never. And swearing as well."

"Ha!" said Tipsy. "That's all you can think of? Insulting my manners. Now who doesn't have a defense? Well, here's mine." She leaned down into May Penny's face. May Penny retracted, a turtle in coral lipstick retreating into its shell. "Your comments are bullshit," Tipsy said.

"What's going on out here?" said Tripp as he walked down the stairs. "Kids are watching old Mickey Mouse cartoons. Y'all's ruckus is drowning out Donald and Goofy."

May Penny's mouth went right side up. "Nothin', honey. Tipsy asked me to help Ayers with the kids."

"You going deaf or something?" Tripp asked. "She asked pretty loud."

"No," said Tipsy. "You know me. I can be loud sometimes."

One of Tripp's gray eyebrows crept up his forehead, but it didn't reach a quarter of the way to his hairline. "All right then. Ayers texted me. He's on his way."

"I'll go then." Tipsy ran up and said goodbye to the kids, who were too enthralled by Mickey to pay her much mind, while Tripp moved his truck to the other side of the driveway.

"Thanks for taking them," Tipsy said from her open window. "Y'all drive safe."

"We will," said Tripp. "Hope you get some good painting time in."

"I plan on it."

"Enjoy your week off," said May Penny. She'd donned her sunglasses, so Tipsy couldn't read her expression. One of the few downfalls of living in a sunny place. People wore sunglasses all the time. A city of hidden eyes and covert expressions.

"Thanks," said Tipsy. May Penny and Tripp started up the stairs. Tipsy pulled her phone from her purse and sent a text to Shelby.

I stuck up for myself. It felt damn good.

Shelby replied: *I knew you had it in you. Sixteen years in the making, but better late than never. XOXO*

———————•———————

Tipsy has never been to a party like this and she's so damn nervous. She clings to her new friend, Shelby. Shelby basically stalked out Tipsy in her dorm room, where Tipsy was hiding and thinking about painting. Shelby's rich family owns a big art gallery in Charleston. It's like her mom's hobby or something. Her family contributes to art scholarships at Carolina and Shelby heard all about Tipsy. Tipsy reckons Shelby is the reason she got a bid from Kappa Zeta, because Tipsy barely opened her mouth to talk to those girls. Everyone else chatted and flipped their hair, and Tipsy was like a mute giraffe. Granna wouldn't approve of Tipsy using some of her life insurance money to pay for friends, but it's the first chance she's had in forever to make any. Besides, with her scholarship and financial aid she's doing okay. Even if she uses a bit of Granna's money for sorority dues she'll still have enough to move to New York after graduation. Tipsy can stretch forty grand out for years after how she's used to living, even in a big city like that.

Shelby is a year older than Tipsy and she knows a lot of people. The party is at a townhouse off-campus. A bunch of guys from Sigma Alpha, SA's, live here. It's the party before the party before the party. Everyone will leave here soon to tailgate, and then go to the football game. Tipsy might be nervous, but she's also crazy excited because she never went to parties back in Martinville.

This place is kind of nasty, honestly. Maybe it's in better shape when there aren't fifty people crammed inside, but right now it smells like cigarettes and beer-soaked carpet. There isn't a square of toilet paper left in the whole place. Someone has strung Christmas lights around the living room. There's a banner over the beat-up couch. It reads, "The South will rise again," and includes a drawing of a skeleton who wears a confederate uniform and waves a rebel flag. Tipsy might be the only person who finds it ironic that the skeleton is looking across the room at a Bob Marley poster.

There's a guy standing on the living room coffee table. He's tall and has broad shoulders, dark shaggy hair and a scruffy beard. Guys and girls sit on the couches and floor around him with red plastic cups of beer. Their heads tilt up at the guy on the table, like Indian warriors cheering on the chief's battle dance. He's playing air guitar and singing "Sabotage" by the Beastie Boys.

"IIIII can't stand it—I know you planned it!" He raises his arms above his head and they strike the rotating ceiling fan. The people around him roar with laughter as he shakes his hands and grimaces. "Imma set it straight— this Watergate!"

"Ayers Collins," says Shelby in Tipsy's ear. "We went to high school together."

Ayers jumps down from the table and the crowd parts like he's Moses. He hugs Shelby. "Shelby girl!" He kisses her forehead. "Who's this?"

"This is Tipsy Denning," says Shelby. "The artist I told you about."

"Well damn, Tipsy. Shelby's mama thinks you're the next Van Gogh, or some shit."

Tipsy blushes. "Thanks, I—"

Ayers winks at her. "Shelby said you were talented. Didn't say you were so pretty." He grins, all shiny white teeth and crinkling, laughing brown eyes. Tipsy blushes harder and grins back at him. Granna's voice rises in Tipsy's head, as its been doing these last few months since she passed.

My word, if he ain't handsome. But remember sugar, you're here to paint.

Shelby shoves Ayers's shoulder but he leans into Tipsy's ear. Tipsy's heartbeat thumps beside his mouth. She's sure he can hear it. "Your crystal ball ain't so crystal clear," *he says.*

Her mouth goes dry and she looks into his eyes for some sign he knows. Someone from Martinville told him she's a freak. But he just keeps smiling. "You like the Beastie Boys?"

She exhales. Of course. The lyrics to the song. "I feel no disgrace, because you're all in my face," *she says.*

"Hell, yeah. You know it." *He laughs up at the ceiling fan that almost dismembered him a few minutes before.* "Come on, Tipsy Van Gogh. Come meet everyone." *He drags Tipsy toward the couch and someone hands her a beer. The rest of the day flies by. Drinks and introductions to umpteen guys who all laugh at Ayers's jokes and nod at every opinion he expresses, from his views on the Gamecocks' chances at a championship (*"I love these boys but they suck a fat one this year."*) to his party-hosting strategies (*"Next time we're buying a keg of St. Paulie Girl for the house."*). The women smile, too, but there are shards of ice in their eyes and the conversations don't go much beyond hellos. Tipsy can't blame them. Who the hell is she, a freshman hick, to be standing here with this man that everyone loves?*

After the game, a deflating loss to Tennessee, Ayers is in a more philo-sophical mood. He and Tipsy sit on the steps leading to the dirt yard behind his house. He puts an arm around her shoulders. "For real, girl," *he says.* "It's cool that you're an artist. You're not like all these other sorority chicks who come here to become first grade teachers and marry a rich guy."

"Thanks. My grandmother said—"

"I'm going to do special things, too. I'm graduating in the spring. Going to go to New York. Be an actor."

"Really? Wow. I've never been, but I'd like to move there someday."

"Come visit me when I go! I think there's all kinds of artistic stuff up there."

"That would be nice. Maybe we could go to the Met."

"I'm not crazy about baseball."

"The Metropolitan—"

"I'll run into some famous actor. Like in a bar or at the dentist or something. They're all over the place up there. Once I meet, like, Tom Hanks or those guys who directed that Something About Mary *movie, they'll see I can do it."*

He lights a cigarette and blows smoke toward the September moon. For a moment, a smudge of foul smelling gray obscures that white sliver. Ayers rests his hand, the cigarette free one, on Tipsy's knee. He taps the end of her nose, and then kisses her. He tastes like smoke, but there's something else there as well. Maybe it's Skittles or Hubba Bubba. She doesn't care. His mouth is sweet. "What do you think, Tipsy? Can I do it?"

Tipsy nods, because she's already soft spoken and he's struck her dumb. In that moment, she's sure Ayers Collins can do anything.

Chapter 9

Tipsy never had this much time to herself, so no matter how crappy she felt, she wanted to make good use of her week without the children. She finished her sketch Monday night after leaving the kids at May Penny's. On Tuesday, after work, she set up on the front porch again. She'd come to love that space, with its creaky wicker furniture and even creakier ceiling fan. She even loved the daddy long legs that hid in the corners. She thought of them as her crawly little art critics.

She was adding white paint to the walls behind the figures of Jane and Henry when a brown UPS truck stopped in front of the house. She'd ordered some new brushes from her favorite online art supplier. She popped the old ones into the plastic cup beside her easel and clipped down the stairs to meet the UPS guy in her cutoff jean shorts and bare feet.

He handed her a large, cushioned envelope. She slid it under her arm and signed his electronic signature pad, foreboding swelling in her chest.

Overkill for a few paint brushes, said Granna.

Tipsy sat on the wicker sofa on the porch, and broke the envelope's seal. As she dumped out a pile of five-by-seven glossy photographs, a sickening taste traveled from her hollow stomach, through her constricted throat, and into her dry mouth. She slowly flipped through them. Here was Tipsy sitting on the bench in the St. Phillips graveyard, smiling and talking to someone beside her. Except, of course, there was no one beside her— Proctor didn't show up on film. In the photos on

Water Street, she gesticulated through the wrought iron fence of the old Robinette house, into a garden that was empty of anything but lush wisteria bushes and carefully maintained flower beds.

Next, to her shock, there were photos of Will's boat out at Morris Island. She couldn't believe that Ayers had actually paid the PI to take an afternoon boat cruise across the harbor, just to spy on her. The Tipsy in the photos was laughing, dancing, carefree. She held a beer in her hand. In one, she was kissing Will Garrison. His hands stood out in stark relief against her white bikini bottom.

Tipsy's hair about stood on end in mortification. Goose bumps bloomed on her arms and legs. There was no return address on the envelope. There was no note. Just these invasive screenshots of her life. They portrayed a wacky bimbo, not a responsible mother.

"Oh my God," she said. *"Oh. My. God."* She slammed the envelope onto the coffee table in front of her.

"What's wrong?" Jane appeared in the adjacent rocker.

"Wrong—it's these photos—Ayers—" Tipsy shut her mouth, her eyes widening. She stood, her eyes racing up and down Bennett Street.

What if the PI was out there right now, watching her?

Taking pictures of her, wherein she would appear to be talking to the daddy long legs and their brethren? Her mind raced. *Maybe he has videos, too.*

Oh dear, replied Granna. *Could be. Hard to send those in the mail.*

She stuffed the photos into the envelope and hustled into the house. She closed the door behind her, and locked it.

Jane reappeared, this time in front of her. "Tipsy?"

Tipsy dropped the envelope of photos on the foyer table and strode into the living room. She closed the blinds, choking back sobs. Jane followed her. "Are you ill again?"

Tipsy shook her head and ran up the stairs to her room. There was Jane, again, sitting demurely on the puffy old chair where Tipsy draped the clothes she couldn't fit in her tiny closet. When she yanked the curtains shut, Jane's blue effervescence somewhat made up for the sudden lack of sunlight.

"Tipsy?" Jane asked again.

Tipsy spun around. "I'm *fine,* Jane! I'm not sick. And I'm *not crazy*. But Ayers is going to make me *look* like I am. He'll get some good ol' boy judge to think I'm a floozy for good measure. And then he'll take my kids. My kids—"

Tipsy gasped, even though there was plenty of air in the room. *This is what a panic attack feels like,* she thought.

"I can't talk to you anymore. Or Henry. The PI might see me somehow. Please stay away from me." She wished she had an inhaler. It always seemed to work for Mimi.

Tiffany. A voice rose in her head. At first she couldn't hear it very well over the sound of her own clamoring thoughts. She thought it was Granna again, but Granna never sounded so fey.

Tiffany, Jane said, in Tipsy's mind. *Ayers will not take your children.*

She flopped on the bed and turned her tear-streaked face toward Jane. *You don't know him.*

You're right. But I've seen enough to know he's miserable. He's doesn't understand why. Being angry with you is a good enough reason. I don't think he truly wants to take them. She smiled. *I have some experience with angry, miserable men.*

I know you're right, but I still don't know how far he'll take it. The only predictable thing about him is his unpredictability. I have to prepare for the worst. The compassion on Jane's face made Tipsy cry harder. *I need some time to myself. I'm so sorry.*

Don't apologize, said Jane.

A new voice in rose Tipsy's head. *Can I help in some way?*

Henry stood on the other side of the room. He watched Tipsy with the same solemn empathy. Tipsy thought her heart would break. She shook her head.

Tipsy is afraid to speak with us, said Jane.

I see, Henry replied. *Well, we are accustomed to long silences. Being as we are, it does not surprise me that she'd reach that conclusion.*

I'm sorry. Tipsy rolled away from them and buried her face in her pillow. She cried herself to sleep. Evening turned to dusk, and dusk to the black of her darkest charcoal pencil. Tipsy slept all night. At some point she stirred when someone draped a blanket over her increasingly thin shoulders. *Thank you, Henry,* she thought, vaguely hoping he'd hear her. She woke to a gray morning and the sound of light rain on the roof. She jumped out of bed in yesterday's clothes, and ran down the stairs in a panic.

To her great relief, her easel, the new painting, and her supplies were carefully set up in the dining room, safe from the elements.

"Thank you, Henry," she whispered it, but she did say out loud.

She walked back upstairs to shower and get ready for work.

———•———

The storm cleared by Wednesday evening. She summoned her courage and returned to the porch with her art supplies. Before she started painting, she walked to the sidewalk and looked for suspicious cars or someone she didn't know, but for now at least, she couldn't find Ayers's spy. She finished the walls, the porch floors, and railings, the door, and the joggling board. When she got to the figures, she first focused on Jane. She felt compelled to bring to life the anguish Jane had felt when Henry rebuked her, and told her to find someone else to love. What

Tipsy had further seen on her face as she sat on the dock and wrote that hopeless letter to her lover.

But it would not be obvious. Jane would not grimace, or weep, or cover her face in shame. She'd stare straight out of the painting, solemnly, into the observer's own eyes.

She was adding pale blue paint to the iris of Jane's left eye when a green pickup truck pulled into the drive. With so many pickups in Tipsy's life, sometimes she found it difficult to keep them straight. By the time the truck stopped, she recognized her brother-in-law.

"Hey, Jimmy," she said. She stuck the brush in a cup of water so it wouldn't harden as it dried, and sprayed water over her palette. "You come by to do some work on the house?"

He joined her on the porch and kissed her cheek. "I need to get started, but it's kind of hard. Working on this place. Thinking about selling it."

"You grew up here. Of course it is." She wiped her hands on her old running shorts and added streaks of lavender to a slew of white, black and green drips and splats. The poor shorts looked like a Jackson Pollack painting had thrown up on them.

Jimmy ran a hand over one of the porch columns and picked at a few flecks of peeling paint. "Gonna bring some guys over to look at that water heater next week."

"Sure." Tipsy waited for Jimmy to say something else, but he stood there, a forty-year-old man in a visor and flip-flops and a Charleston Angler tee shirt. Except for his tired blue eyes, he looked like a college student who wasn't ever going to be ready for graduation. If Mimi was the picture perfect Charleston wife, blonde-haired Jimmy Lathrop, who'd played football for the Citadel Bulldogs and spent three years in the Navy after graduation before attending law school, was the picture perfect Charleston husband. Like Tipsy, Mimi had supposedly struck spousal gold.

"I—damn, sorry to bug you when you're working," he said. He spun his heavy Citadel ring around his finger. The Band of Gold, they called it. He sometimes let Little Ayers wear it. Tipsy knew the inscription on the inside because her son had asked her to read it to him. *JTL, Romeo Company, Honor & Brotherhood.*

"You're not bugging me. I live in your house. I owe you. Is something up?" she asked, but she already knew the conversation's trajectory.

"Has Mimi talked to you at all? About us?"

Tipsy shook her head, her promise of silence ringing in her ears.

"We're having some problems. I don't need to get into it…but…I thought, maybe she'd told you what she's planning to do. I think she's going to leave me."

Tipsy treaded lightly. "How do you feel about that?"

"I don't want a divorce, Tipsy." His words came in a rush. "But I don't want to keep fighting like this, either. I'm worried about the kids…and money. When we fight about it, Mimi always brings that up—how much she'll get. Seems like that's all she cares about."

"I'm sure she's just scared."

"I'm down for trying whatever she wants. I know I don't help her around the house. I probably don't take her out enough, or bring her flowers."

"You want to try. That's more than I can say for how I felt about my marriage."

"Didn't Ayers want to work at it?"

"He did, but I was too far gone." Guilt swelled inside Tipsy like an ice cube that had frozen, expanded, and cracked the tray. She wondered if she'd ever stop feeling guilty, and not just for breaking up her children's home. How could she still feel weirdly responsible for Ayers, when he was actively trying to ruin her life?

"Everyone's different," she said to Jimmy. "Maybe y'all can figure it out."

"Yeah, well. I guess we'll see." He started down the stairs and she followed him. "Thanks for talking with me. Don't tell her I came by, okay?"

"I won't." So now Tipsy kept the confidence of both Mimi and Jimmy. Equal opportunity secret-keeper.

Jimmy drove off, and Tipsy walked back toward the house. Her phone rang. She didn't want to miss a call from the kids, so she picked up the pace. As she clipped up the stairs the front of her flip-flop caught on the edge of the top step.

She fell forward. Henry stood before her, with a look of surprise on his face and his arms extended as if to catch her. That didn't work, of course. She kept going toward the floor, right through him.

<hr />

She's in the parlor of Miss Callie's house once again, and the wallpaper is fleur-de-lis. It's daytime, and someone has been baking. Maybe a pie, or maybe cookies. The sounds of an argument clash with the sweet smell, like a political rant in the middle of a lullaby.

"What are you saying to me?" Henry stands behind one of the armchairs. He clenches both sides of it, as if he might lift it over his head and throw it. His straining fingers remind Tipsy of her father's hands on her grandmother's flimsy kitchen chairs. Maybe a man needs something to hold onto when he's about to lose it.

"I'm saying I'd like a divorce." Jane sits in the other chair with her hands folded in her lap. She only needs a teacup and saucer to round off the picture of serenity.

"Divorce is illegal in South Carolina," says Henry.

Jane shrugs. "I'm sure there are ways to get around such things. Mary Pickford divorced that Irishman so she could marry Douglas Fairbanks."

"Mary Pickford is a famous film star in California. Not a girl from a good Charleston family."

"Times are changing," says Jane.

"They're not changing here." Henry is suddenly a man of tradition. *Tipsy wonders if F. Scott Fitzgerald or Ernest Hemingway would approve.*

"You could leave town," said Jane. *"Go to New York City. Finish your books and chum around with the great writers of our century. Divorce is legal in New—"*

"You've certainly thought this through." Henry's gaze lights up, but it's the glow of lupine eyes peering from the woods at night. *"No—none of this is coming from you. It's from him. He's infiltrated your brain."*

"I have thought about it—"

"You're not jesting? You want to leave me—for him? This mystery man?"

"I love him."

"You're supposed to love me."

"I don't understand why you're so angry. You told me to find someone else."

"I meant someone to dally with. Perhaps a gardener. Or one of the grocery boys. I didn't say anything about falling in love."

"Henry, that's absurd. You think love has certain parameters, as if it's impossible to fall in love with a grocery boy. And I would never break my vows to you for a silly thrill. You don't know me at all. Another reason we should part ways."

"Tell me who he is. Tell me or I'll go mad."

"You don't know him."

"We know everyone in this state. I must know him, or you'd say his name!" He spins around with his hands in his hair. When he faces Jane

again, it sticks up in triumphant flames on his head. "My brother, Edward! It's my brother—damn him."

"Don't be ridiculous. It's not Edward."

"Your parents will never allow it. The Robinettes would be the talk of Charleston."

"Once I explain to them, perhaps they will understand. And if they don't…" *Jane takes a deep breath and slowly releases it. Lamaze exercises to ease the pain of shattering her life.* "I'm a grown woman. I can vote now. I can make my own decisions."

"Little Miss Suffragette! This is exactly what our senators were worried about when the Republicans pushed for that amendment. Women running amuck. Society coming apart at the seams."

She laughs. "Now you're concerned with society. You detest society."

"Don't laugh at me, Jane. You're breaking my heart."

"You broke mine a million times." *She stands and balls her fists.* "You kept beating at it until it finally cracked. Now you're standing in the pieces, and you want me to be concerned with yours?"

"So you no longer love me?"

Tipsy feels Henry's abject befuddlement. He looks as if someone just informed him that Galileo and Isaac Newton were both wrong. That the world is flat and there's no such thing as gravity, so he'd better be careful, lest he fall off the edge or float away.

In a rush of artistic adrenaline, she vows to capture his volatile confusion in the silent, staring eyes of the figure in her new painting.

"I came to you," *Jane says.* "Over and over. And you bid me find love elsewhere. How can you rage at me now?"

"Fine!" *Now Henry had progressed from yelling to screaming.* "Do it! Divorce me and be a trollop and carry on with whoever he is, but you'll not stay in this house! I'll not see you under this roof for one more day!"

"It's my house as well. I've spent many more hours within its walls that you have."

"Then I'll go. The sight of you...you who love another man. It's slaughtering me."

He strides out of the room. The knick-knacks and framed photographs on the mantel jump when he slams the door behind him. Jane moves to the couch. She lies down, curls into a ball, and rolls over. Tipsy sees only the back of her yellow dress and the black soles of her shoes. Her face is hidden. Tipsy cannot tell if Jane is awake or asleep, if she's crying or laughing.

Henry stands on the front porch. He watches his wife through the window. Tipsy walks toward him, but before she can see anything beyond his hateful expression, he turns away. The yellow and black lights appear. It's Henry's memory, and she can't see what he doesn't see.

That night, Tipsy's headache was so bad that she dreamed her head was stuck in a too tight football helmet, and she couldn't pull it off. When she woke up the next morning, it was still there, like her brain had been replaced by an agitated porcupine. Two Aleve cut the worst of that ailment, but painkillers couldn't do much for the nausea that also plagued her.

She had to deliver a painting in Mount Pleasant, so she met Will for lunch at Poe's Tavern on Sullivan's Island. It was a cloudy day, but they sat outside anyway. She wore her gym clothes and sweat had dried on her skin. Every few minutes the breeze picked up and she shivered. Around the white picket fence that separated the restaurant's patio from the sidewalk, people milled like seagulls circling a picnic basket. Each time a table cleared the flock descended before the servers had a chance to remove leftover plates and glasses.

Tipsy told Will about the PI, albeit a version that didn't include the photos of her talking to invisible people. He scowled. "Can he do that? Y'all are divorced. You can date who you want to date."

"Yes, but he can still hire a PI and try to prove I'm an unfit parent. Make me look like some drunk party animal."

He crossed his arms over his chest. "That's ridiculous."

"That's Ayers."

"So what are you going to do?"

"I have to lay low for a while. It's probably best if I don't, like, go out much. I'm definitely not drinking, at all."

"You mean we can't even go to dinner and have a few beers? What about the boat?"

His comment annoyed her. She was talking about losing her kids, and Will was worried about beers and his boat. "For now. Is that really a problem?

Will shook his head, but Tipsy sensed he was placating her. "Of course not," he said. "We can Netflix and chill, right?"

She couldn't help but smile at that. He reached across the table and they clinked glasses above their burgers and obscenely large portions of fries. Will had a beer, but Tipsy had a Coke. Despite its acknowledged unhealthiness, she'd taken to drinking at least one a day. The carbonation did for her stomach what the Tylenol or Aleve did for her head. It had to be the real sugary thing; she couldn't stand diet. With all the weight she'd lost since she moved to Miss Callie's, she wasn't worried about calories, anyway. She blessed Will for picking a lunch spot that practically necessitated she eat greasy, stomach-calming comfort food.

She picked a happier topic. "Shelby sold *The Sleeping Man*."

"Hot damn, baby. That's great."

"Thanks," Tipsy said. "I can hardly believe it. Forty-five hundred dollars. I should finish *The Joggling Board* in the next couple days.

Shelby already has two different buyers waiting, so it could be bid off. And she's had people calling. Asking about my work. I guess that woman who bought *Stepping Off The Porch* has been doing a lot of entertaining and showing it off. Word is getting around."

"Wow. You must be excited."

"I am, but it's a little stressful." She took a bite of her burger, chewed and swallowed gingerly, and set it down. "I don't want to lose buyers because I don't have enough paintings."

"Better to have too many buyers and not enough paintings than the opposite problem."

"True, but nothing's come to me since *The Joggling Board.*"

"Can't you just make something up? Like you said you did with the painting of the sleeping guy?"

"Umm, well…maybe. It's not always that easy."

"It sounded like it was, from the way you described it. You saw some guy with red hair and came up with a painting."

"That was kind of unusual."

Will pointed at the table across from them, at a baby in a high chair. "That baby. Could you add her to a painting of babies? People like babies."

Tipsy fidgeted. "I have to go to the bathroom."

She walked up the stairs and into Poe's. Edgar Allan Poe was stationed at Fort Moultrie during the late 1820's. The beaches, marshes, and creeks of Sullivan's Island and its people inspired his story *The Gold Bug*, and legend said he wrote the poem *Annabel Lee* about a doomed local beauty. In his honor, the tavern's walls were covered in every kind of Poe kitsch imaginable. Some defied imagination, like the rock in the shape of Poe's head on which someone had painted his melancholy visage. Tipsy squeezed into the tiny women's room and shut the bathroom stall door.

Why am I annoyed? she asked herself. *I'm the one who isn't being truthful with him, but ugh; he will not let it go.*

Granna answered, as she was wont to do when Tipsy asked herself questions. *He doesn't seem like the type to quit until he gets a real answer.*

Tipsy leaned her forehead against the wall. It was covered in pages from Poe's books, all shellacked into place. The complete works of E.A. Poe, flattened bathroom version. She stared at the type before her eyes until it came into focus.

I could not be sure that she was sane; and, in fact, there was a certain restless brilliancy about her eyes which half led me to imagine she was not.

She read it again before washing her hands and returning to the table. Will picked at his French fries and watched cars pass down Middle Street. He'd pushed his sunglasses back onto his head as it got cloudier. She sat down. "I've got to tell you something."

"Okay." He faced her. "I thought you might."

"You're going to think I'm crazy."

He scowled, and looked very much like the Will of her first passing meeting with him. As if she'd never discovered tenderness hidden under his glare. "Just tell me. Don't drag it out."

"You know how we went out to the Old Cannon to ask Mrs. Childress about Jane and Henry Mott?"

"Yeah. The people who were killed in your house."

"The man in the paintings. The sleeping man, and the one on the joggling board. That's Henry Mott."

"Oh—okay. You painted it from the photo she gave you?"

Tipsy shook her head. "Not exactly. The woman in *Stepping off the Porch.* And also in *The Joggling Board.* That's Jane."

His eyes darted over the table, as if the explanation could be found amidst the condiments. "Did you find some other old pictures of them in the attic?"

223

She shook her head again. "No. I painted them as I saw them."

"What do you mean? They've been dead for decades."

"They are dead. But I painted them as I saw them."

Comprehension dawned on his face. "Are you saying you saw them in the house? Like ghosts or something?"

She nodded.

His brow furrowed to the point where it looked as if someone had tried to sew his eyebrows together. Then he laughed. "Gimme a break, Tipsy."

"I'm serious. They haunt my house."

"And you can see them?"

"I've been able to see ghosts my whole life. My grandmother saw them, too."

"You really think these people are in your house? Ghosts walking around—like…" He held up his hands and wiggled his fingers. "Boooooo!"

She flinched. "Jeez, Will. You asked how I saw those paintings. I'm trying to tell you the truth."

"You expect me to believe that the people in those paintings are ghosts? They look like regular people."

"That's how they look to me! Not like bloody sheets or something! This isn't an episode of Scooby-Doo."

He laughed again, and Tipsy thought she might cry. "No—this is real life. That's what this is." He threw his napkin on the plate. "If you have some other guy coming around, you don't need to lie to me about it and make up some crazy story. I don't like people lying to me."

"I'm not lying to you!" she said. "I've never told anyone! Not Shelby. Not even Ayers."

"So why would you tell me?"

"Because I thought I could. I thought you—you loved me and you'd understand. Or at least try to understand. Guess I'm wrong."

"First, I'm not ready to say I love you yet."

His words hit her like a fist.

"Maybe I would have been soon…but now…man, this is bullshit." He stood and threw a fifty on the table. "I have to go back to work. I'll talk to you later." As he waited to cross the street, he pulled a round green can from his pocket and stuffed a wad of dip into his mouth.

Although she sat outside, several hundred yards from the wide-open ocean, Tipsy felt as if all the air had left the vicinity of her lungs. A man in a tank top with a swirly gray mustache approached her table, a middle-aged seagull swooping in on an opening basket. "You leaving, sweetheart?"

She asked the server for the check, stuck Will's fifty in her purse, and put the bill on her credit card. She didn't want him paying for her lunch after his reaction to her candor. It felt like charity dolled out to a mental patient. She'd give the money back to him next time she saw him.

If I see him. Why did I tell him?

Ain't your fault, sweetheart. You did the right thing. Maybe Will Garrison has his own ghosts. The kind no one can see, not even the likes of you and me.

———•———

Since Will's first appearance in the GQB, nearly two months past, Tipsy hadn't gone a day without communicating with him. The past few weeks, she'd spent all of her kid-free time with him, when she wasn't painting. As the hours since their argument stretched into two days, the sadness around her got thicker and clingier. She felt as if she were walking through a bog. Hopefully by the time the children returned from

Disney she'd be over Will Garrison and able to give them the genuine smiles they had the right to expect from their mother.

Saturday evening found her on the front porch. She'd finished *The Joggling Board* and safely delivered it to the GQB that morning. In the piece, Jane and Henry sat on the board, stark white walls behind them. Somehow, the emotions Tipsy had felt in their past—Jane's humiliation and sadness, and Henry's flummoxed rage—were conveyed in their anxious, staring eyes and the awkward tension that writhed and squirmed in the empty air between them. Shelby referred to it as Masterpiece Number Three.

She had no new painting ideas, so she had nothing to work on. In the moment, she didn't feel anxious about it. Just terribly sad. She'd set up a new bank account for potential attorney's fees. She'd saved twenty-five hundred dollars, so far. Ayers's attorney, Clark Middleton, was an old friend of Tripp's. He was the most expensive, and feared, divorce lawyer in town. She knew through the grapevine that he charged six hundred dollars an hour, and took a minimum ten-thousand-dollar retainer. She needed a lot more than two grand and some change to hire anyone who could realistically challenge him.

She had a couple weeks before she absolutely had to reply to Ayers's Summons and Complaint. If she didn't get any new painting ideas, or if she didn't sell any paintings she managed to produce, or if she failed to win the lottery, she'd have to clean out her meager savings. Granna's remaining life insurance money.

I can't think of a better use for it, said Granna.

I know. Thank you. But once that's gone, I have zero safety net. And before I know it, I'll have to start paying rent somewhere. What am I going to do?

She sensed Granna humming reassurance, but she didn't have a concrete answer any more than Tipsy did.

Her phone dinged. She read a text from Lindsey. She and P.D. were at Saltwater Cowboys for drinks, but Lindsey awkwardly hinted that Will would join them. Hence, while things between them were on the rocks, Tipsy was out. It hurt Tipsy's feelings, but didn't surprise her. P.D. and Will had been friends forever, and Lindsey always stepped back and let P.D. run the social show. Shelby was also MIA — she'd been on the boat with her brother all day— she was already in bed.

Tipsy replied to Lindsey, *No problem! Y'all have fun!* ☺.

She wasn't feeling gregarious anyway. She shut off her phone once she'd talked to the kids, so she couldn't check for a text or a missed call from Will. She rested her bare toes on the coffee table and pushed the rocking chair back and forth. The now familiar creak of wicker on wood brought her some comfort, and her headache was blessedly in submission. She sipped a Bud Light and nibbled on Cheez-its. Her remaining appetite had gone sailing out the window with her relationship, but she'd never been able to turn down those salty orange squares.

Jane blinked into existence on the other rocking chair. "Why are you sad?" she asked. Her hands twirled in her lap. "I thought— perhaps you'd like to talk. Connie and I used to talk about our troubles. But I understand if you don't, and I'll go."

Tipsy sighed. Her other friends were busy, but she still had one with a willing ear. She'd done some research, and Ayers couldn't legally break into her house and record her talking without her knowledge. One person in a conversation had to be aware of the recording. The fact that no one could else could hear the other side of her conversations would probably pose some interesting legal questions, but the principles were sound. She'd be damned if she was going to let Ayers take every bit of comfort from her.

For good measure, she asked Jane, *have you and Henry seen Ayers, or anyone else, come into the house when I'm not here? Come in and like, sniff around?*

Goodness, no. Never. Not even Miss Callie's son, Little Jimmy, who is grown now.

Would you know if someone came in?

I sense when people come and go from this place. I believe Henry and I are almost part of its beams and walls, after all this time.

Tipsy stood. *Let's go inside.*

Jane nodded, and Tipsy went into the house. They sat in the living room—Jane's old parlor. Tipsy closed the blinds and turned on the table lamps. She waited for Jane to choose a spot, in one of the two club chairs, and she took the spot furthest from her, on the edge of the sofa. Hopefully, if Jane made any abrupt movements, Tipsy could back off before Jane touched her. There was no crackling fire in the fireplace, just some plastic ivy plants that Miss Callie must have stuck in there in the 1980s, but it was still cozy.

She told Jane the story of her argument with Will. Jane faded somewhat as Tipsy talked, as she often did when she thought hard on something, and Tipsy saw the fireplace through Jane's face. She went solid again when she spoke.

"That's a difficult circumstance, for I can see how many people would have the same reaction." She corrected herself. "The *disbelief.* Not the anger about it."

"I've never seen that side of him. So defensive. And I never would have imagined he'd disappear like this."

"I'm *certain* he'll make amends. And if he does not, he's not the man you want. Y'all aren't meant to be if he can't accept your truth. I know that's easier for me to say than for you to believe." Jane pulled one bare foot up under her body. The other one bounced above the

Oriental rug, a pale pendulum. "Have you kept this secret *all your life*, about seeing the dead?"

"It wasn't so hard when my Granna was alive. We could speak about it, since she saw the same things."

"Could your mother have seen us?"

Tipsy shook her head. "Granna says it skips a generation. My mother, no. My kids, no. But I'll watch for my grandchildren. I don't want them to feel afraid and alone."

"I didn't know Henry saw such apparitions until after we died. I was so *frightened* when I found myself in this state. But Henry wasn't even *surprised*. As if he'd always thought he'd linger on for all eternity."

"How exactly did you come to believe Henry killed you both?"

"Well, in those first few weeks we actually got on better than we had in *years*. Neither of us knew what had happened, and we had only each other for comfort. It seemed a blessing. A warped one, but a blessing nonetheless."

"It brought you back together."

"Yes. The house was empty, except for a maid who came and went, and she never said a word. It wasn't the *simplest* thing, coming from the peninsula to Mount Pleasant, in those days. The ferry."

"Right." Sometimes Tipsy forgot that Charlestonians had once vacationed in the Old Village. Mount Pleasant wasn't a suburb in Jane's day. It was a destination. "Y'all didn't go into town very often, did you?"

"We went more than most of our neighbors. I always stayed overnight with my parents. I often left Henry at home. He had trouble getting away from the warehouses."

"I can't see Henry in a warehouse."

Jane nodded her agreement. "He *hated* going to that place. He complained that it smelled of barley and spilled vinegar. Henry had traveled all over the *world*. Charleston itself had become a village to him. Our marriage deteriorated faster when we moved to this side of the Cooper. Henry hated the neighbors, and I had trouble befriending *anyone* with a well-known sour puss for a husband. I tried going to church, to Saint Andrew's Chapel, but I missed St. Philip's. It didn't have to be unpleasant. We had a beautiful home. We could walk on the beach or to the post office, or to Patjen's Grocery Store. But all Henry saw were the muddy streets and the neighbors' chickens and barefoot children."

"It's amazing how much it's changed," said Tipsy. "Nowadays, this is one of the nicest neighborhoods in the state."

Jane defended her adopted hometown, even if its rural character had probably contributed to the collapse of her marriage, and hence her death. "Even then, people were friendly and things were slowly changing. More shops. Better roads. I heard tell of the new bridge a few years after we died. The new owners spoke of it."

"Grace Memorial," said Tipsy.

"And then another bridge after that, and then both of them torn down for that great huge thing." She pointed in the direction of the Ravenel Bridge. "If Henry and I had lived, we would have seen Mount Pleasant go from country to town to a right little *city*. But that wasn't meant to be."

Tipsy returned to her original line of questioning. "So you heard about your deaths from someone here in the house?"

"Finally Mama and Constance came to the house to sort through our belongings. I heard Mama say she'd not been able to face the task. I followed them through the house. Henry joined me, although he'd never been partial to either of them. He thought they were silly, with all their gossip and trading of recipes and dress patterns. But we were both desperate to know that the world still went on."

"And you heard them speak of the murder?"

Jane nodded. "They carried on about it from one room to the next. They cried on the front porch, sobbed on the first floor, and wailed when they went upstairs. They said Henry stole me from them. They called him a brute and a monster. Me shot through the heart, and him through the head. And over and over, they lamented over the pistol found in his hand. They speculated that it was all for money. Constance said money was the only reason he wanted to marry me at all. I don't really know if I ever really believed Henry did it for the money, but no matter the reason behind it..." Her almond shaped blue eyes, so pretty and sad, were teardrops turned sideways. "Henry kept saying, *No, no, Jane. I would never have hurt you. No matter what passed between us. I always loved you.* He screamed at my mother and sister that they were liars and frauds, only trying to save face in town."

Tipsy pictured them. Jane silent and mortified. Henry shouting his innocence to the rafters, unheard. "How awful."

"There's no other explanation, Tipsy. We had a hard time, those months before we died. So much unhappiness..." She trailed off, and Tipsy almost asked her about the affair. Jane had to remember it, if only the last week or so of her life had disappeared from her memory. Tipsy decided against it, however, because she couldn't come up with a viable reason why she knew about Jane's indiscretions.

"I wish I could help you," said Tipsy.

Jane smiled. "You have helped me. By being my friend. I haven't had one in many a year."

"Do your feet get cold? They're always bare."

Jane shook her head. "No. I can see and smell and hear, but I cannot taste. Or feel."

"But you still feel—" Tipsy put her hand over her heart. "Here."

"Oh yes," said Jane. "Those kind of feelings never go away. I wish they would. I wish I could forget everything, not only that last week of my life."

"It does seem unfair." Henry sat in the other chair with his legs splayed out before him and his hands laced behind his head. His casual posture made Tipsy cautiously optimistic that, like the last time he'd joined them on the porch to watch the children, he'd come for a chat, not a battle. "That we should be forced to remember how despondent we were before we died." He smiled. "Good evening, ladies. It's a lovely one, isn't it? Tipsy, I'm so pleased you've decided to speak with us again."

"I still have to be careful, but—"

"We weren't *always* despondent," said Jane. "That is to say, *I* wasn't always despondent."

"We had some enjoyable moments, true. I recall our wedding day as reasonably pleasant."

So far, Tipsy had only seen Jane as the reactionary, on the defensive from Henry's attacks. This time, however, she sensed that whether Henry meant to or not, he was starting to piss her off.

"I begged my father to allow us to marry for months. My parents hosted the wedding of the year. You shed tears of joy on the alter, and gave a speech claiming to be the happiest, luckiest man alive. Yet you remember it as *reasonably pleasant?*"

Oh, Jesus. Here we go. "Jane— it's a nice night—can't we just—"

Henry leaned forward, his elbows on his knees, with the beginnings of a smirk on his face. "No, Tipsy, let the little lady have her tantrum. Go on, Jane. Show us some of that dramatic talent for which you were *so famous* in life."

"Why must you be so infernally mean? I know what Tipsy and her friends would call you." Her pale face flushed purple. She looked

232

heavenward, as if afraid her mother might hear her. "You're— you're an *asshole!*"

"How ladylike. And poetic."

"You're the one who is supposed to be able to write poetry. Not me." Jane's eyes

narrowed, and she went in for the kill. "*You never actually wrote anything*. Nothing worthwhile, anyhow."

Jane and Henry stood over her, ranting and raving. Tipsy pressed her fists into her eyes. Soon Jane would cry, and Henry would probably chuck the table lamps across the room. The thought of sweeping up broken porcelain and explaining to Jimmy what happened to his mama's lamps pushed Tipsy over the edge.

"Would y'all shut up, please?" she said, as she stood. "I am so freakin' sick of listening to you! Both of you!"

Jane and Henry froze, agog.

"Why should I even risk talking to y'all? One minute it's a pleasant chat, and the next you're about to kill each—uh—" She threw her hands up in frustration. "You know what I mean. You're worse than my kids! I swear— it's like living in a war zone. You've been around for over a hundred years. You both need to get over yourselves and *grow up!*"

"Tipsy— darling, I'm so sorry—"

"How rude of me—"

They both disappeared, and reappeared even closer to her. As they pressed in, Tipsy tried to shrink. She wrapped her arms around her head. She was freezing. Their smells, mint and lemon, filled her nose, like she's taken a deep drag off a cold cup of Thera-flu.

"Okay—please, ya'll, give me some space."

Still they hovered around her, appearing and disappearing, so she couldn't focus on either of their anguished, imploring faces. Her knees buckled. As she reached for the floor, her hand passed through one of Henry's shiny black shoes.

———•———

At first she doesn't know what happened—she's back on the porch. But then Tipsy notices that the furniture is different. It's wrought iron with red beaded cushions, not wicker with upholstered green and white seashells. There are no ceiling fans. The flowers in the tall pots surrounding the furniture are in varying stages of dying.

Jane and Henry sit across from one another. She's perched on the edge of a rocking chair. His chair is stationary. Two cups of untouched tea sit beside a floral china teapot on a narrow glass-topped table. The tabletop is a transparent moat that Henry seems to want to cross.

"Are you cold?" he asks Jane.

She shakes her head and pulls the heavy woolen shawl tighter around her shoulders. It's gray with purple stripes and has numerous pockets. Tipsy wonders if Jane knitted it herself. She cannot see the rest of Jane's clothes, for both feet are tucked up under her. She looks like a thin, female Buddha, or a tribal shaman waiting to hear a spiritual request. Dark circles ring her eyes.

"Thank you for letting me come home," Henry says.

"You're welcome." It's a harsh whisper in a hoarse voice. From yelling, or crying.

"Jane...I..." Henry leans toward her with his hands on his knees. He wears the same white shirt Tipsy has always seen him in, and she wonders if he has shirts in any other color, but his trousers are dark brown. "I've thought long and hard on your request for a divorce."

Jane nods.

"I was so angry, but I've realized I had no right to rage against you, as you called it."

Jane blinks but says nothing.

"I'm—" His voice catches, and he swallows a harsh sob, so the sound that comes out of his mouth is something like the bark of a dog trapped in a tight muzzle. "I'm so sorry. I've treated you horribly. Abysmally."

"Pardon?"

He rushes on. "What husband tells his wife to seek another man's arms? I cannot understand how I said such words to you. I've been so consumed by my work. My—let's say true. My inability to work. I've had enough time to produce five novels. I have nothing."

She tugs at the shawl. "I bothered you…distracted you—"

"No, dearest. You only asked of me to pay you some mind and treat you kindly."

She sucks in a hitching breath. "I would have spoken on anything you thought important. I would have read your work, or talked of novels. I love books."

"Do you? Of course you do. I should have asked for your opinion." He covered his face with both hands. "I was so cruel to you, at Johnny's last party. It pains me to admit it, but couldn't stand to see everyone celebrate you. They say there's a loving woman behind every great man. I couldn't bear to face the fact that in our case, I'm the man behind the great woman. Without the loving part."

"I shouldn't have brought up your book that night. I made it worse. I'm sorry."

"Jane. Please. I'm begging you. Do not ever apologize to me again for my own boorish behavior."

His appeasement so differs from the shocked fury of her last memory visit. Tipsy finds it hard to process, as if those old feelings still linger in her veins. She has not yet flushed his rage from her system. Two Henrys are competing for firepower in her emotional arsenal. It's creepily unpleasant, and for the first time, she's ready for the memory to end before it does.

A few minutes pass with only the chirping of fall crickets. "Will you not say anything?" he asks.

"I don't know what to say."

"I'm asking you to forgive me. Give me a chance to show you that I can be different."

"Oh, Henry—"

"If you truly do not love me anymore…if this other man has stolen you from the fool I was…I will grant you the divorce you want. I'll find a way. Even if I have to leave the state. If I can finally make you happy by ending our marriage, I will."

Jane covers her face with her hands. "I don't know—I don't. I'm so confused, and I'm not the same person you dismissed so casually."

"Dear God, what I wouldn't give to change that. To pummel the ass that I was." He reaches over the table and rests his hands on her lap. "Will you think on it?"

She nods, her face still hidden. "I will, but I need some time alone. I think I shall go into town and stay with my parents. Just for a night. Maybe two."

He sits back. "As you wish. You won't hear from me until you choose to tell me your decision. And I shall sleep in one of the guest rooms tonight. But…can we sit here, for a while? Maybe until the sun goes down."

She nods. "Yes. It's a lovely one tonight, don't you think?"

To Tipsy's relief, Henry's reply is muffled, meaning she's heading back to her own life.

"Yes," Henry says, as the porch disappears. "Lovely."

Chapter 10

On Monday afternoon, as she drove Mary Pratt and Olivia Grace to acting camp after dropping Little A at the surfing camp bus stop, Tipsy peeked over her shoulder at the twins in the middle row of seats. They stared out their mutual windows, reverse mirror images of the same child. She took a sip of Coke. She'd downed her morning Tylenol, so the headache from her Saturday night trip down memory lane was in remission, but this qualified as her longest lasting spectral hangover so far. To borrow some mommy-speak, her tummy was still not happy. She hadn't eaten much since the Cheez-its. She made a mental note to force herself to choke down something of substance later today. Her butt and boobs were deflating faster than week-old helium balloons.

"Let's hear more about Disney, girls," Tipsy said. She held in a burp. "Mary Pratt, you still didn't tell me which ride you liked best."

"Peter Pan," Mary Pratt said.

"Me too," said Olivia Grace.

Tipsy pushed her sunglasses onto her head. Sometimes she envied the numerical distribution of other families, for she firmly believed the third kid put you over the edge. You were brutally outnumbered, and as Tipsy's Sociology 101 course had taught her, triads are notoriously unstable. Two against one seemed to be the permanent dynamic among her kids.

She'd fully expected one to pick It's a Small World and one to go with Thunder Mountain. The discrepancy should have come along with an argument in which one yodeled *It's a world of laughter, a world of tears* while her sister hollered at her to *Staaaaap!*

"Girls, what's up? Are y'all still tired from the trip?" They'd only come home the night before. "Maybe I should have kept you home today. Or y'all can come to the gallery with me."

Olivia Grace said, "I want to go to camp."

"Okay. If that's what you want."

"Mama?" said Mary Pratt. "Why don't we all live in one house anymore?"

Tipsy turned off the radio, silencing Rhianna mid-caterwaul. "We've talked about this before, M.P. Mommy and Daddy are still friends, but we decided it's best for us not to be married anymore. Sometimes that happens with mommies and daddies. It's a hard choice, but we hope everyone will be better for it."

"Daddy said you started it. You told him he had to go live in that apartment. Then when you moved to Miss Callie's, he got to come back to our house."

"Did you hate our house?" asked Olivia Grace.

"No. I didn't hate our house. Why would you ask that?"

"Daddy said you hated it."

"Okay..." Tipsy pulled onto the frontage road on Route 17, the main thoroughfare through Mount Pleasant. She passed multiple law firms, most advertising specialties in family law, before pulling into a pawn shop parking lot. She put the truck in park and turned around. "What else did Daddy say?"

"He said you stopped loving him." Mary Pratt's big brown eyes were pools of brackish worry. "Are you going to stop loving us, too? Me and O-Liv and Ayers?"

Tipsy got out of the car and opened the back door. She wrapped one arm around Mary Pratt, and reached for Olivia Grace with the other.

"Sweet girls, never, never ever. That will never happen. I will always love both of you, and your brother."

"But you don't love Daddy," said Olivia Grace.

Tipsy bit back her anger and said what her girls needed to hear. "Your Daddy is a special guy. He loves y'all. I've known him for many years, and I will always love him, as my friend. But that does not mean I'm going to be married to him."

"Not ever?" asked Mary Pratt. "He said maybe you would. Get married again."

Tipsy straightened. "No, girls. Daddy and I won't ever be married again."

Mary Pratt's lip trembled, and Olivia Grace turned toward her window. She spoke over her narrow little girl's shoulders. "I don't like the new house so much, Mama. Sometimes it's happy and sometimes it's sad."

Tipsy reached across Mary Pratt's lap to touch her twin. "Most places are happy and sad, sweetheart, but I know what you mean."

Olivia Grace faced her mother. "Daddy said if we really don't like it, we can live with him. He told us we could. And then he talked about it with Mr. Middleton on the phone in the car."

"And y'all could hear him?"

O-Liv nodded. "It came through the speaker." Tears leaked over her eyelids. "But I don't want to live away from you. Not all the time."

Mary Pratt joined the conversation again. "Daddy isn't good at fixing our hair. Or putting on tights."

Tipsy squeezed each child's knee. "I promise y'all, I'm going to fix our house. Now, nothing is happy-happy-happy all the time, but you give me a bit and I'll make that big old house as happy as it can be."

M.P. nodded, but O-Liv wasn't finished.

"Daddy asks us a lot of questions about you, Mama," she said.

Tipsy squeezed the door handle. "Like what?"

"If you're real tired and sleeping a lot. If you're crying. I've never seen you cry, except when Elsa saved Anna."

Despite herself, Tipsy's lip twitched. That scene from *Frozen* always got her.

"And he asks about Mr. Will. I never know what to say."

"Hmmm. You know, grownups really shouldn't ask kids those kinds of questions," Tipsy said. "But you can ask me anything. Anytime y'all have questions about your daddy and me, and what's happening with our family, you just ask."

Both girls nodded, and Tipsy gave them her usual Pillsbury Dough Boy belly pokes, which elicited a few good giggles. She got back in the driver's seat and drove onto the main road.

"O-Liv, did you like Mini Mouse or Daisy Duck best?" asked Mary Pratt.

"Minnie."

"Daisy is better."

"No," said Olivia Grace.

"Yes."

"No! Mama—who is better?" Mary Pratt's face had reddened at her sister's nerve.

"Minnie is the best mouse and Daisy is the best duck," said Tipsy. "But what is Goofy?"

"A dog," said Olivia Grace, as Mary Pratt said, "A donkey."

"M.P., donkeys don't have round noses," said Olivia Grace.

"Dogs can't talk," countered Mary Pratt.

"Duh—neither can donkeys, poophead."

"O-Liv!" Tipsy said. "That is not nice. Where did you hear that?"

"Ayers," said both girls, and so it went.

Tipsy manned their bickering during the rest of the drive to acting camp. Their childish anger was a grain of sand compared to the ever widening beach of her animosity toward her ex-husband. As if the blatant attack of the custody case wasn't enough, he was actively involving the children in his grotesque maneuvering. She couldn't believe that he'd blame the divorce on her, after they'd both decided never to disparage one another in front of the children. She'd kept up her end of the bargain, but who knew how long Ayers had been throwing her under the bus? Never mind the years she'd subtly defended him to the children throughout their marriage.

Daddy is tired, y'all...let's be quiet.

Daddy will be home soon...let's make sure we clean up and make him proud of y'all for being such good helpers!

Daddy didn't mean to say that...he loves you to the moon and back!

And to give the girls hope that they might get back together... The adultery charge that Ayers had slammed on Tipsy not only got him out of paying her alimony, it allowed for a quickie three-month divorce, rather than the usual one year waiting period required under South Carolina law. In the throes of a rage against Tipsy that had rocked their family like the stomping strides of a fairy tale giant, he couldn't wait to be finished with her.

The thought that he'd planted the weed-like seed of the children living with him made her want to run over his foot with spiked tires. And she never imagined he'd stoop so low as to talk to his lawyer about it in front of them, or, God forbid, ask them questions about her mental state and her personal life. By the time she dropped the girls at camp, they were both smiling and whispering *poophead* back and forth as if Tipsy couldn't hear them. Their mama, on the other hand, couldn't wait to give Ayers Lee Collins IV, a piece of her mind. Maybe enough time had finally passed for anger to outweigh guilt. The choice words she planned on using made *poophead* sound like a term of endearment.

•———•———•

Mimi invited all three kids to spend the night at her house for her daughter's birthday, so on Thursday, Tipsy had a rare mid-week evening off. By the time she got off work, she felt reasonably normal— no headaches or nausea— but not strong enough to go to the gym or go for a run. She still hadn't come up with an idea for a new painting. In retrospect, the financial pressure she'd felt before she moved into Miss Callie's seemed trite compared to today's burden. Her poor kids were getting sucked into the mess, so she might have to budget for therapy for them, too.

Even though she knew it was unimportant in the big picture of financial survival and keeping her kids, she still hadn't talked to Will, and it hurt more than she cared to admit. It freaked her out to realize how quickly she'd come to rely on him, as if he were already a permanent fixture in her life. Everything felt dangerously out of her control.

As she drove over the Ravenel Bridge, she longed for something she could act on—something she could fix. She kept coming back to Jane and Henry. If she could figure out their problem, at least she'd be able to exist in Miss Callie's house without feeling like she lived in a vintage, spectral episode of *The Jerry Springer Show*. Plus, she felt guilty about losing it on Jane and Henry the other night. No matter what her lot in life was right now, it was not as bad as theirs was in death.

Granna had suggested she find another way to help them. And maybe another way to get some painting inspiration. Her last accidental visit to Jane and Henry's past had given her more insight into their lives and their emotions, but so far, nothing solid had taken shape in her imagination and demanded to be transferred to canvas. An idea dawned on her. A possible means to both ends.

She kept going down Coleman Boulevard, past Shem Creek, and drove out to Sullivan's. Dark clouds swirled over her head as she parked at station fourteen. Proctor said the Huger's cottage sat on the southern end of the island, in the area known as Moultrieville, where the oldest homes clustered around stations eleven and twelve. More history surrounded those early cottages: old Stella Maris Catholic Church, the Revolutionary War-era battalion of Fort Moultrie, and historic officers and soldiers' quarters that had been renovated into private homes and condos.

Tipsy had learned a good bit about Sullivan's on multiple school field trips to Fort Moultrie. She'd kept one ear in the guide's monologue, while trying to wrangle Little A and his buddies into paying attention. About 400,000 enslaved Africans had passed through Sullivan's, during the years it served as a quarantine zone. Those who had miraculously survived the Middle Passage, and were still deemed healthy enough, were forced on to the great tragedy of the old slave market downtown, giving historians good reason to liken the fort to a sad sort of southern Ellis Island. Early in the Revolutionary War, the colonists successfully defended Charleston from the British during the battle of Fort Sullivan. One of the most popular restaurants on the Island, the Obstinate Daughter, was named after an English political cartoon of the day, which likened the American rebels to England's stubborn progeny.

The Huger place had to be around here somewhere, but she hadn't been able to find any records of where it stood, if it still existed. Maybe it had washed away in some long ago storm, or been bulldozed, or the land had been partitioned in the chaos of what passed for zoning on the Island. She figured John Huger had most likely drowned close to his parents' house. If he happened to be lingering, a la the rest of her ghostly friends, she'd find him along this beach.

You sure you don't want to come back another day, sugar? Asked Granna. *Tide's already pretty durn high.*

It's my only free night this week, Tipsy replied.

So how 'bout next week then? Storm's coming too. Thunder rumbled overhead. A light drizzle started in to boot, as if Mother Nature decided to back up Granna's position. *And what about the PI? Maybe he's lurking.*

People walk this beach in the evening all the time. There's nothing weird about it. Even in the rain.

But the thunder—

And I don't want to wait that long. Tipsy sensed Granna taking a breath to reply. *Don't say anything about how long he's been out here and how he ain't goin' nowhere.*

Hmph. Granna sounded miffed, but Tipsy didn't care. The need to find John Huger, and have him answer her questions, overpowered her. His memories of those days would surely provide some clarity for Jane and Henry. If he was the killer, perhaps he'd even admit it. As a ghost, what would he have to lose?

And maybe, just maybe, talking to John would give Tipsy a new painting idea, without having to risk a trip back in time.

You talked to Proctor, and Luisa. They gave you nothin', said Granna.

Tipsy clung to her plan. *They were just remembering gossip and rumors. If John loved Jane, or was actually there when they died, who knows what I could glean from talking to him? Maybe something even purer than Jane and Henry's memories. Maybe I'll see a painting of John himself.*

I suppose. Granna did not sound convinced. *Don't seem like talking can equate with peekin' in someone's head.*

Tipsy's flip flops ground into the sand, kicking up rough grains onto the back of her calves as she plowed her way toward the ocean.

The wind picked up, grabbing at her ears, trying to pull her back. She sensed Granna's disapproval, heavy at the base of her skull. Tipsy, the Obstinate Granddaughter.

The beaches around Moultrieville suffered more erosion issues than those on the middle of the island. Breach Inlet battered the north end. The south end wrapped around toward the harbor, where multiple rivers flowed into the sea. The town and the property owners had set up stone jetties and retaining walls to defend the dunes and private property, and once the tide came in, there would be no beach left for Tipsy to wander. The waves would smack against the rocks and retaining walls. A huge, permanent sign warned of the dangers of the currents— SEVERAL DROWNINGS, DON'T BE NEXT.

So better get going, if you're going to do it, said Granna.

So Tipsy walked the beach. She cleared her mind of everything but John Huger's handsome face. She listened to the complicated rhythm of her heartbeat, the switch-switch of her flip flops on wet sand, and the wind jumping from one side of her head to the other as she craned her neck for any sign of a ghostly glow.

John Huger? Are you here? I need to talk to you. Do you remember Janie? She needs your help.

She walked as far as station nine and turned around, into the wind. Grains of sand stung her cheeks. The ocean slithered close, and then retreated in a babble of frothy giggles, as if Tipsy were playing tag with the waves and she was It. Lightning sizzled past the Ravenel Bridge, pale against the steel gray sky. For a few seconds, the bridge shone like the white skeleton of an abandoned fairy tale castle. A clap of thunder followed, making Granna jump. Her agitated presence rattled against the inside of Tipsy's skull along with the reverberating thunder.

The water is coming in.

As if it had been waiting on Granna's cue, the first wave of the in-coming tide, warm and deceptively pleasant, sloshed over Tipsy's feet. She picked up the pace, and looked at her phone. She'd tucked it into her bra to avoid the rain, but it was wet anyway, like the rest of her. She'd been walking for over forty-five minutes.

You got to get off this beach.

Just a little longer, Granna. I can find him. Tipsy climbed over a jetty. She leaned down to keep her balance on the slippery rocks. A gull screamed at her. She jumped onto the sand and kept walking. She passed the sign for Station 13.

Tiffany! This beach is three miles long. The man could have died any-where along here. He might not even be out here! You know most people go on. They don't linger. Perhaps John Huger drowned and went on to his death with not a worry on his rich, spoiled, pretty boy soul.

How could he go to his death peacefully, if he had a part in Jane's death?

She jumped as water covered her feet. When the waves came in, they hit mid-calf. The clouds above her head opened up, swollen gray water balloons pierced by the lightning prongs slicing the sky. Even if John Huger appeared, she might not be able to see him, unless his appearance coincided with a lightning strike.

She screamed for him inside her own mind, compelling him to come forward and solve her problems for her. Give her information that would bring peace to her home, and end her friends' eternal speculation. She willed him to appear in front of her—the perfect model for her next painting, complete with handsome face and turbulent emotions and the beautiful background of the restless sea.

She could almost see it in her mind. But it wasn't right. She could paint from her imagination—she could draw anything, and draw it perfectly, if she had to. Even during her painter's block. But her best work—her *realest* work— had always come from *seeing* her paintings through the lens of her unexplainable mental camera. If she painted John Huger without it, the emotions would be hers, not his. The perspective would be off, even if the ocean perfectly met the horizon.

And the result certainly wouldn't be up to par with her last three paintings. Panic seized her. What if she could never paint again, without supernatural influence?

Tipsy yelled, and pleaded, and finally cursed at John Huger.

You killed them! That's why you're hiding. Show yourself and own it!

Nothing.

Worse yet, she didn't sense any ghosts, anywhere. She thought her calling might rouse other spirits, for there had to be some lingering on this stretch of sand, between the soldiers and the slaves who had died here. What if there was something wrong, or her powers weren't working at all, and no one could hear her?

Or maybe whatever other ghosts haunt this beach don't give a damn you're out here. This is plain stupid, Tipsy! Tipsy hadn't felt Granna's anger in decades.

She stopped. The water rose up her legs and deluged down on her head. She strained to see something— anything— in the cloudy dampness around her. She stood in the water like a lightning rod, with the irritable ocean tickling her thighs, and a wall of unforgiving boulders between herself and the nearest footpath out of here. She noticed her teeth were chattering.

She thought: *The wind came out of the clouds by night, chilling and killing my Annabel Lee.*

Tipsy realized she'd lost her breath, as if she'd been running. She looked at her phone again. She was lucky it was still working. She'd been out here, pacing around on the beach for almost two hours. Not only was she risking life and limb, she was potentially giving the PI good fodder at this point. Only a crazy person would put herself in this position. *I gotta get out of here.*

The water rose above her knees. She waded toward the closest boulder. Her toes caught painfully in rocky crevices. Barnacles scratched her palms and snagged her clutching fingernails. One of her flip flops slipped off. It floated away before she could grab it.

She clambered into the tall grass atop the boulders. Tipsy stood on the dune overlooking the water, bent over and gasping, with tears and rain streaming down her cheeks. She looked around, but saw no one in the dunes, or along the path to the beach. The downpour had muted the edges of the footprints on the path, and no fresh tracks disturbed the wet sand. She prayed that if the PI had followed her out here, the weather had chased him away before things got too weird.

Sugar, you beat the tide, but you could still lose to the lightning.

Tipsy's obstinate side had come out on that beach, along with a heaping side of (hopefully undocumented) crazy, but unlike the rebellious colonists, she didn't play the stubborn offspring for long. She listened to her Granna, and hauled ass out of there.

●————•————●

Once she got home and dried off, Tipsy picked up her phone to touch base with Shelby. She stared at the name on the screen as if she'd forgotten how to read.

Will Garrison Text Message

She swiped the screen and read his message, sent over an hour ago, *Can I come by tonight once the kids are asleep?*

They're at Mimi's for a sleepover. You can come over now. I'll leave the front door open.

She brushed her teeth and hair and sat at the kitchen table. She decided against jumping in the shower. If he didn't want to see her messy after a day of running the kids around, working, and ghost hunting, and if he couldn't accept the circles under her eyes that missing him had put there, screw him.

The front door creaked and Will called out, "Hello?"

"I'm in here," Tipsy said.

He sat across from her. She searched his face, but he betrayed nothing, aside from his eternally furrowed brow. He folded his hands in front of him on the table. "So, I guess I should tell you something, too. If you want to hear it."

She nodded.

"Remember how I said I made the final decision on ending my marriage?"

Tipsy nodded again.

"It's because I found out...my wife got fired from her job. For stealing pain medication out of the dispensary at Greater Mount P Regional."

"Jeez—"

"She was addicted. Percocet and Vicodin, mostly, but sometimes she got a hold of OxyContin. Her boss called me while I was out on a job site and told me she'd been caught. I confronted her about it, and it all came out."

"How does she work as a nurse now?"

"She didn't work for almost a year. Because of her father's friendship with her boss she didn't lose her license. Her dad begged the guy not to press charges. So nothing came of it legally, thank god."

"That must have been rough on you and the kids."

"You have no idea. Once I understood the reality, it was so obvious. All her evasiveness, and how she seemed confused and forgetful sometimes. Depressed, too. She called in sick to work a lot the previous year. I'd blamed it all on our marriage problems." He rubbed his jaw. "It

249

took her over six months to get clean. She'd stop taking the pills for a week or so…and she'd be crying and sweating and had muscle pain and headaches. Then she'd fall back off the wagon. She had them hidden all over the house. Even buried in the freakin' backyard."

Tipsy pictured Will scouring his house for hidden envelopes of pills.

"I couldn't leave the girls with her. My mother came up from Beaufort to help, and her parents were there all the time, too. Finally, I couldn't take it. I moved out with the girls, into a two-bedroom apartment. That's when she joined NA—you know, Narcotics Anonymous, like AA for drug addicts. She wanted me to come back, but I was so far gone then…"

"I can't imagine. Why didn't you tell me?"

He shrugged. "It's kind of embarrassing for me. And I'm embarrassed for her. She has it together now. She goes to NA meetings all the time, and has another job. In a doctor's office, so she doesn't make the kind of money she used to make, but she's stayed clean. She really is a good mom. I feel sorry for her. And guilty that I couldn't make myself try."

"I know that feeling."

"I can't believe I didn't see what she was doing. Was I that stupid, or naïve? Or too caught up in work and fishing and hunting to realize my wife was killing herself right before my eyes?"

"You trusted her."

"I know—but, God help me, I will never be that clueless again. I put my kids in danger because I had my head too far up my own ass to see that everything she said to me was a lie. And it's not just that. I— like you so much, Tipsy. You're smart, and funny, and you're a great mom from what I see. Your artwork is amazing. And you're beautiful, to boot. You're the total package."

She appreciated the compliment, but sensed something unpleasant behind it.

"I want this to work out," he said. "But also— I— damnit."

"Go ahead."

"I still want to hunt and fish."

She shrugged. "I never said you can't hunt or fish."

"I know you didn't. It's more than that though. Even if it was a huge part of my marriage falling apart, I like the freedom to hunt and fish when I feel like it. Or go barhopping when I get the urge. Or even take the boat to freakin' Morris Island and party my ass off like a college kid every once in a while. I know you don't want to do that stuff."

"No. I really don't."

"And the bullshit with Ayers— part of me is like, do I really want to deal with that? Worrying about some asshole causing drama? Not being able to go out because you can't?"

As it had at Poe's, that stung. "You don't have to stay home because of me."

"I feel terrible even admitting I think like that. I start to feel trapped, even if you're not trying to rein me in. Sometimes, I don't want to answer to anyone. Except my girls, of course. What does that say about me?"

"It says you're like a lot of guys."

"I feel like a selfish asshole."

She tried to lighten the mood. "At least you realize you're a selfish asshole. That says you're *not* like a lot of guys."

"Maybe I'm not capable of giving a woman what she deserves."

Tipsy's heart sunk. It seemed like Will was giving her the *it's not you, it's me* speech. "So you want to stop seeing each other?"

"No. That's the thing. I don't. Maybe I'm just freaking out. I was married for years, and I feel like I've been single for a few minutes. We can slow it down some, but—can you be patient with me? I don't want to ruin this."

Tipsy took his hands across the table. "Yes. If you can be patient with me, too. If you've been single for minutes, I'm still at seconds. And I've never heard you talk so much in one sitting."

He exhaled, and Tipsy heard the relief in it. "Thank you. Now you know I can run off at the mouth like anyone else." He squeezed her hands. "Are you serious about this ghost stuff? You're really, truly serious?"

She nodded. "I swear it, Will. I would have checked myself into the nuthouse long ago if it weren't for my Granna confirming what I saw from the time I was a little girl. I wouldn't believe me either, but..." She dropped her voice to a whisper. "It's hard being crazy all by yourself. I'm sorry I burdened you."

He shook his head. "No—I'm sorry. I needed to think...and I..." He closed his eyes, as if self-imposed darkness might make it easier to admit to the reality she presented him. "I believe you."

"Perhaps I can be of assistance."

Tipsy looked up. Henry stood over them like a pale scarecrow. "You think? How?" she asked.

Will's eyes opened. "Who are you talking to?" His chair shot back from the table with a goose bump-inducing screech of wooden chair legs against rough tile. "Is there someone here with us right now?"

"It's okay—it's Henry."

"The murderer?"

"Stop, now—he's trying to help us."

Tipsy had left a notepad, preprinted with the motto "Stuff We Don't Really Need and Things I Don't Really Need to Do," on the table. A blue pen, ironically emblazoned with the name of Will's ex's former employer, Greater Mount Pleasant Regional Hospital, sat beside the pad of paper.

Henry flexed both hands, as if preparing for a clean and jerk. He picked up the pen with his left hand and flipped the pad of paper to a blank page.

"Holy shit," said Will. "That pen is floating."

"No—you can't see him. Henry is holding it."

"He can do that?"

She nodded. "Henry can. Jane can't."

Tipsy leaned toward the pad of paper. She beckoned to Will. "It's okay—he's trying to tell you something."

Henry's loopy script slowly filled the page. He held the pen as if it were the handle of a hot saucepan and he couldn't let go, lest he spill supper. She read around his clenching fingers.

Will,

Last night, when you tucked your two small daughters into bed, you sang them a song about wise men and fools who can't help falling in love. You kissed them goodnight and whispered something in their ears I couldn't quite hear. You asked the older girl about the book she was reading, and she said it was a story about rabbits who take a long journey to find a new home. She fell asleep with the book on her chest, and you placed it on the desk beside her bed and pulled the sheets up around her shoulders.

I watched you, because I know that Tipsy has been pining for you, and I want to know that you're worthy of her affections. After seeing you with your children, I think you are a good soul.

I will not come to you again. I'm sure the idea of me watching you is distressful, and I saw enough to believe in you. Help Tipsy by believing in me.

Henry Whitestone Mott

"Sweet Jesus," said Will.

The pen fell from Henry's hand. He grabbed at his wrist, and moaned. For the first time, he sounded straight out of Scooby-Doo.

"Thank you, Henry," she said. "Go, please, and rest."

He nodded and blinked out of existence.

Will pulled the sheet of paper closer and reread it. His finger traced Henry's words as if they were a pirate's directions on a treasure map. "That's exactly what happened last night."

"Are you angry at him for spying on you?"

Will rested his elbows on the table. "No. It definitely feels strange, but I'm not angry. He's looking out for you, after I acted like a jerk." He chuckled. "This is all so weird, Tipsy."

"I agree, wholeheartedly. It's totally, completely weird." She reached for his forehead and smoothed the lines between his eyes.

He leaned into her hands. "So, did you ever figure out if he killed his wife?"

"Not yet. I'm still working on it."

"Well, keep me in the loop. I want to know what happened," Will said. "If I decide to believe in something, damnit, I'm going to believe in it whole hog."

❦

The next night, once the kids were asleep, Jane appeared in Tipsy's bedroom. Tipsy made sure to close the curtains, and they sprawled beside one another on their stomachs, like two teenage girls at a slumber party. Tipsy broke her own rule against eating in bedrooms by nibbling Cheez-its.

"Those smell *interesting*," said Jane.

"Jeez, it's probably rude to eat in front of you."

"Not particularly. I'm not hungry, you see. And I don't know that I'd enjoy those. The color is rather *unnatural*."

Tipsy laughed. "You're so right. They're probably ninety percent food coloring and preservatives, but whatever. I'll go to Whole Foods and pick up some organics tomorrow."

Jane didn't ask for clarification. It seemed she'd gotten over their generationally garbled communication, as if Tipsy sometimes lapsed into short bursts of Chinese and Jane concentrated on the English phrases.

"I'm sorry I yelled at you and Henry the other night. I'm just so stressed out."

"I understand. Since we died, no one in the house has been able to hear us carrying on. We've forgotten our manners." Jane shrugged. "I'm glad you've made amends with your beau."

"Me too. Although... we'll see." Tipsy felt good about her conversation with Will, and happy they were going to keep seeing each other, but she now had a more realistic view of their relationship. In the grand scheme, she hardly knew him, and they both had a lot of baggage left to sort out from their marriages. Dating post divorce was a lot more complicated than getting up the nerve to ask someone to the KZ Fall Semi-formal. "It's so funny to hear you call him my beau. I love when you get all southern belle on me."

"I didn't use that term often, myself. Even for me it felt old-fashioned. But my mama did. She always referred to Daddy as her beau. It was *real sweet*."

"Did your parents love each other?"

"They did. Did yours?"

Tipsy shrugged. "I don't know. They're nutty. Both of them."

"Your grandmother raised you?"

Tipsy nodded. "Pretty much my whole life. We always lived with her. Mama and Daddy were there with me, until he took a job in Charlotte. But even then before they left..." Tipsy didn't feel the need to spray air freshener on a bag of memories that contained more than a few rotten tomatoes. "Honestly, my daddy is a redneck drunk. And Mama, she never got up the will to throw him out. They'd been together since they were fifteen, and they were nineteen when I was born. She didn't know life without him. She treated me as well as she could, but she's a flake."

This didn't pass Jane's language filter. "What's a flake?"

Tipsy had to think a moment. *Flake* was a term like *tacky*, or *frumpy*. Hard to explain, but you knew it when you saw it. "Someone who is weak, and has poor character. Someone you can't count on."

"Do you ever see them?"

"They missed my wedding. Ayers's parents paid for the whole she-bang, and let me tell

you, those were fun times." She rolled her eyes. "They did come to Charleston once, after Little Ayers was born. May Penny almost had a heart attack at the way Mama kept bouncing that baby on her knee. She thought Mama would give him brain damage, and for once I agreed with her. It was a disaster. I speak to her every six months or so. Never talk to my daddy. They still live around Charlotte somewhere."

"I'm surprised it doesn't call up more sadness in you."

"Granna made me who I am. She taught me right and wrong and made me feel safe. My parents leaving me paled in comparison to losing her." Tipsy laid her head on her pillow. "But because of what I am—how I can see and talk to you—I still feel close to her. I know she's still with me." Tipsy didn't elaborate. Maybe even a ghost would think she was crazy if she said she talked to spirits other dead people couldn't see.

Jane rested her head on her arm; their noses weren't but twelve inches apart. "What I wouldn't give to be close to *my mama* again." She closed her eyes. She didn't display the normal signs of sleep, like deep breathing or fluttering eyelashes.

Judging from the wintery weather in Tipsy's last few memory visits, the answer to the question that had dogged Jane and Henry for a century was just out of her reach. She hadn't been able to find John Huger, but maybe Jane could give her more clues.

And maybe something in whatever she saw would spark a new painting idea.

She thought twice before she acted. The kids were fast asleep. She lay on the bed, so she wouldn't risk a fall. Ten feet from the toilet, if she needed to throw up. She had a brand new, industrial sized-bottle of Tylenol to wipe out her inevitable residual headache.

Tipsy, like innumerable other women, had powered through her pregnancies in varying states of physical discomfort. Nausea. Headaches. Exhaustion. Hunger pains. Back pain. Hip pain. Swollen hands and feet. Constipation. Hemorrhoids. You name it, she'd dealt with it, with as much grace as she could muster, like every other mom. At the wire, Little Ayers came so fast, she pushed him out with no epidural. The twins had weighed over six pounds each, and she'd carried them to full term and popped them out, too. She'd sat in a sitz bath, her nether regions so inflamed that the thought of an adult male phallus made her want to scream in terror. She'd pumped her breasts when they felt like they might explode, and emotionally traumatized her with their turgidity for good measure.

When she put it that way, her recent headaches and queasiness seemed the smallest of potatoes. She was tough enough to handle another short voyage through time, to help Jane and Henry. And to search for painting ideas, to help her fight for her children.

Tipsy braced her mind, like she had on the afternoon when Jane walked through her in the foyer. This time, she focused hard on Jane's letters, and the enigmatic person on the other side of the correspondence. Once Jane fell into whatever state of quiet consciousness she needed to rejuvenate herself, Tipsy rested her hand against her friend's pale cheek.

———•———

This foyer isn't Miss Callie's house, but maybe it's the Old Cannon? An ornate wooden staircase towers above red and brown and black oriental rugs. There is a drippy crystal chandelier over Tipsy's head and a rounded bay window to her left. A quick look out the windows lets her know she's in the city, not the country. Antique-y cars sparsely line the cobblestone street. Tipsy presses her face against the pane. She can't feel the coolness of the glass, just pressure where she can go no further. The garden is familiar, although the trees are smaller, so everything feels more open. There are no climbing wisteria bushes, only a thick line of roses that are no longer in bloom. It's the Robinette house on Water Street.

Jane is huddled at a delicately carved wooden table by the landing. She sits, hunched like an old woman with a bad back, with the base of the phone in her lap and the receiver to her ear. She talks in frantic whispers, so Tipsy creeps close. She kneels by Jane's side. Her conversation flows by Tipsy, frustratingly one sided.

"I cannot come see you…yes, I remember what we talked about, and you had me convinced it could happen. Perhaps I just wanted it to be so… But he's right. The law makes it so difficult, and my parents will never— no, I haven't spoken to them about it yet."

The speaker on the other end must be going on, because Jane closes her eyes and grinds her teeth, and tears leak down her cheeks.

"No—nothing has changed. Or maybe it has—I don't know…" She pauses. "Please, keep calm. The party line—if anyone picks up… I'm not saying I won't…I need more time."

Again she goes silent. Tipsy can hear muffled bits of the other person's speech, but not one intelligible word.

"Please be patient with me," Jane says. "Yes—yes, but it's not so simple—don't speak to me so, please... Of course I forgive you. I'm sorry I'm making you so distraught."

She covers both ends of the phone and buries her hands in her lap. "Henry," she whispers.

And Tipsy can hear the person on the other line for a moment, a man's voice. "Jane? Jane!"

"I'm here...I am. Please give me a day or two." She asks her lover to be patient, just as she'd asked her husband. "I must have time to think."

More muffled talk, and then Jane says, "I'm going home tomorrow."

The man on the other end responds with a frantic, "No! No!"

"I have to go! You don't understand. There is so much at stake...yet you demand I rush ahead."

A woman's voice from an unseen room. "Janie? Darling—who are you talking to—and are you alright?"

"Yes, Constance—I'm speaking to Henry." She drops her head toward the table and whispers into the phone. "I must go. I'll speak to you as soon as I'm able." She hangs the phone on the hook and sets it back on the table. Frantic wiping of her face and straightening of her dress make her presentable before Constance walks around the corner.

Constance is taller than her sister and has lighter hair, but they have the same arresting blue eyes. "Does Henry have a telephone at his warehouse now?"

"What? No, why?"

"It's two o'clock in the afternoon, and you said you were speaking with him. I assumed he'd be at the warehouse."

"Oh—" Jane adjusts the phone on the center of the table and pushes the chair against the wall. "No—he has a touch of a head cold. So he stayed at home today. Pity I'm not there to care for him. So I'll be leaving in the *morning." She walks toward whatever room lays beyond the stairwell. A parlor, or perhaps a library.*

In this memory, the overriding emotion is guilt. Guilt for lying to Connie; guilt over putting off her lover; guilt over breaking her wedding vows; guilt for not being the person her parents think she should be. Strangely though, there's no regret in her contrition. She would do it all again if given the choice.

"Don't leave," says Constance. "You only just arrived."

"He's my husband, Connie, I have to look after him if he's ill."

"Of course you do. Although you'd better take care. I suspect he's a right bear when he's ill, that man."

"Stop, now. Have some compassion." Jane disappears from Tipsy's view. Constance follows close behind her, trailing a red silk shawl and a string of apologies.

Chapter 11

O n Monday, Lindsey followed Shelby and Tipsy from one exhibit room to the next while they dusted paintings and sculptures and adjusted lighting. Lindsey's daughter, Emma, was away at sleep-away camp in North Carolina for a week, so Lindsey had taken to popping into the GQB in the afternoons after she'd exhausted all her conversational options in Mount Pleasant. Lindsey's divorce settlement had rendered employment unnecessary. Apart from some part-time assisting of her interior designer when she had a wild hare, she really didn't do much of anything except gossip and go to the gym. Such a person normally would have annoyed Tipsy with her purposelessness, but she couldn't find it in her heart to begrudge Lindsey the life of leisure. Besides, she paid her dues in ten years of marriage to Barker, salacious old goat numéro uno.

Shelby kept up with the torrent of Lindsey's updates, but Tipsy found her mind wandering. She sipped her Coke and tried to eat a banana. A gross combo, but it settled her stomach. She dipped in and out of the conversation.

"...so, I finally figured out the deal with Mark and Jennifer—you know, the red Mercedes couple," said Lindsey. "It's her ex-husband's ex-wife's ex-husband's money."

"Say that again," said Shelby.

"There was a couple, and they got divorced...and she got his money. Then she got remarried, and then divorced, and he got the money. Then he married Jennifer and they got divorced, and she got his money, and then she married Mark. So they're living off money from a few marriage generations back."

"How much money did the first dude have?" asked Shelby.

Tipsy drifted away from them. She focused on an oil painting of an apple, a chickadee and a lamp, set against a night sky. An odd combination, but it worked. She admired the depth of color. She'd worked in oils in the past, when she didn't have a sense of urgency. She didn't have weeks, or even months depending on the layering of the paint, to waste on drying time.

"...you know him. Sergio. That tall skinny guy who docks his boat at Morgan Creek, on the Isle of Palms. He's there all the time. He's from Bulgaria, I think. Or maybe it's Latvia. One of those *ia's*. His family owns a circus."

"No way," said Shelby. "Like Ringling Brothers?"

Lindsey nodded. "Supposedly they're loaded. He told me he's been shot out of a cannon."

"Is that his pick-up line?"

"Maybe. It seems to work. He's always got lots of young chicks hanging around."

Shelby put one hand on her hip and shook her feather duster. "Hey, baby. Come to my place. I teach you to sa-ving on zee trapeze. I shoot my cannon at you."

"Ugh, Shelby, that's gross," said Tipsy, but she laughed. She left Shelby and Lindsey on the first floor. She huffed and puffed through a head rush, up the stairs, into one of the upper exhibit rooms. As she adjusted the lighting over a set of blown glass spheres, she thought of the ugly sculpture with which Henry had tried to brain her and Will. The tingly energy that had allowed her to deflect it against the wall had happened twice since. When she'd also deflected Henry's anger toward Jane, and then pushed Rosie clear of that wave.

I wonder if I can do it again. If I can do it right now. She stared at the glass spheres—which looked like giant blue and green and yellow gumballs—and pictured them levitating in the air in front of her. She even lifted her hands, as if she were waving at the figures in the paintings across the room. She strained her brain in a mental grunt. The spheres sat stubbornly on their pedestals, bubbles that refused to float.

"Umm...Tips, you okay?" asked Shelby. She peered into the room.

"Oh—yeah." Tipsy pointed at the spheres. "Making sure those things are centered."

Lindsey blabbed on as she and Shelby joined Tipsy. "...so I was saying, she doesn't *do anything.* I see her at the gym every day, and I heard she lives off her ex—"

"Ah, Lindsey, you don't *do anything* either," said Tipsy, "and Barker supports you."

Lindsey dismissed that logic with a sniff. "Barker could support three ex-wives and still vacation in Europe every other week. The weird part is, there's some other guy who gives her money. I think he's married. But she flirts with everyone she sees. In her perfectly matched workout get ups and coordinated neon shoes. She looks like a clown, bless her heart."

"Maybe she can join Sergio's circus," said Shelby. "She'd fit in the cannon."

"So every time I talk to her, she's all, *I don't need a man. I'm so happy. I'm so content.* Then I see her out and she's falling-down drunk before happy hour even ends. She must be miserable. Can you imagine being the secret mistress of a married man? At our age?"

"Hey, y'all," said a soft voice over Tipsy's shoulder.

"Hey, Mimi," said Shelby.

"Who are y'all talking about?" Mimi asked.

"Just my neighbor. Claire…umm…Claire what's-her-face. Curly blonde hair. Her kids go to Pinegrounds. Do you know her?"

Mimi shook her head. "Can I talk to you for a second outside, Tipsy?"

"Sure." Tipsy handed her feather duster to Lindsey. "Get 'er done."

"Yes, ma'am," said Lindsey, and saluted.

Tipsy joined Mimi on the bench outside the GQB. The sun glared off the pastel buildings across Queen Street. Tipsy closed one eye. "I'm ready for it to cool off some. Aren't you?"

"I thought y'all were talking about me, just now. The mistress of a married man."

Tipsy squeezed Mimi's knee. "You know I'd never say anything. Besides, you're not like that Claire chick. I've seen her at the gym. Lindsey's right. She's a train wreck. And everyone in town knows about her mystery married guy. She gets drunk and tells people about it."

"Remind me not to drink," said Mimi. "Anyway, now I'm the former mistress of a married man."

"Did you end it with Brad?"

"Yes—no. But it's over." She held her inhaler in her lap. "I told him…I was going to…leave Jimmy. I said he needed to leave his wife, too, if we were… going to keep… seeing each other."

Foreboding welled up in Tipsy's stomach. "Let me guess."

"He broke it off. He said he wasn't leaving her. That had never been part of his plan. Kids…money…he even brought up God and sin and said he'd been going to church." She laughed, shrill and bitter. "He wasn't so holy last week when we were making love at the Courtyard Marriott on 17 at two in the afternoon."

"Oh, sugar—"

"I thought if I put his feet to the fire he'd leave. Even though he said he wasn't ready. I was sure if I threatened to end it he'd come with me.

He came on so strong last fall, like a Mack truck going downhill. We were so—it seemed so—oh my God, Tipsy. I'm so stupid."

"You're the second person in my life who has recently claimed stupidity because of someone else's problems." She took Mimi's hands. "Look—I'm not saying what you did was right. Cheating on Jimmy. Mimi, you know it wasn't."

She nodded.

"But Brad Humphries obviously has his own issues. You got caught up in them. Now…you need to give yourself some time to heal from this—"

"I don't know if I can go home. I feel like there's a hole in my chest and everyone will be able to see through me."

"You've got to go home. If not for Jimmy, for your kids. If Brad contacts you, and you know he might, do not answer."

"What do I tell Jimmy if he asks what's wrong?"

"For now just say you're struggling with y'all's problems. Y'all haven't been getting along, right?" Tipsy asked, even though she knew full and well the answer, since Jimmy had told her. "If you want to come clean once the dust has settled, that's your call."

Mimi nodded. "Okay. I'll do that." She sucked on the inhaler the way an alcoholic might toss back a shot of bourbon.

Tipsy hugged Mimi, and her sister-in-law climbed into her Volvo station wagon. As she pulled away, Shelby joined Tipsy on the sidewalk. "What's up with Mimi?" Shelby asked.

"Same kind of stuff that seems to be up with everyone in this town," said Tipsy. Before Shelby asked for further information, Tipsy switched to the subject she knew Shelby wanted to raise. She squeezed her friend's arm. "No, Shelby. I haven't started a new painting yet."

As Tipsy turned to follow Shelby back into the GQB, she noticed movement in a Toyota sedan on the other side of Queen Street. Her eyes narrowed. "I'll be right back," she said to Shelby.

She walked across the street. The man behind the steering wheel sat up straighter. He fired up the car's engine, and pulled away from the curb. Before he put on his sunglasses, Tipsy looked deep into his dark, watery eyes. He was middle-aged, bald, and had a receding chin. He licked his lips as the Toyota slid past her. She'd never forget that face. She could have painted his portrait, if she had any desire to produce something unsavory and unsettling that no one would want to buy.

She turned and stormed back to the bench. She texted Ayers. *You're really paying that slimeball in the Toyota to follow me around?*

As she predicted, his reply came within a minute. *If u had your shit together I wouldn't have to.*

A few photos popped up in the message window. She laughed when she opened them. There she was, walking around on the beach at Sullivan's. The photos were taken from a goodish distance, so the PI must have used a long lens. It was gray and drizzly, but no downpour or lighting. There were a couple other people still lingering on the beach, watching two golden retrievers play in the surf.

Tipsy: *So what? I went for a walk on the beach.*

Ayers: *He said u were still out there when a mother of a storm came through. You're crazy.*

I guess he was worried about his big fancy camera and didn't stick around, because I don't see any big storm. Just me and some dog lovers on an evening stroll.

Whatever. I got enough others.

Tipsy almost ripped into him about her conversation with the girls, but she decided it was too complicated for text. Instead, she sent him a gif—the back end of a braying donkey.

Let him figure out that message.

———•———

The gallery stayed empty most of the day, as if Condé Nast had suddenly declared that Charleston was *not* the top city in America, causing the tourists to flee in droves back to Atlanta and New York and San Francisco. In a business like the GQB, the majority of visitors didn't buy a thing or have a serious interest in art, but Tipsy enjoyed chatting with most of them just the same. After Mimi left, followed by Shelby to a lunch meeting and Lindsey to a chemical peel appointment, the minutes crawled by. Tipsy scanned Facebook and read the HuffPost until she finally resorted to playing one of Little A's zombie games on her phone.

As soon as Shelby returned, Tipsy declared lunch break and swept out of the GQB with the doorbell's clanging admonishments ringing in her ears. She headed down Church Street with no real plan, just the urge to stretch her legs, but once she got to the quirky intersection of Church and Water Streets she hung a left toward the old Robinette House. She'd been inside the house now, in a way, and she wanted to take another look.

She scanned the street. No Toyota, and no one sitting in any of the other cars parked along the street. No pedestrians. And there was nowhere for the creepy man to hide, especially now that she knew what he looked like. He'd have to climb into someone's private garden to get any kind of cover.

Regardless, she wasn't taking any chances. She crossed the intersection, and walked towards Atlantic Street. To her amazement, she saw the Toyota.

This guy is earning his pay, said Granna.

Once again, Tipsy made a beeline for the PI's car. He saw her coming, and this time his eyes immediately disappeared behind mirrored sunglasses. He had to back out from between two cars. He didn't make it out fast enough. Tipsy tapped on the window.

"Hey!"

He looked over his shoulder, and eased the car backward. "Move away from my car, ma'am!" he shouted through the closed window.

"How about you move on out of my life, asshole! Does this make you feel good, stalking people?" Before he pulled away, Tipsy tapped on the window again. "You just lost this gig, brother! I know what you look like! I'd recognize you in a dark alley. So stay the hell away from me!"

The Toyota drove down the narrow street, as fast as one could reasonably go on the cobblestones. Tipsy ran one shaking hand over her hair, pushing loose strands away from her face. She turned around, eager to take care of her business while she knew the PI was at least temporarily out of commission.

She slowed down in front of the old Robinette house and scanned the yard. Once she was certain that the owner wasn't hiding behind one of the short, squat palmetto trees on either side of the stairway, she stopped. Before she ascertained which of the two bay windows she'd peeked out of in Jane's memory, a pale face appeared on the other side of the wrought iron bars. A humming-jailbird.

"You're back!" said Luisa. "I've been waiting for you to come talk to me." She scratched at her absurd bow, first with one hand, then the other. "I've been waiting and you *didn't come.*"

"Jeez, you're right." How unthinking, to give a lonely child a solitary reminder of the pleasures of conversation. "I should have come back sooner." She put her phone to her ear as an extra precaution.

"I looked out the window many times, and saw brown haired ladies passing. I called out, but no one heard me. No one *ever* hears me!" She flickered and stomped her feet, and then hung her head. Her bow drooped. "Beg pardon. Mama wouldn't like me pitching a fit and hollering. She says it's not ladylike."

"Don't worry about it. You're allowed a fit every fifty years or so."

"It's so lonesome without Virginia to talk to. Even if she's been gone for a thousand years."

"Probably more like eighty." Tipsy rested her bottom on the stucco edge of the wall, as she had the last time. Nothing particularly unusual about that on a hot day. "It's interesting that Virginia went away. Tell me more about her."

Luisa nodded, an eager student with the answer to a simple question. "She was lovely! She sang the prettiest songs. Hymns, from church. And songs from where she grew up, near the mountains. About ladies like Barbry Allen and Lady Margaret."

Tipsy smiled. She herself couldn't carry a tune if she superglued one to her hands, but she felt a kinship with this woman, Virginia. As a mountain girl herself, she'd heard those old ballads as a child.

"Sometimes she'd sing all day and all night. You would think that I would have gotten tired of it." Here Luisa went from child to adult within the space of a few sentences. "But I never did. It filled the quiet."

"And she was just gone one day? So strange. What happened again?"

"She said she understood now, and she had to go home."

"Where was home?"

"I don't know. Maybe she went back to the mountains?"

"Did she ever mention that she could see ghosts, when she was alive?"

"I don't think so. She told me she'd never believed in spirits until she became one."

"And she couldn't move things around. Y'all tried, but it never worked."

"No, ma'am." The little girl again. "It sure didn't. And sometimes I would have liked to throw a plate or maybe a pillow at that mean Yankee lady who moved into the house after my grandparents went away."

"What mean Yankee lady?"

"Mrs. O'Brian. She came here with her husband, Mr. O'Brian."

"From where?"

"I think it was New Jersey. Is that where Philadelphia is?"

"No. Good guess, but Philadelphia is in Pennsylvania."

Luisa nodded, and laughed in a grown-up way that clashed horribly with her round cheeks and pug nose and knobby knees. "Of course. How silly of me! Pennsylvania. Grandmother was beside herself, selling the Robinette house to some Yankee, but Grandfather said, *I'm sorry my dear, we haven't another buyer*, and that was that."

"What did she do that was so mean?"

"Oh, she was always yelling at the Negro maids, and the cooks. And even at her own husband. She was only nice to her Yankee lady friends who came here to talk about the things they missed from up north. Theaters and shops and *civilized accents*. They all said Charleston was a black water town."

"A backwater town?"

"Something like that. She didn't want to come here, but her husband Mr. O'Brian had some position running the docks in the harbor where the big ships come in. So I guess she was mad all the time. But Virginia told me the O'Brians weren't the first mean people to live in the house."

"Really? Who was she speaking of?"

Luisa shrugged. "She said it wasn't my grandparents, or my grandfather's grandparents, so it wasn't the Robinettes. What did I care?"

Tipsy leaned her head against the wrought iron. It pressed into her temple, like an idea searching out an entryway into her mind. "She wanted to go home, so she went. Did anything happen in the days before she disappeared?"

Luisa took a moment to reply. "I don't think so. Just one of Mrs. O'Brian's tea parties the day she disappeared. I asked her to sing me a song, but she wouldn't. Then she went away."

That was enough for Tipsy. She put her phone in her pocket, and looked up and down the street again. It was empty, so she reached one arm through the railings, and gripped the cold iron with the other. She planted her feet, as if she were about to do a squat. This time, damnit, she was going to stay on her feet. She expected Granna to warn her against pitching over and cracking her head on the concrete, but this time, Granna doesn't object. Her silent confidence buoyed Tipsy.

Luisa stepped away. "It's alright," Tipsy said, as Granna might have said to her many years ago, when she needed a hand to jump a puddle. "If you can, hold your hand to mine."

"Why?" asked Luisa.

Tipsy closed her eyes. She pictured her own willpower as two tightly clenched, intertwined fists inside her head, jammed up against her forehead, holding her upright. "So I can see…maybe…why your friend went away."

———•———

This time, Tipsy opens her eyes to a new porch. The rounded white columns and railings holding it together are thicker and grander than Miss Callie's, with carvings around each base and elegant moldings along the ceiling. She also senses she's further from the ground. She peers over the railing to her left down into Theresa Robinette's old garden. The sunburnt grass is patchy. Butterflies swarm a patch of daisies and black-eyed Susans. The sound of chuckling water drifts up from a stone fountain beside the stucco wall that abuts the neighbor's house. She's on the third floor piazza.

A buxom woman stands beside her. She wears a tattered dress with a cinched waist and full skirts. It might have once been a pretty daytime gown, but it's definitely been through the ringer. She appears to be about forty years old.

The strange thing about her— her dark blonde hair is much longer on one side of her head, as if someone tried to lop it off with a butter knife.

"Can you see me?" Tipsy asks, because she hasn't had contact with a ghost in one of these memories.

The woman pays Tipsy no mind, and stoops to the level of the child beside her. Luisa grins up at Virginia. Her bow bounces in anticipation.

"Let us join Mrs. Grumpy—" Luisa thumbs her nose. "For a little civiliiiiized con-va-sa-shion."

Virginia laughs. This memory has the feel of high summer, but she smells faintly of spring—honeysuckle and rain. "That sounds lovely. But who shall see us?"

"No one!" shouts Luisa.

They clasp hands and crouch, as if sneaking up on the five women who sit in identical high backed, stiff-looking wicker chairs, like a gathering of minor queens who can't decide which one is holding court. Each holds a blue and white china teacup on her lap. The teapot sits like a scepter beside a stout woman with reddish hair, and the look of tight-lipped superiority on her face tells Tipsy that she's the highest highness on the porch.

Virginia straightens and proclaims, "Good afternoon, ladies!"

And Luisa says, "Good afta-noon. And good eva-ning!" She strolls into the middle of their little cluster. She mimes sipping tea with her pinky fingers sticking out.

Virginia does the same, and says, "Oh, it's dreadfully hot. Let us drink hot tea anyway. And complain the whole while."

"Sweet tea is so uncivilized," says Luisa. She holds her nose, so her repetition is a passable impersonation of a clipped northern accent.

Virginia laughs again, while Luisa stands in the middle of their little cluster and twirls. She's a maypole that spins for the crowd, rather than staying still while the celebrants do the rotating. Her giggles ring out over the women's chatting— someone loudly thanks God for the breeze up here on the third floor. Luisa leans over and shakes her little flickering bottom in its pink silk nightgown right in Mrs. O'Brian's face.

"All right now. Silent!"

Everyone obeys: the four guests, and Luisa and Virginia. For a second Tipsy thinks that Mrs. O'Brian has somehow heard or seen the spectral interlopers, until she says, "Ladies, please. Everyone talking at once is so uncivilized. I have a story, if you'd all be quiet long enough to hear it. About this house."

One of her friends, a woman with steel gray hair and talon-like red fingernails, says, "Doris, your fascination with this house is so quaint."

"It passes the time," says Mrs. O'Brian. "All the old houses with all their lore in this town, and George buys the one that's only been owned by two families in a century. Most of the time by those people who sold it to us. The Robinsons."

"Robinettes!" says Luisa, with her hands on her hips.

"The woman next door finally pried open her lips and said hello, the rude old cat."

"People here are so clannish," says Red Fingernails. "She probably only converses with her relations."

"I caught her in the garden and complimented her camellias. Once I had her talking, she ran on and on." Mrs. O'Brian drops her voice. "She smelled like whiskey."

The ladies sip their tea and murmur disapproval, a circle of slurping and tsk-ing.

"She spoke of the lovely family that lived here before us…such quality people, so forth and so on. But the original owners, now they were the

interesting ones. Some bad things went on in this house in its early years, she said."

All four guests move to the edge of their seats.

"The man who built this house, Mr. Converse was his name," says Mrs. O'Brian, "he took a second wife—herself a widow. The wife had a grown daughter, newly married, who lived somewhere nearby."

The guests nod.

"It seems Mr. Converse had quite a temper. Sometimes his new wife screamed so loudly, the neighbors up and down this street heard her wailing. She'd stay in the house for days after such a hullabaloo, and then emerge with yellowing bruises, and even healing lacerations."

"Dear me, Doris," says Red Fingernails. "This is distasteful. Airing one's family business about town is so gauche."

"Virginia?" Luisa looks up at her friend.

"Hush, now," says Virginia, her eyes on Mrs. O'Brian. "Look into the garden, Luisa. For butterflies. Find me a monarch, if you can."

"It gets worse," says Mrs. O'Brian. "The wife finally left him, and went to stay with her daughter."

"Did she ask for a divorce?" asks the youngest woman in the group.

"Apparently that's never allowed in this state, even under such circumstances. Mrs. Converse could only live separately from him, and beg a judge to make him support her. Which I'm quite sure he didn't want to do."

"I will never approve of divorce," announces Red Fingernails, to no one in particular.

"So, just a few days later, Mr. Converse used conciliatory words to trick his wife into returning to the house to retrieve her belongings. The daughter came with her. When they arrived, he attacked Mrs. Converse—right here on this piazza."

"No," says the young woman.

"Yes! He beat her soundly, and knocked her down. He pressed her face into this wooden floor, and held her there, by her hair. Wrapped his fist all through it, and threatened to snap her neck if she screamed, or if the daughter went for help."

"Beastly," says Red Fingernails.

"It was a rainy, early spring day. When the daughter tried to cover her shivering, wet mother with a shawl, Mr. Converse laughed and wrapped it around himself. After nightfall, he fell asleep. The daughter snuck out here with scissors, and tried to cut her mother's hair to free her. He woke up, and shoved her away."

Virginia runs her hands over her ragged hair. Her left eye twitches.

"At dawn, the daughter was hiding out of their sight, peering through the cracked door. But she heard and saw what happened next, and lived to tell of it."

The porch is silent, waiting for Doris O'Brian's morbid punchline. She leans toward her goggle-eyed friends.

"He finally released his wife's hair. But he said if she ever left him again, her daughter would die the very same day. So Mrs. Converse, she climbed onto that railing, right there behind all of you. And just as the daughter ran on to the porch to stop her— she jumped."

"Oh, dear lord." The young woman stares down into the garden, three stories below them.

Tipsy stops hearing Doris' morbid scandalizing of her flock of chickens and focuses on Virginia. Her face has gone blank. Her eyes, wide and staring. Her mouth hangs open, revealing the hint of a pink tongue. "Oh…my. Oh, my," she whispers. She presses her fingers into her eyes. "I remember. Anna saw me fall."

Luisa returns to Virginia's side. "I didn't see a monarch. What are they talking about, Virginia?" she asks.

Virginia holds her hands out in front of her. She stretches, both arms akimbo. Her gaze travels up and down her limbs. Her eyes widen, if that's possible.

She leads Luisa into the house. They stand in a foyer that's bare except for a frayed woolen rug and a china cabinet full of knick knacks. She kneels, and takes both the little girl's hands and kisses them. "Now don't you think on what Mrs. O'Brian is saying. She doesn't know what she's talking about. The old bat."

Luisa giggles. "She's a fat bat."

"Yes," *says Virginia.* "Hold my hands now."

Virginia closes her eyes, a small smile on her lips.

"What are you doing?" *asks Luisa.*

"Shhh," *says Virginia. Now she stares into Luisa's face. She squeezes the little girl's hands, her brow furrowed. They stay still, the woman on her knees and the child in front of her. Virginia is expecting something, but nothing happens.*

Luisa fidgets, clearly bored. "Will you sing Barbry Allen for me now?"

Virginia bites her lip. "Not now." *She sits on the ground, and pulls Luisa into her lap. Luisa rests her head on Virginia's chest. Tears stream down Virginia's face as she talks.*

"Luisa, you know I've been here a long time. Longer than you."

"Yes, ma'am," *says Luisa.*

Virginia rocks Luisa gently as she talks. "I was sleepy for a long time, till you come. I stayed mostly in the attic, away from the people in the house. I never paid much attention to them. I didn't hear what they said, or take heed of what they did, until I felt you. Alone, and scared, like I was when I found myself dead. Now, don't I wish I'd paid attention all those years."

"I don't understand."

"I know you don't, but now, I do. I can't stay here, sweet child. I can't let that man keep me in this house anymore. Not one more day." *She kisses*

Luisa's hair, and gently pushes her onto the rug. "Luisa, I love you. I'm sorry I can't take you with me. But I must go home."

Luisa watches her with wide, uncomprehending eyes, her index finger in her mouth. Virginia stands, and wipes her face. She smooths her ragged hair again. Then she holds her hands before her, and clenches her fists. For a moment, her lip curls, as if she's in a boxing ring. Facing off against the monster of a man who abused her, humiliated her, and threatened to murder her child. The man who drove her to kill herself, in an attempt to escape him that only trapped her in his house for nearly a century.

The smell of honeysuckle rain washes over Tipsy; so strong, it makes her gag. Her stomach turns, and the vision slips away.

As Tipsy woke, she found herself hanging onto to the iron bars with both hands, but miraculously upright. She cleared her throat and spit into the climbing wisteria bushes. Her pulse banged painfully against her temples, but as the blood relaxed in her veins, the need to throw up retreated. She perused the street again. All seemed clear.

"Why'd you do that?" Luisa asked.

Tipsy leaned over, her hands on her thighs. She took a few deep, cleansing breaths. Her belly grumbled irritably, but as the seconds ticked by, she felt more confident that she wouldn't vomit. She felt a perverse sense of pride— she'd managed a trip back in time, without collapsing or barfing, and her head had not exploded.

She looked through the fence into Luisa's curious face. Virginia's disappearance made some semblance of sense. She grabbed the wrought iron railings again. "Luisa. You don't remember how you died, do you?"

Luisa shook her head.

"Do you remember being very sick?"

She shook her head again.

"You were very ill, Luisa. With influenza. It's a sickness that still can kill people. Mostly old people, but sometimes young ones, too."

"I fell ill?" Luisa's lower lip covered her top one. The corners of her mouth pointed at the grass below her feet.

"Yes. Your mother nursed you, but couldn't save you."

"Oh. Oh."

"You died in her arms. She cried and begged you to stay with her. Not to leave her."

Luisa's eyes widened. "Not to leave her, like my daddy did. In the war across the sea."

"Yes—yes, that's what she said. And she held you until you were gone."

There was no child in Luisa's cry, only an old soul in deepest mourning. "Oh, Mama. I'm sorry I couldn't stay. I never meant to leave you."

"Luisa—"

"Lord, lord." Luisa collapsed on the grass and curled her arms around her knees. She sputtered like a candle fighting a happy birthday blowout.

"Sweet child," said Tipsy, just as Virginia had said. "Look at your hands. What do you see?"

Luisa raised her head, her face a mask of shock and confusion. She held her hands before her face. "It's not what I see. My hands. And my arms. I can *feel* them!" She touched her cheeks. "I can feel my skin!"

"Are you afraid?"

Luisa sniffed back a few watery sobs. "No, ma'am. I'm not afraid."

"Do you know what you need to do?"

Luisa nodded. She wiggled her fingers before her face. She flickered a few times, and then curtsied, a child again. "It was nice to meet you. I think I'm going away now, too."

"Yes. I think you are." Tipsy waved as Luisa spun around and ran toward the house, her arms waving wildly above her head. With each stride, her shimmering quickened, until she blinked out of existence. "Go home, sweet child." Tipsy said, and Luisa ran no more. Not in this world.

Chapter 12

Mimi's oldest son was two years older than Little Ayers. In Tipsy's earliest days of motherhood, when exhaustion had seeped into the deepest level of her being, Mimi told her, "No matter how much you love your baby, Tips, you're always happy when he goes to sleep." Tipsy had believed her then, but that message took on a different meaning the night she freed Luisa from her haunting.

She had the kids' dinner on the table at half past five. She hustled Little A into the shower and the girls into the bath at half past six. "Early bedtime tonight, buddies!"

"Mama," said an indignant Little Ayers, "it's not even getting dark yet."

"School starts in a week."

Ayers peeked around the shower curtain. Shampoo dripped from his hair. "Right. A week. Not like, tomorrow."

"You need to rest up."

"But—"

"Ayers Lee, rinse that shampoo out of your hair and get your butt into some jammies."

She scrubbed both girls and brushed their teeth in record time, before they found something to fight about. By 7:15, three kids stared at the ceiling from three beds.

"I'm not tired, Mama," said Ayers.

"Me either," said one of the twins. Sometimes Tipsy couldn't tell which was which when she couldn't see their faces.

"You will be." She sat in the hallway between their rooms, like she had in June, on their first night in Miss Callie's house. "Close your eyes, my friends."

It took much shushing on Tipsy's part, but all three children slept soundly by a few minutes past eight. She closed and locked the door to her bedroom. Her hangover from the visit to Luisa wasn't nearly as bad as the others, but her headache worsened as she called out, *Jane? Henry? Jane? Henry? Jane? Henry?*

Henry appeared by the door. Jane chose a position by the windows and Tipsy's self-portrait. The ghosts eyed each other, duelists without pistols. "Is something amiss?" Henry asked. "You're very loud."

Tipsy sat on the edge of the bed. In a rush, she told Jane and Henry what had passed at the house on Water Street that afternoon. They slowly crept toward her from their respective corners of the room, until they stood before her. Their faces spoke surprise in volumes. Jane faded in and out as Tipsy talked, but Henry stayed solid.

"So Luisa is gone," said Jane. "Moved on—to someplace else. Someplace she thought was a *good* place?"

Tipsy nodded. "There was no fear, only joy. She's free. Like Virginia said after hearing the story of her own death: she understood, and she went home."

"You told Luisa what you knew. About her passing?"

"Yes. I told her just as Mrs. Childress and Proctor told it to me. I told her what had happened, and she remembered. And she went." Tipsy smiled. "I wish I'd told her months ago. I didn't want to frighten her."

"How does this help us?" said Henry. "There's no one alive who was present when Jane and I died."

Tipsy took hold of the quilt with both hands. "There's a way I can see what happened that day. I've been getting closer for months."

"I don't understand," said Jane.

Tipsy squeezed the quilt and told Jane and Henry the shortened version of what she'd seen, and how she'd seen it. She finished with Jane's phone call from the house on Water Street. "I'm sorry I haven't told y'all. I didn't want to take sides, and honestly, I thought if you knew I could snoop around your heads, you wouldn't want me to."

"It makes you sick, looking into our memories," asked Henry. "Yet still, you did it."

"Sometimes I didn't have a choice. But I want to help." She decided to be honest. "Not only that, y'all and your past inspired my last three paintings. The best I've ever produced. And sometimes, recently, it hasn't been as awful. I think I'm learning how to control it."

Tipsy stopped talking and silence fell over them like a heavy coat on a hot day.

"You were having an affair?" Henry asked Jane. "You must have remembered that. You carried on for months before we died."

"I did. I do remember. But I *don't* remember telling you about it."

"You have kept that from me all this time?" Henry shook his head. "I don't remember you telling me either—"

"She told you in the week before you died," said Tipsy. "The week you don't remember."

"Why have you kept this from me? Is that why you were so convinced I did it? You knew I had reason to act in rage. You never believed your mother and sister's story about the inheritance."

She shook her head. "Perhaps I should have told you...but...now you know why I'm *so sure* you did it."

"I've been so certain all this time I couldn't have done it." He buried his hands in his hair. "But perhaps I did—but you!" He turned on his wife. "You betrayed me—with another man!"

"You told me to do it!"

"That's why you didn't want Tipsy searching for answers in the first place. You were afraid this would come out. You'd be exposed as an adulterer. And all these years you've lorded over me with your false perfection. Who were you whoring with? John?"

"No! You don't know him, Henry. You don't—"

"Wait!" Tipsy said. "You've already been through this. You—" She pointed at Henry. "—realized that you drove Jane to someone else and asked to be forgiven." She pointed at Jane. "And you were trying to make up your mind as to whether you forgave him or not."

"This is insane," said Henry. "I feel like my mind is fracturing."

"Let me help you. If I touch you, I'm sure I can see what happened. I can tell you and you can both move on. Imagine finally leaving this house, forever. Jane—you haven't wanted to know—"

"I do. Now I do. If it can set me free of this house, *yes*. Show me."

"No!" Henry backed away from both of them. "Because now I know…I must have done it. I don't want to remember that."

"But Henry, you don't know for certain what happened. Perhaps you didn't. If you did, then wouldn't you have remembered, hearing Mrs. Robinette and Constance speaking of it?"

"They said I did it for the *money*. That's not why I did it. Someone has to tell us the *whole truth*. Can't you see that, from your stories of Luisa and Virginia Converse?"

"If you did do it," said Tipsy. "You can be set free and go in peace. Jane will forgive you."

"I will. Henry, I don't care if—if I did it myself. I want to go on from this house. My existence is nothing, but it will be even more so knowing I could set us free and I didn't."

Henry's ankle rolled as he backed away. He grabbed for Miss Callie's blue dresser, but solid pine gave way to his fading form. He passed through the dresser, and his fall ended in a huddled mass of glowing bluish light on the floor. "No. I won't remember it. I will not." The blue light went out.

"Henry—" Jane called out, but he didn't reappear. Jane knelt for a moment in the spot where he vanished, then returned to Tipsy. "I'd still like to know."

"Okay. You're sure?"

Jane nodded. Tipsy sat on the edge of the bed. She steeled herself, mind and body, as she had that afternoon on Water Street. Jane held up both hands, and Tipsy raised hers. They came together, cold blue against warm cream.

And nothing happened.

———•———

Tipsy and Jane tried for hours, but finally Tipsy had to give up. The kids would surely equate early bedtime with early wake up time. Jane promised to think on it, and Tipsy spent the next day at the gallery wracking her brain. Since she didn't understand how the memories worked in the first place, she couldn't very easily figure out why they wouldn't work, either.

Granna! I wish you were here to help me.

I'm as good as there, babygirl, and I got nothin'.

The kids were spending the work day hours at May Penny's the last week of summer, so Tipsy had a nice long ride from downtown to Sullivan's to obsess some more. Was it something physical, something wrong with her? She was worn down, and had lost a lot of weight. The supernatural hangovers still plagued her, but she *had* felt a little better since she took control of the memory visits. Maybe the fact that she knew exactly what she wanted to see? But she'd focused on Jane's winter correspondence and the visions had revealed Jane writing a letter on the dock. Was it that Jane *knew* Tipsy wanted to look into her memory?

That one had some possibility, but now that Jane was in the know, Tipsy couldn't change that fact.

Tipsy had a right frazzled brain by the time she pulled into May Penny's driveway, and the sight of Ayers's truck did nothing to assuage her mood. She hadn't seen him in person since he dropped the kids off after the Disney trip. Now, she suddenly had a spontaneous opportunity to elucidate on his jackass status. To his face.

He clipped down the stairs, his belly bouncing as if a child had stuffed one of May Penny's pool floaties down his shirt. Anger growled in Tipsy's stomach, like she'd not eaten any emotions in weeks and the fast had ended.

"Umm, hey," he said, as she got out of her truck. "I stopped by to say hi to the kids."

"That was loving of you."

He stopped at the foot of the steps. "Thanks?"

"You sure do love your children."

"Right. Okay, Tipsy."

She narrowed her eyes at him. "Feels unsettling, doesn't it, when someone comes at you with a bunch of passive aggressive bullshit? Although your bullshit has been pretty straight up lately."

He shook his head. "Whatever. I'm leaving."

"No, you're not."

He paused again, this time with his hand on the door handle. His face reddened. He opened his mouth, but Tipsy broke with years of pointlessly and amiably allowing him to unload on her, and beat him to it.

"What the hell, Ayers—you telling the kids the divorce was all my fault? That I stopped loving you—as if I just woke up one day and said, *I think today's the day. Time to fall out of love with my husband.*"

"Maybe you did—"

"And insinuating that I might stop loving them? How dare you."

"How dare you—"

"And another thing. Over my dead body will the kids live with you all the time. You can sue me all you want. Hire some stalker to follow me twenty-four hours a day. Take it right on up to the Supreme Court. I'll live with the three of them in a cardboard box under the Ravenel before I let you take them. I'll go a hundred grand in debt to lawyers and sleep on the judge's front porch until he sees my side. So you can get that idea right out of your freakin' head!"

She crept close to him and poked his chest with one vengeful index finger. In that moment, Tipsy understood how one person could punch another's lights out. "Leave the kids out of it! Don't you ever—ever say any of that crap to them again. About me not loving them or living with you or us getting back together. Never-ever-ever!"

"Stop screaming—Jesus—"

"Don't you tell me what to do—you can't. Don't—" She poked him again, over and over, with each word. "You—ever—tell—me—"

"Y'all!" May Penny stood on the front porch. "I'm coming down there."

Tipsy retreated, her chest heaving. Her hands shook. Both of them, not just the one that now had several mildly jammed fingers from poking Ayers. May Penny stood in front of Tipsy and Ayers with her arms crossed over the bright purple polo shirt of her latest tennis outfit, like a short and sporty but ferociously opinionated judge. "I've had about enough of people yelling in my driveway, Tipsy."

Tipsy looked at the neighbor's house. A drop of mortification sizzled on the frying pan of her temper.

"But I'll tell you, Ayers," said May Penny, "Tipsy has a point."

"Mama, you don't know what she's talking about."

"I do. Those girls told me the same thing. Everything nasty and manipulative you said about their mother." She held up a hand when he started denying her accusations. Only May Penny could make Ayers shut his mouth so quick. "They also said you keep hinting around that y'all might get back together. I think Tipsy's made it pretty clear that's not happening. Whether I agreed with her reasons or not, the decision's made. No use confusing those children."

"You're taking her side, Mama," said Ayers. He sounded like a little boy with a playground problem.

"I'm taking the side of the kids, first, but yes. I'm taking her side. Because she's right in this."

Ayers let out several huffing but wordless breaths. He got in the truck and backed down the driveway. He didn't pause before swinging into the street. A Honda Civic slammed on brakes to avoid sideswiping him. The driver blasted the horn and flipped Ayers the bird, but Ayers wheeled on down the road. No retaliatory flip off, no open windows, no blaring country music.

"I'll call the kids from the pool." May Penny paused halfway up the stairs. She looked down at her former daughter-in-law with a clear blue stare. No shades. Open eyes. "I know it's not like you, but I won't approve of you poking my son in the chest again. It's not civil."

"Yes, ma'am," said Tipsy.

"Although, the good Lord knows he's probably had it coming for a while."

"I won't. I think I got it out of my system."

"Marrying you wasn't in our plan for Ayers. But then we got Little A, and the girls. I'm sure all this—" She gave Tipsy illustrative jazz hands. "—drama wasn't in y'all's plan, either. But God has other plans for y'all."

"I agree." Tipsy didn't buy into May Penny's version of higher power, but she wanted her overall sentiment to be correct.

"This custody lawsuit, now, that's serious stuff." May Penny shook her head. "I'll talk to him, but I'm warning you, he seems dead set on pursuing it. Hopefully it doesn't amount to anything but wasted money."

"Thank you. I don't have the money for an attorney right now, but I'm working on it."

"Hmmm. I'll call Clark. Ask him to give you some more time."

Tipsy's eyes stung in gratitude. "Thank you. I'm supposed to respond within thirty days, and there's a hearing coming up, too."

"I'll ask him if he can give you another month. I don't know how it all works, but that seems reasonable."

"That would be amazing. And thank you for coming down and helping us sort this out."

"You're welcome." She called over her shoulder from the porch. "Sometimes it takes one outside voice between two hurting people to make everyone see the truth."

Tipsy sat in the truck and waited on the kids. She'd taken little, if any, advice from May Penny in all their years of acquaintance, but that statement rang true.

———————•———————

"I think y'all both need to be here," Tipsy whispered to Jane. They sat on the joggling board on the front porch late. Little Ayers and the girls were playing tag with Mimi's three kids in the front yard. The noise of their game made it relatively easy to have a clandestine conversation with a ghost on a hot Wednesday evening. Still, Tipsy held her phone beside her ear, in case the PI had figured out a new way to spy on her.

"Both Henry and me?" Jane whispered, too, although no one heard her but Tipsy.

"Yes. I need to touch both of you."

"Perhaps you can't see the whole story without both of us."

"Right. Have you seen Henry? I've been calling for him, or, more like yelling for him. It makes my head feel like it's going to pop. He doesn't answer." In fact, Tipsy had pretty much been pacing the house with *Henry-Henry-Henry-Henry!* running through her mind for two days, but Henry refused to show himself.

Jane shook her head. "He's hiding."

Tipsy leaned against the clapboard siding. A skittering black something caught her eye. She leaped to her feet. "Jesus, palmetto bug." She'd never grown accustomed to the Lowcountry's giant flying cockroaches. Some people hated fire ants and no-seeums, and Tipsy wasn't fond of those biting critters either. Even if the roaches didn't bite, however, something about them grossed her out to the core. "Lord, I can't squish it."

"Why?" asked Jane. "I used to mash them with daddy's shoes on a daily basis."

"Gross. They make that cracking sound when you whack them. Ayers!"

"Ma'am?" Little A ran to the bottom of the steps.

"Kill this bug for me, please."

"Mama." Ayers clumped up the stairs. "What do you do when I'm at Daddy's?"

Tipsy's son removed his flip-flop. The roach must have sensed imminent doom, because it raced across the porch like a many-legged mini Ferrari. Ayers went after it, and *bam-bam*, goodbye, roach. Ayers ran into the house, grabbed a paper towel, and scooped up the dead bug. Tipsy clutched her stomach.

"I'll flush it," Ayers said.

"Thanks, little man."

He smiled at her. "I'll kill all the bugs if it makes you happy."

Tipsy took his arm, the roach forgotten. "What do you mean?"

"I'm kidding, Mama. I thought about what you said. About Daddy, and me not having to keep him happy all the time." He slipped his toes into his flip-flop. "There's nice things we do for our parents because we love them. But that's not like having to make your dad or mom happy *all the time*. That's too much work for a kid."

"Wise boy," said Jane.

Tipsy kissed Ayers's hair. "Wise boy," she said, because Jane was right.

He growled and stuck the roach-paper towel under Tipsy's nose. "Ayers!" She swatted him on the rear end as he raced into the house.

Tipsy sat on the board again and picked up her phone. "Anyway, roach assassination aside, I think there might be a way I can make Henry come out."

"How?" Jane joined her on the board. She jumped when Little A slammed the screen door on the way back into the yard.

"That's the problem," Tipsy said. "I don't know how to make it work."

Jane spoke around pursed lips. "Jeez, Tips. That makes, like, zero sense."

Tipsy laughed. "Please don't lose your 1920s charm. If I want to talk to someone who sounds like me, I'll call Shelby." She made a fist, as if to grab the mysterious vibrating energy that had showed itself at random times over the past few months and squeeze cooperation out of it. "I have this way of sometimes making things happen. Pulling at some source of whatever is inside me that lets me see you, and feel close to Granna."

Jane's mouth twitched, but she didn't look convinced.

"It's this weird fuzzy feeling all through my body—and it lets me—" Tipsy's elbows hit her knees. "I tell you, it feels real good to have a *ghost* look at you like you're nuttier than a jar of peanut butter."

"I just don't *follow* what you plan to do."

"I don't plan to do anything right now. I don't know how to control it." Mimi's station wagon pulled into the driveway.

"I'll go," said Jane.

"Okay—let me know if you see Henry. I'll keep trying, too."

Jane vanished and Tipsy met Mimi on the steps. "The kids are having fun. Sit a minute. Want a Coke?" Tipsy asked.

Mimi wiped at the top step, as if a few swipes of her hands would protect her white shorts from the dirt of hundreds of passing bare feet. She sat on the step's rough edge. "No. I'm okay."

"You in a hurry?" Tipsy asked.

Mimi shook her head and for a couple of minutes they watched the kids race around the yard.

"We don't have to talk about it, Mimi," Tipsy finally said. "It's your business. I just want to know you're okay."

"It's embarrassing. Remember how we talked about owning our dirty laundry? I'm trying... but I've never had any this nasty." Mimi hugged her knees to her body.

"Like those gym clothes that you wash over and over but they smell as soon as you start sweating."

"Ha, right." Mimi shifted toward Tipsy. "Jimmy and I are going to try to work it out."

"Really? That's great. If you can put your heart into it and try, you should." Tipsy put a hand on Mimi's knee.

"I've done a lot of thinking. Most of the divorced people I know... it's the wife that pulled the plug."

Tipsy nodded. Notwithstanding Lindsey's lecherous older husband, she agreed.

"We keep putting up with so much crap. Until we're just over it. But we're not prepared to deal with what comes next. I guess I imagined myself...still living in my house. Being a mom. Doing my usual routine with the kids, and the gym, and getting my nails done. I just wouldn't have to...deal with Jimmy anymore. That's not reality."

Tipsy thought of her daily struggle to make ends meet. She remembered being jealous of her divorce attorney, and her kids' pediatrician. Women who had made different decisions. They had something to fall back on, and more control over their lives.

"If your hubs is Barker, it's reality. Otherwise, nope. And we've got it relatively easy. Some women are really stuck. The ones with kids to support, who work minimum wage jobs, and have husbands who beat them up." Even on her worst days, Tipsy tried to keep things in perspective. It helped her stay sane. "We have educated white woman problems."

She nodded. "I never even realized what that meant until now. I would have been the first one to say, *they should just leave.* If their husbands hit them. Now...look at me. I'm scared to go...and I'm way better off. They must feel so trapped." She wiped her eyes. "I don't know how much we owe on our house...or what's in any of Jimmy's retirement accounts. I don't have a job, or any prospects. But somehow...I was planning to leave my marriage, like nothing would change. Except maybe an idyllic Brady Bunch life with Brad." She rolled her eyes. "From one man to another. I don't know who I am...except someone's girlfriend turned fiancée turned wife. I feel like a child, Tipsy."

"Well, now is a good time to start growing up." Tipsy took her hand. "Have you told Jimmy about Brad?"

Mimi shook her head.

"He might find out anyway. This town."

"Maybe I will tell him. I really don't know what's best. It's all so delicate right now."

"If it's truly over with Brad, maybe there's no point telling Jimmy and you learned a lesson. One the other hand, there's something to be said for brutal honesty."

"You always see all the angles, Tips," said Mimi.

Tipsy thought of her constant struggle to choose sides, and not just when it came to everyone else's problems. She had a historical tendency to allow the opinions and instincts of others to swamp her own, especially when it came to her ex-husband. "I guess. That's not always a good thing. Sometimes life is easier if you see everything in black and white."

"I'm going to think about it before I decide whether to tell him," said Mimi. "Maybe call our counselor and ask her."

"Y'all going back to counseling?"

She nodded. "It hasn't worked before, but he seems more willing to try now. He's always dismissed all my concerns. Made me feel demanding or unreasonable… or plain crazy. But—he really wants to change. He said he'll help me more around the house. And that we can plan a date night once a week. Go out more, together."

Tipsy chuckled, and Mimi said, "What?"

"Nothing. It sounds like you and Jimmy are on the same page. Every couple is different. I hope y'all find a way to come together again."

"I'm not saying I'm convinced. There's a lot of fixing that needs to happen. But now with Brad out of the picture, at least I can try with a clear head. And I'm going to start thinking about what *I want*. What *I* need. How I can take care of my kids and myself. So if it doesn't work out… I'll be ready to face it." Mimi took Tipsy's hand. "Thanks for listening to me through all this…and not judging me. You know you'll always be my sister, divorced from Ayers or not."

"You needed me. You need me again, I'm here. No matter what happens with you and Jimmy."

A shriek from the yard drew their attention away from their tender moment. Mimi's seven-year-old son had Mary Pratt in a headlock. The looks on both children's faces showed that this wasn't part of the game.

"Jack!" Mimi yelled. "Jack Lathrop—you let go of your cousin *this instant!*"

Jack spun and Mary Pratt flew out of his arms like a shot put with a ponytail. *"Jack!"* Mimi ran down the stairs, but not before Little Ayers took care of business.

Jack was a full year younger than Ayers, but he was an offensive tackle to Little A's running back. Regardless, Ayers grabbed hold of his cousin's arm and wheeled him around. "Don't you touch my sister like that!"

"She called me a poophead!"

"So what? You're *waaaaay* bigger than she is. You push her again I'll knock your head off." Little A's nose was at level with Jack's chin, but all the better for Ayers to see Jack's quivering lip, as far as Tipsy could tell.

"Fine!" said Jack, and he sat in the grass in a huff.

Tipsy and Mimi intervened. Apologies were delivered all around, along with the typical mommy-isms: *poophead isn't nice, we don't hit when we're angry, you all love each other so let's be kind.* Mimi thanked Tipsy for keeping her kids and shuffled them into the car.

"I'm so ready for school to start," said Mimi as she leaned against the station wagon's door.

"Me too. Sorry for the poophead and Little Ayers going all commando."

"Jack needs to control his temper," said Mimi. "And Little A was protecting his sister. Wonder where he gets that from." She winked and punched Tipsy's arm.

"He'd better watch out, going after a kid that outweighs him by twenty pounds."

"You've heard those stories about mothers lifting cars to save children trapped under them." Mimi slipped into the driver's seat. Before she closed the door she added, "When you're protecting... someone you love, you can do anything."

Chapter 13

Tipsy texted Shelby the next morning after Ayers picked up the kids for his weekend.

I'm going to be in late today...like noon, ok?

Sure no prob. You painting?

:(not exactly...have some stuff to take care of!

Sigh. Ok see you then!

Tipsy decided to attempt the unexplainable in the front parlor, beside the fireplace where she'd seen Henry tell Jane to love another man, and then scream at her for following his advice. When Jane appeared, Tipsy explained, albeit poorly, what she wanted to do.

"So if he appears," Tipsy said, "I need you to be beside me. I don't know how much time I'll have."

Jane nodded. "I'm at your disposal."

"Don't put too much stock in this. I have no idea what I'm doing."

"You're the only being that's given me reason to have faith in many years. Try. If it doesn't work, Henry and I are no worse off than we are now."

Tipsy nodded. She'd pulled her hair back into a tight, high ponytail, as she did before running or lifting weights. She wore a loose fitting tee shirt and a pair of old cut off shorts. She didn't want any hindrances.

She pictured the destroyed ceramic statue with her artist's eyes. The rain of colorful sharp shards and the poorly defined faces of the two figures staring up at her from the floor. The feel of Will's heart beating against her own chest. Her frantic relief that the blood on his arm wasn't on his face, which had taken only a few minutes of easy conversation to become dear to her. She moved on to Henry's anger and Jane's fitful combination of defending herself and cowering before him, a doe with a confused sense of fight or flight. Tipsy relived her own admiration of Jane's defiance. The kind of rebellion Tipsy hadn't been able muster against her own husband. Lastly she saw Rosie's terrified face and a wall of uncaring water. She heard Will splashing toward his little girl with the slow steps of one caught in a dream where he knows he must *run, run, run,* but his legs won't cooperate.

She felt it. The first vibrating twinges, like newly metamorphosed butterflies were sitting on her limbs and testing out their wet wings. Her head and her stomach rebelled, but she ignored the pain and the nausea. She shifted her mind to the here and now. She called out to Henry, with all her desire to bring peace to a house that had hidden despairing memories under layers of subsequent happy ones.

She felt Henry, just out of reach and fighting hard. His thoughts leaped before her closed eyes, panicked rabbits in a cramped hutch.

I told you I don't want to remember!

It's not only for you, Henry. I can't set Jane free without you.

Still he pulled away. *No. No. No.*

So Tipsy focused on Jane, in all her various incarnations. Damaged phantom. Giggling girlfriend. Heartbroken wife. Vital young woman in white on a hot Lowcountry Thanksgiving Eve, with her whole life in front of her.

Tipsy took hold of Henry's arm and yanked. His pale, panicked face materialized before her. *Please, Tipsy,* he said. *I don't want to know I'm a murderer.*

You're my friend, Henry. But I won't leave Jane in the dark because you're afraid of the truth.

Tipsy reached for Jane. Jane's lips moved, but if she whispered prayers, Tipsy couldn't hear them. Henry cried out as Tipsy took Jane's hand.

———•———

Miss Callie's? The Old Cannon? Water Street? Or maybe she'll turn up somewhere she's never been, on the turf of Jane's unnamed lover. Tipsy strains for a sight line past the clearing yellow and black and silver, as if she's been dropped into a cave and her eyes will somehow adjust to the light.

Once her vision comes into focus she gets the quick relief of the familiar stairs and windows of Miss Callie's foyer. There's no screen door, just solid wood, so she looks out the window to get a sense of time. Dry brownish grass tells her winter or fall, but it's hard to interpret the time of day by looking at the grayish, clouded-over sky. She walks the loop between the foyer, the parlor, the dining room and what in Jane and Henry's when is a study, but in Tipsy's when is a TV room. She peers into the kitchen at the back of the house, and up the rear staircase. No one seems to be around.

Just as she's wondering how the hell this can be a memory without a person to remember it, there's a knock at the front door. Tipsy walks into the foyer and stands in annoyed helplessness. She stares at the door, a wooden rectangle of opaque Charleston green, hiding the visitor's identity. No one comes to open it, not the black maid that a movie would have logically placed into the scene—"Welcome, sir-or-ma'am, can I take your coat?" The visitor knocks again.

Quick footsteps on the second floor and Henry descends the stairs. His bright red hair is slicked down with pomade. He wears a pair of beige trousers, shiny black shoes and the requisite white shirt. "I'll be right there!" he calls out.

He pulls a handkerchief from his pocket and wipes his hands and face before opening the door. "Well!" he says. "What a pleasant surprise!"

It's not John.

On the porch is standing a trim man with salt and pepper hair and pleasant, even features. He wears an overcoat and a red scarf. "Hello, Henry," he says.

Henry claps the man on the shoulder. "What are you doing on this side of the Cooper?"

"I had some business over here."

"In your line of work, I guess you go where you're called." Henry stands back. "Come in. It's rather fortuitous you're here. I've been meaning to visit you, but…I've been distracted. Can I take your coat? Beatrice isn't working today, being Sunday afternoon."

The man hugs himself and rubs his arms. "I think I'll keep it on, if you don't mind. This is a cold February." He winks. "Although I'm sure I'm a victim of the thin blood of our kind."

Tipsy can't remember the faces of the other men from John's party. She struggles to place the visitor.

"Jane's upstairs, resting."

"Is she unwell?"

Henry lowers his voice. "Truth be told, I'm worried about her. She's not physically ill, but… you'll see." He stood at the bottom of the stairs with one hand on the banister. "Jane? Come down, darling. We have a visitor." He leans toward the man in the overcoat and speaks again in hushed tones. "I'm sure she'll be happy to see you. Come, I'll pour you a bourbon, to warm up."

Henry and the visitor enter the parlor and Tipsy is torn between waiting on Jane to come down and losing the chance to hear their conversation, or following them. Perhaps something will happen on either end of the memory that she needs to see. Jane makes the decision for Tipsy by appearing at the top of the stairs. Her gray shawl is wrapped around her shoulders. She's barefoot, despite the chill that the visitor described, and she looks as if she's just woken from a long nap. Her feet hit the stairs hard, one step after another, as if she's walking on peg legs. The dark circles under her eyes appear to have become permanent features.

It's taking her too long, and Tipsy wants to know what Henry is saying to their guest, so she leaves Jane to her slow progress and joins the men in the parlor.

"You're in unusually buoyant spirits," says the visitor.

"Truth be told, I'm not," says Henry. "But I've had some revelations of late. Evaluating my actions, so to say, and perhaps my temperament. I've been thinking Jane and I should get away for a while. Perhaps a trip down to Florida. She has cousins in Tallahassee—" Henry sets his glass of bourbon on an end table when Jane enters the room. "Darling, let me help you."

He's walking toward her, but she's stopped in her tracks. Her bare toes twitch. They grip the rug beneath them, like she's a squirrel clinging to a falling tree. She stares at the visitor over Henry's shoulder, as if she and Henry already exist alone in the house, and she's long removed from the company of other human beings.

"Hello, Jane," says the visitor.

Henry steers Jane to the couch, and eases her gently onto the cushions. "Can I get you anything?"

She shakes her head.

"Henry tells me he's worried about you." The visitor sits across from her. The tumbler of bourbon dangles between his knees. "Perhaps I can help you unburden yourself."

Tipsy clings to her conclusion about Jane and John, a scientist with a suspect but rational hypothesis. Perhaps this man knows something about them. And he's going to rat them out.

Jane cracks a smile. "How nice of you to visit us. But I'm not much in the mood for unburdening at the moment."

"I was just saying," says Henry, "it's funny how old friends turn up when you need them."

"It is," says Jane. "Even when they've not been invited."

"Do I need an invitation?" asks the visitor.

"Under the circumstances, yes."

"Jane," says Henry. "Don't be rude to our guest because you're tired. He's always welcomed us with open arms."

The visitor motions Henry to the chair beside him. "Not to worry, Henry. It can be taxing on one's manners when one is in mental distress."

Jane stands. "Henry told you. I'm not well. I'm not prepared for visitors." She opens the gray shawl to reveal the bodice and one sleeve of a lavender dress. "I'm not dressed properly, and I'm not in a conversational mood. Perhaps you can return another day, when we're more prepared."

"Jane—really—" says Henry.

The visitor holds up one hand. "I take no offense."

"I want to go back to my room," Jane says, "but I can't retire until you've taken your leave, sir."

The visitor leans forward. "Perhaps if we all sit a spell, you'll be able to reach a decision. Once it's made, you'll be at peace."

Henry stands, and rakes a hand through his hair. He destroys the pomade job in one swipe. His neat part disappears. "I'm sorry for my wife's behavior. You're right. We can't continue in this state. It's obviously affecting your clarity of thought, Jane. You must make your choice—" He looks down at the guest's head. "Wait—I didn't mention the need for a decision. Did I, Proctor?"

And Tipsy can see the ghost from the St. Philip's Cemetery. The Proctor she knows has white hair and a beard, but he's there in the hazel eyes and long slim fingers of the man before her.

Proctor James shakes his head and removes his red scarf. A white priest's collar peeks over the top buttons of his overcoat. Henry looks between Proctor and Jane. He points at one, and then at the other, as if calculating a particularly difficult arithmetic equation in his head. "You—you're." And he stops.

"I am."

Adrenaline floods Tipsy's bloodstream. Oh my god. Not John. Proctor.

"You're. You." Henry has apparently lost the ability to craft complete sentences. *"You're. You. Him."*

If possible, Jane is whiter now, as a living being, than Tipsy has ever seen her in death. Her eyes start from her face like blue signal flares. "I'm going back to my room now."

The parlor door slams shut behind them, although it's not within anyone's reach. Henry's flaring nostrils shoot out whistling breath and suck it back in so quickly that Tipsy wonders how he doesn't pass out. There can't be any oxygen left in that little patch of recycled air. "I thought, maybe John Huger."

Tipsy almost laughs at their colossally incorrect mutual assumption.

"Or even the new gardener. That strapping big bumpkin." Henry points at Proctor. "But you're *stealing my wife away from me?"*

"With your blessing, from what I've been told."

"Blessing!" Henry's laughter is an explosion. Jane jumps in place, a kernel of corn in a just-hot-enough skillet. "You blessed our marriage. Now you'll be blessing our divorce?"

"That's not yet come to pass. Aren't we here to make this decision?"

Henry grabs Proctor by his overcoat and jerks him to his feet. He drags the priest toward the mantel. "I will kill you. I will smash your pious, hypocritical skull into a million pieces and burn you to ashes in this fireplace. You'll have a straight, hot path to hell."

"Who is the hypocrite? The man who throws his wife willingly to the arms of another, or the man who catches her with the intent to love her like she should have been loved for years?"

Without warning, the china candelabras on the ends of the mantel tip over and smash in a spray of blue wax and white glass. The sound breaks Jane's paralysis. The gray shawl falls from her shoulders as she stands. She hoists it up again with one hand and grabs Henry by the shoulders with the other. "Let go of him. Henry—Proctor, let go!"

Henry detaches from his erstwhile spiritual adviser and falls against Jane. "You told me I didn't know him. You said I didn't know him!" *he screams down into her face.*

"Because I knew this would happen—"

"You couldn't prepare me? As if you'd leave me for him and I wouldn't find out? I cannot...I cannot survive this."

Oh my god, *Tipsy thinks.* He is going to do it. He's going to kill Jane, and then kill himself.

Jane's hands are on Henry's chest. "I haven't made a decision—"

Proctor steps away from the mantel. "Jane—don't succumb to the guilt he heaps on you. Think of how we've been—how happy we've been—"

"Shut your mouth!" Henry screams. A row of books fly off the book-shelves, leather-bound, knowledge-filled dominoes.

"I've loved you your whole life. I've proven it to you in laughter and kindness and patience. Remember?" asks Proctor. His brownish-greenish eyes plead with Jane to see what he sees. "Don't abandon our plan now."

Jane backs toward the couch, and Henry follows her. She slumps onto the cushions and wraps her arms around her knees. Her toes stick out from the hem of the lavender dress. Henry and Proctor bear down on her like the comedy and tragedy masks. Henry's face blotchy and wild, Proctor's calm and beseeching.

"Jane, don't do this to me. I promised you I'll change—"

"We will be as we have been—always—"

Jane covers her ears with her hands and screams. It dies off in a whimper. "Proctor." She looks up at the priest. "You have to leave now. Please... please go."

He straightens. "Is that truly what you want?"

She nods. "Yes—please."

Henry grabs at her hands. "Thank you—my love—my dearest—"

She pulls her fingers from Henry's and stands. She shoves her hands into the deep pockets of her lumpy purple shawl. "Don't you dare touch me."

She backs toward the mantel. Tipsy's stomach drops again. Does she have something in those pockets? A gun? Holy shit. Jane did it.

Henry follows Jane, and Proctor follows Henry. Henry is still begging his wife, and she's replying in some way that doesn't seem to satisfy him, but Proctor's voice rings clear.

"Henry. Henry!"

Henry turns around. His admonishments end mid-syllable.

"Are you right- or left-handed?" Proctor asks. He has his arms crossed over his chest. His hands are tucked inside his coat, Napoleon style.

"What?" Henry says, as if Proctor asked him to dance a waltz in the middle of a surgical procedure.

Proctor repeats himself, and Henry says, "Left."

"I was right. Pardon the pun." Proctor take two strides in Henry's direction. A flash of silver, and a blast like nothing Tipsy has heard before outside of the few times she went to the shooting range with Ayers. Then, however, she wore sound protection over her ears.

The left side of Henry's head explodes. Blood sprays across the parlor, red on green upholstery, a macabre early holiday display. Jane stumbles against the wall with her arms before her face. Her shawl has fallen to the ground, and her husband's blood stains the sleeves of her lavender dress a dark magenta. If the furniture has been dyed in Christmas colors, Jane's clothes smack of Easter.

Jane lowers her arms, her eyes huge and lemur-like. She cries out and lunges at Henry's crumpled form on the floor. She rolls him onto his back. At the sight of his destroyed face, a mass of red and purple and white bone and what must be, dear Lord in heaven, gray brain matter, she retches onto the hearth. "Nonononono—" It's one word.

"Jane," Proctor says, as he creeps toward her. "Now it's easy. You're not obligated to him anymore."

She looks up at him, hysterical horror and disbelief running under the contortions in her face like frantic, tunneling moles. "The telephone—Proctor. The telephone in the foyer. Call the doctor—call my father—call someone."

"No, don't you see? You're a widow now. He killed himself. He was always so glum and sullen."

"Killed himself?"

Proctor smiles, all crazed reassurance. "Or—a thief. We can say a thief killed him."

"Henry—Henry?" She shakes Henry, in final denial of the brutal truth that stares up at her from one remaining dark blue eye. "Oh, my god... sweet Jesus, Henry?"

Proctor's arms slump at his sides. The gun dangles from his thumb. "You're free now, Jane."

"You're insane!" She screams up at him, as she rocks Henry's body. "You're insane—you murdering lunatic!"

"No—I did this for us—I—" Proctor's cheek twitches, and suddenly Tipsy wants this vision to end. Right now. "You'd chosen already," Proctor says. "You'd chosen him."

"How can you talk of that, when you killed him in cold blood? I don't know what I would have done—but what does it matter now? Henry... my love. I'm sorry—I'm so sorry..."

"You always loved him. You didn't love me at all."

"Yes, I did—I—stop. Proctor, please stop talking."

"So now I've done murder—and you loved him. You wanted him."

She doesn't reply. She cradles Henry's lolling head and whispers to herself.

Proctor lifts the gun.

Jane! Tipsy screams. Jane! Jane! Move—run—*Jane! But of course Jane doesn't hear her. Tipsy tries. She reaches for that protective power, but she cannot find it. Not while she's living in the memories of others.*

"I know your secret, Jane," says Proctor.

Jane looks up. Her eyes widen at the sight of the gun pointed into her own face.

"I know you're a whore. For that's what you must be, to have abused me like this."

She shakes her head. "Proctor—no."

"We share secrets, now. You know I'm a murderer. And no one can know that. The world will know a man of God. Not a broken-hearted killer."

Jane scoots away on her bottom. She clings to Henry's limp arm, as if she might drag him with her. "Proctor—I'm sorry—"

The bang sounds again. It rings through Tipsy's head like her thoughts have broken the sound barrier. By some gift of a merciful angle, Tipsy cannot see Jane's chest blow apart as she saw Henry's face do the same, but she does see Jane's body shoot backwards across the floor like a tossed rag doll.

And it's Tipsy who is screaming, and as sometimes happens in nightmares, she screams loud enough to wake herself up.

———◆———

Tipsy's scream died off in her own ears and she opened her eyes. Miss Callie's parlor was firmly replanted in the twenty-first century. Her phone was charging in the dock on the end table beside a leather couch. Not a hint of splattered blood and guts. Henry and Jane above her, both pale and smudgy on the edges but whole. No dismantled face for him, no concave chest for her.

The vision had been too powerful for her to stay on her feet. At some point she'd hit the ground, but fortunately, the old rug was thick and well made. She rolled from her back to her side, and wrapped her arms around her knees. "I'm going to throw up."

At Henry's bidding a small trashcan floated to her side. She winced as bile rose in the back of her mouth. The hearth to her right. Were those patterns in the marble or ninety-year-old bloodstains?

She grabbed the trashcan. For what felt like an hour, but was surely only a few minutes, she hurled up the little she'd eaten. Even when there was nothing left, her stomach kept surging, as her body tried to rid itself of something other than sustenance.

When she thought it safe, she leaned against the sofa. Her eyeballs hurt. She wondered if she'd busted a blood vessel or two, like she had when she gave birth to Little Ayers. Jane knelt beside her. Tipsy held up both hands. "Give me a minute, please. I'll tell you what I saw—but I need a minute."

"You don't need to tell us," Jane said gently.

"I don't?"

Jane shook her head. "Perhaps it was both of us showing you, or maybe Henry's abilities and yours together, but I saw. Proctor killed Henry. And then he killed me. Henry—did *you* see?"

Henry nodded, his face expressionless.

"I would never have thought him capable," Jane said. "He was the *gentlest* of men."

Tipsy shook her head. "I feel like I'm more disturbed by this than you are."

Jane sat beside Tipsy and crossed her legs. *Crisscross-Applesauce*, as Tipsy always said to her kids. "I feel as if you've reminded me of something. As if I've had a word, or a whole *speech*, on the tip of my tongue all this time."

"Are you angry? At Henry—or Proctor? Or yourself?"

"I have nothing *left* to be angry about. It's done. I played my part, and I've suffered for it. But so has Henry. As Proctor must have, too." She closed her eyes, and Tipsy saw the old woman she would have become, had fate been kind. "I want to go home."

"Can you feel your hands, like Luisa said? Or your arms?"

Jane smoothed her hair with her elegant fingers. "I can. It's like my soul is back inside itself. Where it belongs."

"So you'll be going." Tipsy's lip trembled, and she bit her pinky nail to quell it.

"Yes. And for so long I've dreamed of a way to leave this house. Now, I'm going. But I will miss it."

"It's been your home a long time."

"No. It's been my prison. I won't miss its walls. I'll miss the late-incoming friend who calls it home now."

"I'll miss you, too, Jane." Tipsy took a hitching breath. "And now that I know…that I don't have your problems to think on…" *Kids-money-fear-divorce-paintings-lawsuit-worry-house-job.* Themes like chapter titles in a book called *How To Watch Your Life Fall Apart.*

"You're going to be fine, Tipsy. Your now— it lets you be what you want to be. You do *right* by that opportunity."

"I'll try, Jane. I promise."

"I *know* you, darling. You're not just going to try. You're going to *kick some ass.*" The ghost of Jane Robinette Mott winked and brushed Tipsy's cheek with her own in a cool goodbye kiss. She stood and faced her husband. "Are you coming with me?" she asked.

"Not just yet," he said. "I'll be along."

"Don't wait too long. I'm quite *accustomed* to you." She flashed a smile at Henry. Her deep dimples and bright eyes shone from a face that already seemed to have more color. Henry winced, and Tipsy sensed a direct line from the tightening of his face to the constricting of his heart. Rather than waving her arms or clenching her fists, as Luisa and Virginia had done, Jane wrapped her arms around herself, in the first real hug she'd had in decades. The very first time Tipsy laid eyes on Jane, only a few months ago, she'd recognized Jane as a ghost by her smudgy edges. As Jane slowly disappeared, Tipsy saw one painting of her friend flash by in different styles and in varying media—a sharp, bright oil portrait melted into an impressionistic watercolor, until Jane finally disappeared in a fading abstract.

Tipsy stood. "Can you feel it too?"

"Yes," said Henry.

"Are you angry with Jane? For keeping the secret about Proctor all this time?"

"It would have made it worse, had I known all these years that she'd been in love with Proctor before we died." He let out a long breath. "Jane and I have been slowly going insane for decades. That knowledge would have added speed to that process for me. Perhaps she protected me from myself."

"You knew she was hiding something."

"Not until you raised the idea of hunting down the truth, and she didn't want to know it. That's when I became suspicious. Before that, it was simply her mother's claim against mine."

"But you know now. You didn't kill her."

"Didn't I? I don't think I've thought about that conversation, when I told her I didn't care if she strayed. Not once, in life or in death, until you reminded me of it."

"You didn't remember?"

"No. It existed in my mind, but it had no significance. I said it so casually, without a thought, and moved on. But it was that discussion that killed us, as much as Jane's secrets or Proctor's unhinged pain."

"I'm going to miss you, too, Henry," Tipsy said, "and whether it matters to you or not, I'm glad you didn't do it."

"I'm not leaving yet."

"Why? It won't hurt. You can be gone from here now, forever. No more house calling you back."

Like Jane, Henry's edges became smudgy, as if he couldn't stay within the lines of his own coloring book page.

"I'm not ready," he said. "I have more to think on."

"You can think on the other side."

"How do you know?"

Tipsy shrugged. "I guess I don't?"

"Perhaps I will not be me at all when I pass through that doorway. Perhaps I will wake as someone else. Or became part of some..." He quivered, like the last leaf on a winter branch. "...some other being or consciousness?"

Henry's sudden inability to stay solid didn't set well with Tipsy. "You won't know until you get there. But from my limited experience, others seem compelled to go. And most people, the millions who don't end up like you and Jane, they go on without much fuss."

"But I'm not like everyone else." He walked toward Tipsy. Just a few days ago, she might have held her ground and let him pass through her, with the hope of catching a memory, but there was nothing left to see. She stepped out of Henry Mott's way. He disappeared.

"Henry?" Tipsy called. He didn't answer, but Tipsy was fairly certain he heard her.

Chapter 14

Tipsy took a shower, got a huge fountain Coke from McDonalds, and drove downtown, chiding herself for the heaviness in her heart. She knew she should celebrate Jane's freedom, not mourn her own loss. Still, having Jane in the house had been a bit like college all over again. That precious time when your girlfriends are there when you go to sleep and when you wake up, and all the sad and happy moments in between. No need to call or text or meet for coffee. A time that no woman really appreciates until years after it's gone and conversations with her kids or her husband, no matter how dear they are, just don't cut it. She thought about calling Will to let him know what she'd found, and to tell him that Jane had been released from her long captivity, but decided to wait. One other person needed to know first.

She sat on the stone bench in the cemetery at St. Philip's with her phone in her lap. Every time she came to the cemetery, it got hotter and hotter, as if she stepped closer to hell with each visit. She'd piled her hair on top of her head in a messy bun, and her sunglasses fogged up from the heat that radiated off her face. Sweat ran down the backs of her legs.

"I know you killed Jane and Henry, Proctor." She looked down into her lap, as if she were texting someone.

An elderly woman with a pad of paper and crayons sat on the grass about ten feet away. She looked up from the rubbing she was making on one of the gravestones. "Did you say something, miss?"

"No," said Tipsy.

"You got yourself a nice spot, there in the shade."

"Yes, ma'am, although it's still uncomfortably warm."

"Charleston in late August," said the woman. She wore her hair in a slicked back white ponytail rather than a blonde bob à la May Penny. May Penny's flipped under 'do wasn't as ubiquitous as Mimi's keratin job, but Tipsy still admired this woman for letting her hair go the way nature had meant for it. The woman pushed her sunglasses up on her nose. "You don't sound local, but you don't sound too far away, either. Where you from?"

"Upstate. Martinville."

"Ah, my first husband was born in Gaffney. Not too far."

"No, ma'am, not too far. I've been living in Charleston since I graduated from Carolina."

The woman shook a finger at her. "We're a Clemson family."

Tipsy smiled. "And you seemed so nice."

The woman laughed and waved her orange crayons at Tipsy before returning to her rubbing.

"Friendly conversation everywhere you go in Charleston," said Proctor. He sat beside Tipsy with one leg crossed over the other and his hands around his knee. Hazel eyes and straight, almost boringly even features behind his snowy beard. The quintessential Anglican holy man. The same large hands and long fingers that had gripped the silver gun.

Yes. Tipsy didn't open her mouth, in case the PI was hiding amidst the gravestones. *But lately it seems like every friendly conversationalist has an unsavory secret that's going to come out eventually. In Charleston, you might as well fly your batshit crazy banner alongside your Gamecock football flag.*

"Once everyone knows your troubles, why bother pretending to be perfect? You should try being a minister, if you'd like to hear some disturbing stories."

Is that how you came to be Jane's lover?

He started at her question, and then nodded. "She came to me, heartbroken over Henry. I'd always worshipped her from a distance. I never thought she'd pay me a bit of mind, but we fell together quite easily. Once her love was a possibility, and then a reality, it became my obsession."

And no one ever found out. No one ever discovered your troubles.

"Correct. A rare case of a secret staying secret."

I thought it was John. I was sure he never married out of guilt, and unrequited love.

"John was not the marrying type."

At least he was a true friend to Jane. Unlike you, apparently.

"I wanted nothing more than her happiness, unbelievable as that may seem." Proctor's lips stopped moving. *How do you know all this?*

Jane and Henry showed me. You don't need to know anything else.

So Jane knows now? She remembered it all?

Yes. She's gone home. Like Virginia and Luisa.

I'm glad. He smiled, but happiness fell from his face as quickly as it had appeared. *When you told me that she lingered, as I do...it killed me, should you pardon the pun. The thought of that precious spirit...trapped, as I've been...*

Tipsy wanted to punch him. *Why didn't you kill yourself, right then? If you were so in love with Jane. You killed her, and Henry, and then kept right on living as if nothing had happened.*

He shook his head. *No. Everything changed for me. I never touched another woman. Not that I'd had the nerve to touch many before. The town rumor mill claimed that I had, shall we say, strange proclivities.*

Everyone thought you were gay? Homosexual?

He nodded. *It suited me fine. I preached peace and kindness, and I drank myself into oblivion most nights. For the next twenty-seven years.*

Maybe that's how you died. You're still here, so you must not know.

I know. He pointed toward the other side of the graveyard, in the direction of Jane and Henry's grave. *I froze to death. I used to sit out here, in the middle of the night, and talk to Jane. Almost every night. Usually, I was so drunk I didn't remember what I said, although it doesn't matter. It's not like she heard me. I thought she'd be in heaven and maybe she could. It was a January night. The coldest in years. A drunken southern priest wouldn't think to wear a coat. Or even shoes, I suppose. I passed out, and never woke up. The sexton found me the next morning in my shirtsleeves and stocking feet.*

Proctor lifted one leg. It went solid, and Tipsy saw that the blackness of his slacks ended in equally black socks, not the shoes she'd assumed must be there. He wiggled his toes, revealing a few largish holes. *Bachelor life,* he said. *No one to darn my socks.*

And you remembered what happened? Tipsy asked.

Proctor looked at Tipsy as if she'd failed kindergarten. *No, of course not. Not at first. But the congregation talked about it incessantly. If no one ever knew about my love affair with Jane, they certainly knew more about my drinking than I ever realized. I heard tell within a week or so of what happened.*

So why are you here? Can't you leave?

Yes. I can feel my arms. And even my legs, shady as they are, when I want to feel them.

Why don't you go?

Proctor put both feet on the ground, as if gravity still mattered to him. *I'm afraid. Of His judgment. I spent my life studying scripture. And any Christian knows, thou shalt not kill.*

Are you repentant?

He nodded, vehemently. *Every day of my life, and every day of my death.*

Isn't Christianity about forgiveness as well?

I'm too frightened to find out.

Proctor, I'm not sure why I'm telling you this, but Jane went home with no anger toward you. If she can forgive you, and God is all-powerful and loving, don't you think He can, too?

What of Henry? Has he moved on?

He didn't seem to have any anger toward you last I saw him…but… Tipsy sighed. Something about Henry's befuddled ruminating in those few minutes after he understood the truth bothered her. *I'm worried about him, to be honest. The longer I knew Jane, the more she calmed. They still fought all the time, but she seemed more— more coherent. I thought Henry was on the same path, but once I reminded him of the past, he relapsed. And it got worse once he knew what really happened to him and Jane. It's like she became saner, and he went crazier. I believe he's still in the house.*

Proctor's interest in Henry only went so far. *But Jane forgives me. And she's at peace.*

Yes. I got the impression she'd want you to be at peace, too.

He stood. *Knowing she's in a good place is enough for me.*

But you're staying here? You really aren't a man of much faith if you aren't willing to trust that your god will forgive you.

I stole the fragile heart of another man's wife, and you know what came to pass from that. Perhaps I never had much faith. He pointed at the multiple spires above his head and turned in a slow circle. *St. Philip's. The old Hugenot church. St. Michael's. The Circular Congregationalist place. Over there* —he waved in the direction of Broad Street— *the papists and their cathedral.*

There's a reason they call Charleston the Holy City.

So there is. So much sanctity crammed onto one small peninsula, but our piety runs disappointingly shallow. A creek that purports to be deepwater dockage but turns to a mud flat at low tide.

You wanted so badly for Jane to make a bold choice.

That boldness was a long time ago, Miss Seer. Proctor James walked to the MOTT headstone, the gravesite of the couple he'd murdered. He sat and rested his back against it. He crossed his misty legs at the ankle. Tipsy wondered if that's how the sexton had found him on a cold January morning in 1949.

She wiped her sweaty hands on her cotton dress and shook out the long skirt. "You choose fear, Proctor. So be it."

The lady with the crayons looked up again. She smiled and pointed at Tipsy, and for a moment she reminded Tipsy of Granna, although this woman had the look of good breeding and an easy life, as opposed to Granna's square country chin and work swollen legs. She removed her sunglasses and dabbed her upper lip with a white lace handkerchief. She had sharp dark eyes. "Now you did say something!" she said. "I'm not imagining it."

"Yes, ma'am," said Tipsy. "You're right. Maybe the heat is going to my brain."

"Go get yourself a bottle of water, honey."

"I will."

"You don't want to be sitting in graveyards talking to yourself. People will think you're a little—" She twirled her finger beside her temple.

"They sure will. Don't want that."

"Do you come here often?" asked the woman. "I'll be working in this cemetery for the next week or so. It would be nice to have a chat now and then. These stones sure are quiet. I'm Vivian. Vivian Greenblatt."

"I have been, but I won't have much reason to any—wait, Vivian Greenblatt?" Tipsy left the bench as if it had bit her rear end. She knelt beside the woman. "You bought one of my paintings. *Stepping off the Porch!*"

Vivian wiped bits of orange crayon on her linen shorts. "Tipsy Collins! So nice to meet you." She held out a hand to give Tipsy's a shake, but Tipsy couldn't help herself. She hugged Vivian.

"Goodness!" said Vivian, but she hugged Tipsy back.

"I'm sorry." Tipsy let go and they both stood. "That was an important sale for me. I hadn't worked in a long time, and I needed it."

"Of course, dear. I'm glad I got to it before someone else did. It's one of my favorites. It was my good luck, having dinner with Barker that day."

"I'm so glad you did, and I'm so glad you said hello. I never would have guessed you were Vivian Greenblatt from New York." Tipsy blushed in mortification as soon as the words left her mouth. They were loaded with all sorts of assumptions. "Not that you look—ah, you look like—"

Vivian laughed. "I don't look like a New York Jewish lady? Or sound like one? No bouffant hairdo, or *Oy-vey, dah-ling?*"

Tipsy grimaced. "You called me out. Horrible. I'm so provincial."

"Don't worry about it, bless your heart. We Charleston Jews are a well-kept secret among many of our neighbors. You know, in 1800, South Carolina was home to more Jews than any other state."

"No, ma'am. I didn't know that."

"It's true. I've already studied all the gravestones in the cemetery at KKBE. Kahal Kadosh Beth Elohim." She swelled with pride. "The fourth oldest Jewish congregation in America. I'm working on my family tree, and my daughter married a Christian. Her husband has relations in this cemetery." Vivian said it like those relations were still living. As if she'd come to chat with them in person, rather than record their vital statistics.

317

"Interesting," said Tipsy. "I'm sure my ex-husband has relatives in cemeteries all over town. Maybe when my kids are older I'll do some genealogy research."

"All old southern ladies do it," said Vivian. "Jew or gentile, black or white. We like to know where we came from."

"Honestly, I'm also surprised to learn Barker has friends his own age."

Vivian rolled her eyes. "I've known Barker for years. We were at Clemson at the same time. He knew my first husband very well. Barker was a rarity in those days. He didn't care if someone was a Jew or a Negro or a leper if he thought that person could help him get ahead. He's always had a weakness for pretty women. Unfortunately for him, his definition of pretty never went past the age of thirty."

"He said you were from New York."

"My second husband is a New Yorker. I moved up there with him when we got married. Almost fifteen years ago. I demanded we keep a place down here, near my family. So we summer on Kiawah." Vivian squinted up at the sky. "Goodness! High noon sun. Still, I'll take our good clean heat over muggy New York every time."

Tipsy looked at her phone. "Noon! Jeez, I have to get to the GQB." She hugged Vivian again. "It was so nice to meet you. Thank you again for supporting my work."

"Of course, Tipsy. You're very talented."

Tipsy bid Vivian Greenblatt goodbye and walked toward the cemetery gate. She didn't bother checking to see if Proctor had disappeared. It didn't seem to matter one way or another.

⸻

Two days later, on Thursday evening, the kids went to Ayers for the weekend. Tipsy called in sick to work on Friday. She slept most of the day. By evening, her stomach felt as normal as it had in weeks, and her headache was nothing more than she'd feel after one too many glasses of wine. Her limbs felt light and tingly, and sort of achy in that post workout kind of way— where it hurts, but it feels good, too. She sensed something healing inside her.

That Saturday afternoon, Tipsy and Will arrived at Home Team Barbeque on Sullivan's in advance of their friends, to give Tipsy time to fill him in on the details of Jane's sad-yet-happy departure. They sat at a high table with a pile of nachos before them. She had a glass of ice water. She hadn't see the PI since she confronted him on Water Street, but she figured he could be creeping around the crowded restaurant somewhere, perhaps while sporting a well-placed toupee. Tipsy kept her voice low, although a loud Saturday early-season college football crowd filled the place. The story took longer than it should have, as they had to say hello to numerous acquaintances, both mutual and non. The latter required introductions, which only took away from Tipsy's storytelling time. She had to pause for touchdowns and first downs, fumbles and interceptions, because the volume increased exponentially with the progress of each of the four games on the overhead televisions and the number of beers consumed by the observers.

"Slow down and speak up," Will said, as drained his beer.

"I can't speak up. People might hear me—"

"I can barcly hear myself think."

"—and I want to tell you everything before they get here."

"Okay…so Jane is gone, but Henry isn't."

"Right. Jane is gone." Tipsy felt the sharp sting of tears. She pressed her cocktail napkin to her eyes.

"Babe, didn't you want to set her free?"

"Yes—yes. But I miss her. She was my friend." Tipsy leaned on her elbows. She wore a slouchy tee shirt, and it slipped further over her shoulder. "Don't make fun of me, Will! Missing a ghost."

319

"I'm not!" he said. "But you wanted to help her. You did. Now you should be happy for her."

"I am—I know. You're right—"

He took her hands. "But it's totally legit to miss her."

She smiled at him. "You're so sweet. Validating my emotions."

"I read *Men are From Mars, Women are From Venus*. The Wikipedia summary, anyway."

"It's funny, even though I convinced myself that John was Jane's secret Romeo, now it all seems obvious. Jane being so taken aback when I mentioned meeting Proctor. And when I asked Proctor about Jane and Henry's death he said he couldn't tell me what happened. Not, *I don't know*. He said, *I can't tell you*. In other words, I don't want to tell you."

"And you haven't seen Henry?" Will reached across the table and tugged Tipsy's tee shirt back up onto her shoulder.

She shook her head.

"Maybe he's gone." Will shrugged. "Maybe he didn't say goodbye."

"Maybe."

P.D. and Lindsey joined them. Shelby arrived soon after with a new guy in tow. Tipsy slid around to Will's side of the table. "Oh, lord, another one," she whispered.

He shifted her shirt again. "Let's give him a chance now, Miss Skeptic. And will you watch that shirt? Every time it slips down I imagine slipping it off. I'm going to have to adjust myself when I walk to the bathroom." He motioned to his lap.

"Ha," Tipsy said. "Keep up that talk and I'll be following you in there and adjusting for you."

"What are ya'll whispering about?" asked Shelby. "Say hi to Brian, please. Show him some good southern manners."

Tipsy said hello to Brian, and summed him up as unlike anyone Shelby had dated in the past. He was cute in a pleasant but not sexy way, probably fifteen pounds overweight, and had short brown hair shot through with bits of gray. She learned that he'd recently moved to Charleston from Connecticut, where he'd lived all his life. He was a software engineer for a local start up. He and Shelby met when he came into the GQB to ask after a particular photographer.

"You fish?" asked Will.

"No," said Brian. He took Shelby's hand on the table.

"Hunt?"

"No. I'm not opposed to learning."

"Hmm, okay," said P.D. "What do y'all do up there in Connecticut, for fun?"

"I rowed in college. Still enjoy it. Oh, and I brew beer in my garage."

This caught Will and P.D.'s attention and while the men talked it gave Tipsy time to smile her approval at Shelby. "Third date," Shelby said, and wagged her eyebrows.

"Slooooow down, Speed Racer," said Tipsy.

Lindsey leaned toward Shelby. "He seems really—" Her mouth fell open, and Tipsy and Shelby looked toward the entrance. Glen scanned the crowd from the doorway.

Tipsy elbowed Will. She whispered in his ear. "Did you tell Glen we were coming here?"

He shook his head. "No, I haven't talked to him in a couple weeks. But half of Mount Pleasant is here. It's not surprising he'd show up."

P.D. and Brian were still engrossed in talk of hops, but Shelby had gone as white as Jane in a snow bank. Tipsy locked eyes with Glen. "Damn," she said, as he walked toward their table.

"Hey, y'all," he said.

They exchanged hellos, and Will introduced Brian. "He just moved to town."

"Ah," said Glen. "Yeah, you got that look."

"What look is that?" asked Brian.

"Glen," said Shelby. "You know Mark and Jennifer—over there." She pointed at the red Mercedes couple that Lindsey had described in the GQB, the ones who were living off the money of some poor divorcé who was probably in a nursing home by now. "I heard he's not happy with the charter he's been using to take his friends fishing. You should talk to him."

"You think so."

"Yeah, I do. Why don't you go over there right now."

Glen nodded. "Maybe I will. Thanks for the tip, Shelby."

"You're welcome. Anytime."

Glen didn't approach Mark and Jennifer. He sidled up to the far end of the bar and set about pounding Fireball shots and glaring at Shelby and Brian. Tipsy caught Shelby and Brian's conversation out of one ear.

"Who is that guy?"

"I dated him for a while."

"I figured." Brian's eyes flicked between Shelby's face and the tan, tattooed, rangy figure of Glen at the bar, with his sunglasses buried in his shaggy hair like an additional set of jealous eyes.

"Don't worry about him," Shelby said. "Honestly."

"You sure?"

She leaned into Brian's side. "Yup. I'm sure."

"Here he comes," said P.D. "We don't need this. Grow up, man."

"Damn right. Enough of his B.S. I'll take care of it." Will intercepted Glen. Tipsy didn't catch much of what Will said, except, "Your wife at home."

Glen shrugged Will's hand from his shoulder and pushed through the crowd toward the door. "Lord," Tipsy said. "Good riddance."

Will slid into his seat beside her. "I'm finished with that kind of redneck ridiculousness," he said to no one in particular.

Tipsy could almost see Granna's smile. *Looks like Will cares about more than just fish gettin' caught, after all,* Granna said.

Tipsy smiled back at her Granna, and let the whole table think she was smiling back at them. "Potty— I mean, bathroom break," she said. Sometimes she had trouble switching out of mommy talk, even when the kids weren't around.

Shelby followed her. "What is it about Home Team?" she asked, once they'd closed the door behind them. She reapplied lipstick as Tipsy locked herself in the stall. "I've never been to a place where more grown men get into altercations."

"Fireball shots and egos," Tipsy called over the door. She joined Shelby at the mirror. "Brian seems really nice."

"I think he is," said Shelby. "But you know, even if it turns out he isn't, I'm fine."

"Really? I'm proud of you."

"There's always another one coming down the pike, Tipsy. I'll get lucky someday, and find one that sticks. Look at you, with Will."

"Yeah, but I lived with Ayers for sixteen years. Besides, it's definitely good with Will right now, but let's see how I feel when hunting season really kicks in. Plus, I still got a lot of figuring out to do myself. I'm not ready to lock it in yet."

"True, true. Still, you and Will are the most normal people I know."

Tipsy opened the bathroom door. "Considering the people you know, Shelby, I don't even know if that's a compliment."

Chapter 15

School started a few days later, and with it the relief of returning to an academic year schedule. Tipsy happily traded the scramble of scheduling camps and late afternoon childcare for earlier wakeups and all three kids attending after-care at their elementary school. Little Ayers started third grade with little fanfare. She marveled at his uncanny maturity as he sauntered into his new classroom after bidding the principal a polite hello. The girls were split into two different first grade classes at Tipsy's request. They pined for each other for a few days, for they'd never spent so much time apart. By the end of the week, however, M.P. and O-Liv were planning a sleepover for the new friends they'd made in their respective classrooms. Tipsy dropped everyone at school by half past seven. She had time to hit the gym or go for a run and still make it to the GQB by half past nine to prep for opening.

She'd always been a creature of habit, so the regularity suited her. Still, the looming lawsuit and her continued lack of painting inspiration disturbed the routine, like foreboding clunks and whistles coming from the engine of her well-oiled machine. She'd received a Notice of Continuation from Clark Middleton, Esquire, thanks to May Penny. She had some time, but she still needed to come up with a new painting, stat, and then sell it, double stat, so she could hire her own lawyer.

The lingering question of Henry's whereabouts also nagged her. After over two weeks with no sign of him, Tipsy had convinced herself that Will had been right. He'd probably moved on without saying goodbye.

Seems rude, said Granna.

Well, Henry hasn't always showed himself to be the most well-mannered guy.

Tipsy ran into the house on Wednesday of the second week of school. She took the stairs two at a time. A run on the beach had stretched on longer than she'd planned. She'd been looking for potential paintings in everything and everyone she passed, from other runners to wet dogs to beached jellyfish, and ruminating on sixteen years' worth of unpleasant Ayers anecdotes, as a self-defense strategy against his attacks on her own character. She'd come back to reality a full mile and a half past her usual turn around point. She'd booked it back to her truck, but she'd lost almost thirty minutes of getting ready time. Shelby had an important client arriving at the gallery promptly at 10am.

She stripped off her sweaty, sandy clothes in the bathroom and stared at herself in the mirror. *Is a shower really necessary?*

Uh…not trying to be rude, sugar, but…

Tipsy leaned closer to her red, splotchy reflection and sniffed under one arm. *You're right Granna!*

She grabbed some underwear and a bra and a sundress and piled it all on the back of the toilet. Shower, lotion, a bit of tinted moisturizer. She slicked her wet hair into a tight ballerina bun, but the wavy strands that always framed her face would not cooperate with such utilitarianism, so she pulled a few longer pieces loose in what she hoped lent an aura of purposeful messiness. She whipped out her mascara, began swiping it across her eyelashes, and promptly poked herself in the eye. Both eyes teared up, as if her left sympathized with her right. "Damnit! Forget this." She dabbed makeup remover under her eyes, which were now charmingly bloodshot. *Perhaps this can be my new painting. I will call it* Woman Running Late. *Critics will describe the subject's big gray eyes, which are eerily reminiscent of a heroin addict's.*

She threw on her clothes, remembered deodorant at the last minute, and flung open the bathroom door. She screamed at the sight of Henry on the other side.

"Pardon," he said, as she clutched at the doorframe with her chest heaving. "I've gotten so good at not startling you."

"Okay…okay," she said. "Don't worry about it, but I have to go. I'm late for work. I promised Shelby I'd be there early."

"She's already there."

"How do you know?"

"I thought you were on the beach, but I couldn't find you, so I visited the gallery this morning. I thought you might be there."

"Shelby never gets there early," said Tipsy. She grabbed for her phone. "I'll call her—wait, she texted."

I got in early! Stayed at Brian's last night, down on Broad Street ☺ *no rush! And BTW, I've got something exciting to tell you!*

Tipsy replied, *Ok…what? Don't leave me hanging!*

She set the phone on Miss Callie's blue and white dresser and pointed at her eyes. "At least now I can wait for the swelling to go down. Haven't seen you in a while. I thought you'd left. Gone on."

Henry shook his head. "I'm still not ready."

Tipsy thought of Proctor, and for some reason both men's hesitance struck her as exceedingly annoying. "Lord, Henry. I've seen you writhing in pain from leaving this house for an hour. Now you can go and you're staying put?"

"When I leave the house now, I know where I'm going."

"Writers love drama, right? It's an adventure. Going off to some new world you've never seen. And you're following Jane." She shrugged. "It's kind of romantic, actually. I can see it all laid out in a novel."

"I've never finished a novel."

"No way. All that writing and you never—" She stopped, remembering his sadness when he spoke to Jane about his lack of literary productivity. "No, I get it. I've gone years without being able to paint a thing."

"If I go on now, I won't ever finish."

"Ah, Henry. If you haven't noticed, you're probably not finishing anything here, either. That one note to Will gave me the impression your problems are bigger than a little carpal tunnel syndrome."

"Perhaps I can finish it somehow. I have thought… someone in this day should invent a machine. Where one can speak into it and his words would be transferred to paper."

"Um… there sort of are machines like that. My phone could do it."

"That would be perfect."

"Yeah, but unfortunately the magic female voice inside my phone can't hear you."

"I know it's there," said Henry. "Inside me. THE GREAT STORY."

And that's how Tipsy pictured it, in all capital letters. Perhaps in bold and italic with a fancy font.

Henry rattled on like an intoxicated philosophy professor. "If I go on, what if I'm not me? What if the story goes away?"

"Maybe it will, but you'll be at peace, and from what I sensed from Jane and Luisa, in a place that's full of happiness."

Henry sat on the bed. "I can't write THE GREAT STORY if I'm in a place that's all happiness and contentment. Without sorrow, there's nothing to juxtapose the joy. I don't see how one can exist without the other."

"You've had plenty of sorrow. From what I've seen, you were sorrowful in life, and now you've been sorrowful in death for ninety plus years. Maybe it's time to try something different."

"I can find a way to tell my story." He smiled, and Tipsy noticed a tick under his right eye. "I've started it, in here." He pointed at the side of his head. The left side, that Proctor had blown apart in the downstairs parlor. "I've been reciting the first chapter, over and over."

Tipsy tried another route. "Don't you miss Jane? Especially now that everything is revealed, and if I'm correct, forgiven. You'll be able to see her."

He nodded. "Yes, I miss her. But what if I cross over and I can't find her?"

"I've never heard so many what if's."

That response floated over Henry's head like dandelion fluff. "Besides," he said, "in missing Jane, I love her more than I ever did when we were together. It's a pure love."

"Sorry, dude—"

"Dude?"

"But that's not *pure love*. That's melodramatic, tortured artist crap. If you really loved her, you'd go right now and exist with her in whatever state of joy she's in."

"You don't understand, but that's to be expected. I've met few people in all my years who truly understand me." He muttered under his breath. "*...and he waited, in breathless agony, for her to come home...a man who has seen the sunrise and subsequently been struck blind...*" The fingers of his left hand moved in small circles, like a conductor leading a tiny orchestra, or a man holding a pencil. Tipsy picked up her phone and read Shelby's response.

You're going out to Kiawah Friday morning. That woman who bought Stepping off the Porch, Vivian Greenblatt, wants to commission you!

"Oh, my gosh," said Tipsy. "Sorry—I have to call Shelby."

"I'd like to show you something, if I may."

"Sure—but, this could be what I need to pay a lawyer." Tipsy hadn't had a commission in over ten years. The idea thrilled and terrified her. "Let me at least text her back—"

Tipsy was so intent on typing – *OMG! I wonder what she wants* – that she didn't notice Henry's long fingers close over her wrist until the phone screen in front of her face faded behind a visual cacophony of black and yellow lights.

———————•———————

This memory is different from the others, because Tipsy is sitting in the back seat of an extended cab pickup. Henry sits beside her, to her right. Through the windows, it's all leafy green woods. There's a bunch of stuff around her feet: a camo flask, a Chick-fil-a bag, some empty beer bottles and koozies, and a few cannisters of Buck Bomb, the noxious doe pee extract that hunters spray on themselves to attract male deer.

"Roll down the window," says a familiar voice. It's Jimmy, her brother-in-law. Beside him is Ayers, in the passenger seat. They're not wearing full camo hunting clothes. They're both in tee shirts, but with jeans and heavy boots instead of their usual summer uniform of khaki shorts and flip flops. They must be out on the hunt club land, laying out corn to encourage the deer to visit.

"Nah," says Ayers. "It's too damn hot. The gnats."

"I don't want to go home smelling like weed. Mimi will shit her pants."

"I'll crack it." Ayers rolls down the window about an inch. "You sure you don't want a hit?"

Tipsy leans forward. Ayers has a zip lock bag of marijuana on his lap. He's stuffing the greenish brown shredded leaves into a black pipe with a Dia de los Muertos *skull on the side.*

"Yeah, I'm sure," says Jimmy. "Been a long time. If I get high, I'll probably get paranoid. Think the deer are coming for me, instead of vice versa."

329

"I went about eight years without smoking," says Ayers, as he draws a flame from a blue lighter with a flick of his thumb. "Got used to it again damn quick. I needed a way to relax when Tipsy gave me shit about the kids and work. And everything else."

Tipsy hadn't realized Ayers smoked weed during their marriage.

"I'm still married. And I'm not that slick. Sure Mimi would bust me. We've been gettin' along. I can't deal with a fight tonight."

Ayers takes a long drag from the pipe. He holds his breath for a few seconds, and exhales slowly. "Glad I don't have to worry about fighting with Tipsy anymore. Not every day, anyway. Being divorced is just as stressful. But at least I can get my relaxation in peace."

Tipsy laughs out loud, since no one could hear her, at Ayers's depiction of a marriage in which he was so sorely put upon. She has college déjà vu as the smoke dissipates through the car. She'd never enjoyed weed herself—it made her sleepy the couple times she tried it— but you never forget that smell. Jimmy reaches into the back seat and grabs some Buck Bomb. He spritzes himself, and opens the door.

"Don't leave any of that shit in my truck," he says to Ayers. "It's still illegal in South Carolina."

"Got it, 'Bo. I won't."

Jimmy grabs a bag of corn and walks off into the woods. Ayers sits quietly, puffing as the urge hits him. He checks his phone. He grabs a bag of potato chips from the passenger seat floor and crunches away. Apparently he's got the munchies.

Suddenly, the truck lurches.

"What the fuck," says Ayers. He grabs the console beside him. With a click-click, the doors lock.

Tipsy turns to Henry. His eyes are closed and he's muttering under his breath. The car shakes. Ayers grabs at the door handle. He pushes buttons, then tries to force the lock upright, but it won't move. "Jesus. Earthquake."

The car bounces and rattles. Tipsy's teeth chatter in her head. The seatbelt beside her head clatters against the window glass. Ayers grabs a water bottle and pours some on his pipe. It goes out with a hiss. He stuffs the pipe into a camo backpack at his feet.

"Jimmy!" he screams, and bangs on the window.

The rattling stops, and the passenger door swings open. Ayers starts to jump out, but he grabs the doorframe with a grunt. His mouth hangs open, like the door. Tipsy looks out her window.

The truck hovers about five feet above the dirt and pine needles below. With all the vibrating, she hadn't noticed the levitation. Neither had Ayers. It's good thing he notices now, because he'd probably break a leg if he jumped straight out.

Ayers sits back in the seat and slams the door. He closes his eyes. "Wake up," he whispers. "Wake up. Sober up. Wake up."

The truck crashes back to the ground, and with a jolt, it's Tipsy who is waking up.

———•———

Two days later, on Friday morning, Tipsy arrived at Vivian Greenblatt's beachfront Kiawah mansion at half past eight. She'd woken before dawn with a case of nerves that wouldn't subside, but happily, she didn't have a headache, or feel queasy. She'd showered and dressed in a pair of black slacks and a flowing silk blouse before the kids woke up. Olivia Grace had looked up at her from her pillow, her hair in its usual state of messy little girl bed head, and said, "Wow, Mama. Where you going so early? You got on earrings and everything."

Unlike Sullivan's Island, Kiawah didn't do shabby chic. Every detail of Vivian's house oozed perfection, from her elaborate landscaping to the hand carved knobs on her kitchen cabinets. Vivian showed Tipsy a blank expanse of wall over the white couch in her formal living room.

White on white everywhere, so Tipsy breathed a sigh of relief at the freedom of palette. Vivian had greeted Tipsy with the same grandmotherly friendliness she'd shown in the cemetery, but when they started talking art she was all business, like any serious collector.

"I love your work, Tipsy," she said, "so I'm willing to give you a lot of leeway. I want something that shows the character of the region, but also the grittiness. What's behind our pastel houses and the white beaches and charming accents."

Tipsy nodded. She wondered at what Vivian has seen, and experienced, in her day. She'd referred to Charleston's Jewish population as a well-kept secret, but Tipsy had a hunch that there had been a time when it was easier, and maybe even safer, for Jews to keep to themselves.

"That's what I loved about *Stepping Off the Porch,*" said Vivian. "The sense of something below the surface. I've never seen anything quite like it. I can't promise I'll buy whatever you come up with, but I have a feeling you understand what I'm looking for, and can give it to me."

Vivian offered coffee and scones, but Tipsy demurred. The pressure of Vivian's request had infiltrated her bloodstream, like intravenous fluids administered during a state of severe dehydration. Vivian stopped Tipsy on the way out. She rested a slender but age-spotted hand tipped in perfectly manicured fingernails on Tipsy's shoulder. She had that casual white hair, but her perfect makeup, tastefully Botox-ed brow and robin's egg-sized diamond earrings reminded Tipsy that Vivian wasn't your run-of-the-cotton-mill southern grandma.

"Shelby and Barker told me a bit about you," Vivian said. "I've been where you are. Starting over, with young children and a heap of uncertainty. I took advantage of the bones thrown to me. And I did it before I ever considered getting remarried. A woman's independence is her greatest treasure." She squeezed Tipsy's shoulder. "And I'm not just talking about money."

"My girls will know that," said Tipsy.

"The best way to teach them is to show them." Vivian squeezed Tipsy's shoulder and asked for a sketch of the painting's design within two weeks.

———•———

As Tipsy drove back from Kiawah that morning, through the rural community of John's Island, her eyes darted from one side of Bohicket Road to the other. When she tired of left to right, she glanced up through her sunroof. Flashes of light found nooks and crannies in the canopy of leaves and Spanish moss that turned Bohicket into an asphalt and foliage cathedral aisle. The oaks didn't quite match up to the Old Cannon's behemoths, but they'd been known to stop a car or two. They bumped up against the asphalt, some of them sawed off in strategic places so as not to spill into the road. Striped reflectors on skinny poles stood before each tree, shiny memorials to lives snuffed out on impact. The reflectors served as reminders that the trees had been there long before there were cars to careen into them.

There seemed to be a church every mile or so, although Tipsy couldn't fathom how the island had the population to support so many congregations. A few were traditional denominations, mostly Methodists and Baptists, but some had the colorful titles Tipsy associated with screaming pastors and fainting parishioners. *House of the Good Word Praise Cathedral. Light of the World Tabernacle and Fellowship Center.* The longer the name, the humbler the church. Trailers and ramshackle houses sat alongside private driveways. Engraved signage welcomed guests to estates with names like Osprey Point and Save Haven Farm.

This is what Vivian is talking about, Tipsy said to Granna. *What's below the surface.*

Same thing downtown. Carriage rides taking tourists past the projects on their way to the next mansion.

Tipsy clenched the steering wheel and asked Granna the question she'd asked herself on the beach.

What if I can't paint anything without them?

Granna didn't reply, so Tipsy drove on. She retraced the sketching and painting of each of her three last paintings in her head. Undoubtedly her best work. Each piece inspired by the conundrum of Jane and Henry, her erstwhile muses. Jane lost to the victory of a solved mystery and Henry to his own perpetual tragedy, so it seemed. And it had been a month since Tipsy had felt the moment of revelation that inspired *The Joggling Board.*

A woman's independence is her greatest treasure.

It's funny, how men were supposedly less emotional than women, yet their feelings had dominated Tipsy's life. She had molded her notions of what constituted correct reactions, not based on her own feelings, but on theirs. Much had changed for the better in Charleston since Jane's day, but these nebulous, private quandaries with no black and white answers—they lingered, subtle and insidious, wreaking gory emotional fallout. Jane hadn't been able to live the life that was expected of her, let alone the life she may have truly wanted. Still, Jane had found a way to move on. To release her old sorrows and hardships, along with the expectations others had created for her, and those she'd placed upon herself.

Tipsy could do the same, if she was brave enough.

———◆———

The gallery was unusually busy that day, due to a cruise ship at port. Tourists streamed in and out. Tipsy answered questions about artists, gave color scheme advice, and sold and made shipping arrangements for three sculptures and two large paintings. She enjoyed herself, and knew Shelby would be thrilled, but she didn't get a chance to think much about her own commission. The pressure returned as she locked the gallery doors and walked to her truck.

As she drove up East Bay Street toward the Ravenel Bridge, she squeezed the steering wheel with both hands and glared through the windshield, like Superman trying to penetrate Kryptonite with x-ray vision.

Vivian Greenblatt had tossed her a bone. She had to chew on it.

She spoke a quick text into her phone, thanking May Penny for picking up the kids from aftercare. She drove down Coleman Boulevard and turned onto Rifle Range Road, on her way to Target to grab art supplies for Little A's science project ("Bugs of South Carolina"). She rushed through her shopping, and escaped with a poster board, some construction paper, and a less than twenty-dollar tab. To her annoyance, traffic on Rifle Range Road crawled along. A stalled car, or maybe an accident.

She gazed out the window, at Mount Pleasant's version of *below the surface.* On her right, tiny cabins and single-wides once again crouched beside a busy thoroughfare. Some advertised firewood for sale, or produce, or sweetgrass baskets. To her left: a new subdivision of large coastal "cottages" and Nuevo Charleston singles. Most streets branching off Rifle Range led into neighborhoods of varying age and grandeur, but some were dirt roads, leading back to additional hamlets of humble living spaces.

Most of the people Tipsy saw coming and going from these homes and seemingly out-of-place country roads were African American. She'd read enough about gentrification in Mount Pleasant to know that their families had lived on the land for generations, going about their daily business of working and playing and falling in and out of love, while the town slowly tried to swallow up the evidence of them. Some of their predecessors had sold to developers, and she hoped those people were living comfortably wherever they'd chosen to go. But she admired the ones who remained. Their ancestors had survived slavery, Reconstruction, Jim Crow, and the Civil Rights movement. They were still here, making the best of whatever passed for equality in this day and age. Over the years, Charleston had absorbed parts of the Gullah-Geechee heritage into its pretty postcard. Their food. Their music. Even the ubiquitous sweetgrass baskets. All the while trying to ignore or stamp out the identity of the real live human beings who had created those things.

But they keep on livin', said Granna.

Yes, they certainly do, Tipsy replied. She was suddenly exhausted. She wished she were home in her bed with a commission idea simmering in her mind and her children sleeping peacefully down the hall.

She leaned her head against the window. Movement down the road caught her eye, and she smiled at the familiar figure.

In her own mind, Tipsy called her the Walking Lady. She was a petite, wiry black woman with salt and pepper hair that she wore in long braids. She wore glasses with pink frames, and Tipsy guessed she was near seventy. Every day, so Tipsy had come to believe after several years of seeing her, she walked at least three miles up Rifle Range Road in the morning, and three miles back in the evening. She did this rain or shine, and Tipsy even saw her making her sojourn during a freak snowstorm. In the warm months, she usually wore long simple dresses and white tennis shoes. When it got cold, she switched to jeans and boots. She added a raincoat when needed, and in the winter, a puffy red coat with a fuzzy hood.

She always had a large purse slung over her shoulder. The first couple times Tipsy saw her as she zipped by, she thought she might be a ghost, but her weather related clothing changes indicated that she was perfectly alive. Tipsy figured she was going to work somewhere, although she never seemed to be in a hurry, one way or the other. She had actively looked for her in the stores and businesses along Coleman Boulevard, but had yet to find her place of employment.

Tipsy sometimes thought about offering her a ride, but something about the woman's ramrod stance, her purposeful stroll, and her dogged routine made Tipsy think she might be offended. There had been a few times over the years when Tipsy hadn't seen the Walking Lady for a couple weeks, which always made her worry that something had happened to her. It must have just been bad timing on Rifle Range, however, because eventually, she always picked her out on the sidewalk.

Usually, as Tipsy drove past in her car on her way somewhere, she only got quick glances of the Walking Lady. Creeping traffic gave her a chance to watch her closely. When she was only about ten feet away, the woman's dark eyes met Tipsy's own.

Embarrassed to be caught staring, Tipsy leaned back against her seat and closed her eyes. The darkness reminded her of her sleepiness. *I'm so tired*, she thought. *Are you, Walking Lady? You've been traveling much longer than me.*

To her shock, a new voice rose in her mind. *Yes. I sure am tired.*

Tipsy opened her eyes and stared out the window. The Walking Lady met her eyes again and smiled, but she didn't slow down.

Can you hear me? asked Tipsy.

Yes.

Tipsy pressed her nose to the window. *Can you see the ghosts, too?*

Yes. I can. You're not alone.

Thank you. Tipsy smiled back at her.

But now I got to keep going. You keep going, too. The Walking Lady turned back to her path as a blonde woman with earbuds in her ears jogged past her.

Tipsy saw lines and colors, as she always did, but she saw hints of the Walking Lady's story. Tipsy would never be able to tell her whole tale—she couldn't truly understand what this woman's long life had been like, even if they spoke for hours. But they shared something anyway. A way of communicating without words, and seeing the world, that had nothing to do with painting. Still, Tipsy's craft could reveal something of their kinship to a discerning viewer.

Like everyone else in Charleston, it seemed the Walking Lady had a secret. The grittiness below the surface wasn't just in the contrasting roads and buildings. It was in the people of this beautiful, complicated city; the place that called Vivian Greenblatt home from the glamour and bustle of New York. It was in the characters as much as the setting.

When she finally got home that night, she used one of the kids' number two pencils to sketch the design of the painting on a piece of computer paper. An antiquated cabin on the right, and a half-built McMansion on the left. In the center, the Walking Lady on the sidewalk in a yellow dress, smiling knowingly at the viewer. A white woman in black yoga pants, about to run out of the picture. Tipsy took a photo of the sketch with her phone and emailed it to Vivian.

She got a response back two hours later. *Way to catch that bone.*

Bones are caught, and bones are dropped. Some are buried in the back yard and aren't properly chewed on until years later.

───────•───────

Sometimes Granna is so loud in Tipsy's ears, it's hard to remember that no one else can hear her. That she won't actually be at Tipsy's college graduation. Tipsy pulls at a stray thread on the sleeve of her black graduation gown. Granna wouldn't have her looking sloppy.

"I'm telling you, Tipsy," says Ayers. He sits on the edge of Tipsy's bed with his legs splayed out in khaki pants. His flip-flops whap-whap-whap nervously against the bottom of his feet. "You'll hate it there."

"I've always liked it when I visited you." She looks around at all her stuff. She's started sorting through everything, since she'll be moving out in a week or so. She's been living here, in the sorority house, for three years. As a senior she finally got a single room. It's tiny, but it's home. She picks through the pile of KZ paraphernalia she's accumulated since freshman year. Mugs, sweatshirts, picture frames, shot glasses. She plans on giving it all to some of the younger girls. She won't have room for it, and it's time to move on, anyway. She's not going to be one of those people who won't let go of the glory days. Besides, she doubts the artsy New York people she imagines herself schmoozing it up with will be decked out in Crush Party and Bid Day tee shirts.

"You've only been up there three times," says Ayers. "You don't know anything about it except the damn Met and Ruth's Chris. Living somewhere is different from visiting."

"Ayers, that's where I need to go. Shelby's mama can introduce me to people at the galleries—"

"Where are you going to live? You don't have shit for money." He's really working a piece of gum, like a bull that's pissed off at his cud. His chewing makes little scrunching noises that grate on Tipsy's nerves, but she never mentions it. She's sure she has habits that annoy Ayers, too.

"I got a little from Granna."

"What about us?"

"You could move back to New York." Even as Tipsy says it, she knows Miss May Penny and Mr. Tripp will never allow it. Ayers had shown up there for Easter, twenty pounds lighter and with shaking hands and twitchy eyes. He'd said, "Acting isn't what I really want to do, it's all bullshit," but he wasn't fooling anyone. Mr. Tripp must have known the five grand Ayers *needed to tidy up loose ends would go to his coke dealers, but as long as Ayers was coming home to South Carolina, the Collinses were content to pretend he was paying the maid.* "Or we could keep up the long distance thing," Tipsy says. "I won't stay up there forever. Maybe a couple years. Just long enough to make my mark." *She ruffles his hair.* "It's too cold up there for me."

Ayers isn't having any of her attempts at humor. "I'm done with long distance."

"I waited for you. Can't you—"

"I'm done with New York, too. I need to be here. With my own kind. With you."

"What about that last agent you talked about? Can he get you any—"

He stands and pulls her close. Her fingers splay across his chest. For a moment she pushes, but he doesn't give her space to do much. "Why don't we move back to Charleston? You'll love it. There are galleries there. Mrs. Patterson will give you a job while you paint. Do you really need to be in New York? Nah."

"What will you do?"

He shrugs. "Work for my dad, I guess. A lot of my boys are back in town. Their girlfriends are there, too. Shelby's getting married in a few months—"

"If they make it down the aisle before she drops his sorry drunk ass."

Her inadvertent humor succeeds in making him laugh. His bubble gum breath is warm in her hair. "It cracks me up when you bust out with shit like that. Miss Sassy." *He squeezes tighter.* "Don't leave me, Tipsy. You know I've been struggling… with the… you know."

"Yes." *They hadn't spoken directly about the habits Ayers had picked up in New York. Maybe when you know, you really know.*

"I don't know how I'd stand it if we weren't together."

Tipsy hugs him back and says yes to Charleston. He's right. She can paint in Charleston. She can paint anywhere. New York has probably always been a pipe dream. Now she's got Ayers, and he needs her. Feeling needed gives her the warm fuzzies.

Ayers's family is in Charleston, his parents and his sister and his cousins. Most of their friends are there. And she's never seen a more beautiful place in all the world. Not even during the European vacation Ayers's parents took them on last year. They'll be happy in Charleston. And besides, what more is she really looking for?

Chapter 16

Shelby gave Tipsy a few days off to start on the new painting, to make up for the lack of free time over kid-weekend. On Thursday morning she set up in one of her favorite spots by the old vegetable garden. Her workbench was in its usual satisfying state of organized chaos. She wore a visor to keep the sun out of her eyes as much as possible, for she wouldn't think to wear sunglasses while painting. The commission was too important to risk color errors. Or any errors.

She'd witnessed her ex-husband smoking marijuana, an illegal activity, via the intervention of an unpaid, undead private investigator. She couldn't state *that* in a responsive pleading, or swear it under oath before the court. Her best option would be to hire a real PI to track Ayers— get some evidence that was of this world— and PIs weren't cheap. She couldn't imagine how much money Ayers had paid the creepy bald Toyota man. If she wanted to put the nail in his coffin (pardon the pun), she needed Vivian to buy the painting.

She was eyeballing her progress so far— she'd already knocked out most of the unfinished home and moved on to the old cabin— when Ayers pulled into the driveway.

Speak of the devil, said Granna. *And that's* not *a pun.*

Tipsy started dabbing paint on the canvas as Ayers approached her. "I need to grab M.P.'s ballet slippers before I pick them up from school," said Ayers. "She's outgrown the ones at my place."

"Okay," said Tipsy. "The ballet bag is in the hall closet."

Ayers returned with a handful of pink canvas and stood over her shoulder. "Good you're working so much," said Ayers. "You selling anything?"

"Yes."

"I probably should have, you know, encouraged you more."

She paused. Her brush dripped gray paint that would eventually materialize into the sidewalk. A few layers of gradated, textured tone would create the impression of pebbles and scattered sand.

"Maybe I wasn't ready to get back to work," Tipsy said. "Kids being so little and all."

"Yeah, but I never paid any attention to what you wanted to do. Even before the kids." He poked at his gums with a toothpick. "It's funny. When we met, I liked you because your painting made you interesting. Guess I forgot over the years."

In the past, Tipsy might have appreciated his apology. Or maybe it would have made her mad. On this sunny morning, she just said, "Thanks. I'm working now." His contemplative, relatively pleasant demeanor made her wonder if May Penny had talked to him, as she'd promised she would. She pointed at the little blue stick in his hands. "Something in your teeth?"

"Nah. Dentist thinks I'm chewing too much gum. Weird, huh?"

Tipsy nodded. "Weird."

She remembered Lindsey's predictions about mundane conversations in the middle of World War Collins. *Welcome to the Divorce Twilight Zone.*

"Toothpick gives me something to do with my mouth, I guess." He ran his tongue over his lips and Tipsy's skin crawled. "I'm thinking of getting into the restaurant business," he said.

"Yeah?" Tipsy hadn't known Ayers to be particularly interested in food, beyond Chick-fil-a and whatever she or May Penny cooked for him.

"Uh huh. Buddy of Jimmy's is going to open a sushi place on the Isle of Palms. I'm helping him some with the design. Found these light fixtures with feathers on them from a Swedish furniture designer that's been showing in Atlanta."

"Cool."

"I think this could finally be it. What I'm meant to do. Get a string of restaurants going. Make a shitload of money. If I retired by forty-five...man. That's the stuff that makes a man happy and gives him satisfaction." He sighed. "Not much to be happy about now. ColSouth is such a waste of my time. My parents are going to help me with the investment, in case you're wondering." His chin jutted, and the Ayers she knew, who cared nothing for sushi but loved Scandinavian furniture, returned. "Don't worry. Your child support check will keep coming."

"What are you going to do with the kids this weekend?" She touched her brush to the canvas again, and added a gratifying swooping streak to the sidewalk.

He shrugged. "Maybe take them out to the beach. You know, Dad promoted Brad Humphries to VP of Marketing, over me. His own son."

Tipsy's skin crawled again at the mention of Brad Humphries, but at the same time, she'd heard nothing but praise for his work ethic and people skills from Tripp. "Maybe you should watch Brad and learn from him."

"Whatever. Brad is an idiot. I've heard he screws around on his wife all the time, too. Maybe Dad doesn't know that."

"That's not really any of your business." Now he was starting to get on her nerves, even in the divorce twilight zone. Only Ayers could apologize, snark, snarl, and lament the perpetual meaninglessness of his professional life— all in one conversation. Against the background of his lawsuit against her, no less.

"Shit, Tipsy. You'd think you'd have a little more sympathy for me. I'm busting my ass every day to take care of our kids."

She faced him with her hands on her hips. The paintbrush pointed at him like a half drawn sword. "Look, Ayers, you got a lot of nerve, asking for sympathy from me when you're trying to take my kids from me. And thanks for going to work everyday, but most people do it. And I know you've always fancied yourself meant for greatness. So I hope this restaurant thing does great and you make a zillion bucks and become the next reality TV restaurant critic. I've been pitying you for a long time. Guess I still do. But not for the reasons you think I should. And honestly, it's not my job anymore."

She braced for him to scream in her face, but instead of gale winds and pelting rain, she got a drizzle. His lower lip stuck out. He opened his mouth, closed it, and opened it again. "Thanks, Tipsy. Thanks a lot." He huffed across the grass, a gloomy large round man, as Jane had once described him, carrying ballet slippers.

She lowered her paint brush. Something a little dark, and a little calculating, settled over her. It felt foreign and scary, but oh, so right. "I haven't hired an attorney yet," she called out. "Clark gave me an extension."

He grunted acknowledgement. "I know. But I'd like to get on with it. Finally get past all this."

"Yeah. Me too. So that's why I have a question for you. Can you pass a drug test?"

"What? Of course."

"Really. I hear tell you've gone all Snoop Dogg with the weed."

"I have no idea what you're talking about." His face reddened.

"Your cute little pipe? With the skull? And a big fat bag of dope out at the hunt club? Jimmy has more sense than you. No one looks kindly on a father who does illegal drugs."

"You're not allowed to bug his truck—" His mouth clamped shut, and his eyes widened.

"I bet you felt so high, Ayers." She sauntered toward him. "Like you and that big old truck were going to float on out of there."

"Stop it."

"I'll tell you something. If you don't drop this lawsuit, then you'll come *crashing to the ground*." She turned and strolled back to her easel. "You know exactly what I mean."

She heard him shuffling toward her. She spun around, prepared to reach inside herself for the first time in weeks, find the power that lived inside her and inside Henry, and defend herself.

Sweat had broken out on Ayers's cheeks. "Fine. I'll drop it."

"Everything stays the same then. Except no more PI. And you'll quit your weed habit. I think a few extra years of smoking, as a grown ass adult, is more than enough."

His jaw jutted toward her, for approximately the ten millionth time in their long acquaintance. Still, the shock in his eyes made her think he might shed a few tears. Instead, he said, "Agreed. I'll tell Clark to dismiss."

He called back over his shoulder. "Jimmy decided not to sell so soon. He wants to see if the market keeps going up. So you can stay put in this house. Thought you might like to know that."

"That's great news. Tell him thanks."

He got into his truck. He fiddled with his phone, and then the stereo. She almost burst out laughing when he slowly backed down the driveway with Carrie Underwood's plaintive request for Jesus to take the wheel wafting from his open windows.

Tipsy returned to her painting, but she didn't put brush to canvas right away. She glanced down at her tubes of paint, and the blobs of mixed colors on the palette. It crossed her mind that this painting would not require any Charleston green. No forest tones concealed in the darkness, like the long forgotten consequences of Henry and Proctor's collective jealous rage. Or the blurry choices Tipsy made, many years ago, when she was young and afraid. Hell, even those she made not so long ago, when she was a lot older, but still pretty damn scared. She closed her eyes, her eyebrows drawing together. She didn't like to think much while she painted, and so she took another second to determine if Ayers's departure required any more contemplation. Once she was sure she didn't feel anything but the urge to get back to work, she did.

———•———

Will came over the next day after work. They tossed around the idea of Friday happy hour out at the beach, or an evening boat cruise, but in the end they sat in the center of Miss Callie's freshly repainted joggling board and drank a few beers. The slight dip in the middle of the board pushed them together, just as Tipsy had imagined it might when she'd seen Jane and Henry on its opposite ends. Will's leg felt solid and warm beside hers, his jeans soft against the bare skin beyond her shorts.

"It might get chilly later," he said.

"I'll change if we go out."

"Let's not. I don't feel like yelling to be heard in a loud bar. And I like looking at your legs."

She rested her head on his shoulder, until movement in the garden below them caught her eye. She peered between the porch railings.

"What is it? Henry?" asked Will.

She nodded. Henry walked down the slate walkway leading to the gate in the picket fence. With each step he raised his foot almost to waist level, like a soldier in slow motion, or a child playing *step-on-the-crack-break-your-mother's-back*. His lips moved, although Tipsy couldn't hear him from across the yard. The fingers of his left hand stirred whatever stew of words and sentences and paragraphs made up THE GREAT STORY.

"Has he talked to you lately?" Will asked.

"Not much. It's like he's lost the ability to do anything but repeat THE GREAT STORY over and over to himself."

"What's it about?"

"Who knows? But according to him, it's GREAT."

Henry spun around and walked toward the house. He met Tipsy's eye. She stood. Will took her hand, but she squeezed his and let it drop. She walked to the edge of the staircase. Henry stopped, and his spinning hand went still.

"I'd like to move on," he said.

"I think that's wise."

"But I want to finish the story first. I understand it now. I never understood it when I was alive, or since I've been dead." He chewed his lip, and asked her, almost shyly, "Will you help me? Perhaps I can tell it to you, and you can write it down for me."

Tipsy smiled. "Sure. I can do that. But it will take a long time."

"I've been writing it for a hundred years. I'm in no hurry." His fingers started spinning again. "Let me think on it some more."

"Okay," Tipsy said. "Neither of us is going anywhere. Henry, thank you for helping me fight Ayers. Not like, fist fight him—" She punched the air in front of her. "But, you know." She closed her eyes and whispered nonsense, the way she'd seen Henry mutter in the truck.

"My pleasure, Tipsy. You must still be careful. Your former husband strikes me as a man who does not like to be outshone." He smiled ruefully. "Many men share that unfortunate quality. Among others. We are a flawed sex."

"We all have flaws. And some men learn from their mistakes," she said. She glanced at Will, who watched her with his usual solemn curiosity from the porch. He might not be perfect. He might have a lot of baggage, but she wasn't perfect either, and she had plenty of the same. She believed that he had faith in her, in more ways than one. That seemed as good a place to start from as any.

"I can't help Jane blossom," said Henry. "I lost that chance, long ago. But perhaps if I'm around for a while, I can be of use to you."

Henry turned on his heels and resumed strolling along the walkway.

"What did he say?" asked Will, as she sat.

"He wants me to help him, like, transcribe his novel."

"Whoa, that could take years. Kind of ironic, isn't it? Him finally really going crazy after all this time."

She took a deep breath. "Maybe he's not crazy. Maybe he just needs to finish his work. I'll help him, if I can."

Like he's helped you. They both helped you, said Granna, her voice warm and comforting in Tipsy's mind.

"It doesn't surprise me that you want to help him," said Will with a chuckle.

"I feel sorry for him."

"You feel sorry for everyone."

She faced him. "I don't feel sorry for you, Will."

He laughed. "Wow, thanks."

"No, you don't understand."

"I think I do. I don't feel sorry for you, either. And I've told you, you're stronger than you look."

"Thank you, but—"

"You really don't have to explain."

Tipsy shook her head. Will might not be partial to verbosity, but there were some things that couldn't be understood unless spoken, plain and simple. "I've never loved a man that didn't need saving."

He put one hand on her cheek and kissed her. "I love you, too."

She returned her head to his shoulder. The cicadas in Charleston refused to give up. They didn't care that the calendar said fall was approaching. They buzzed and whirred as if winter would never come. And really, in Charleston, it rarely did. Although once, many years ago, it got cold enough to kill a heartbroken, homicidal priest who'd consumed too much bourbon and forgot to wear shoes. Tipsy watched Henry's methodical progress up and down the walkway. It seemed like a parade toward nowhere, but perhaps he needed more time to find his destination.

"What do you want to do tomorrow? It's Saturday," Will said.

"Paint. Maybe go out on the water, if you want to take the boat on a little cruise up the Intercoastal. Make love to you."

"That sounds perfect. Except I'll read the paper while you paint."

Tipsy found she didn't need to think much beyond that. Many people would have called her crazy if they knew the nutty situations she'd gotten into of late with folks both alive and dead. But she was plenty sane enough to appreciate a late summer Saturday in the Lowcountry.

The End

Acknowledgements

T he narrative of *Charleston Green's* literary journey from first draft to publication could be a novel unto itself. I wrote this book several years ago in a burst of amazing inspiration, but it took countless ups and downs, many steps forward and just as many stumbles back, to finally see it in print. To that end, I am most grateful that I can finally hold the book in my hand and share it with my readers.

There are, as always, too many people to thank, but I'll give it a shot. Thank you to my friend Veronica Light for introducing me to the book's namesake color, Charleston green. An artist's tale is well served by such a colorful moniker, and the shade became a lovely metaphor for many themes in the story. Thank you to Caroline Staley, also known as the Gallavantor, for the wonderful cover art. If you're ever looking for highly original Lowcountry artwork, check out Caroline's colorful Instagram account (Instagram.com/gallavator). Thank you to Kathy Meis and Shilah LaCoe at Bublish, Inc., another local Charleston enterprise and a tremendous resource for writers in the rapidly evolving publishing space. Bublish gives authors like me, whose work is considered outside the traditional publishing box, the power to take control of our careers, put out a great product, and make sure it reaches potential readers.

Thank you to Maisha Grant Rounds, who took the time to talk with me about the Gullah Geechee people, including the sensitivities around language, and her personal experience growing up within that vibrant culture. For more information about the Gullah Geechee community, please look to the College of Charleston's Avery Research Center. I also wanted to acknowledge the late Mrs. V.L. Converse. I came across her lawsuit while doing research on domestic violence in South Carolina. *See, V.M. Converse, by Next Friend v. A.L Converse*, 9 Rich.Eq. 535 (1856). Her brave alimony lawsuit inspired the story of Virginia, a woman who chose death over life with her abusive husband.

Tremendous gratitude to my agent, Stefanie Lieberman of Janklow & Nesbit Associates, New York, New York, and her wonderful assistant, Molly Steinblatt. These women saw something in this book from the get go. They supported it for years. They put it in front of people who contributed to its positive evolution, even if it didn't quite turn out how we hoped. Regardless, *Charleston Green* is a stronger novel for their involvement. I'm so fortunate to have a smart, dedicated agent like Stefanie behind my work.

Thanks are always due to Haley Telling, my cousin who is more a sister-meets-BFF. She helps me stay positive and think of creative outlets for my work. My mother, Dianne Wicklein, is quite simply the most inspiring person I know. My children, Eliza, Harper, and Cyrus, are my muses. I am so proud of the amazing young people they have become over the years while I toiled on various novels. They have become the protagonists of their own adventures.

Thank you to my husband, Jeff Cluver, to whom I dedicate all my work, one way or another. No husband could be more supportive, patient, and inspiring. In *Charleston Green*, Tipsy makes a wry comment about marriage when she says, *you're not meant to keep at it for all eternity*. I now know she says that because she doesn't have a Jeff Cluver (not yet, anyway). You are my always, in this world, and the next... whatever that may be. I love you!

Lastly, this story, and these characters, are my love letter to Charleston, South Carolina. A beautiful, flawed, unique, complicated city. I am grateful I live here, and I have raised my children here. I hope *Charleston Green* gives readers some insight into this quirky, charming place.

Best,
Stephanie

Made in the USA
Columbia, SC
08 September 2022

66832731R00217